PROVENDER GLEED

ARTS COUNCIL
ENGLAND

Also by James Lovegrove

Novels
The Hope
Escardy Gap (co-written with Peter Crowther)
Days
The Foreigners
Untied Kingdom
Worldstorm

Novellas
How the Other Half Lives
Gig

Short Fiction
Imagined Slights

For Children
The Web: Computopia
Wings
The House of Lazarus

PROVENDER GLEED

A Bildungsroman

James Lovegrove

GOLLANCZ

LONDON

The right of James Lovegrove to be identified as the author
of this work has been asserted by him in accordance
with the Copyright, Designs and Patents Act 1988.

First published in Great Britain in 2005 by
Gollancz
An imprint of the Orion Publishing Group
Orion House, 5 Upper St Martin's Lane, London WC2H 9EA

A CIP catalogue record for this book
is available from the British Library

ISBN 0 575 07683 6 (cased)
ISBN 0 575 07684 4 (trade paperback)

1 3 5 7 9 10 8 6 4 2

Typeset at The Spartan Press Ltd,
Lymington, Hants

Printed in Great Britain by
Clays Ltd, St Ives plc

www.orionbooks.co.uk

PART ONE

From *Kin*! magazine – 'Your Weekly Guide to All That's Hot and All That's Not in the World of the Families':

Provender Turns 25

Provender Gleed hits the quarter century next Tuesday, and ClanFans all across the country will be holding street parties to celebrate.

But Prov himself has no plans for a bombastic birthday beano.

A Gleed Family spokesman commented: 'The young master will treat the day just like any other. He attaches little importance to anniversaries and other such events.'

Of course, with the Gleed summer ball this weekend, Provender will probably be all partied out by the time his personal silver jubilee comes round.

Blue-eyed Prov is very much the dark horse of the Gleed Family, a man of mystery who shuns the media spotlight, unlike the majority of his relatives.

Even at almost 25, he is still unmarried, which is a source of consternation among the Gleeds, with Provender being the firstborn (and only) male child on the Family's primogeniture bloodline.

Insider Gleed sources say that his mother Cynthia is tearing her hair out trying to match him with a suitable bride.

But apart from last year's brief dalliance with Adèle Fforde-Nevant and a trial date with Inez Lamas, a distant cousin on his mother's side, Provender has not been successfully linked with any potential marriage material, Family or otherwise.

His continuing single status, however, is a ray of hope for countless female ClanFans. Organisations such as One Bride For One Provender and Thicker Blood have dedicated themselves to sourcing the Gleed heir a mate from the ranks of ordinary folk.

Members of The Wives of Provender have gone a step further, taking a vow of chastity that will end only when one of them is wed and bedded by the man himself.

Then there's Beardless, the militant gay pressure group who insist that Provender should not be forced into marriage when it is obviously against his inclination.

And what does Provender make of all this?

As he hardly ever ventures outside the grounds of Dashlands and never gives interviews, it's a moot point. The official Gleed line is: 'No comment.'

Still: happy birthday for Tuesday, Provender!

Next week's *Kin!* will carry full pictures of the arrivals at the Gleed ball, plus analysis and commentary by Family experts.

From the Court and Social section of the *Daily Dynast*:

The Gleed Summer Ball

will be held at **Dashlands, Berkshire,**
on **Saturday June 30th**

The theme is **Renaissance Venice** and guests
are expected to attire themselves appropriately.

Start time is **8.30 P.M.** for **9.00 P.M.**
Carriages at dawn.

*Entry will be refused without valid invitation.
Unauthorised guests will be shot.*

1

Your invitation to the Gleed Summer Ball, had you one, would have arrived by courier six weeks in advance of the occasion. It would have come in a bonded-vellum envelope, eight inches by six, the flap sealed with a blob of crimson wax bearing the imprint of the Gleed Family seal, which depicts a nutmeg drupe, partially split open to reveal the kernel, and the legend 'In Condimentis Pecunia'. The invitation itself would be printed on card of extraordinary smoothness, with an icing-sugar-like finish which would seem to cry out to be stroked. Holding it close to your nose, you would detect a faint aroma which you would find delicious but hard to identify – sandalwood, cinnamon, ginger, something like that. The card would appear to have been impregnated with a scent redolent of the original source of the Gleed Family fortune, spices.

As for the text on it, this would have been printed in an elegant sans-serif font designed specially for the Gleeds some eighty years ago by none other than Eric Gill. Indeed, in printers' typeface catalogues the font is known by the name 'Gleed'. Its contrasting thick and thin verticals might suggest to you expansiveness coupled with caution, or perhaps, if you were of a more cynical bent, financial satiety gained through the impoverishment and starvation of others.

Be that as it may, you would not be paying much attention to the font, or even to the way the characters project from the card, thermographically raised, shinily black, like flecks of jet. Rather, you would be concentrating on the words themselves, and in particular that all-important opening line: 'You are cordially invited to . . .'

Now, with this invitation you would be entitled to approach the main gates of Dashlands, the Gleed Family seat, on the appropriate date at the appropriate time. You would doubtless be clutching the invitation tightly as your vehicle turned off the M4 and began to navigate the tortuous labyrinth of country lanes leading, eventually, to those gates. Holding the invitation in your hand would not in any way hamper your driving abilities because you would not, of course, yourself be driving. A chauffeur would be doing that for you. If you did not have a chauffeur, if you were in some sort of automobile that was not a limousine, then you would not be attending the party in the first place. You would have no right to.

At the gates you would encounter the first line of security. Your car would be flagged down by a group of intense-looking, large-torsoed men dressed in jumpsuits and body armour, with sidearms bolstered at their waists. They would peer in at you, scrutinise your invitation, check its watermark with a UV light, compare your face against a register of guest names and photographs, frown at you in much the same way that a hungry fox might frown at a hen, and eventually, and with seeming reluctance, wave you through. Meanwhile a mob of paparazzi and TV cameramen would be jockeying behind barriers for a clear shot of your face through the open window of your limo. Flashbulbs would be flickering like lightning. If recognised by this jostling journalistic throng, you would hear your name being called, howled, ululated, in order to get you to turn a certain way. In the unlikely event that you were someone nobody recognised, you would still be photographed but you might be subjected to a few sneers and jeers as well from the press pack. You might even hear such remarks as 'Who are you?', said almost indignantly, and 'You're nobody. Even you don't know who you are.'

Kept further back from the gates than the newshounds, you would spy numerous ClanFans, popping away at you with their little cameras, their Instamatics, their Polaroids. You would not, if you had any sense or self-respect, pay these people any heed.

Past the gates – high gates, towering iron structures topped with gilded spikes, gates that would not disgrace the entrance to heaven – you would cruise along a drive lined with immense cedars. It being the height of summer, the trees would be at their lushest and most frondsome. They would resemble, you might say to yourself, great blue cumulonimbus clouds.

Then, a mile on, you would come to a second line of security, a manned barrier flanked by tank-traps – twists of steel girder wreathed in barbed wire. This second appraisal of your identity and your invitation would be to ensure that no one else had manifested inside your vehicle since you entered Dashlands – no one had emerged, perhaps, from a place of hiding under the seat or in the boot (this has happened in the past). It would also be to ensure that your limo had not, for some reason, left the drive and taken a detour across the grounds, an act which could only be construed as nefarious. In other words, you hadn't tried to smuggle in some gate-crasher and you didn't have some sinister ulterior motive for being on the Gleed estate.

Safely through the barrier, you would find yourself on the final approach to the ball. Dashlands House itself would just be coming into view. You would have a glimpse of its multiplicity of pitched and flat roofs, its jutting monolith-like towers, its sideways-protruding concrete balconies, its sliver-thin windows, its open-face stonework . . . and then your car would be guided off the drive by an official with fluorescent orange batons, who would direct you towards another similarly equipped official who, in turn, would direct you towards yet another such official who would instruct you, or rather your chauffeur, to park the limo in a cordoned-off area at the end of one of several long ranks of already-parked limos. Your vehicle would then become just one of many top-of-the-range marques and models – Cowley Torpedoes, VW Haifisches, BdM Atalantas, Dagenham Grey Spectres, Savage Ariels – and the splendour of its tailfins and hood ornament and whitewall tyres and running boards and spoiler and metallic paintjob would be signally diminished by proximity to cars of the same calibre, in the same way that an individual diamond, whatever its carat count, will lose its lustre when placed among a host of other diamonds, the dazzle of the whole subsuming the beauty of the one.

Still and all, this would not matter to you, for you would have a party to attend. You would be about to partake of the famously lavish Gleed hospitality. You would have your costume on. Let us say that in keeping with the theme of this year's ball you had adopted the traditional Venetian *bautta*, consisting of a tricorne hat, a cape, a white mask, and a large black, full-cut mantle coming down from your head to cover the top half of your body – stifling to wear on such a warm night but striking apparel nonetheless. Or else you had come as a *dogaressa*, a chief magistrate's wife, with a pointed cap and a high-collared brocade cloak worn over a silk ballgown. You would, quite naturally, be feeling resplendent, socially accepted, top of the tree, as you left the limo and followed a path towards the site of the soirée. The ball would not be taking place at the house itself but at a specially constructed venue set apart from the building. Not only would signposts be directing you towards it, the glow of light against the dusk-steeped sky would be drawing you, moth-like.

But before you got there, a third and final line of security. This one perhaps the most daunting of all.

Greeting you at the perimeter of the party site would be Carver. Carver, the Gleeds' major-domo. Carver, the head of the under-the-stairs household. Carver, right-hand man to the wheelchair-bound Gleed patriarch, Great.

Carver would be standing there dressed in a frock coat finished with gold epaulettes and braid, his hands all but covered by lacy shirtcuffs, buckled shoes on his feet, a periwig perched on his head. You would catch sight of him, and whoever you were, however important you were, whatever your net worth, your status in the world, there would inevitably be a catch in your step, a falter in your stride, a brief, trepidatious hesitation.

For Carver is a forbidding presence. He would gaze on you with a respect that was somehow just a shade away from cold contempt. He would bow to you, ever so slightly, and as his eyes looked up at you

9

through their beetling white brows they would be narrowed, ever so slightly.

It would strike you, if you had never set eyes on Carver before, that this was a very old man, in his eighth decade at least, if not his ninth. It would also strike you that this was a very tall man whom age had not, as it does so many, stooped. You would mark the breadth of his shoulders and the power that they still seemed to contain. You would note the economy of effort in that bow he made, and the lack of stiffness. This was not, you would conclude, someone who suffered from any of old age's physical shortcomings, or if he did, did not let it show.

Most of all your eye would be ineluctably drawn to the deep scar in Carver's left cheek, the result of a wound inflicted long ago in his youth. You would, if you knew anything of the life history of this domestic servant, recall that Carver served as an infantryman in the last world war. You would be aware that he accompanied Great Gleed as batman during the protracted and bloody Eastern Front campaign. You would know that he saw action in Riga, Gdansk and Poznan; that he helped defend the vital rail link between Vilnius and Minsk; and that he took part in the Siege of Prague, the final and decisive battle of the conflict, after which victory was pretty much a mopping-up operation. It was in Prague, on the Charles Bridge, before the big push into Wenceslas Square, that Carver received a bayonet-thrust in the face, courtesy of a trembling teenage Czech conscript who seemed more alarmed than elated at what he had done and became further alarmed when Carver seized the bayonet with his hand, calmly detached it from the barrel of the conscript's rifle, slid the blade out from his cheek, and proceeded to bury it hilt-deep in the conscript's own head. Eschewing medical attention, for the rest of that day Carver continued to fight using his right arm only, his left hand occupied with holding the two sides of the gash together.

So now this weathered face, with its disfigured left half, would be staring at you, waiting for you to say your name. You would be trying not to stare back, most of all trying not to fixate on the scar and how horribly puckered the scar was at its edges and the way the scar pulled down the outside corner of Carver's left eye . . . and then you would collect yourself, moisten your strangely dry tongue, and give your name.

Carver would then turn and announce you. In a voice sepulchrally deep, like the grating of a stone door in some vast cellar, he would let the guests already arrived know that one more had been added to their number. And then, instantly forgetting you, he would turn to the person waiting in line behind you; and you, not without some relief, would move on, stepping forward to immerse yourself in the brightness and bustle, the opulence, the sumptuousness, the sheer astonishing profligacy that was the Gleed Summer Ball.

Yes, all this would happen if you had an invitation.

But of course, you don't.

Who are you?

You're a nobody.

Even you don't know who you are.

And what do you think *you've* done to deserve being invited to a Family occasion?

2

'Where *is* Provender?' said Cynthia Gleed, and sighed, knowing full well the answer. *Not here.*

She was addressing her two daughters, Gratitude, the elder, and Extravagance, the younger. Both girls were dressed in billowing shot-silk gowns, both sported half-face masks with large noses that hid their only-somewhat-less-large real noses, and both wore wigs so ludicrously high-piled and heavy that they had to be supported by steel rods attached to purpose-built, truss-like undergarments. This arrangement restricted movement considerably, and Gratitude and Extravagance had spent much of the past week practising how to walk in their party get-up. What they had come up with was an oddly stately, swan-like gait which gave the impression of being effortless but was anything but. For the most part, so as not to exhaust themselves, they kept still.

Cynthia herself had opted for an equally fabulous gown – hers beaded with freshwater pearls and fitted with saucily revealing organdie panels – but she had decided against a wig, preferring a teeteringly tall tiara set atop her own hair. She was no longer young and did not think her spine would accept the weight of an enormous wig, truss or no truss. (Her daughters, she predicted, would be suffering for their vanity for days to come.) Like them, she did have a mask, but hers was a basic black domino framed by an array of glossy blue-black magpie feathers and set, lorgnette-style, on the end of a wand so that she could cover her face if she wanted to but also reveal it if she wanted to. Cynthia knew she was still beautiful at fifty-three. She knew, too, that she devoted a great deal of money and effort to remaining beautiful at fifty-three. Why hide what was so hard-won?

Gratitude, in response to her mother's query, gave as much of a shrug as her outfit allowed. 'Haven't seen him.'

Extravagance assayed a nod. 'Me either. Not since lunchtime.'

Cynthia sighed again. Really, that son of hers . . .

'Bet he's still in his room,' said Gratitude.

'Moping,' said Extravagance.

'Probably not even in costume yet.'

'He's such a miserable sod.'

'And a party-pooper.'

'Sometimes, you know, I can't believe we share the same DNA.'

'Now, girls,' warned Cynthia, although it was hard to contradict anything they had said. 'None of that. Anyway, till your uncle Fortune arrives, strictly speaking the party hasn't started. So Provender's not late. Not yet.'

'Wonder what Uncle Fortune will do for an entrance this year,' said Gratitude. 'He won't arrive by elephant again. Not after last year, when he fell out of the howdah and nearly broke his neck.'

'Besides, the theme was maharajahs then,' said Extravagance. 'Do you think possibly he'll abseil from a helicopter again? Not very Venetian, I know . . .'

'Doubt it. And I'm certain the bungee jump from a hot-air balloon isn't going to get a repeat performance. Remember? They got the cord length wrong. An inch lower and he'd have smashed his skull open.'

'Uncle Fortune,' said their mother, 'will try and top himself. Not literally, but you know what I mean. Outdo himself. Uncle Fortune always does.' She brisked her palms together. 'Now then, we can't stand around nattering to each other. We must go and mingle.'

Obediently, Gratitude and Extravagance turned and, grimacing with exertion, glided off. Cynthia herself turned and surveyed the party.

So far, an hour in, things had gone swimmingly. There had been no upsets – nothing, at any rate, that she had been told about or observed. If there were crises happening behind the scenes, they clearly hadn't been so severe that the domestic and catering staff couldn't sort them out. Cynthia was all set to step in if summoned and straighten out any kinks in the smooth delivery of hospitality to her guests. She had, however, spent hundreds of hours organising the ball and drilling various employees on their roles and tasks, precisely in order to ensure that nothing went wrong that could be foreseen to go wrong.

All that hard work paid off here, at this moment, as she looked upon the replica of Venice which had been erected in her back garden. A team of set-builders from Pinewood Studios had come in and worked for a month re-creating all of *La Serenissima*'s architectural features and landmarks. This second Venice of polystyrene, plywood and custom board, covering the equivalent of three football fields, was thronged now with the great and the good of Britain and a fair selection of the great and the good from other countries as well.

Cynthia was standing at one corner of the Piazza San Marco. To her right was the Basilica, wherein a sprung dance floor had been installed and an orchestra waited to play later on in the evening. To her left rose the Campanile, thirty yards tall and, as in the real Venice, crowned with a Golden Angel. The party's version of the Grand Canal ran alongside the piazza's far edge, winding through the rest of the 'city' on a circuitous loop, passing beneath a Bridge of Sighs and a Ponte de Rialto along the way. Gondolas and a couple of *vaporetti* were plying the waterway, ferrying guests on round-trips or between different 'boroughs' of the party site, perhaps to San Polo where the revellers could try their luck at the gambling tables on the Rialto itself or else to Castello where, at an ersatz Arsenale, they could shoot twelve-bores at luminous clay pigeons. There was a Lido (swimsuits, towels and changing rooms were supplied, although there would be few takers, few guests willing to unpick their elaborate costumes and hairdos just for a brief dip) and near that there was a stage where a troupe of circus performers were putting on a continuous programme of juggling, fire-eating, unicycling, and high-wire walking, some of them doing all four things simultaneously. Food, naturally, was in plentiful supply – nowhere were you out of sight of a buffet table – and waiting staff dressed as Harlequins and Columbines circulated bearing salvers of drinks.

Nothing had been left to chance. Many millions of pounds had gone to ensure no guest could claim, by the night's end, that he or she had not been thoroughly, amply, unstintingly, repletely entertained.

To judge by the faces Cynthia could see, lit up by the myriad strings of light bulbs festooned across the piazza, the ball was well on its way to achieving that aim. There were smiles everywhere she looked, and where there weren't, there were frowns of the mildest sort – the frown of someone forced to choose between a dozen different kinds of stuffed olive, the frown of someone listening avidly to another's words, the frown of someone unable to decide which of the many amusements on offer to partake of next.

Her eye then alighted, however, on one disgruntled face which didn't have a mitigating excuse for its expression, a face which was genuinely, miserably frowning.

Great, parked halfway along the piazza's west side in his wheelchair, glared at the party-goers who flocked to and fro in front of him. The Gleed patriarch, oldest living member of the Family, was not happy.

But then, when was he ever?

Feeling a tug of reluctant obligation, Cynthia went over to him. Fluffing out her skirt and petticoats, she crouched in front of him like a deflating hovercraft, so that he and she were eye-level with each other. His glittering blue gaze settled on her and took a moment to place her. When it did, his scowl eased, if only slightly. The horizontal lines thinned but remained put, looking like a musical stave on which the innumerable liver spots that dotted his brow (and the rest of his pate) resembled so many crotchets and minims.

Great tried to open his mouth, but all the action achieved was a drooping of one corner of his lower lip which exposed a couple of slanting brown teeth. At the same time, the only part of his anatomy other than his face that was not paralysed began to move. His left hand started to beat sideways against the wheelchair's armrest, his signet ring hitting the tubular-steel frame with a sharp, resonant tap.

'Hello, Great,' said Cynthia. 'You're having a nice time I trust.'

The rhythm of Great's taps increased, becoming irregular.

'How many summer balls does this make it?' Cynthia went on. 'A hundred and seven? Something like that.'

Great's head jiggled in such a way that he could either have been nodding or shaking it.

'I hope it meets with your satisfaction. We've gone all-out this year, haven't we. No expense spared. After all, what use is it being Family if we can't show off the fact that we're Family?'

Cynthia fancied she saw agreement in his eyes. Great's eyes were the one feature of him that remained truly expressive. Usually baleful, sometimes they seemed to register approval of what they saw, as now. But that, Cynthia thought, might just be her own imagining. Eyes, when the face around them was slack and all but immobile, gave away very little.

'Carver's got another forty minutes or so till he's done with his announcing duties. I expect you'll be needing him by then.'

Carver not only attended to all of Great's physical requirements, such as feeding him and changing his incontinence pants; he also had an uncanny, almost supernatural ability to interpret Great's thoughts and wishes. Having served Great for many a decade, first as batman, then as personal valet, Carver had developed an understanding of his master that went beyond intimacy and bordered on the psychic. Since the old man's paralysis had set in, Carver had become his mouthpiece, his messenger, his intermediary. When you spoke to Great in Carver's presence, you actually spoke to Carver, and when Carver replied, that was Great replying.

Which was why Cynthia liked to talk to Great when Carver was *not* around. It might not be a dialogue as such, but at least she felt she was communicating with Great himself rather than with his glowering dragoman.

'Well, anyway,' she said, rising. 'Nice chatting with you, Great. I must go and grin at a few more guests.'

Great's head jiggled again. The leathery wattle that hung below his jaw quivered.

'And,' she added, with a speculative glance around the piazza, 'if Provender doesn't show soon, I may have to go and roust him out from wherever he's hiding.'

Mention of Provender's name appeared to excite further agreement (or perhaps disagreement) from Great. His head jiggled more agitatedly. His wattle quivered so much it almost vibrated.

Cynthia strode across the piazza. She had just spied her husband, whom she recognised without difficulty even though his features were almost entirely hidden beneath a *larva* mask. Her husband was busy chatting up an attractive young woman. Cynthia made a beeline for him.

En route, she was accosted by: one of the most successful movie directors in the world; a Saudi princeling; the editor of the UK's most

Family-friendly broadsheet newspaper and his tabloid counterpart; a Texan oil baron; Greta von Wäldchenlieb, wife of the head of the premier Teutonic Family; a pop star whose name Cynthia did not know but whose face she did because he had been given Gleed patronage and was riding high in the charts on the back of that; a duchess tangentially related to the British royals; and a peer of the realm who had done the Gleeds several favours in the House of Lords. While Cynthia could have happily stopped and made small talk with any of these, and indeed should have in order both to play the gracious hostess and to reinforce her and her Family's superiority over them, instead she bypassed them all with a wave and an airy smile. Her husband was her target and she could not afford to be diverted from reaching him. Just a few moments' delay, and next thing she knew, he would no longer be on the piazza and neither would the attractive young woman.

'Prosper!' she cried, pulling up alongside him. 'I've been looking all over for you.' She placed a hand gently but proprietorially on his elbow. 'We must talk. Oh, but who's this lovely young creature?'

Prosper Gleed shot his wife the fiercest of glares before composing himself and introducing her to . . . 'Ahh. Awfully sorry. I don't think I caught your name.'

The attractive young woman was not amused. 'Sophie,' she said, in such a way that it was clear she had already told him, perhaps more than once. 'Sophie Kilverton.'

'Oh yes, that's right!' said Prosper. 'And you're one of our artistic protégées, aren't you. A poet.'

'A novelist.'

'Yes, that's what I meant, a novelist.'

Cynthia grinned at Sophie Kilverton – ostensibly a grin of greeting, really a grin of victory. She had been almost certain her husband would not have remembered the girl's name. Prosper was nothing if not predictable – predictably drawn to nubile females, predictably unmindful of such minor details as what they were called and what their occupations were.

'Well, Sophie,' she said, 'if you've no objection, I shall just drag my husband away.'

'No objection,' said Sophie Kilverton, frostily. 'None at all.'

'Cyn, honest, it wasn't how it looked,' said Prosper, when they were out of the girl's earshot.

'Prosper, you know as well as I do that it was exactly how it looked. And while I couldn't give two hoots about your infidelities, attempted or otherwise – I'm way past caring about those – don't you think you could give it a rest, just for one evening? It is our party, after all. People are watching us.'

'They wouldn't necessarily know it was me,' Prosper said, touching his mask. The *larva* was made of fine waxed cloth, with large eyeholes.

Undoubtedly it disguised Prosper but it also left enough of his physiognomy visible that you could still tell he was good-looking, in an ageing, roguish, roué way. There were those grey eyes, in their charming beds of wrinkles. There was that bifurcated chin with its small underflap of skin that spoke of a man well-preserved for his age but displaying just an enticing hint of dissipation.

'Of course they'd know it's you,' Cynthia said. 'They'd know it's you by the puddle of drool around your feet. And anyway, why were you bothering with her?'

'What do you mean?'

'She's English. You've done England already. You've done all the major countries. It's only the smaller nations left on your checklist now. Djibouti, Tajikistan, São Tomé and Principe, Vanuatu . . .'

Prosper had made it his goal in life to commit adultery with at least one representative of every known country. He had never actually admitted as much to Cynthia but she had heard about it from reliable second-hand sources and indeed read about it in the Family column of one of the more scurrilous tabloid dailies. Prosper Gleed would, it seemed, not rest until he had philandered his way across the entire globe. Rather in the manner of the great empire builders of old, he hoped to see the map of the world coloured red with his conquests.

'Well, yes, but . . . You can't blame a chap for trying. Besides, I think she may have had some Welsh ancestry.'

'But you've done Wales too.'

'Wales. Ah yes, Wales.' Prosper's eyes took on a wistful, faraway look. 'There was certainly a welcome in *her* valleys.'

Cynthia ignored the remark. 'So you're adding hybrids to the list now, is that it?'

'Actually, that's not a bad idea.'

'Prosper . . .'

'No, dear. No, I'm not. Just kidding.'

'Ha ha.'

'So, what did you have to talk to me about?' Prosper snatched a flute of champagne from the tray of a passing Columbine, giving the girl the once-over as he did so. Sheer force of habit. 'Something important? Or was it just a pretext to sabotage my chances with the delectable what's-her-name – Sophie?'

'Both. But mainly I was wondering if you'd seen Provender yet.'

'Here? Can't say I have. Why, should he be here?'

'Of course he should. Apart from anything else, it's only polite. His absence will be noticed.'

'Well, I'm sure he'll make it.'

'I'm not.'

'And I suppose the reason you want him here is you have some fine, marriageable little filly lined up for him to meet.'

'Naturally. Two of them, in fact. You may recall my mentioning them at breakfast just this morning.'

'Yes, absolutely,' said Prosper, evidently having no memory of the conversation in any way, shape or form. About which Cynthia was not surprised. Half the time, things she said to her husband simply did not register. He might nod and go 'Hmph', as though he were listening, but she knew the information was pouring down some bottomless hole in his brain as fast as it arrived there.

'You may also recall my saying that I have a good feeling about these two,' Cynthia went on. 'Neither's Family, but they're both well-born, interesting, intelligent, attractive . . .'

'Attractive?' Prosper perked up. 'Don't suppose I ought to meet them, eh? You know, check them out beforehand. Vet them. Just to be on the safe side.'

'Dearest husband, I am not letting you anywhere near those girls.'

'Not even just a look?'

'Not even that.'

'Spoilsport.'

'Prosper,' Cynthia was becoming annoyed now. 'This may all seem terribly funny and trivial to you, but it's no laughing matter. We're talking about your son. We're talking about the last and only male on the primogeniture line. The only branch left on the trunk of the Family tree. The future of the Gleeds. Provender must marry. He must produce an heir. If he doesn't – if, God forbid, he dies without leaving a son – then we're sunk. We fade into obscurity. We lose continuity and status and all that makes us a Family. You know this as well as I do, and yet you still can't seem to take it seriously. And here I am, doing my best to get our son paired off, going to all this effort on the Gleeds' behalf, and I'm not even a born Gleed, I just married into your damn—'

She broke off, interrupted by a salutation from a guest, some jowly non-Family plutocrat whose name temporarily escaped her but whose obeisant overtures could not go unacknowledged. By the time she and her husband had finished assuring the plutocrat that yes, he was 'in' with the Gleeds – and she had consented to the man's request of the honour of a dance later – Cynthia had lost the head of steam she had built up. She was still angry with Prosper, still incensed that she alone was bearing the burden of finding a mate for their son, but the moment had passed. Continuing to remonstrate with her husband was not going to get her anywhere. Tonight was not the time for it; the party was not the place.

'Look,' she said, 'I realise how you like to appear frivolous, Prosper. I realise how important it is to you to be the playboy, the rake, the frequenter of casinos and racetracks. It's all very lovely and beguiling, believe me. It's why I fell for you, and even as I married you I hoped I might be able to change you while knowing I never would. The point is, deep down I know you care about this Family as much as I do and I know you're keen to see Provender settled down and I know you wouldn't exactly hate the idea of a grandson – never mind the continuity a grandson represents – simply because you'd love to play grandfather to one. So just . . . help me, that's all. Support me. That's all I ask.'

Prosper looked chastened, though not for long. Contrition wasn't really in his repertoire. 'Whatever you say, Cyn,' he said. 'Point taken. You're the boss. No argument here. Et cetera, blah blah blah.'

Cynthia, for the third time in the space of quarter of an hour, heaved a sigh. She wheeled away from her husband and took herself to the waterside end of the piazza, where she rested her elbows on the balustrade and peered out over the Grand Canal. The sky was twilight purple and the canal was dark, though its surface glittered intermittently with reflected light. The water itself came from the mains but had been dyed to an authentically green Venetian murk. A gondolier paddled past, yodelling an operatic aria. He was one of several dozen tenors from the Gleed Academy of Music, Drama and Dance who had undergone a fortnight's intensive coaching, courtesy of genuine Venetian gondoliers, in the art of propelling and steering that particular mode of transport. The genuine gondoliers had grumbled that no amateur should be piloting a gondola, even around a fake Venice. None of them, however, could sing opera, and that was the main criterion for the job at the ball. Besides, they had been well paid for sharing their expertise with the tenors, so the grumbling had been perfunctory, more for form's sake than anything. It allowed them to go home with their consciences clear, the Gleed money that stuffed their wallets rinsed satisfactorily of the taint of professional compromise.

Cynthia thought of this and all the other snags she had had to deal with on the way to making the ball a reality. It was the same every year – a horde of obstacles to overcome, pitfalls to anticipate, wounded egos to soothe – and no sooner was one ball over than she had to begin making plans for the next. She gave this Family her all. She did everything for them. She dedicated herself, sacrificed herself, for the greater good of the Gleeds, and asked little in return. And yet for all her efforts she was still unable to furnish them with the one thing they needed most. And this was becoming more and more anguishing to her.

Oh, Provender.

Cynthia glanced up at the sky. When it was fully dark . . . No, when Uncle Fortune came. Then Provender would be joining the party, whether he liked it or not.

3

'I'm scared,' said the Columbine, in a quiet voice. 'Really scared.'

'Don't be,' said the Harlequin. 'Everything'll be fine. This is going to work.'

'But what if something goes wrong?'

'It won't.'

'And what if he doesn't even notice me? What if he just ignores me?'

'He'll notice you, not a doubt about it. Especially with that little lot on show.' The Harlequin gestured at the Columbine's breasts, which were naturally large and whose largeness the balconette bustier of her dress was doing very little to disguise. Her breasts, indeed, appeared to be in competition as to which of them was going to squeeze itself free of the bustier first.

The Columbine placed an arm across her cleavage, unhappy at the Harlequin's leering scrutiny.

'What's the problem?' the Harlequin said. 'You shouldn't be ashamed. Tits like those. Should be proud. And anyway, it's not as if I haven't seen them before.'

'It's different.'

'If I remember rightly, you even wanked me off with them once.'

'It's different,' the Columbine insisted. 'Things are different now.' Colour had come to her cheeks and she could not meet the Harlequin's gaze. 'I'm not your girlfriend any more.'

'That could change.'

'No, it couldn't.'

The Harlequin let it lie, although his eyes said he didn't believe her. She was protesting too much. She still fancied him. Of course she did. Bloke like him? Strong? Worked out at the gym a lot? Smart? Committed? With a cause? Irresistible.

'Listen,' he said, his voice softening, becoming almost gentle, 'you're going to do fine. I mean it. The plan's sound. You – you're intelligent, beautiful. You'll play your part just right. I have every confidence in you.'

The Columbine looked up at him again. In spite of her better judgement, against every instinct she had, she was consoled by his words. She wanted to believe in him. He had hurt her in the past. He could be cruel. But she was convinced that at heart he was good. She was sure she could trust him. And if he had confidence in her, there was no reason why she shouldn't have the same confidence too.

'All right,' she said, and she took a deep breath which helped stiffen her resolve and which was also, from the Harlequin's point of view, a good thing because it resulted in a temporary increase in the ratio of exposed breast flesh to unexposed. 'All right,' she said again, exhaling. 'I'm fine. Everything's going to be fine.'

She picked up a salver of drinks, the Harlequin did likewise, and together they exited the catering marquee, returning to Venice and the party.

4

Uncle Fortune – Fort for short – had elected to arrive at the ball this year by parachute.

For him, in all sorts of ways, this was no mean feat. For one thing, Fortune was not of a naturally athletic build or disposition. He had the kind of figure that was most politely described as cuddly, the kind that, far from being aerodynamic, best lent itself to plummeting like a stone. For another thing, he was notoriously bibulous. He seldom did anything without alcohol in his veins (and that included eat breakfast).

The parachute instructor he hired to teach him, however, was aware of his reputation and impressed on him the unwisdom of skydiving while under the influence of alcohol. One might, the instructor said, if one jumped drunk, make a careless mistake. An irrevocable mistake. Such as, for example, forgetting to pull one's ripcord.

So it was a strange and novel experience for Fortune to embark on a potentially life-threatening enterprise without his customary cushion of inebriation. But he knuckled down and got on with it. First in tandem with the instructor, the two of them joined by a harness like Siamese twins, and then solo with the instructor alongside him, Fortune performed a series of jumps from his private dirigible at ever increasing altitudes. By the end of the course of lessons, he had become a proficient parachutist, able to hit a ten-foot roundel painted on the croquet lawn at the back of his manor house every time without fail. Apart from slightly spraining his ankle during one landing, he had not suffered any sort of injury and was proud of that.

Now, on the night of the ball, shortly before nine p.m., his dirigible nosed across Dashlands at a height of two thousand feet with its running lights doused so that it was all but invisible – if spotted, it would in all likelihood be taken for a cloud. Below, the party site glowed bright, unmissable. Fortune strapped on his parachute pack, went through his final equipment checks, slid open the cabin door, bid farewell to his pilot, reflexively groped for his hip flask, remembered he hadn't brought it, and threw himself out into the night.

Everything went according to plan – almost. After a ten-second freefall Fortune yanked the ripcord, the parachute billowed open above him with the customary explosive *snap*, his harness constricted around him, not unpainfully, and for a while he swung dizzyingly to and fro. When things settled down, he grabbed the guide-rope handles and began steering. Venice loomed beneath his feet and the party-goers swelled from milling dots to identifiably human shapes. The Piazza San Marco was his goal, although landing in the Grand Canal remained a possibility – he hated the idea of a soaking but the stunt would be funnier and more memorable if he came down with a splash.

Soon Fortune was low enough that he could even make out, or so he thought, his brother. He was about to yell out Prosper's name, and thus alert everyone to his imminent arrival, when a sudden crosswind caught him. In order to counter it he dipped one side of his parachute, but he could still feel himself being driven relentlessly and inexorably off-course, away from the piazza, towards the rooftops. The Campanile rushed up at him. *Please, O Lord, don't let me die*, was Fortune's brief, fervent prayer. *Not like this. Not sober.* Then he screwed his eyes tight shut and braced himself for impact and possible impalement.

When he dared to open his eyes again, he found that he was dangling some thirty feet above the piazza's paving stones. A crowd had gathered beneath him and anxious voices were calling up, wanting to know if he was all right. He looked up and saw that his parachute had got hooked over the Golden Angel. He was suspended helplessly but harmlessly from the Campanile like some sort of novelty decoration.

Fortune began to chuckle.

When someone below informed him that a ladder was being fetched, he chuckled even more. 'Tell them to bring up a snifter of brandy while they're at it,' he called down.

Ten minutes later, Fortune was safely on the ground and receiving applause from the assembled party-goers. The applause, as was often the case, had a note of sycophancy to it. Applause usually did when you were Family. Nonetheless he accepted it with a gracious nod, and then he hugged Prosper, kissed sister-in-law Cynthia lavishly on both cheeks, made a typical bachelor-uncle fuss of nieces Gratitude and Extravagance, and in no time had a bottle of claret in each hand and was well on his wassailing way to total inebriation.

His costume, incidentally, was that of a devil. Red bodysuit, horns on his head, scarlet face-paint, short three-pronged pitchfork, and a fake goatee beard of hellish blackness.

Uncle Fortune having arrived, Cynthia could not put it off any longer. Provender would be coming to the ball even if she had to grab him by the scruff of the neck and drag him here.

She left the piazza. She threaded through the thoroughfares, the *salizade*, the canalside *fondamente*, till she reached the edge of Venice. Then she took off along a lamp-flanked path of crushed quartz that led towards the house. The party dwindled behind her, the sounds of conviviality fading, the shotgun reports from the Arsenale becoming nothing more than faint popcorn *cracks*. By the time she arrived at the house, all Cynthia could hear was the crunch of her own footfalls.

Dashlands House invited her in through a square archway into a courtyard which gave onto another courtyard via another square archway which in turn gave onto yet another courtyard via yet another square archway. The last courtyard, the largest of the three, boasted a rectangular lily pond which butted up against the lofty, narrow windows of the largest drawing room. A broad, low loggia led to one of the house's two main entrances. Twin teak-panelled doors swung inward, affording access to a chamber that was as much atrium as entrance hall – cylindrical, capped with a conical ceiling made up of arcs of iridescent glass. Gold-patinaed sconces held candle-shaped bulbs which shed a buttery light over the marble floor and the cuboid table-and-chair set that occupied a space next to the passageway into the drawing room. A rising concrete staircase hugged the inmost half of the wall, complete with wrought-iron handrail. But the hall's dominant feature was the twenty-foot chryselephantine statue which stood dead centre.

She was called Triumph and she held a pose that was part exaltation, part ecstasy, her legs together, her hips and breasts thrust forward, her head thrown back, one arm stretched in front of her, the other upraised with its fingers knifing to the heavens, like a gymnast about to begin floor exercises. Her face was incongruously inexpressive, with blank eyes and placid mouth, but then it did not need to convey much when her body was talking so eloquently. She was, it seemed, on the verge of something, some vast and longed-for release. Solid and gleaming and chunky, she had lines like a locomotive, and she waited, she only ever waited, poised, ready to commence. Triumph.

Depending on her mood, Cynthia could find the statue daunting, inspiring, oppressive, and, occasionally, vulgar. This evening, with certain matters weighing heavily on her mind, she thought Triumph looked silly and vain, an old tart in a posture too young for her, hoping for admiration. She passed around the statue and ascended the stairs, noting halfway up that Triumph's left shoulder bore a thick coating of dust. She would have a word with Carver about that.

Nowhere on all the acres of land it occupied was Dashlands House more than three storeys tall. It spread, it sprawled, but even its highest roof apex was a mere thirty feet from ground-level. Contained within it, however, was any number of midways and mezzanines. Rare was the room that shared the exact same horizontal plane as another room, and rare the corridor that did not terminate in a short flight of steps. Some of the larger rooms were in themselves multi-tiered, with platforms and pits denoting various separate sections. Sometimes, to Cynthia, the place felt like an indoor obstacle course. It was impossible to walk through it at any speed because every dozen or so paces you were obliged to break stride and turn a corner or go up or down. Frank Lloyd Wright had had a hand in its design, but you could be forgiven for thinking Maurits Cornelis Escher hadn't also been somehow involved.

Eventually she came to its northernmost wing. As she neared the door to Provender's suite of rooms, she heard the rattle of brass keyboard keys. Provender was at his videotyper, probably hammering out another entry in that journal of his. Cynthia tapped softly on the door with the rim of her mask, expecting that he would not hear this above the furious clatter he was making. He didn't, and so she opened the door uninvited, knowing that if Provender complained about the intrusion she would be able to tell him in all honesty that she *had* tried knocking.

The blinds were drawn. All the lamps were switched off. The only illumination in the suite's main room came from the videotyper's screen, in front of which Provender sat hunched, staring fixedly into its small glowing oval. His brow was ploughed in concentration. His shaven head nodded as he typed. On the desktop beside him, the videotyper's operating unit whistled and droned in its brass housing. It was a Japanese make. In spite of the fact that the Gleeds owned several patents on British circuit-board technology, Provender insisted that the Japanese produced better machines and so purchased with money what everyone else in the Family could get for free. If medals were handed out for perversity, Provender would have a lapel-full.

Cynthia did not step into the room yet. She stood in the doorway and studied her son, who remained oblivious to her presence. She saw a slender, well-proportioned nearly-twenty-five-year-old who until recently had sported a head of lustrous Cavalier curls but now wore just a down of shorn hair, like a velvety pelt. She saw a grown man. But she also saw the infant Provender had been, the chubby, babbling creature whom she had held and fed, fussed with and dandled, and watched over through many a wakeful night. She could not look at him and not think of the clear, unblinking eyes that used to gaze up at her while he was at suck and not remember the smell of his scalp, rich and yeasty like baking bread. His gestures, his mannerisms, had all been there, ready-formed, and had changed little in adulthood. Provender was and ever would be her baby boy, and come what may, she adored him.

But that didn't mean there weren't times when she thought he could do with a good hard smack.

Cynthia gazed on Provender for a further minute or so, then loudly and fulsomely cleared her throat.

5

The question which needs to be addressed, wrote Provender, is whether extreme wealth is incompatible with an ethical life.

No doubt there are many people for whom this question would seem otiose, even absurd. They would love to be in a position to ask themselves such a question. They would love to have that luxury.

But for those of us who do have that luxury, and have an ounce of self-awareness, it is the only question worth asking. It is the question.

For an answer, one might look back to the early years of the Gleeds, in the seventeenth century, when the family was not yet a Family.

Rufus Alexander Gleed (b.1649–d.1707) was a merchant trader, and a successful one, specialising in the import of spices, particularly nutmeg, which was then gaining currency in European cuisine.

He did well in a cut-throat business. British spice traders were in perpetual competition with the Dutch, and Indonesia and most of the Southern Seas had become a virtual battleground. Merchantmen raced one another to secure the latest crop, and clashes between ships of either country were not uncommon as they homed in on the same harbour, each hoping to be the first into port to secure the best bargains. Since most merchantmen were accompanied by a naval escort for protection, the skirmishes were known to cost vessels and lives.

Neither the British nor the Dutch government was any too happy to keep supplying military support in this manner. It was a huge drain on their budgets and resources. Yet they continued to do so, grudgingly, because the national economic interest demanded it.

Rufus Gleed's stroke of genius, if one can call it that, was to decide to bypass government involvement. He began employing privateers to escort his trading fleet. He took on the defence of his own ships as a business expense. He was even able to defray the outlay against tax. He made piracy in effect a tax write-off.

His privateers, unhindered by rules of engagement, were fiercer and more aggressive than any Dutch naval captain. They would attack without provocation. They harried Dutch ships mercilessly. With them there was never any parley. They argued with the voice of the cannonade.

From being merely successful, Rufus became unimaginably affluent. His ruthlessness (and that of his privateers) paid off to such an extent that he began to consider himself eligible for Family status. In a letter written to a nephew in 1693, and now kept at Dashlands in the Gleed archives, he states his intention thus:

'In that I am now among the richest men of Englande, and am blest with issue in the forme of three Sonnes and lately a Grand-sonne, it seems that it should be my purpose to raise myself and my progeny to the rank of Family; and this being so, to that end I have made Supplication to the Borgia de'Medicis of Italy, who as the very first and original of the Families are endow'd with the Responsibility of bestowing or otherwise said Privilidge, and it is my full Expectation soon to be in receipt of Documents confirming their accession to my Desire . . .'

However, not long after his 'Desire' became a reality, Rufus found himself in a direct conflict with a fellow spice trader, also recently Familied: Pieter van der Ebb. Van der Ebb had decided to adopt the same tactics as Rufus and furnish his fleet with a privateer bodyguard.

What ensued was a protracted and violent spice war whose effects are still being felt to this day (its most trivial legacy may be found in certain Gleed forenames, including my own, embarrassing, never-to-be-mentioned-here middle name). Eastern Indonesia, and especially the tiny archipelago known as the Banda Islands, where most nutmeg is grown, saw an increasing incidence of bloodshed both on and off land. Down through the decades thousands of Bandanese were killed, caught in the crossfire between opposing groups of mercenaries employed by the Gleeds and the van der Ebbs. Several hundred Chinese immigrant workers met the same fate.

The fighting was still going on even in the late 1800s, albeit sporadically. By then the van der Ebbs had, pardon the pun, ebbed in influence and power. As a result of a series of bad marriages and the premature deaths of a number of sickly offspring, more and more the van der Ebbs were finding themselves subsumed into the Kuczynski Family. Their name was dying out. The Kuczynskis were taking over their business interests and their lineage, and the van der Ebbs were shrinking to a rump. Over them fell the deepening shade of the Kuczynskis' rapidly expanding East European umbrella.

Animosity toward the Gleeds, however, remained. The Kuczynskis subsumed that too. It entered into their bloodline and infected it, and has festered there ever since, bursting out at regular intervals and engulfing whole nations with its venom.

It is also, undeniably, reciprocated. My father, for one, cannot mention the Kuczynski name without spitting.

And this draws me to my point. There can surely be no Family which doesn't owe its fortune and status to the exploitation and the suffering of others. Somewhere in every Family's history there lies a heavy weight of guilt, never referred to, never expressed. We have built our empires on huge piles of nameless, forgotten corpses. We continue to sustain these empires in that way. We never admit it. It is too immense, too appalling a fact ever to be uttered.

In the Gleeds' case, all we ever care to say – the official line, inculcated from birth – is that we started out earning our money from nutmeg.

Such an innocent thing. Nutmeg. Everyone loves it. Everyone uses it. You put it in Béchamel sauce and mulled wine. Dopeheads say you can get high on it, although this is disputed. Its hallucinogenic properties are weak, if they exist at all. You have to ingest a hell of a lot to get a result, and more often than not that result is a bad case of vomiting follow by a cracking headache. I know this from experience. Never again.

(Nutmeg also yields mace, a less innocent-sounding product, derived from the thin leathery tissue between the stone and pulp of the fruit. But mace, for all that by etymological accident it shares its name with a medieval weapon, is harmless. Merely another spice.)

So it eases the conscience just to say 'nutmeg'. It glosses over the awkward parts of Gleed history. In two soft syllables it sweetens the unpalatable past.

How, then, to change that? How to tackle the truth of all the Gleed Family did – and still does – in the name of furthering its own ends and feathering its own nest? How to undo the sins of the forefathers?

I come up against this time after time. I wrestle with it at night. I ponder on it by day.

The irony isn't lost on me that my sleepless nights are spent on a well-sprung bed between the softest of sheets, or that my daytime ponderings often find me strolling through a palatial house and a huge estate amid a host of domestic servants who call me Master Provender and would doubtless drop to their knees and lick my arse if I ordered them to (not that I ever would).

All the same, if I didn't have these thoughts and feelings, these doubts - this urge to somehow make amends - I would consider myself less than human.

What I have yet to establish is how to go about

The sudden throat-clearing shocked Provender out of his skin.

'Mother!' he yelped, crossly. 'For God's sake! How long have you been standing there?'

'Not long,' said Cynthia.

'Christ!' Provender rapidly tapped out a sequence of keystrokes, saving the journal entry and then blanking the file from the screen. 'A man's entitled to some privacy, you know.'

'Not when there's a party going on that he should be at.' Cynthia strode into the room. Glancing through a doorway to her right she saw Provender's bed. His costume was laid out on it, untouched, exactly as she herself had left it that afternoon. Provender was still in his day clothes – open-necked shirt, corduroy trousers, brogues. 'And you're not even dressed. Really, Prov, this isn't good enough.'

'Um, what time is it?'

'Gone nine. You promised me. You promised me you wouldn't be late.'

'I . . . lost track of time.'

'I don't care. A promise is a promise. I'm very disappointed.'

Provender tried to look as if her disappointment did not mean anything to him. 'It's just a stupid party.'

Cynthia tried to look as if she did not resent her summer ball being described as stupid. 'In that case, then surely it needs someone like you to come along and raise the intellectual tone.'

'Ooh, nice going there, Mum. Cunning piece of psychology.'

'Yes, I thought so.'

'And just how many nice young ladies are going to be paraded in front of me when I get out there?'

'I don't know what you're talking about.'

'Come on. Two? Three?'

'It's possible I may have a couple of people I'd like you to meet.'

'Female people?'

'Well, if you must be so gender-specific – yes.'

'Mum.' Provender reached down and switched the videotyper off. 'You're a modern woman, wouldn't you say? Emancipated. Liberated. Doesn't this whole finding-Provender-a-wife malarkey strike you as just a bit, you know, anachronistic? Not to mention chauvinistic. At the very least, shouldn't I be left to do it myself, in my own time? You know, hunt my own fiancée fodder?'

Cynthia shrugged and nodded. 'I can't disagree, it *is* an anachronism. But it's also tradition, and Families are nothing if not traditional. Tradition is our bedrock. It's what people like about us. Bloodline. Take away the money, and that's the main source of public fascination: bloodline. I'm afraid it's your responsibility to be a part of that, and it's *my* responsibility to make sure you discharge *your* responsibility, and that's an end of it. Believe me, I'd happily let you, as you so charmingly put it, "hunt your own fiancée fodder", if I thought there was the slightest chance of it happening. I would, I'd step aside and leave you to it like a shot. But since you don't seem able to even get up off your backside and start looking, I've no choice but to get all matchmaker on you. I'm sorry you find it all so irksome, but— Well, no, I'm not sorry at all. It's just tough *mierda*.'

Provender, in spite of himself, smiled. His mother no longer believed, as she used to, that it was all right to swear in front of her children as long as she stuck to her native Spanish. However, the habit had become so ingrained that she continued to do it even now, when they understood perfectly well what she was saying. Not only that but, instead of preserving her children's innocence, she had managed instead to teach them a second set of obscenities to go along with the Anglo-Saxon ones they had picked up anyway from their schoolmates and peers. They were now, thanks to her, doubly proficient at swearing – expletive-bilingual.

'*Mierda, madre?*' Provender said.

'Oh, don't start.'

'Wherefore this Iberian invective?'

'I mean it. Stop.'

'This Castilian castigation?'

'Stop it now. Put your costume on. Come to the party. Do as I say.'

'This—'

'Provender!'

Her eyes flashed with pure exasperation. Anger would surely follow if Provender wasn't careful, and his mother's temper, when aroused, could be fearsome. It was the slumbering tiger you tiptoed around.

'OK, I'll come, I'll come,' he said.

'Good. Thank you.'

Cynthia crossed over to the row of windows that occupied all of one wall, giving access to a balcony. She rolled one of the windows open, to let in some air. The main room of Provender's suite was the size of a tennis court but even with all that space it could start to smell musty and stifling if he spent too much time there. A breeze wafted in around her ankles, bringing with it the scent and sound of waterfalls. There was a cascade directly below the balcony, a sequence of sluices and rock-pools that decanted into a stream and thence to a forest-fringed lake. Above the rushing water the night air thrilled with insects and misty spray.

Turning, she said, 'Do you need a hand getting your outfit on?'

'Twenty-four, Mother,' Provender replied, mock-wearily.

'I'll wait out in the corridor then.'

'Do that.'

'Five minutes.'

'*Fine*.'

6

Five minutes later, mother and son were making their way through the house. Ten minutes after that, they were approaching Venice.

By then Provender was already regretting his choice of costume. He had elected to go as the Medico from the *commedia dell'arte*, a kind of private joke since the character's look was derived from the outfits worn by real Renaissance doctors during times of plague. It amused Provender to think of himself at the ball as the one healthy individual among a batch of the diseased.

However, he was in a long black linen cape, which was hot and itchy, with a flat broad-brimmed hat, also hot and itchy, and worst of all was the mask, with its elongated beak-like nose and small round spectacles perched in front of the eyeholes. Navigating in this was phenomenally difficult. Wherever Provender looked, the nose was always in the way, obscuring a significant portion of his field of vision. He cursed himself for not having tried the mask on beforehand and wondered at what point he would be able to dispense with it – at what point he would feel his ironic statement had been sufficiently made.

On the plus side, he was equipped with a baton-like stick, like the ones the Medico (and the real Renaissance doctors) carried in order to be able to remove patients' garments from a safe distance. Even if no one 'got' Provender's costume, there was always the option of whacking party-goers around the head with the stick to show them what he thought of them. No, not really. But he didn't doubt that he would at some point tonight be sorely tempted.

First to greet him on the Piazza San Marco was Uncle Fort, several sheets to the wind by now. Rocking unsteadily, Fort regaled Provender with an account of his arrival, pointing with pride to the parachute which still engulfed the Golden Angel like a squid, its severed ropes dangling tentacularly. 'Thought I was a goner for sure this time!' Fort exclaimed, and his breath was the sweet-sour stench of a hundred vineyards, strong enough to assail his nephew's nostrils even through the Medico mask's prodigious proboscis.

Then came Gratitude, followed closely by Extravagance. Like galleons on a calm sea they sailed towards their brother, homing in. Cynthia, meantime, had melted into the crowd, and Provender knew it wouldn't be long before she was back with one or both of her marriage prospects in tow. He tried not to think about it.

His sisters gave him grief, in a sisterly fashion, for not turning up when he should have and for making their mother go to the trouble of fetching him. He in return, in a brotherly fashion, told them they could stick it up their wigs.

'You have obligations, Prov,' said Gratitude. She was his elder by two years but often behaved as if it was more like ten.

'Fuck obligations,' he replied. 'I don't see why I should have to be here if I don't want to be.'

'Oh, very mature,' said Extravagance, who, though seven years younger than him, also behaved as if she were a decade his senior. 'And what sort of costume is that? This is a ball, Prov, not a Halloween party.'

'Really? So why are there witches here then?'

Extravagance went through an elaborate charade of not understanding the reference, then understanding. 'Oh, I get. You mean us. Gratitude and I are witches. How clever. Sharp as ever with the put-downs, Prov. Obviously, spending hours on your own in your room does nothing to blunt the wit, does it?'

'Is that the best you can do, 'Strav?' Provender replied. 'Have a go at me for preferring my own company to that of others?'

'Oh no, I can do much better. I'm just getting warmed up. For instance, your slothfulness on the marriage front. I mean, what's it going to take for you to realise you *have* to get some poor girl up the aisle, ASAP?'

'And if I don't, ASAP? What the worst that can happen? I get to spend a few more years single. Not such a bad alternative.'

'Not for you maybe. Probably not for your putative wife either. But you know what's at stake, and still you faff around.'

'I don't see you in any hurry to get hitched,' Provender said. 'You either, Grat.'

'It's not so important for us' said Extravagance. 'We can leave it as late as we like. No Y-chromosome. Sorry!'

'Best not leave it *too* late. There's a limited shelf-life for the Y-chromosome-less, and spinsterhood can creep up unexpectedly. One moment you're young and lovely, the next you're a crocheting old hag.'

'Cheap shot. But seriously, Provender, what if something happens to you? What if there's an accident or you get ill or something? What if—'

Gratitude stepped in. As the oldest sibling it usually fell to her to make peace between the other two. It had been that way since they were little, and she would not have minded so much if the level of the bickering between her brother and sister ever rose above childish, but it never did and probably never would.

'Listen, both of you,' she said, low-voiced, stern. 'Not now. Not here. We're on our best behaviour. You can argue all you want tomorrow. Tonight, we're one big happy Family. All right?'

Provender and Extravagance glared at each other, the tips of their masks' respective noses almost touching. Then both of them nodded, reluctantly, surlily. As the three siblings parted company, Extravagance turned and popped her tongue out at Provender. He, in response, brandished his stick at her. Each felt this constituted the last word and so was able to walk away satisfied, victorious.

Spying a Harlequin with a drinks salver, Provender made for him. He was almost at his goal when a party-goer stepped in the way, blocking his path.

'Provender. It is Provender, isn't it, under all that?'

'It is,' said Provender, warily.

'Thought so. I'm pretty good on posture and gait. Got an eye for it. And yours are pretty distinctive. You always look like you're expecting something bad to happen.'

It just did, Provender thought. 'Arthur,' he said.

'None other,' said the party-goer, and executed a sweeping bow.

Provender's cousin had, like Provender, chosen his ball outfit from the ranks of the *commedia* characters, but his was that of Scaramouche. Consisting of a multicoloured, gold-buttoned tunic, a feathered hat, a swirling moustache, and a sword at his side, the costume lent Arthur a swashbuckling look, which was let down somewhat by the fact that Arthur was a shade over five feet tall, five-two if he was wearing his lifts, and had ears that wouldn't have been out of place on a football trophy. Height, it would seem, was a prerequisite for successful swashbucklery, and so was a set of aural appendages that did not stick out sideways.

Arthur was the son of Prosper's other younger brother, the late Uncle Acquire. Uncle Ack, as he was known, had been the black sheep of that particular generation of Gleeds, turning his back on the Family and going off to live on a remote Scottish isle where he met, and for a while shared his humble croft with, a local girl who became Arthur's mother. Whether she and Uncle Ack were ever actually married was a question nobody dared ask. Ack died without mentioning her or her child in his will, at any rate, and so the Family chose to regard their union as not having the legality of even a common-law bond.

That was until the product of their union left the island in his late teens and came to the mainland, presenting himself at Dashlands and demanding to be treated as a proper Family member or else. What the 'or else' consisted of was never made clear but it seemed likely to have something to do with the legitimacy or otherwise of Arthur's birth. Arthur appeared to be threatening to expose himself publicly as a Gleed bastard if he didn't get what he wanted, and rather than face that PR nightmare the Family decided instead to welcome him to its bosom, purchase him a fine London town house, furnish him with a handsome allowance, and help him get on in whatever trade or profession he might wish to pursue.

Arthur wished to pursue the craft of acting, and so was enrolled at the

Gleed Academy of Music, Drama and Dance, from where he graduated *summa cum laude* and stepped straight into his first starring role in a TV series in which he played a dashing police detective who solved crimes while moonlighting as a cabaret singer in his spare time. That Arthur was neither dashing, nor old enough to be a detective, nor any sort of singer, was not perceived as a hindrance to his getting the part. His principal qualification was that he was a Gleed. To have that surname in the cast credits guaranteed good viewing figures.

Thereafter, Arthur had never been out of work. Movies, comedy, radio drama, musicals – whatever type of role he set his heart on, he got. Some critics grumbled that he had no charisma or presence or discernible talent, that listening to him recite his lines was like listening to a washing machine running through its spin cycle. Not many critics expressed such opinions in their reviews, however, and few who did lasted long in their jobs. It wasn't a wise career move to be anything less than unstinting in your praise of a Gleed.

To say Arthur was smug would be an understatement. Being kind to him, one might aver that his smugness was warranted in so far as he had successfully blackmailed and bluffed his way into the Family's acceptance and then had shot to the top of the thespian tree despite his negligible acting ability. One might even admire him for his sheer nerve and gall.

Then again, one might, if one was Provender, dislike him intensely for that very reason. One might, indeed, make a point of trying to annoy him every time one encountered him, just to demonstrate one's feelings towards him.

'So, Art,' Provender said, 'how's tricks?'

Arthur did not care for 'Art', but let Provender get away with it this time. 'Not so bad.'

'Haven't seen you on telly lately. Got any work? Or are you resting right now?'

Beneath the curlicued moustache, Arthur's lips went rigid. ' "Resting", Prov?' he said.

Gotcha, thought Provender.

During the time he had lived in England, Arthur had successfully managed to eradicate all traces of Scots brogue from his accent. He spoke Received Pronunciation with greater precision than many of those who were born to it.

' "Resting",' he said, in his archest, RP-est tones, 'is a word used only by people who aren't in showbusiness – people who like to think they're in with the jargon and know what's going on and what acting's all about. You will never, ever hear anyone in showbiz say "resting". No actor worth his salt would dream of letting the word pass his lips. And do you know why?'

Provender did, as a matter of fact. He had heard Arthur deliver this diatribe on at least two previous occasions, using almost the exact same words, with the exact same degree of pompous indignation. 'Resting' was a red rag to this particular bull; or, if you prefer, it was the cue that invariably prompted Arthur to launch into a lengthy and probably self-penned soliloquy.

'Because,' Arthur continued, 'it isn't resting. It's anything but. When you're between jobs, you don't spend the time sitting at home making toast and waiting for your agent to ring. You're out there putting yourself about, going to audition after audition, callback after callback. You're phoning people, you're having meetings with producers, it's one long constant slog, and it's exhausting, let me tell you, it's not *resting*, it's the complete bloody opposite.'

'OK, right,' said Provender. 'Yes. Silly me. Thanks for setting me straight on that one.'

'No problem. You're welcome. But honestly, it does get on my tits when I hear someone say "resting". They clearly have no idea what they're talking about.'

'Clearly.' Provender paused, then added: 'But – forgive me, Art – but has there ever been a time when you've actually been between jobs? You seem to know all about it but, as far as I'm aware, you've never had a problem getting work and you're always saying how your diary's booked solid for the next three years.'

Arthur's eyes narrowed, and his teeth came together with an audible *clack*, and his neck straightened, and Provender congratulated himself on a hit, a palpable hit.

'I am speaking, not for myself, but for all actors,' Arthur said stiffly. 'All my brethren and sistren in the craft. All us jobbing thesps. I've been fortunate, yes, I won't deny it, luckier than most, but it's a precarious living, acting. Who knows, three years from now I might be looking at a diary full of blank pages. I doubt it but there's always the chance. Besides,' he said, recovering some of his previous vim and vituperativeness, 'at least I *have* a job. At least I do something to earn a living. There are those of us who can't say the same, aren't there, Prov? Quite a few names spring to mind.'

Provender tried not to flinch; not to let Arthur know that the barb had struck home. 'You don't need to work, Arthur.'

'And yet I do,' Arthur replied. 'I choose to. It would be perfectly possible for me to swan around all day long, the living epitome of the idle rich, all "la la la, look at me, I've never put in a day's graft in my life" – but I don't. I get out there. I roll up my sleeves, muck in, *achieve*. And I have to say, doing that makes it a damn sight easier to look at myself in the mirror every morning.'

Provender bit back the obvious retort. Too easy; and more to the point, he was suddenly finding himself on the losing end of the exchange, and a cheap crack about Arthur's looks would only incite his cousin to attack with even greater viciousness.

As it was, Arthur did not seem willing to relent just yet. 'Yep,' he said, 'having a job sets you free, definitely. It sends you to bed with a clean conscience. It gives your life structure and focus. It prevents you from getting obsessed with yourself, bogged down in your own thoughts. Generally a good thing, Prov, work. Take it from one who knows. Oh, and in answer to your original question, yes I'm working right now. Well, not right this moment, but you know what I mean. I've no idea how it's passed you by, when *everyone's* talking about it. I'm doing *Hamlet* in the West End.'

He left a pause, waiting for Provender to be impressed. When Provender just gave a non-committal nod, he went on, 'Yes, I've never tackled Shakespeare before, but it's only right and proper that I should. We're about to open at the Shortborn Theatre on New Aldwych. Previews tomorrow and Monday, first night Tuesday. It's a challenge, and frankly I'm nervous as hell about it, but then something would be wrong if I wasn't. You don't brave the Bard lightly.'

'And you're playing . . . ?'

'Who do you think I'm playing!'

'Well, I just thought I should check. You know, me not being part of the acting profession like you are, not a brethren or sistren thesp, somebody could say to me, "I'm doing Shakespeare in the West End," and for all I know they mean they're Third Servant or the stage manager or an usherette or something.'

Arthur looked askance at his cousin, unable to decide if he was really as naïve as he sounded. 'But I'm not somebody, Prov.'

'No, that's true.'

'And there can't be many actors better suited than me to portraying the Prince of Denmark. I do have a unique insight into that sort of world. Families in castles. Strange relatives and relationships.'

'Yes?'

'Yes. In fact, you really ought to come and see it. I can arrange comp tickets for you. In the Family Box.' Arthur struck Provender as surprisingly in earnest. 'You'd enjoy yourself. It's quite a production. You could even attend the first night. You're not doing anything on Tuesday, are you?'

'Don't think so.'

'No plans? Not likely to be otherwise detained?'

'Otherwise detained? Not as far as I know.'

'There you go, then. It's settled. I'll sort out tickets for all of you. You could make it a Family night out, the five of you.'

'Well, we'll see.'

'No, no, you have to come. Leave it with me. Now, I think there's someone over there I need to see. Nice chatting with you, Prov.'

Arthur sauntered off, and belatedly it occurred to Provender that even if he didn't have anything planned for Tuesday night, he should have said he did. It was, after all, his birthday.

Well, Arthur could arrange tickets if he wanted to, and Provender's parents and sisters could go see Arthur's *Hamlet* if they wanted to. Provender was pretty sure he would be staying put that night. He had no pressing urge to travel to London and watch his cousin massacre one of the great Shakespearian roles. Arthur's performance as the Dane would, he was sure, be tragic in all the wrong ways.

Provender scanned the piazza, looking both for someone with a drinks salver and for someone he might possibly want to talk to. Neither was immediately apparent. He swung his head this way and that, picturing the mask's nose as the barrel of a piece of field artillery, sighting along it and taking imaginary potshots at guests. He stopped when Great became his next 'target'. It didn't do to lob hypothetical artillery shells at your great-grandfather. Or was it great-great-grandfather? Or even great-great-great? Great being so old, so fantastically antiquated, there was some confusion about his genealogical status. The line of descent had become blurred, and nobody was quite sure any more where, exactly, he fitted in. It was possible he was not a direct ancestor at all, not several steps up the primogeniture bloodline from Provender but rather a distant uncle, a remote cousin several times removed. He was, though, undeniably the ultra-patriarch, the senior-most Gleed. For all his useless body, his threadbare scalp, his inability to communicate, his helplessness, he remained the root and figurehead of Britain's foremost Family.

Provender debated whether to go over and speak to him. What decided him against was the presence of Carver at Great's side. Carver stood sentinel, hands behind back, coldly viewing the party guests. Great's own expression seemed not much less cold. Nearby, Provender spotted a waitress bearing beverages. He made for her instead.

7

The Columbine did not, at first, recognise who the dark figure swooping towards her in fact was. The hook-nose mask, flat hat and swirling black cape made him a startling apparition, and, already in a state of heightened anxiety, the Columbine experienced something akin to mortal dread as he closed in on her with purposeful stride. For a few appalling seconds she thought this was not some party guest, but rather punishment, nemesis, doom, all rolled into one, coming to claim her. Had the figure been carrying a scythe instead of a stick, it would not, to her, have seemed at all out of place.

In her consternation, she nearly dropped her salver. But the figure reached her just in time to seize her wrist and steady it, levelling the salver before the drinks slid off, and his grip was warm and firm and plainly that of an ordinary human being, and his voice was that of an ordinary human being too as he said, 'Whoops, careful there. Be a shame to waste all that booze before I've had a chance to sample some.'

The Columbine blushed. She could scarcely believe her own foolishness. Thinking this was some supernatural entity. Honestly! How ridiculous was that? Get a grip on yourself, girl.

'Drink, sir?' she said, faltering only slightly over the words.

'Absolutely,' said the party-goer, 'now that they're not spilled all over the floor.' He let go of her arm and she lowered the salver so that he could peruse the selection on it.

'I do apologise about that, sir.'

'Oh God, don't worry. Accidents happen. Or don't, as the case may be.' The party-goer's hand hovered to and fro over the various glasses like that of a chess player trying to decide which piece to move next. 'Ah, bugger it, I can barely see what I'm doing.' He grabbed his mask by the nose and yanked it down beneath his chin. 'That's better. Now then . . .'

It was Provender Gleed, and the Columbine had realised that it was Provender Gleed an instant before he exposed his face. She ought to have known who he was as soon as she set eyes on him, and would have, had she been thinking straight. She had, after all, been told what costume Provender would be wearing tonight. It had been described to her in detail, right down to the fake spectacles on the nose. She had been supposed to be looking out for somebody dressed just like this.

Again, she told herself to get a grip. She needed to stay calm and focused. She needed to have all her wits about her. If she didn't pull herself together, she wasn't going to be able to do what the Harlequin wanted her to do, the plan would fail, everything would be in vain . . .

She remembered the Harlequin telling her earlier how he had faith in her. Even though they were no longer lovers, he had a way of making her feel capable of anything, everything. Not only that, his approval was still important to her, his happiness still mattered to her.

Thinking of which instilled her with strength. She could pull this off. She *would*. She peered across at Provender Gleed, who appeared unable to make up his mind.

'So, what'll it be?' she asked, and she accompanied the query with a small giggle. At the same time, she widened her eyes slightly, tilted her head to one side, and arched her back, thrusting her chest forward. Old tricks. Obvious tricks. But they seldom failed.

Provender noticed. He glanced up from the salver. His eyes flicked to her face. Searched there for a moment. Then he smiled.

It was, the Columbine noted, a nice smile. He was, indeed, a good-looking boy, better so in the flesh than in photographs. In some of the pictures of him she had seen, his nose looked enormous, as though transplanted from somebody else's face, someone twice his size. But up close, it fit. Big yet dignified. Characterful. A perfectly-in-proportion nose would have left him looking bland, she felt. Ordinarily handsome. A run-of-the-mill pretty boy. The largeness of it gave him stature. And of course, such a nose was a physical trademark of his Family – without it, he would be far less of a Gleed. The shaven head worked for him as well. On someone else it might have looked thuggish. On him, it emphasised the sensitivity of his features, making him seem vulnerable and open. She vaguely recalled reading somewhere that that was the reason he had lopped off his long locks, as an outward expression of honesty. That, and to distance himself from the current vogue among young Family males for collar-length hair.

It crossed her mind that she oughtn't to be so taken with his looks. It seemed a betrayal of her principles. He was Family, and she hated the Families. She consoled herself with the thought that if she found Provender fanciable, there was no harm in that. It made what she had to do easier. She could play her role more credibly.

'There's champagne,' she said. 'White wine. Red. Rosé. That's a *kir Famille* there. That's a margarita, of course. And there's a G and T, and that one's a vodka-tonic, I think. If you'd like something else, just say. Anything. Anything at all. If you don't like what you see . . .'

It was a perfect lead-in, but for some reason Provender didn't take advantage of it. Instead he said, 'Did you know that every drop of alcohol on that tray comes from a Gleed Family vineyard or plantation?'

'I didn't know that, sir,' replied the Columbine. 'How fascinating.' She widened her eyes a fraction more, and a fraction more breast flesh swelled into view just above the level of the salver. 'It must be quite a thing, owning all those vineyards and plantations. I can't even imagine what it must be like.'

'It's . . . As a matter of fact,' he said, with a shrug, 'it's pretty meaningless.'

'Meaningless, sir?'

'I've no idea why I even brought it up. It doesn't bother me in the slightest where all that booze comes from, and I don't see why you should care either.'

'Because, um, because I might be interested to know what I'm serving you with?' said the Columbine. 'Its provenance?'

'Provenance?'

He grinned at her. Like his smile, his grin was nice too, the Columbine thought. Fresh and sincere, as if it was something he didn't do too often.

'That's a good word,' he said. 'Not one you hear every day. Provenance. I suppose if you hang around auction houses and museums you'd hear it a lot, but . . . Do you hang around auction houses and museums at all?'

The Columbine wasn't sure how to answer. Definitely, Provender was flirting with her, and that was good, that was the plan, that was the reason behind all her eye-flaring and her bosom-thrusting and her awed-ingénue remarks. His flirting, however, wasn't taking any form she was familiar with. He was attracted to her but showing it in none of the commonly accepted ways, by complimenting her, for example, or showing off. That line about vineyards had sounded sort of boastful but he had undercut it straight away. And now he wanted to talk about *auction houses*? One thing was for sure: Families were not like ordinary folk.

'Museums,' she said. 'Sometimes I'll go to a museum. But not that often, really. I've been meaning to visit the Gleed Gallery, the new one on Millbank, but . . . But . . . I haven't had the time.'

'You're busy.'

'I am.'

'Doing jobs like this?'

'No. I mean, yes. Working, generally. Earning a crust. Some of us have to.'

Provender was suddenly unsmiling. 'The implication being some of us don't?'

'No. Oh no, sir.' Idiot! 'It was just a figure of speech. I didn't mean that—'

He waved a hand and laughed. 'I was teasing. Sorry. Unfair of me. I apologise. "Earning a crust" – I like that, too. You come out with all sorts of interesting conversational wrinkles.'

'So do you, sir.'

'Do I? Thanks.' He sounded genuinely flattered. 'I like to talk with people. Properly. You know, not the standard hello-how-are-you-lovely-weather-we're-having crap, the nonsense that passes for conversation at occasions like these, everyone agreeing with everyone else. I like *discussing* things, the way you and I are doing. Aren't we? I get bored out of my mind if there isn't some kind of depth to a conversation. I'd rather have an argument with someone than listen to them jabber on about mutual acquaintances and the last holiday they went on and isn't so-and-so looking positively radiant this evening? It's an attitude that doesn't make me very popular, but then life isn't a popularity conte—'

'Provender!'

Both he and the Columbine swung round in the direction of the cry. She saw a middle-aged woman striding towards them with another, younger woman in tow. The latter the Columbine did not recognise but the former she knew was Provender's mother. That afternoon, Cynthia Gleed had stood up before an assemblage of all the catering staff and told them what she expected of them at the party tonight (not much, just total dedication and immaculate efficiency). She had struck the Columbine then as a forceful personality, someone not to be messed with. Enviably beautiful, too. Now, resplendent in ballgown and mask, she looked no less beautiful and no less indomitable. She steered her young companion towards her son by the wrist, and it didn't take a genius to intuit what she had in mind for the two of them. The girl was in her twenties, slim, pretty in a vacant posh-girl way, and Provender's mother had a glint in her eye that said she was sure her son and this lissom lass were going to hit it off, and if they didn't, she would want to know the reason why.

'Prov, not interrupting anything, am I.' It was not a question. Cynthia Gleed shot the Columbine a look that was mercilessly – or, depending on your viewpoint, mercifully – brief. It appraised and dismissed in the same instant. 'Only, this is the most amazing coincidence. I was just talking to Gentian here and she, can you believe it, went to the same finishing school in Zürich as Cousin Inez. Isn't that a thing?'

Provender had no alternative but to fix on a smile and hold out his hand to the willowy Gentian. The Columbine, for her part, had no alternative but to shrink away with her salver. Cynthia Gleed's look had made it plain. The Columbine was not wanted there. Superfluous to requirements. She must look for someone else to serve.

Just before turning to meet Gentian, however, Provender had given the Columbine a wry roll of the eyes, then winked. Suddenly there was complicity between them, and in that complicity, connection. When the Harlequin sidled up to her a few moments later and said he'd spotted her talking to Provender and asked how it had gone, the Columbine was able to tell him, with complete honesty, that it had gone well. When the Harlequin then asked if she and Provender were going to be meeting up again later that night, she was able to say, also with complete honesty, that yes, she was certain they were.

And hearing this, the Harlequin smiled. A broad smile, but a wolfish one too. Not like Provender's. Not nice at all.

8

It wasn't until nearly midnight that Provender was able to speak to the Columbine again.

Dealing with Gentian took half an hour. She was a pleasant enough person, hard to find fault with. They talked about her horses, whom she loved, her parents, about whom she was more ambivalent, and about his cousin Inez, with whom, in Zürich, she had learned deportment, cooking, etiquette, and all the other hunting skills a girl needed in order to bag herself a well-to-do husband. She didn't balk when Provender made a joke about finishing schools being so called because they *finished* any chance their pupils had of becoming independent, free-thinking individuals. She responded by saying, with just the right amount of rancour, that learning how to behave correctly in polite society didn't always mean turning into some kind of mindless social robot. You stayed who you were inside, just a little more polished on the outside. Did he think Inez had turned into a robot?

He didn't, and said, with truth, that he liked Inez a lot and didn't believe her time in Switzerland had inflicted any lasting damage.

'There, then,' said Gentian, her point made.

Briefly, Provender recalled his date with Inez, which their mothers had fixed up. He had flown to Seville in the Gleed dirigible, met Inez for lunch at the Lamas Family hacienda, found her appealing but much too like his mother for comfort, and returned home the same day. His mother was still, a year on, smoothing the Lamas feathers that had been ruffled by his swift departure.

Gentian felt she had to prove that she wasn't as bland and conformist as Provender clearly thought she was, and told him of her three-day-eventing escapades, the nasty tumble she had taken just the other day at Hickstead, and her ambition to run a stud farm once she retired from competitive riding. She could see his interest waning by the second, and her opinion of him, at the same time, coagulated. He really was as stuck-up as everyone said. Not just Family-arrogant – intellectually arrogant. Thought he was smarter than everyone else, and thought that made him better than everyone else.

She was therefore relieved when Cynthia Gleed arrived with another girl for Provender to meet. Provender, likewise, was relieved . . . although his relief turned to dismay soon enough, as he was forced to spend the next hour in the company of Blaise Wynne.

Blaise made no bones about it; she wanted to marry into a Family. She didn't care which one and she didn't care whom she married. Provender Gleed would do as well as any.

Within five minutes of being introduced to him she had raised the subject of babies twice *and* offered Provender a blow job (with the bonus of simultaneous rectal stimulation, if he wished). Smoking incessantly, with quick hard sucks on liquorice-paper cigarillos, she talked of not having to work for the rest of her life, of knowing that men liked their wives to be whores in the bedroom, of injecting a shot of dynamism into a decadent household, and of looking forward to using the speedway circuit at Dashlands so that she could indulge in her favourite pastime, which was driving like a bloody loon. Provender barely got a word in edgeways. As she thundered on, however, he felt panic beginning to rise. Every instinct he had was urging him to get away from this woman. She was a shark – aggressive, relentless, tenacious. If he let her get her teeth into him, she would never let go.

He excused himself – needed to pee. When he emerged from the gents lavatory, in which he had spent an inordinate length of time, there she was, waiting patiently for him outside. Somehow she inveigled him into taking a gondola ride. They looped through the party site, and Provender was glad of the gondolier warbling at the stern, because the man was singing so loudly that Blaise could not make herself heard over him. However, near the end of the journey, Blaise decided to substitute deeds for words and lunged for Provender, her mouth wide. He genuinely thought she was going to bite him with those cigarillo-greyed gnashers of hers, but it turned out to be worse than that: an attempt to kiss him. He ducked his head to the side just in time and her lips mashed the side of his neck, harmlessly. But she wasn't done with him. As the gondola approached the candy-striped mooring posts at the edge of the Piazza San Marco, Provender felt her hand on his thigh, groping towards his crotch. There was still a gap of a few yards between the gondola and the piazza, but he leapt and somehow made it onto dry land. It was possible that in his fright he actually walked on water.

Thereafter, it became hunter and hunted, predator and prey, Provender scurrying through the crowds of merrymakers, Blaise stalking him. He bumped into his father, and Prosper Gleed was puzzled to see his son looking so hounded and harassed.

'What's up, Prov?'

Provender glanced over his shoulder. Prosper followed the direction of the look and saw Blaise Wynne at the other end of it, making her inexorable way towards them. He assessed the situation, grinned, and gave Provender a hearty slap on the arm. 'Attaboy! Hard to get. Sometimes that's the way to play it.'

Provender stumbled off and, not paying attention to where he was going, narrowly avoided a collision with Carver.

He recoiled, appalled that he had nearly touched the manservant. Carver: the bane of Provender's boyhood. Carver: like some ghost that haunted Dashlands. Carver: who, it seemed, had always been just around the corner when Provender accidentally broke a vase or put a scratch on a parquet floor or generally did something he ought not to have done. Carver had not ever scolded Provender – it was not his place – but his eyes had conveyed reproof far more sharply and eloquently than words ever could, and so too, in its way, had that scar of his.

Carver bowed deeply, with just a touch of obsequiousness. Great, beside him, was fast asleep. His chin was lodged on his collarbone, and every vein and tendon in his neck strained against the skin and looked ready to snap. His eyelids were so papery thin, his corneas stood proud through them like two buttons.

Provender backed away, mumbling an apology. He sought refuge in the jovial orbit of Fortune, catching the tail-end of the joke with which his uncle was regaling a small crowd:

'. . . so the third missionary, he's seen what's happened to the other two, he's watched through the chink in the wall of the mud hut as they've been buggered by every single tribesman and then allowed to stumble off into the jungle, and he thinks to himself, *Well, hold on, I'm a good Victorian gentleman, I'm a servant of the Lord, my body is His temple, I'm not going to allow these heathens to defile it in this ghastly manner.* So when the chief comes to him the next evening and makes the same offer, "Death or ooga-booga", the missionary says, "I choose death." And the chief smiles a great big smile and says, "Very well then. If that is what you wish. Death by ooga-booga!" '

As gales of laughter exploded around Uncle Fort, Provender turned away, and before he knew it he was in Blaise's clutches once more.

Realising that it was hopeless trying to flee from her, he adopted a different tactic, letting her know in no uncertain terms that he was not now or ever likely to be in the market for marrying a woman quite as pushy as she was. Weirdly enough, the blunter and ruder he got, the more, not less, confident Blaise became that he was the one for her.

'I like a man who speaks his mind,' she said. 'I like a bit of fire. There's nothing worse than a man who lacks spunk. In more ways than one.'

Even as she chortled at her own crudity, Provender was forming the impression that Blaise Wynne was, in fact, completely mad. He was all for women who knew what they wanted, but this was a woman who didn't know anything other than what she wanted and who simply could not tell when what she wanted did not want her in return. Perhaps she had been normal once, and sane; if so, her dream of attaining Family status, whatever the cost, had driven her stark staring bonkers since then.

Rare was the occasion that Provender had cause to give thanks for his cousin Arthur, but at that moment, as the diminutive Scaramouche lurched into his eyeline, he could not have been more grateful.

Arthur, it seemed, wished to have words with Provender. Arthur, it also seemed, had recently visited a small room off one of the lesser piazzas where intoxicants of a non-alcoholic nature were available. His nostrils were red-rimmed and his eyes had a vacant, slightly belligerent sheen and did not appear to be focusing on the same thing as each other. Drugs, of course, couldn't *not* be offered at a party like this one, and Cynthia Gleed, as any self-respecting hostess would, had laid on a premium selection – pure uncut Ecuadorian cocaine, some very pungent and potent sensimillia, and a smattering of downers and uppers to counteract the effects of the first two. At her insistence, their supply and ingestion was restricted to one discrete (and discreet) corner of the party site, so as not to offend the sensibilities of the more strait-laced guests. She herself didn't necessarily disapprove of the use of narcotics, but there was no need to rub people's noses in it.

Rubbing his own nose, Arthur lumbered up to Provender. His shoulder butted against Blaise's and he turned and peered at her as if he hadn't even realised she was there. Then, facing Provender again, he addressed him as though the two of them were already in the middle of an argument.

'And another thing, Prov,' he said, 'if anyone ought to be bloody on the bloody primogeniture line, it ought to be bloody me. I mean, I'm the bloody one with the acting career that's going bloody well even if I do say so my-bloody-self. I'm the one people bloody see on the TV and the cinema screen all the bloody time. Who'd be better as the next bloody Gleed heir? Who'd be better to carry on the bloody bloodline? Not bloody you, Prov, mate. Me! Bloody well me! Someone people know, someone people bloody see, not someone who bloody hides away all day. And someone whose bloody blood hasn't been bloody thinned like some bloody blood I could ment—'

'Arthur,' said Provender, stemming the blood-flow, 'have you met Blaise Wynne? Blaise, this is my cousin Arthur. In case you hadn't guessed, a Gleed.'

Blaise required no further prompting. In an instant, Provender was forgotten. It was as if he had never existed. She grabbed Arthur by the arm, hard, sinking her claws into him. Arthur winced with pain and tried to prise himself free, but she held grimly on.

'Arthur Gleed!' she crooned. 'Yes, I know you. Well, I've *seen* you. I watched you in that series, what was it called . . . ?'

Provender sidestepped smartly away. Only when there was a decent margin of safety between him and Blaise did he brave a look back. She was bent forward over Arthur, still clutching his arm. Arthur was shrinking from her, bewildered, trying to fathom what had just happened to him. Who was this woman? Why would she not let go? Provender saw him touch the hilt of his stage-prop sword, no doubt for reassurance, but perhaps wondering whether to draw it. Somehow Provender didn't think the weapon, wielded, would deter Blaise. She'd regard it, if anything, as a sexual come-on.

A quick check of his watch told him it was just gone half-past eleven. There was a fireworks display scheduled at midnight. Provender loved fireworks and knew he ought to get down to the southern end of the party site so as to find a spot with a good view. Of greater urgency, though, was the need for a drink. He was also keen to find a certain member of the waiting staff again. There were several Harlequins and Columbines within sight, all bearing beverages, but he ignored them. He was after one particular Columbine and would take a drink off no one else's salver.

He hunted for her through Venice. He could not say exactly what it was about her that had so intrigued him. She was extremely pretty, she had bright, clever eyes, was alluringly curvaceous – but looks alone were not the whole story. *Pert* was the word that kept occurring to him. It seemed to sum her up. *Quirky* also applied. And she hadn't been overawed by him, by what he was, and he liked that, too. She had called him 'sir', but in her job that was how you addressed every man, it was just one of the rules; and even as she was being polite and deferential towards him, Provender had been able to tell that she didn't think he was any better than her. She wasn't Family-struck, as so many people were. She had given no indication that the accident of birth which made him a Gleed was, in fact, of any consequence to her. As far as she was concerned, he was a person, just as she was a person. They were, essentially, equals.

She had been in his thoughts while he was with Gentian and even more so while he was with Blaise. She had been lodged in his brain unshakeably from the moment he met her. Even if he had liked either of the other two women, they wouldn't have stood a chance. The Columbine towered head and shoulders above them. He must find her!

She wasn't anywhere he looked. She seemed to have vanished. He searched through every alley, every narrow Venetian street. Guests greeted him from time to time. He blanked them, forging past, head down. He could have put his mask back up in order to spare himself this awkwardness, but he didn't want to be hampered in any way. He needed his eyesight unconfined – full peripheral vision. Where was she? He scanned every piazza he came to. He began to wonder if she wasn't hiding from him, spooked, perhaps, by the way he had talked to her. Maybe she thought he was like his father, a chip off the old block, hounding after anything in a skirt. Or maybe she thought he was just *odd*. He might not have given the best account of himself during their brief exchange of words. But that simply made it all the more imperative that he find her, so that he could have a stab at redeeming himself.

Eventually, as midnight loomed, persistence was rewarded. Provender was crossing the Bridge of Sighs for what seemed like the dozenth time, and feeling, as he did so, the full appositeness of the bridge's name – and there she was, coming the other way. She spotted him at about the same time as he spotted her. As their eyes met, she looked pleased, and then she looked thankful – not quite the same thing. This perplexed Provender for all of a nanosecond. He had found her, that was all that mattered. She hadn't fled the party or anything. He hadn't scared her away. Here she was.

All at once, he was stuck for what to say. He stammered out a sentence, 'So we meet again,' something along those lines, fumbling and banal. She, with marginally greater confidence, said, 'You never got a drink off me, did you?'

He said, 'I never did.'

She said, 'Now's your chance, then.'

He said, 'Indeed.'

She said, 'Wine, maybe?'

He said, 'Why not?', and cringed, because it sounded like an attempt at a pun. He grabbed a glass of rosé off the salver and downed it in a single, hurried gulp.

'So,' he said, gasping.

'So,' she said.

'They're going to start shortly.'

'What?'

'Sorry. The fireworks.'

'Ah.'

'Do you like fireworks?'

The Columbine's mouth curved up at one corner. 'I don't *dislike* them.'

At that moment, a Harlequin strode past, coming from the same direction the Columbine had. Provender threw him a glance – big, sturdy fellow, muscles bulking out his black-and-white diamond pattern leotard. He looked back to the Columbine. Her eyes, which had also been on the Harlequin, flicked back to Provender's face.

'Do you have a name?' Provender asked.

It was a straightforward enough question. He wanted to know the answer. But at the same time, both of them knew he was asking for a whole lot more. If she told him, she would be opening up the border between professional and personal, stamping his passport and giving him the go-ahead to walk through.

'I don't think I ought to—'

'No, no, of course.'

She paused, deliberating, then said, 'Is.'

'Eh?'

'That's my name. Is.'

'Really? Short for . . .'

'Just Is.'

'Oh. Unusual.'

'Says a man called Provender.'

49

He smiled. 'Yes. Quite. So then . . . Is. Those fireworks. Would you like to come and watch them with me?'

'I can't.'

'Ah.'

'I'd like to, but . . . you know, I have a job to do, and if my boss catches me watching fireworks when I should be serving drinks . . .'

'He'll give you a rocket.'

This time the pun was intentional. That didn't make it any funnier, though.

'Right,' said Is.

'Is that the only reason?'

'The only reason . . . ?'

'You won't come and watch them with me.'

She thought about it. 'Yeah.'

'Then not to worry. You won't get into trouble, I promise. I'll sort it out. I'll go and see your boss afterwards. I'll say I gave you permission to take half an hour off. I thought you'd been working so hard, you could do with a break. Actually, fuck it, why don't you take the rest of the night off? Spend it as my personal guest. On full pay.'

'I don't think . . .' She shook her head uncomfortably. 'No.'

'OK, just the half an hour then. For the fireworks.' Provender was thinking he had lost her. He had pushed too hard. Been greedy. 'Please?'

But he hadn't, hurrah, lost her. 'Perhaps,' she said slowly, 'just for the fireworks, I could, I suppose . . .'

'Brilliant!'

'You promise you'll talk to my boss afterwards.'

'Swear. Cross my heart.'

She took a deep breath. 'All right then. Aren't they about to start?'

Provender consulted his watch. 'Any minute. We'd better hurry if we're going to get a good position.'

She nodded at her salver. 'I need to find somewhere to put this down first.'

'Leave it here.'

'Can't do that. The catering marquee's just that way. It won't take a moment.'

'I'll come with you.'

She cocked her head. 'If you like.'

He followed her down one of the narrower alleys. His mother had told him the streets of Venice were categorised under various names, according to size and proximity to water. The narrow residential type, which this alley aped, was called a . . . *ruga*? Something like that. He thought about sharing this little factlet with the Columbine, Is. But he didn't want her to take him for a show-offy know-all.

Soon they were crossing the perimeter of the party site, and the catering marquee appeared in front of them, voluminous and candy-striped, like a huge canvas cake. From within came a clatter of cutlery and glassware, and also the sizzle of cooking and the sound of chefs shouting at one another. Is entered through one of the flaps, emerging empty-handed a moment later. Provender, eager, pointed towards Venice's south edge.

'That way,' he said.

'Why don't we go over there instead?' said Is, gesturing past the side of the marquee.

Completely the opposite direction. Nothing lay that way except a copse of silver birches, an expanse of lawn, and beyond, the untended pasture and woodland which constituted the majority of the estate.

'There's a rise,' she explained. 'I saw it this afternoon. I bet up there we'll have an uninterrupted view. No one else around to get in the way.'

Provender took this in; thought he knew what she was implying; liked it.

They headed off side by side, into the dark. Provender was delighted at how things were turning out. He didn't the least bit mind Is taking the lead in this way. He knew, of course, the rise she was referring to. He pictured her and him sitting atop it. She was wrong about the view from there being uninterrupted. Most of the ground-level detonations, the Roman candles and Catherine wheels, would be obscured by Venice, but the rockets and mortars, the big loud airbursting bangs which were really the point of a fireworks display – these would be visible in all their scintillating, percussive glory. And if his hand should happen to settle next to hers on the grass, if their fingers should brush, their shoulders touch . . . it would not be an unwelcome development at all. Provender was expecting no more than that. He wasn't expecting Is to pounce on him, Blaise-style. He didn't want her to, and didn't think she was that sort of girl. Just her presence beside him, her companionship, while the night sky exploded, was all he required.

They were passing the copse. The ground was starting to slope up-wards. The light from the party site threw everything into dim relief.

To Provender's right, at the periphery of his vision, something moved. He thought it was the trunk of one of the silver birches, swaying in a sudden breeze.

Then he saw that it was a figure. He glimpsed diamond-shapes, black on white. Someone who had been perfectly camouflaged amid the piebald trees.

Bearing down on him.

Before he could say or do anything, an arm banded around his chest. A hand clamped over his mouth.

'Quick!' a hoarse voice yelled, right next to his ear.

Provender struggled, but the man holding him was stronger, much stronger, than him.

He saw Is fumbling among her skirts.

'Quick! Fucking get on with it!'

From a pocket she produced a small, thin, cylindrical object. It gleamed.

A hypodermic.

Provender struggled harder, but no more effectually. He yelled, but with his mouth muffled the yell came out a growl. Belatedly, he remembered the stick he was carrying. He had forgotten he still had it with him. He lashed backwards with it, going for his assailant's head, but the angle was awkward, he couldn't get in a decent blow.

With almost casual ease, the man batted the stick out of his grasp. It spun uselessly away.

Is moved in with the hypodermic. She grabbed the sleeve of Provender's cape and yanked it up to expose his bare arm.

A needle winked, poised over his biceps.

'Do it, for fuck's sake!'

Provender felt the jab. A sting, then deeper, muscular pain.

And suddenly brightness, a wash of crimson over the scene, followed immediately by a huge, hearty *thump*.

Distant cheering.

And further flashes of brightness followed, and a thunder peal of *thumps*. The tree trunks were lit up in a succession of colours. Is's face was lit up too. Provender watched her, even as his legs began to grow numb and crumple under him, even as the man braced him so that he remained upright. Is was growing further and further away, shrinking, and her face, as it receded and blurred, shifted through a palette of hues: sombre magenta, fierce scarlet, deep gold, shrewd green, cruel blue.

More cheering. Whoops of firework joy.

Coming from a far-off world.

Somewhere in dreams.

9

'Where *is* Provender?'

This time Cynthia Gleed said the words less with a sigh, more with a frown.

A fusillade of explosions erupted overhead, like dandelions made of fire, one overlaying another in rapid succession. The party-goers oohed their appreciation. Faces were upturned, mouths agape. Fireworks made children of everyone.

Cynthia, the only one not looking upward, studied the crowd by the flickering play of pyrotechnic light. No sign of her son in his sombre, somewhat sinister get-up. She could see Gentian, though, and Blaise, the latter with her arm around nephew Arthur (although the embrace, from certain angles, looked not unlike a headlock). Neither girl had found favour with Provender, and Cynthia, while disappointed, was also not surprised. In hindsight, Gentian was perhaps a little too winsome for him, and Blaise was definitely far too forward. Cynthia had had her hopes . . . but she perceived now that her choices had not been right. Ah well. She was learning from her mistakes. Soon she would have narrowed down the perfect woman for Provender. She already had the next couple of candidates in mind, and she also had a network of friends, relatives and acquaintances quietly, discreetly looking on her behalf, rifling through their address books, winnowing out likely young ladies to submit for her consideration. In time, she would find the Girl, the One.

There was a series of immense silver starbursts. Shrieking white dervishes whizzed off in all different directions.

Cynthia saw her husband. She saw her daughters. There was Uncle Fortune, sweaty and satanic. There was Great, craning his bony neck, peering up fiercely at the display.

All her Family. All her *family*.

Except Provender.

The likeliest explanation for his absence was that he had returned to the house; he was back in his suite, probably bashing away again on his damn videotyper.

Yet Provender loved fireworks. It was highly unusual that he wasn't here watching them.

On the ground, several dozen Roman candles ignited at once, and a host of golden sparks tumbled in a shimmering curtain.

Deep within her Cynthia felt the first faint pangs of misgiving.

She tried to ignore the feeling. She tried to convince herself she was being foolish.

She didn't quite succeed.

PART TWO

10

Between them, Damien bearing most of the weight, they carried Provender's inert form to the car and bundled him into the boot.

This, for Is, was the riskiest and most terrifying part of the plan. Security personnel were patrolling the grounds. There was no way of pretending there was anything innocent about two people lugging the sedated body of Provender Gleed to the catering-staff car park and depositing him in the back of one of the vehicles there. It was not possible, if caught red-handed, to claim this wasn't what it appeared to be. Up till then, everything could be explained away, she was just chatting with Provender, they were just getting on with each other, they were just going for a walk in the grounds to find a vantage point to watch the fireworks from. Now, from the moment Damien grabbed Provender and she administered the muscle relaxant, there was no longer the safeguard of a plausible cover story. What they looked like they were doing was exactly what they were doing: they were kidnapping him.

But they made it to Damien's car safely. They saw no one. No one saw them. No one challenged them. The fireworks afforded the ideal diversion. Everyone's attention, including the security personnel's, was on the display. Plus, it provided illumination to see by.

Is hated to admit it, but Damien had thought the whole thing through really pretty well. He had had help, she knew, but nonetheless . . .

Damien lowered the lid of the boot and clumped it shut, leaning on it with all his weight. The catch was temperamental, sometimes not working and sometimes working too well, so that you had to thump the lid to get it to open. That was the problem with Chinese import cars like the Dragon Wind Compact. Not only were they unreliable but replacement parts, so often needed, were hard to come by. And with Dragon Winds in general there was the additional flaw of a crude catalytic converter which gave the exhaust emissions an unusually sulphurous stench. This had prompted motoring journalists to crack many a predictable joke about the brand name.

Tonight the god of felony was in a benign mood and the catch on the Compact behaved itself. Damien raised his hands slowly, experimentally. The boot lid did not spring open. He allowed himself a quick, tight smile.

'Right. Let's roll.'

They drove out along one of the estate's back roads, the Dragon Wind's headlamps combing the dark. Is, in the passenger seat, sat with her fingernails digging into her palms. They weren't free and clear yet, far from it. There was the gate to get through. To be precise, there was the security presence at the gate to get past. She knew Damien had prepared for this contingency, but that didn't in any way help to calm her heart rate or unclamp the tightness in her belly. She was half-dizzy with fear and adrenalin.

Damien, by contrast, seemed to be thriving on the excitement. He was confident in the driving seat, his fingers tapping out a merry rhythm on the steering wheel. As Is looked at him, studying his profile, she remembered that he was handsome. It was an odd revelation. How could she have forgotten? But there it was. He had a near-spherical head which betokened, she thought, integrity, and eyes which, though a mite too deep-set, shone with a zealous gleam. His jaw, with its pronounced overbite, could have detracted from his looks but somehow didn't. *Piranha-esque*, a girlfriend of hers had once called it, but Is didn't think that was quite right. (Besides, the remark was made after Is and Damien broke up, when slagging off the ex was considered fair game, indeed was a vital part of the post-relationship healing process.) He was well-built, too. Even wearing that absurd Harlequin outfit, he had physical presence. Damien was not someone people took lightly or dared laugh at.

Up ahead, the gate hove into view. Is glimpsed the brick-built guardhouse by the road's edge, with its open arched doorway. The guardhouse had been occupied by a member of the security staff when she and Damien had arrived this afternoon, a thickset monster of a man with hod-carrier shoulders and a face that looked like it had received more than its fair share of punches. He had leaned out to inspect their passes like some troll from its cave. Now, as far as she could tell, the guardhouse was empty.

Damien drew to a halt in front of the gate. 'Better make this quick.' He eyed the dashboard clock's phosphorescent dial. 'We've got a half-hour window and it's closing.'

Is leapt out of the car and hurried over to the guardhouse. As she neared the doorway she slowed and peered cautiously in, just to be sure. Yes, empty. The security man was off chasing shadows in the grounds. If interrogated, he would claim he heard suspicious sounds out in the woods and went to investigate. She couldn't imagine how large a bribe it must have taken to convince a trained security professional to abandon his post on a bogus pretext and, in so doing, jeopardise his entire career. All Damien had said was that it was a lot of money. He had also said that they had to be through the gate before the security man returned. If they were still there when he came back from his wild-goose chase, he would have no alternative but to challenge them. The elasticity of the man's conscience stretched only so far.

Is ventured into the guardhouse and quickly located the gate-operating mechanism, a wall-mounted control panel with two buttons on it, one with arrows pointing together, the other with arrows pointing apart. She punched the latter, and with a deep, heavy clank the gate unlocked itself. Its leaves swung ponderously apart and Damien steered the Dragon Wind through.

As Is got ready to hit the button that closed the gate, she thought she heard the thump of footfalls. Her breath caught in her throat. She leaned out of the guardhouse and scanned the darkened woods, her eyes panic-wide, expecting to see the security man come lumbering out from among the trees, sidearm drawn.

Not religious, she nevertheless sent up a small prayer. *Please, God, no.*

Then she heard the thumps again and realised it was the firework display. Three miles distant, a series of rockets detonated and then crackled like splintering tinder.

Slamming the gate-closing button, Is sprinted out of the guardhouse, darted through the narrowing gap between the gate leaves, ran to the car and jumped in. 'Go.'

Damien, seeing how spooked she was, smirked. 'We were fine, you know. Five minutes to spare.'

'I don't care. Fucking drive!'

It wasn't until they were a mile down the road that Is was able to draw a steady breath again. She vowed never to put herself through anything like that again. Ever.

'That stuff you injected Provender with,' Damien said as he negotiated a junction that took them off the lane that ran alongside the perimeter of Dashlands and onto another lane. 'The comatose thingy . . .'

'Comaphase.'

'Thank you. How long's it supposed to last for, again?'

'It was fifteen migs. Should keep him down for three-quarters of an hour.'

Damien checked the dashboard clock. 'Right, so in about twenty minutes, we find a lay-by, pull over and give him a second dose.'

'If we have to. But he'll probably stay groggy even after he's come round. His head'll be fuzzy and he won't know what's going on. It's best not to give him two shots in a row if we don't have to. He might not react well.'

'It's twenty miles to London. Half an hour at least.'

'Let's risk it, Damien. Honestly, even if he wakes up, he'll be in a stupor. He won't be shouting for help or trying to escape or anything.'

Damien remained unconvinced, but nodded. 'OK, if you say so. But we hear the slightest funny noise from back there, anything at all, we stop and jab him. Agreed?'

'Agreed.'

'So load up your hypodermic just in case.'

She did, steadying herself against the car's rocking as she drew off a further fifteen milligrams of the sedative from the ampoule which she had raided from the hospital supply closet and smuggled out of the building in her pocket. She flicked the syringe to raise the air bubbles, then depressed the plunger till a bead of clear fluid welled at the needle's tip. The needle, she noticed, was still smeared with Provender's blood.

Family blood.

When you looked at it, it was just blood, no different from anybody else's, same colour, same consistency. But to a Family it was everything. In what it represented, it was immeasurably precious.

For the first time, Is had an inkling that what Damien had in mind for Provender, the rest of his plan, was feasible. She hadn't dared believe this before. It had seemed dangerous to hope for so much. But the blood on the needle offered a kind of symbolic assurance. It said the Gleeds needed Provender returned to them. They would give anything, pay anything, accede to any demand, in order to get him back alive.

11

Leafy Berkshire – kept nice and rural because that was how the Gleeds liked their home county – gave way to the outskirts of London. The scattering of houses on either side of the dual carriageway became clusters of houses, then knots of houses, revealed by their lighted windows. A greater glare of light denoted Heathrow Aerodrome, where passenger and cargo airships swung at their tethers, white-bellied, like slumbering whales. The road veered towards then away from a stretch of tram track, part of the network that webbed the entire country, an automated transport system for the exclusive use of Family members. Beneath spark-spitting wires a lone tram was barrelling along, its lamp-lit interior furnished with leather armchairs and teak fixtures. No one was aboard. It was estimated that, on average, less than half of one per cent of the trams on the network were occupied at any time. An absurdly wasteful and costly means of getting about; yet the Families loved it, cherished it, and begrudged not one penny of the expense of running and maintaining it.

The glow of London brass-burnished the sky ahead. Suddenly the stars were gone. The city, jealous, would not have them. Suburbs stretched and flexed like a rising tide. Buildings crested upward, the troughs of street-lamp radiance in-between deepening. London massed itself; began to tower. Spikes and spires and skyscrapers, equalling Manhattan's for size, bristled all around. Height was the measure of a capital's worth, and London reached for altitude as keenly as any of its main rivals. Soon, if the Risen London Authority's plans went ahead, there would be cable cars operating between street-level and the summits of the tallest edifices. They were doing that in New York. They were doing it in Paris and Warsaw as well. They would be doing it here.

The road, single carriageway now, wound between the bases of the skyscrapers or sometimes tunnelled straight through. It roller-coastered along a series of elevated sections. It fissured off into slip-roads, or fused with an adjacent road. Traffic, at this hour, was light, and consisted primarily of taxis and electric buses, with the occasional freight lorry bumbling along on a fart of diesel fumes.

Now Damien steered the Dragon Wind off at the appropriate exit and, after negotiating a warren of dingy streets, drove through an entranceway that was neither gate nor outlet but rather indicated transition, a passage from one state of existence to another. On one side, the rest of the world. On the other . . .

The name arched above the entranceway in iron:

Each character was sharp and heavy, like a guillotine blade about to drop. You seldom went under them, even in a vehicle, without a reflexive hunching of the shoulders. And once you were through, the side on which the rest of the world stood seemed just that bit cleaner, just that bit brighter, than where you were now. The difference was hard to define but there was definitely a difference.

The tower blocks of Needle Grove, numbering fifty in all, were thick-bodied and many-tiered. They didn't climb straight but rose in staggered sections, narrowing, like irregular ziggurats. They were thinner at top than at bottom and yet, confusingly, through some architectural optical illusion, the higher up you went the less space there seemed to be between them. They didn't, in all, behave as normal residential buildings, or any sort of buildings, should. Their bulk intimidated rather than inspired.

Threading between the blocks at almost every level there were over-passes and underpasses. There were cantilevered communal areas – concrete plazas suspended in mid-air, where, if you were lucky, some greenery grew, a tree, a shrub, a clump of grass, failing that a weed. There were spiralling outdoor staircases that threw off exit arms like spokes on a spindle. All these, from dawn to dusk, cast shade. They eclipsed one another and cumulatively occluded the ground. At any hour of the day, whatever the weather, down on the ground it was perpetual overcast twilight.

Damien drove along roadways where, if you saw another car, it was either in motion or a burned-out husk. Teenagers roamed, shrinking from the headlamp beams as though the light scalded their faces. They were kitted out according to various gang-tribe dress codes. Young Moderns sported slicked-down hairdos and three-piece suits with what appeared to be fob-watch chains across the front of the waistcoats (but they were longer than ordinary fob-watch chains and those switchblades at the end were no timepieces). The Radical Flappers looked like square-heeled good-time girls out for an evening's Charlestoning, but cross them and you'd soon learn what damage a wire-strung feather boa could do. The Technologists resembled robots as closely as it was humanly possible to do, while the Changelings, acknowledging that styles and fashions were protean and altered almost daily, wore a gallimaufry of types of clothing, diversity their uniform.

There were dozens of these gangs and night was their time. They roved in bands, bug-eyed on Tinct, looking for trouble and very rarely failing to find it. Fights were so commonplace, no one bothered calling the police to come in and break them up. A fatal knifing or shooting was an almost weekly occurrence, and when this happened the police *would* turn up, but only to cart away the body and inform the deceased's parents, if no one else already had, that their son or daughter was dead. The crime was never investigated. As far as the cops were concerned, in Needle Grove, among a certain age group, a gang slaying was tantamount to death by natural causes.

At the foot of Block 26, Damien pulled up at the entrance to the basement garage. He wound down the driver's-side window, leaned out and entered a number into the code-lock mechanism, prodding the stiff steel keys firmly. With a *clunk*, then a reverberant warping *twang*, the segmented steel door began to rise.

Parked in his allotted space, Damien turned off the engine and rested his wrists on the wheel for a moment.

'Done it, Is,' he said, looking sidelong at his accomplice. 'We've done it. We've got him home.'

'Not quite. We're not upstairs yet.'

'Yeah, but. We've done the hard part. And I've got to say, you were brilliant. You really came through. I couldn't have managed it without you. You're a star.'

'I did my best.'

'No, I mean it. You're fantastic. You did everything absolutely right. The timing was perfect. You kept your nerve.'

'There were moments . . .'

'But you didn't lose it. It's all right to be scared as long as you don't lose it, and you didn't, and that's true class.'

'Thank you, Damien.'

His eyes took on a mournful look which, alas, she knew only too well. 'Why did we ever split up, Is?' he lamented. 'What happened? What went wrong? Why did we just . . . fall apart like that?'

There were a hundred possible answers, and almost all of them ended with . . . *because you 're a possessive, jealous, tantrum-prone egomaniac, Damien.* Is chose instead to deflect the question with a shrug, saying, 'Let's just concentrate on this, eh?' She nodded towards the boot. 'Leave the soul-searching for another time.'

Damien studied the backs of his hands for several seconds, then opened the door and climbed out. Opening one of the rear doors, he leaned in and took a pair of overcoats off the back seat. He handed one to Is and donned the other. With the overcoats buttoned up to the neck, their Harlequin and Columbine outfits were hidden.

From one pocket, Damien drew out a scarf-like length of fabric. Then, standing over the boot, he raised his fist and brought it down on a spot just above the catch. The lid creaked upward.

12

Minutes (hours? seconds? weeks?) of juddering motion, in perfect darkness. Smells of oil, grease, sulphurous exhaust, warm metal. Up then down, down then up. Swaying this way, that way. Someone's knees butting intermittently against his chin.

Those are my knees, Provender thought. *This is me, lying embryonic.*

It was a rare instance of lucidity, and it came in a flash and vanished almost as quickly. For the most part thoughts – any thoughts – were jigsaw-puzzle things that demanded a great deal of effort to piece together. Sometimes Provender seemed to have hold of a fully-formed concept, only to find it crumbled into fragments just when it was about to make sense.

There were memories, too. Strange, flirting-phantom recollections of recent events.

Is the Columbine, at the ball.

The Columbine Is.

The Columbine is – was – Is.

Leaving Venice with her.

Hypodermic.

Hypodermic.

And her face, in firework light. Colour-splashed with fields of brilliance.

And so now he was travelling. He managed to comprehend, eventually, that he was travelling. In motion.

And he was also lying paralysed, unable so much as to twitch a finger.

And the hour-second-week minutes rumbled by, until finally, abruptly, they stopped.

The travelling had stopped.

He had stopped.

Provender attempted to roll his head, because that seemed to him like something he might be able to do now that nothing else was in motion. His head lolled rather than rolled, but at least it moved. He had volition. Rollition. Lollition.

Then there was a booming *thud*, and a sudden influx of yellow light. He screwed up his eyes and loll-rolled his head sideways to escape the brightness. Next thing he knew, there was cloth over his eyes. The cloth was being tied behind his head. A blindfold. No more brightness. And the same hands that had put the blindfold on him then grabbed him under the armpits and manhandled him up, out, onto. He was jack-knifed over someone's shoulder. Fireman's lift. He was being carried, through some low-ceilinged, echoing place. Head dangling downward. Nose pressed into the fabric of someone's overcoat. Human lumber.

A soft *ping*.

A rumble of doors.

The vibration, sway, rattle, trundle of a lift ascending.

Ascending.

Ascending for a long time.

Halting.

Doors rumbling again.

'Coast clear?' said the voice of the overcoat, which was also the voice that had shouted by his ear when he was ambushed at the birch copse.

A pause, then 'Yes'. Another voice. He knew this one as well. The Columbine's.

More walking. More nosefuls of overcoat odour.

A door being unlocked; opening.

Provender was carried for a few more steps, and then the person bearing him dolloped him down on the floor with a grunt of effort, a hiss of relief.

'Fuck, *he* wasn't getting any lighter, was he.'

Provender lay on carpet. Coarse, cheap-feeling carpet. He didn't move. Didn't want to, even if he could have.

His brain was marginally clearer than it had been. Sense was becoming that much easier to make.

He was starting to grasp what was happening to him.

And not to move, not to draw attention to himself, not to do anything that might be construed as defiance or resistance – this, under the circumstances, seemed a very sensible course of action indeed.

13

'Carver?'

'Mrs Gleed.'

'A word, if you please.'

'Of course, ma'am.'

Cynthia drew Carver aside to a quiet corner of the Piazza San Marco. She did this without touching him, her hand hovering near his sleeve.

The sky was brightening, taking on a pewtery pre-dawn sheen. The ball was starting to wind down. Some guests had already tendered their thanks and left. There would soon be a mass exodus, once the sun rose and its gleam broke the spell of the night irrecoverably. A few diehards might linger on, dancing till the mist dispersed and the dew evaporated, but most party-goers understood that a perfect night finished when the night itself finished.

'Great's gone to bed?' Cynthia enquired.

'I wheeled him to the house and tucked him in a couple of hours ago. He would appear to have had a very pleasant time.'

'I'm glad to hear it. So you have no other duties to attend to.'

Carver decorously stifled a yawn. 'I was anticipating being able to retire myself, in the not-too-distant future.'

'Before you do, I've a small favour to ask.'

'But of course.'

Tallness in men was not something Cynthia had a problem with, *per se*, but in Carver's case it wasn't an attractive or appealing quality. Whenever she spoke to him he hulked over her, demanding to be looked up *to* as well as *at*. He knew he was doing it, and Cynthia considered it inappropriate in a domestic servant. Notwithstanding that Carver had been with the Gleeds far, far longer than she had, he remained an employee whereas she was Familial. He ought not to behave as if his decades of servitude meant that he outranked her.

She had the measure of him, however. You treated Carver as you would a dangerous dog: looked him straight in the eye, didn't betray an ounce of intimidation.

'I haven't seen Provender since well before midnight,' she said.

'You've checked his room, I take it.'

'Twice. He's not there. I've no idea where he can have got to, and I think . . . I have this feeling . . .' She faltered.

Carver's scar creased crookedly as he smiled. 'You're worried something may have happened to him? Feminine intuition, ma'am?'

'It sounds foolish, I know.'

'Not in the least. Who can fault a mother's instincts? More often than not they are right. However, in this instance, I would like to think they are mistaken, and indeed I'm sure they are. I'm sure no harm has befallen Master Provender. He is almost certainly somewhere on the premises, sequestered perhaps in some remote corner of Venice here. Perhaps a little drunk, who knows? He's apt to take after his uncle in that respect, especially on social occasions.'

'I've scoured the party site.'

'Nevertheless. It is a large site and you are just one person. But in order to set your mind at rest, ma'am, allow me to organise a more substantive search. I'll mobilise a number of security personnel and supervise them personally. We'll find him, have no fear of that.'

'Thank you, Carver. It goes without saying you'll be discreet. I don't want anyone getting wind that anything might be amiss.'

'Invisibly discreet, ma'am. Give me an hour and I shall undoubtedly be able to report back to you with good news.'

An hour passed, and the sun cracked free of the horizon, and the full flow of departures commenced. Cynthia fielded the guests' farewells automatically, clasping hands, pecking cheeks, scarcely knowing whom she was saying goodbye to, or caring. 'Wonderful,' some of the party-goers told her. 'The best yet,' others said. 'Unsurpassable,' said still others, as if throwing down the gauntlet for next year. Cynthia just grinned and nodded, while her gaze kept flicking to the left and right for sign of Carver. What was keeping him? Why was he taking so long to get back to her? She couldn't help but think that the longer the search continued, the less likely it was to yield a positive outcome. The misgiving in her belly was now a knot so tight it hurt. The worst of it was, she simply could not fathom what sort of awful thing might have happened to Provender. She just had this sense, this amorphous inkling, a formless notion of Badness, all the more disquieting because for it to have occurred within the confines of Dashlands, this most protected of places, the Family sanctum, it must be a very bad Badness indeed.

Threats were constantly being made against the Families – the Families in general, certain Families in particular, sometimes specific Family members. There was a lunatic fringe out there who, for no logical reason, found it impossible to feel anything in their hearts except hatred for those who happened to be better and wealthier than they were. These people penned and published anti-Family screeds, went on television to deliver anti-Family diatribes, made placards and gathered for anti-Family rallies in city squares. They were few in number, thank God, and they were, as a rule, reviled and repudiated by the general public, but still they existed, a virulently vocal minority. And sometimes their sentiments went beyond mere disapproval; sometimes they maintained that the Families were evil and must be destroyed. For the most part this was nothing more than impotent ranting, the caterwaul of lost, sad souls who needed someone else to blame for the mess that was their own lives. The Families were a convenient, high-profile scapegoat for all the ills of the world. But you could not be absolutely certain that one of these madmen might not one day graduate from words to actions – indeed, it had happened. Hence a reasonable level of security was necessary at all times, a bulwark against the remote but tangible possibility that some mad, malevolent malcontent would try to take a Family life.

But how mad and malevolent would you have to be to strike at a Family member in the grounds of their own home? You would have to be utterly determined and quite unhinged. You would have to have no respect for life, your own or anyone else's.

Cynthia suspected she was letting her imagination run away with her. She was visualising wild-eyed psychopaths where there were none. Still, she couldn't shake the idea that her son was even now lying sprawled and cold on a lawn nearby, victim of a killer so crazed, so puffed up with self-righteous anger, that he actually felt he was doing the world a favour, ridding it of Provender Gleed.

Come on, Carver. What the hell's keeping you? Put me out of my misery.

Carver was, as it happened, standing right behind Cynthia as the imprecation ran through her mind, as if the same near-psychic affinity he had with Great enabled him to intuit *her* thoughts as well. He alerted her to his presence with the most minuscule of coughs.

'Carver! You've found him, haven't you? You've found him and he's fine.'

'Ma'am . . .' It was hard to tell if his mood was graver than normal. Carver habitually looked grave. It was his default demeanour. 'There is something you ought to come and see.'

He would not be persuaded to reveal more. When pressed, he simply reiterated that she had to come and see, in order to make up her own mind. He did not wish to prejudice her interpretation of the evidence.

Evidence?

Cynthia followed him, her thoughts in such turmoil that merely setting one foot in front of the other was a major accomplishment. They headed east out of the party site, exchanging ersatz cobbles and paving stones for morning-moist greensward. Soon they were nearing a small copse of silver birches, beside which stood a handful of security personnel. None of them could meet Cynthia's eye as she approached. Their attitude was one of furtiveness, almost of embarrassment.

'Well?' she said. It would have sounded more authoritative if her mouth hadn't suddenly gone dry.

'Over here, ma'am,' said Carver, pointing. 'This patch of grass. There are signs of trampling.'

'So what?' She was doing her best to be haughty. Somehow that made it easier for her, gave her something to hide behind. 'Nothing suspicious about that. Obviously some guests came out this way.'

'Maybe, ma'am. But if I might draw your attention to . . .' Carver pointed again, this time with precise emphasis.

Cynthia looked.

On the ground, to the edge of the trampled area of grass, lay a short length of wood.

A stick.

Not a tree branch – a lathed utensil.

Cynthia tried to recall where she had seen it before. Sometime during the past few hours.

In Provender's hand.

The earth seemed to give a lurch. There was a dull hum in her ears. Carver was talking to her, saying something to the effect that this wasn't necessarily as sinister as it appeared, no one should jump to any conclusions, there might be a perfectly innocent explanation . . . Cynthia barely heard him. She stared at the stick, nestled there among those overlapping footprints, dropped, lost.

It seemed to point to something.

No, to nothing.

A headless arrow.

Provender . . .

14

Some time ago his captors had transferred him to a bathroom. He knew it was a bathroom by the cold tiles underneath him, the faint scents of soap and mildew, and the short shuffling echo that attended every sound. They had removed his cape and bound his wrists and ankles with lengths of plastic-coated cord – electrical flex? Then they had left him there, lying on his side on the floor, still blindfolded, with only his dread for company.

Nobody had told him he wasn't allowed to move. Nonetheless there was a kind of talismanic allure about staying still. Frightened animals did this, froze, hoping it would somehow render them invisible to carnivores prowling near. To be static was to invite harm to pass you by. So Provender had lain in the same fixed position, until eventually a severe case of cramp made it impossible to continue to do so. Slowly, with the utmost reluctance, he stretched out his arms and straightened his legs. Having completed this manoeuvre without inviting unpleasant consequences, he dared to ease his wrists and ankles around inside their bonds. His hands and feet tingled painfully as the blood flowed into them again.

By this stage, the effects of whatever drug his captors had injected him with had almost completely worn off. He still felt a little floaty, in a way that reminded him of when he was a child and had spent too long swimming in the sea – the up-and-down of the waves continued to wash within his body for some time after. His mind, however, had regained clarity. His thoughts weren't foggy and fuddled any more, although he might perhaps have preferred it if they were. He comprehended, now, exactly the predicament he was in, and wished he didn't.

He heard the bathroom door open. A pull-cord switch clicked and an extractor fan wheezed into life. No doubt a light must have come on too, but behind the tight-tied blindfold Provender remained in darkness.

He cringed as hands touched him, but he sensed almost immediately that the hands didn't belong to the man, the Harlequin. They were Is's.

'Sit up,' she said.

He did, with her assistance, resting his back against the side of the bath.

'I'm just going to roll up your sleeve. OK?'

His body language must have conveyed why he didn't much like this idea.

'I'm not going to give you another injection. I'm taking your blood pressure, that's all.'

The cuff of a sphygmomanometer was placed around his upper arm, secured with its Velcro fastenings, and inflated. Is then pressed the business end of a stethoscope into the crook of his elbow and let the air out of the cuff.

'One twenty-five over seventy,' she said. 'That's not bad, given how your heart rate's elevated. I'll check again later, but I'm sure you're going to be fine.'

As she unfastened the cuff, she added, 'You can speak, you know. You don't have to sit there like a statue.'

'I can?'

'Just don't try yelling for help.'

'Oh. No. Never crossed my mind.'

'Because there's no point. That's why you're in the bathroom. No windows, no outside walls. Pretty good soundproofing. We'd hear you. No one else would.'

'I understand.' He gave an uncomfortable little cough. The back of his throat was feeling achey and constricted.

'Don't try removing the blindfold, either. We'll be able to tell if you have.'

'What don't you want me to see? Your face? I already have.'

'There are other reasons. Look, I realise you must be scared, Provender. All I can say is, if everything goes the way it should, there's no need to be.'

He forced himself to ask, 'And if everything *doesn't* go the way it should?'

There was the minutest of pauses. 'To be honest, how all this pans out isn't up to us. It's up to your Family. Their response determines *our* response.'

'We have money,' Provender said quickly. 'Lots of money. You know that. Name your price. Any amount, I'm sure my fath—'

'We'll discuss it later,' said Is. There was a soft clatter as she gathered up her medical equipment. 'I'll be back in an hour to do your BP again and give you some breakfast. Till then – please try not to worry, Provender. And get some sleep if you can.'

The extractor fan rattled and whirred for a few minutes after she was gone, then lapsed into silence.

Try not to worry. Get some sleep if you can.

Provender would have laughed, if he hadn't felt so much like weeping.

15

In the open-plan vastness of the second largest of Dashlands House's six main drawing rooms, Prosper Gleed, Cynthia Gleed, Gratitude Gleed and Extravagance Gleed all sat, none of them saying a word. In front of them, on various tables, lay trays of victuals. Clusters of untouched cups encircled cafetières of undrunk coffee and pots of cooled, stewed tea. Croissants and bread rolls, brought hot from the oven, were stacked stone-cold beside melting curls of butter. It was nine a.m. Sunlight gleamed behind blinds that no one had thought to furl. Around the room several table lamps shed their own muted illumination. Each lamp took the form of a classical figurine, cast in spelter, either holding aloft or cavorting alongside a crackle-glass orb that served to shade the bulb. It was as though, in miniature, gods and nymphs were playing with planets.

On one sofa, Extravagance lay with her head resting in her mother's lap. Cynthia, in turn, was stroking her daughter's hair, just as she might have done when Extravagance was eight or nine. The action, performed mindlessly, soothed them both. Gratitude, meanwhile, had a faraway stare, and Prosper was absorbed in dark inward contemplation. The faces of all four showed, to a greater or lesser degree, a grey-tinged tautness – exhaustion compounded by shock, shock amplified by exhaustion. They had all changed out of their ball costumes into day wear. The party seemed to have happened a long time ago, and its pleasures and excesses had been consigned to memory along with the masks and the wigs and the make-up. The mood now was as sombre as it had been, for the duration of the night, frivolous.

Gratitude was the one who at last broke the long silence. 'This better not be some stupid stunt he's pulling, that's all I can say. Some practical joke.'

'He wouldn't, Tudey,' said her mother. 'He wouldn't dare. He knows I'd kill him.'

'He's got such a strange brain, though. It might be his idea of fun. "I'll go missing for a while. Pretend I've been kidnapped. Give everyone a scare." He's probably feeling unappreciated and this is his way of getting everyone to notice him and take him seriously again.'

'I was mean to him,' Extravagance said. 'At the ball. The last time we spoke we were sort of having an argument and I was sarcastic to him and—'

'Don't,' said Cynthia, patting her. 'Don't even think that way. This has nothing to do with anything you said to him, I'm quite certain of that.'

'But I wish we hadn't been arguing.'

'You two are always arguing,' said Gratitude, meaning it as comfort.

'But if I'd known something like *this* was going to happen . . .'

'But you didn't, 'Strav.'

Extravagance settled her head in her mother's lap once more, disconsolately. 'I promise I'm going to be nicer to him from now on. Every chance I get.'

Implicit in this statement was the belief that Provender would be coming back to Dashlands sometime in the future, alive and well. Nobody thought to suggest to Extravagance that she was wrong to think that way. Nobody wanted to say such a thing aloud.

'If he has been kidnapped,' Gratitude said, slowly, 'if that *is* what this is, then won't we be hearing from the kidnappers soon? You know, a message with their demands, or whatever.'

'Let's hope so,' said her mother. 'And let's pray that all they're after is money.'

'What would it be if it wasn't money?'

'They might' – Cynthia chose her words carefully – 'try to make political capital out of holding Provender. They might try and blackmail us into making . . . compromises that would injure us as a Family. Force us to sacrifice certain rights and assets.'

'Such as?'

'Our controlling stakes in major corporations, for one thing.'

'Why?'

'To humiliate us, of course. Remember that Japanese Family a few years back, the Omarus? No, you wouldn't, either of you. You were both very small when it happened. Some radical activists, members of some kind of religious brainwashing cult, I forget what they called themselves, stole the youngest son of the main branch of the Family. He was barely a week old. He had been born premature, and they took him from the hospital, incubator unit and all, right under the noses of a dozen security guards. They just dressed up in white coats, pretended they were doctors, and wheeled the poor little thing out to a waiting car.'

'I sort of have heard this story, I think. How horrid!'

'And then they went on TV and ordered Kenji Omaru—'

'Kenji was the baby's father?'

'Correct, and the head of the Omarus back then. They ordered him to sell off all Family stocks in the main Japanese *zaibatsus* and then read out a speech on prime-time television, which they'd written for him, basically saying he was corrupt, Families were evil, no one should have that much money, the wealth belonged to the people, it should be shared out more

74

evenly, et cetera, et cetera. It was about twenty pages long, that speech, and Kenji was supposed to deliver it to camera with the whole world watching, and you know how the Japanese are about pride and honour. It was intended to break him. It was tantamount to a death sentence. Also, these people – the Cult of the Orange Shrine, something like that – they just hadn't thought the financial side of it through. If the Omarus tried to sell off that much stock all at once, there'd be a huge drop in share values across the board. The stock market would crash. The whole regional economy would collapse. Perhaps they wanted that as well. Social and economic chaos. Who knows how these people's minds work. Anyway . . .'

'What happened?'

The bitterness of Cynthia's tone gave way to wariness. 'No, well, come to think of it, it's not such a relevant story after all.'

'Mother, what happened?'

She shook her head. 'I wish I hadn't brought it up now. The circumstances aren't similar to ours, not at all.'

'*Mother* . . .'

'Kenji refused. Point-blank. Refused to do as they asked. He wasn't going to destroy himself and his whole Family, and heap financial ruin on so many others as well.'

'He refused. So what about the baby? His son?'

'He . . . he thought it better to let the boy . . . It was his youngest son. He had three others.'

'Oh my God.'

'They . . . Police found the body a month later in marshland outside Kobe. They had a tip-off and apprehended the cultists too. There was a trial. Death sentences were passed.'

'But he let the baby . . .'

'He had to. Had no choice. Too much else was at stake. He felt it was the right decision. He said Family is about more than parents and offspring and relatives.'

'What a bloody wonderful little tale,' said Extravagance from Cynthia's lap. 'Thanks for sharing that with us, Mum. I feel a whole lot better now.'

'I know, I'm sorry, it was just to illustrate what some people might be prepared to ask from us, how far they'd be willing to go. I really don't believe it's the same here with—'

' "Some people",' said Prosper. He, of all of them, was the one who had said the least since they assembled in the drawing room. His brooding had been deeper and more intense than anyone else's. Now that he had piped up, it was clear that he had come to some conclusions and wished to air them.

'Yes, dear?' Cynthia said.

Prosper looked at his wife and daughters, steely-eyed. 'I don't think this was "some people". I don't think this is about ransom either.'

'What is it about, then?'

His voice dropped so low, it was almost a growl. 'I think we're under attack.'

'What?'

'I think this is the opening salvo. Someone's gunning for us.'

'Really?'

'Really.'

'Where's the evidence? What makes you say this?'

'Instinct. Gut.'

'Who, Dad?' said Gratitude. 'Who's gunning for us?'

'Who do you think?'

'Another Family?'

'Not just any other Family. One particular Family.'

It didn't take much hard thinking to work out who he was referring to.

'No,' said Gratitude.

'They wouldn't,' said Cynthia.

'Why not?' said Prosper.

'They – they wouldn't go this far,' Cynthia said. 'It's always been strictly business between us and them. Buyouts, takeovers, forced mergers. Yes, we fight them, but only in boardrooms, only in industry and commerce. We compete. We don't . . . It doesn't come to this. Not actually attacking Family members. I don't believe for one second they'd stoop that low.'

'Don't you?' said her husband, flatly. 'I'm not so sure. Face it, we've waged wars with them in the past. Literal wars. Twice this century we've virtually razed Europe, battling them. Oh, it *looked* like it was about armies invading territory, annexation, occupation, political power blocs colliding – *we* know it wasn't. This Provender situation, it's clearly just an extension of that. A new form of war. A new battlefront opening up.'

'No, you're wrong, Prosper. This is paranoid talk. There's just no way they'd, out of the blue, they'd—'

One of the drawing room's three doors sprang wide open and Fortune came striding through.

'Right!' he said, thrusting the door shut behind him. He was still in his devil get-up, although he had relinquished his horns and pitchfork and, for the sake of warmth and decorum, had donned a smoking jacket borrowed from his brother. He was also still not entirely sobered up, although his drunkenness had been mostly alleviated by a sense of mission, and by several cups of espresso from the kitchen. 'This is the situation out there. Prov's definitely not in the grounds. They've done sweeps of the estate, grid-pattern, military-style. Carver's running the whole shebang and you can take the man out of the army but you can't take the . . . and so forth. All the guests have gone. All the catering staff and that lot have been allowed to leave too. The set breakers have been put on hold. All they've been told is that we don't need them yet. The excuse is you lot want a lie-in, don't want to be disturbed by a bunch of blokes hammering away all morning. We'll have to let them come this afternoon at the latest, otherwise it'll look like things have gone awry.'

Fortune pronounced the last word *or-ree*, for reasons unknown even to himself. It was just one of his little verbal tics.

'So,' he went on, 'we've got the rest of the morning to keep searching, though somehow I don't think we'll have any more luck. The main thing is, as far as I'm aware nobody knows a thing about this except us and the security personnel, and we can be pretty sure they won't tell a soul. They're trained to keep schtum and they know that if one of them blabs and we find out who, he or she will never be employed anywhere else again ever. So that's your information blackout right there, Prosp. This isn't going public unless or until we want it to.'

'Or the kidnappers want it to,' said Cynthia. 'Any idea how they got Provender off the estate?'

'Carver's looking into that. Seems there might be some sort of anomaly. Something to do with the catering staff. It may be relevant, it may not, who knows. Carver's on to it, at any rate. Frankly, if I was the chap in charge of catering and I'd made a goof of some sort, I'd be quaking in my boots right now.'

'And has Great been informed?'

'Still asleep, apparently.'

'He'll need to be told, but it should be broken to him gently. Someone in his state of health . . .'

'I'm sure the man with the scar will know how to handle it.' Fortune eyed avidly the items of breakfast food ranged around the room. 'Blimey, I'm famished. Mind if I tuck in?'

'It's not at its freshest. We could ring for more.'

'Not too fussed about freshness.' Within moments Fortune's cheeks were bulging with buttered and marmaladed roll, which he washed down with slurps of room-temperature coffee. Glancing up from his repast, he noticed that his arrival had done little to raise morale. The faces around him were as glum as when he had entered. This perturbed him. If Fortune Gleed had any particular talent, it was the ability to lift the mood of a room. Usually all he had to do was walk in.

'Oh come on,' he said. 'This is going to turn out fine. Of course it is.' He took another look around. 'Isn't it?'

16

Is spoon-fed Provender the last of the corn flakes and held up the glass of orange juice for him to sip. Some of the juice missed his mouth and dribbled down his chin. She swabbed the drips away with a wad of paper towel.

'I feel like I'm six months old,' he said.

It wasn't much of a joke, and the laugh he chased it up with wasn't much of a laugh either. All the same, Is felt a prickle of admiration. In his position, would she be capable of making wisecracks?

'I wouldn't know about six months old,' she said. 'I've fed sixty-year-olds like this, though.'

'You're a nurse, aren't you?'

She hesitated, cursing herself. Damien had been adamant that they gave away nothing about themselves. No clues to their identities whatsoever. She wasn't sure, however, if this was a practical precaution or if Damien was insisting on it because that was what kidnappers conventionally did: remained anonymous to their victims. When all was said and done, this wasn't a conventional kidnapping.

She decided it didn't matter. After all, she had already given Provender her real name. She hadn't meant to, but he had surprised her by asking for it at the ball, and her mind had gone blank. Instead of mustering up a false name, she had let the real one slip out. There was nothing she could do about that now, and similarly, there was no point trying to deny she was a nurse. Even if it wasn't obvious from the injection and the sphygmomano-meter, that remark of hers about sixty-year-olds put it beyond doubt. She resolved, however, to be more careful in future.

'Good guess,' she said. 'Well done.'

Provender nodded. 'The way you are with that blood pressure thing. Very professional. And,' he added, 'you seem like you're used to caring for people.'

'This an attempt to get on my good side? Win me over? Because if so, it's not going to work.'

Had his eyes been visible, she knew she would have seen them wince.

'No, I only . . . It was an observation, nothing more.'

'Right, then. Fine. Just so's you know. We're not going to be getting into any hostage–hostage-taker bonding here.'

She clacked the empty juice glass into the cereal bowl, with finality, and stood up to go.

'Um, Is?'

'Yes?'

'I'm sorry, I don't want to be a pain or anything, but . . . I've been holding it off, and I can't any more.'

'Holding what off? Oh. You need to pee.'

'I need to pee. Quite badly, as a matter of fact.'

She set down the glass and bowl. 'All right. Listen, though. You're going to have to do this with my help because I'm not untying your hands or taking off the blindfold.'

'I'm not all that comfortable with—'

'Tough. Now, stand up. I've got your arm. I'm taking your weight. Both feet flat on the floor. I know it's difficult with them tied together. Yes, that's it, there we go . . .'

She stationed Provender in front of the toilet, lifted the lid, and briskly unzipped his fly. As she delved into his trousers, he tried to bat her hand away.

'I can manage.'

'No, you can't. Men have bad aim at the best of times. God knows what you'd be like blindfold.'

'I could always sit.'

'Don't be such a baby.'

Provender fixed his jaw in an awkward jut as she groped through the flap in his underpants and fished out his penis.

Is had handled more strangers' penises than she cared to remember – all in the line of duty, naturally. Dealing with a male patient's appendage was one of a nurse's less agreeable tasks, although it was far from being the worst (wiping off vomit and cleaning up shit vied for *that* honour). The trick was to think of the penis as just another anatomical part, no more interesting than a toe or a nose. Failing that, you had to try to regard it as just a functional object, a tube that just happened to be made of flesh. Normally, of course, she would be wearing latex gloves, a thin but crucial barrier between clinical and intimate. She made a mental note to buy some. This wasn't going to be the last time she had to help Provender pee.

'Your fingers,' Provender said with a hiss. 'Cold.'

'That's your excuse, is it?'

'What?'

'Nothing. Sorry.'

Provender screwed up his face, then gave a sigh.

'I can't. Nothing's coming.'

'Relax. Try to pretend I'm not here.'

'Difficult.'

'Count yourself lucky. We did think about catheterising you.'

'You wouldn't.'

'But I could.'

Again, Provender concentrated.

'Still nothing?'

'Nope,' he said, pained.

'I'll run a tap.'

Water spattered into the basin.

'I really—'

'Think watery thoughts. And unclench your pelvic floor.'

He turned his head towards her, as though he could see her through the blindfold. 'I don't have a pelvic floor. Do I?'

'Of course you do.'

'I thought only women had . . .'

'Well, you're wrong.'

The water continued to pour, but it was the only thing that did.

'Can we talk about something maybe?' Provender said. 'You know, as a distraction. Take my mind off the problem at hand.'

'What would you like to talk about?'

'How about the name Is? It's short for something, right? Isabel?'

'No.'

'Isadora?'

'No.'

'Isolde?'

'No.'

'I'm all out of Is-es.'

In spite of her earlier resolution, Is felt that giving him one more tiny nugget of information couldn't do any harm. He had half her name already, and the other half was identical to that half. Effectively, she was giving him nothing new.

'Isis.'

'Isis?'

'Ancient Egyptian goddess. Wife of Osiris. Mother of Horus. Associated with nature and fertility. Symbolised by—'

'I know who Isis is. My parents spent a shit-load of money so that I'd be educated to know things like that.'

'Ooh, well, aren't you the lucky one.'

'No, I didn't mean it like that.'

'How did you mean it, then?'

'I . . . I don't know. Not like that, though.' He tried an ingratiating smile. 'So it's Isis, is it? It's a nice name.'

'My mum thought so. I don't.'

'What's wrong with it?'

'For one thing, who wants to be named after a goddess? Talk about raising expectations. Also, it looks odd, written down. Repetitive. An 'is' too far. So I shorten it.'

'Why the second syllable, though? Normally people go for the first.'

'Right, I'd really want to be called "Ice". I just prefer Is. Is is sort of . . . what it is. It just is.'

'Very "in the moment".'

'Don't mock.'

'Very existential.'

'I'm warning you.'

'Ow! Not so tight!'

'Then don't mock, *Provender*. Hang on, what's this?'

'Oh, thank Christ. Finally.' A smile of something close to bliss crescented Provender's lips.

'That's it. Don't lose it now. Keep going. Stay calm. Don't clench up. Relax.'

'Oh, that is *so* much better . . .'

17

Prosper Gleed's study was a symphony in wood. Oak-panelled walls, inset with oak bookcases, stood between a parquet floor and a beech-beamed ceiling lined with cork tiles. A mahogany desk and matching chair dominated the centre, with a teak coffee table nearby on which various wooden ornaments rested, including a lacquered-ebony inro box – gift of the Takeshis, Japan's other main Family beside the Omarus – and a carved cherrywood bust of Rufus Gleed, the likeness of the Family's founder copied from the only extant portrait of him, which hung elsewhere in the house. The louvred window shutters, which stood open, were wood. The inkwell and even the fountain pen on the desktop were wood, as was the housing for Prosper's videotyper screen (for the record, dark-stained ash). The lighting sconces, shaped to resemble candelabra, were wood. Anywhere you looked, wherever wood could be used, wood would.

As Cynthia entered, she saw Prosper's Phone was stationed in one corner of the room, looking, it must be said, somewhat wooden himself. There wasn't much to do, when you were a Phone and not in use, except stand and stare into the middle distance, sentry-style. You must never yawn or shuffle your feet. Above all you must never give any sign that the communications unit strapped to you, all sixty pounds of it, was starting to get heavy. To be a Phone was a job only for those with a strong constitution and a high boredom threshold. Others need not apply.

Prosper, at his desk, was absorbed in contemplation of something on his videotyper screen. To judge by the red-highlighted figures in the right-hand margin, he was studying that subset of the Family accounts which related to the Gleeds' boardroom battles with the Kuczynskis, the only field of fiscal conflict in which the Family's losses currently outweighed its gains.

'Prosper?'

He looked up. Blinked.

'Would you send your Phone out for a moment?'

Prosper frowned, then turned to the man in the corner and clicked his fingers. The Phone stepped smartly out of the room.

Cynthia perched on the edge of the desk near her husband and folded her arms.

'Tell me you were showing off back there,' she said, nodding in the direction of the second-largest drawing room. 'Tell me it was just manly breast-beating.'

'I don't know what you're—'

'You know perfectly well what I'm talking about. It was for the girls' benefit. So that you could look more like a father. You don't sincerely believe the Kuczynskis are behind all this.'

'On the contrary, I'm trying to think of reasons why they might *not* be.'

'I gave you reasons. Plenty of them.'

'And none, in my view, holds up against the fact that our two Families have been at loggerheads for two centuries, more or less. They hate us. They'd stop at nothing to undermine us. Won't you at least admit, Cynthia, that if any Family was responsible for kidnapping Provender, it would be the Kuczynskis?'

'I agree, but—'

'There we are, then.'

'Let me finish. I was going to say, I agree, but without any form of proof, all you're doing is making wild and potentially dangerous accusations. Wouldn't it be better to wait till we know more? Till, for instance, we actually hear from the kidnappers?'

'And what if we don't hear from them? What if Provender is halfway to Warsaw by now? You have no idea what the Kuczynskis are like, Cynthia. You don't have to deal with them like I do. You don't have to sit with them at the Annual Family Congress and watch those beady red eyes and those white faces and those ridiculous filed teeth of theirs. You don't have to watch them sip blood from wine goblets and smack their lips with relish. Blood freely donated by East European ClanFans. Ugh! They're disgusting. They're worse than monsters – they're humans playing at being monsters. Real monsters, if such things exist, can't help being what they are. The Kuczynskis can. So don't tell me this isn't something they'd do, because I know them and this is exactly the sort of thing they'd do.'

'Then why not contact them? Get the Phone back in and ring them right now? Speak to Stanisław Kuczynski and ask him straight out: do you have my son?'

'Because, for one thing, it's mid-morning in Poland. They'll all be fast asleep. And for another thing, he'll almost certainly lie and say he doesn't have a clue what I'm talking about. And for a third thing, I've had a better idea.'

'Which is?'

'All in good time. You know, though, Cynthia, it does upset me a bit.'

'What does?'

'The fact that, here am I, I'm faced with a crisis, our son's been taken, our Family's been attacked in its own homestead, bearded in its lair, and I'm trying to do something about it, and all I get from you is grief. Not support. Not encouragement. My own wife, who's been harping on at me for years not to be such a wastrel and a layabout – and those are just some of the kinder names you've called me – my own wife is unwilling to back me to the hilt when I need her to.'

'I'd back you, Prosper,' Cynthia said. 'Of course I would. If I believed you were doing the right thing. If I didn't feel you were about to take some precipitate course of action that could lead to God knows what.'

'So much for a wife's unconditional love for her husband. So much for man and woman becoming one flesh. Were you asleep during our marriage vows?'

'Oh, *Dios mío*, Prosper! Don't talk to me about "unconditional love". Don't you dare. *¡Hipócrita!* This from a man who'll screw anything in a skirt. A man who'll disappear for days on end and I don't know if he's in a casino in Monte Carlo, at the Kentucky Derby, holed up in some high-class Bangkok brothel, or what! If I've given you anything over the years it's love, patience, tolerance, devotion, way above and beyond the call of duty. I've stood by you while any other woman would have divorced you long ago and made it as public and traumatic as possible. I've put up with your behaviour, I've taken more shit from you than anyone deserves, and damn it, if that doesn't give me the right to tell you when I think you're making a bad decision, I don't know what does. Bah!' She spat. '*¡Hijo de puta!* Sometimes you disgust me.'

'I understand you're upset by all this, Cynthia.' Prosper's hands came up in a placatory gesture. 'It's hardly surprising. We're all under incredible strain right now, and if—'

She hit him, open-handed, intending more to shock than to hurt. The fact that the blow clearly did hurt, however, a lot, was not exactly a source of displeasure to her.

When he had stopped rubbing his cheek and hissing through clenched teeth, Prosper said, 'Well. Hmm. I'll put that down to heat of the moment. Lack of sleep. Time of the month, maybe.'

'Put it down to whatever you like,' she replied, icily. 'You know as well as I do you've had it coming for ages.'

'You won't change my mind, Cynthia. No matter how many times you slap me.'

'A skull as thick as yours, it'd take a sledgehammer to get through to you.'

'I'm convinced the Kuczynskis are behind this. Convinced. And the first thing I'm going to do is get them to confess it. And the next thing I'm going to do is threaten them with dire consequences if they don't give Provender back.'

'You're mad.'

'No, I'm someone who knows what's best for his Family and will do whatever it takes to protect his Family.'

'This isn't just some game, Prosper. This isn't a spin of a roulette wheel or a draw at blackjack. Lives could be at stake here. Thousands, perhaps millions. You'd go to war with the Kuczynskis without even knowing for sure they're guilty?'

'I'll find that out first, and then, if war's what it has to be, then war it is. Phone!'

'Prosper, I'm begging you. Wait.'

'Wait for what? The Kuczynskis to take Gratitude as well? Extravagance? *Phone!*'

The study door open and the Phone poked his head in. 'I'm sorry, sir, did you want me?'

'Dammit, man, are you deaf? I've been shouting for you for hours.'

'Prosper . . .'

'Come over here,' Prosper said to the Phone. To his wife he said, 'I'm invoking an Extraordinary Family Congress. I'll get word out to Massimiliano Borgia de'Medici. He'll do the rest. I want Stanisław Kuczynski to look me in the eye across the Congress Chamber and tell me he doesn't have my son. I want everyone to see that shifty vampire wannabe squirm as he lies to my face.'

'Prosper, I can't condone—'

'Not asking you to.' He snatched the receiver handset off the Phone's back. The Phone, meanwhile, reached over his own shoulder and hurriedly raised the retractable aerial on his backpack, then pressed a lever on his chestplate that flipped up the rotary dial.

'Prosper—'

'Borgia de'Medici,' Prosper said to the Phone. 'Come on, get on with it.'

The Phone dialled the number, and Prosper tapped his fingers while waiting for the connection to be made.

Cynthia spoke her husband's name again, in vain.

'Hello! Yes!' Prosper barked into the receiver. 'Signor Massimiliano? Prosper Gleed here. *Buòn giorno. Come sta?* No, not so good here, I'm afraid. Now listen . . .'

18

Damien had asked to be woken at midday. Venturing into his bedroom, Is was struck by the messiness of it. Heaps of clothes cluttered the floor. Drawers were wide open, cupboard doors the same. The rattan window blinds hung at angles. Damien's collection of books, of which he was so proud, had fallen into disarray, filling their shelves haphazardly, most of them canted rather than upright. Worst of all, the whole room reeked. Unwashed laundry. Unkempt male. It had never, Is thought, been this untidy or this malodorous when *she* had been a semi-regular occupant here. Back then, when she and Damien were lovers, he had made a concerted effort to clean and be clean. Six months on, that was no longer the case. When she had let him go, he had let himself go.

She spent a few moments inspecting the books, seeing if any new titles had appeared. This was Damien's ideological library, set apart from the run-of-the-mill hardbacks and paperbacks that could be found elsewhere in the flat. The books in the bedroom were the ones he returned to again and again, the ones he cherished. Academic treatises and works of political philosophy rubbed shoulders with less reasoned but more impassioned tomes. Anthologies of anti-Family writing. Tracts deploring the Families' stranglehold over ordinary people's lives. Angry denunciations of the public's fascination with all things Familial. And of course the famous what-if? novel, penned by Anonymous, *The Meritocrats*, which posited a world where the Borgias and the de'Medicis had not joined forces in the Sixteenth Century and become *de facto* rulers of Italy and therefore had not inspired the rise of Families in other nations. Utopic in outlook, and a dense and immensely dull read, *The Meritocrats* had arrived on the anti-Familial underground scene roughly three years back and swiftly become a sensation. It was reputed to have found a home in more than a million households across the world, despite being available only in blurrily-printed and badly-bound foolscap *samizdat* form, and was a particular favourite among university students, who passed it around like a naughty secret. Is herself did not know anyone other than Damien who owned a copy and thought the 'million' estimate might be something of an exaggeration. She had also, despite several noble attempts, never managed to finish the book. She was somewhat ashamed of that. It was a seminal work. As Damien once said, 'Anyone who hates the Families and hasn't read *The Meritocrats* doesn't truly hate the Families.' And maybe that was so and maybe Is didn't truly hate the Families – but she thought she did, and she thought that hatred wasn't all you needed to get you through to the end of Anonymous's 750-page doorstop. The patience of a saint and the endurance of a marathon runner were also required. It was a novel in name only. In lieu of plot there was a series of barely connected events. In lieu of characters there was a cast of ciphers who parroted the author's opinions. Each time she had borrowed Damien's copy, Is had vowed to plough all the way through. Each time, usually somewhere around page fifty, it had defeated her.

She leaned down and shook Damien by the shoulder, and kept shaking him till he surfaced blearily and bleatingly from sleep. Swinging his legs over the side of the bed, he sat up and stared at his knees while he sorted his thoughts. Damien was never at his best, newly woken.

'Kettle's on,' Is said.

He grunted approval.

'And Provender's fine,' she added. 'As fine as you'd expect, anyway.'

He half nodded.

'I've fed him, relieved him.' She paused. 'He seems pretty docile. I was wondering . . .'

'If you're going to say what I think you are,' Damien said thickly, 'forget it.'

'I doubt he'd try to escape.'

'Of course he would.'

'But he looks so uncomfortable.'

'Boo-hoo. My heart bleeds.'

'At least we could untie his ankles. Or if not that, take off the blindfold. He's seen my face already, for heaven's sake, and possibly yours too.'

'That's not what the blindfold's there for. It's there to keep him disorientated. Standard military practice with captives: deprivation of light, to make them acquiescent. Like hooding a falcon.'

'And to dehumanise him as well, maybe? So you don't have to look him in the eye?'

'Is.' Damien fixed her with his gaze. 'No. Let's not have any of this. No compassion for him. He's a Gleed, for fuck's sake.'

'That's not *his* fault.'

'I can't believe you said that.' Damien levered himself up off the bed. He was naked except for underpants, and the act of standing showed off his musculature to full effect. The whole of him tautened or flexed, a massed rippling of lean, fatless flesh. The rippling continued as he pulled on a plain shirt and a pair of cords. He wasn't innately graceful, but everything in his body moved and meshed just as it should and that lent him a kind of fundamental physical harmony.

Buttoning his shirt, he turned to face Is. 'No Family member is innocent. You know that. They can't hide behind "Ooh, it's not my fault, I didn't ask to be born". They're part of the cabal from the moment they're conceived. Because it's genetic. It's in the blood. They go on about it all the time, don't they? Blood, lineage, and so on. It wouldn't matter if it wasn't all-important to them, but it is, and so they can't have it both ways. Either they're Family, every last one of them, or their entire massive con job falls apart. There are no exceptions. Think of it like the Catholics and Original Sin. They're all tainted, and no amount of denial or distancing's ever going to alter that.'

He jabbed a finger at her.

'Are we clear?'

Is said, 'It doesn't mean you and I can't show him a little humaneness.'

'Humaneness,' said Damien, 'is what the Families have never shown towards the millions of people they've exploited, harmed and killed over time. Besides, we're not starving him. We haven't hurt him. If you ask me, he's come off pretty well, all things considered.'

In the main room of the flat, the kettle began whistling. Damien strode out of the bedroom, and minutes later was to be found hunched at the table gulping down slices of toast and the first of several cups of tea. He had the television on, tuned to one of the news channels.

'Nothing about us,' he said to Is, gesturing at the TV. 'The Gleeds have sat on it, just like I thought they would. Keeping it in the Family.' He smirked. 'What I wouldn't give to be a fly on the wall at Dashlands House right now. I'd be able to watch them all flapping around like arseholes. *And* I'd be able to leave little dots of shit all over their windowsills.' The smirk became a guffaw. 'Oh come on, Is, you have to admit that was pretty funny.'

Is, rather than admit anything, got busy in the kitchen area, preparing a lunchtime sandwich for herself and for Provender.

Damien paid a visit to the bathroom, and she heard him chatting to their prisoner while he took a long and loud piss. Damien's tone was jovial but, she thought, mockingly so. This was confirmed when she looked in on Provender shortly afterwards. He didn't appear in any way happier about his situation. She noticed splash marks on the uppers of his shoes and a few dribbles of urine on the floor by his feet. *Damien.*

She gave Provender his sandwich and sat on the toilet seat to eat hers.

'Thanks,' was all he said, when he had finished.

'Whatever he said to you,' Is said, meaning Damien, 'take it with a pinch of salt.'

'Oh, he was very friendly. I'm your honoured guest, apparently. And if I have any complaints about the living conditions, I'm to take them up with the hotel manager, whose name is Mr Couldn't Give A Toss.'

'That's his idea of a joke.'

'No, really?'

Damien, when Is emerged from the bathroom, was on the phone. 'Yup,' he said, 'all trussed up, nice and tight. He's not going anywhere.'

He listened briefly, then said, 'How long do you think I should leave it, then? I mean, they're expecting a note, aren't they? A phonecall at the least.'

More listening.

'Fair enough. And what's it like over there? What's your impression? All hell breaking loose?'

A grin appeared on his face, and broadened.

'Nice. Very nice.'

The grin vanished.

'I wasn't gloating. I wouldn't call it that at all.' For Is's benefit, he sneered and made a masturbatory gesture at the receiver with his free hand. 'I was just . . . Yes, I know. Nope. Yes. No.'

Now Damien began wagging his head from side to side, the universal sign language for The Person I'm Having This Phone Conversation With Is Beginning To Get On My Nerves.

'All right. So you'll call me when you want the next phase to start. OK. Yup. Fine. 'Bye.'

He clanked the receiver onto its cradle, then said to the phone, 'Your wish is my command, fuckwit.'

'That was your insider?' Is said. 'Your mole?'

'No, it was my mother.'

She brushed the sarcasm aside. 'So everything's going according to plan?'

'Seems that way.'

'So why aren't you pleased?'

Damien pondered this. 'I suppose because I'm the one meant to be running the show and yet I feel like I'm taking orders a lot of the time and that really wasn't how I saw this going.'

'Why not tell him that? Your insider?'

'Who says it's a him?'

'Or her. Why not tell her?'

Damien shrugged. Is thought there was something furtive about the shrug, but then Damien was perennially touchy on the subject of his contact within Dashlands. Cagey as well. It was as if the less Is knew about the person, the less important it would be that Damien had needed inside help to formulate his kidnap plan. His vanity demanded that he appear solely in charge of the operation.

'Anyway . . .' Damien stood up, grabbing a jacket. 'I'm off out. Breath of fresh air. Need anything from the shops?'

Is shook her head, then remembered she did need something. 'Latex gloves, please.'

'Eh?'

'Disposable ones.'

'For what?'

She waggled a hand at him. 'For this. For stuff I have to do with Provender.'

'Oh. Oh, right. OK.'

'Not washing-up gloves, either,' she said, as Damien headed for the door. 'Proper ones like I use at the hospital.'

'I'm going to find those around here?'

'Don't see why not.'

Damien sniffed. 'Well, I'll try.' From a small, low table by the door he took his wallet and another object. The wallet went into a pocket of his jacket. The other object he strapped to the back of his belt and carefully covered with the jacket flap. Then he went out.

Is pottered around the flat for a while, tidying, then glanced in on Provender once more. He was sitting crouched against the bath, as ever, head down. He looked small. Waiflike. Lost. She wanted to say something that would lift his spirits, even just slightly. Nothing sprang to mind. Gently, she shut the door.

19

At school Damien had been known as Disgrace. The nickname was coined by a Fifth-Form master, Mr Sudworth, who fancied himself something of a stand-up comedian though in truth was as tedious and mirth-free as the subject he taught, geography. Mr Sudworth's brilliant stroke of wit was to take Damien's name as it appeared on the school register, D. Scrase, and pronounce it in such a way that *it sounded like the word 'disgrace'.*

Hilarious!

Mr Sudworth thought so, at any rate, and never tired of the joke. Each time he addressed Damien as Disgrace, he would chortle heartily as if the nickname had only just occurred to him. Damien's classmates, for their part, found it amusing once, perhaps twice, but thereafter could barely muster a titter.

By rights, then, Disgrace ought not to have stuck. It wasn't an especially clever nickname, nor did it lend itself to shortening or further mutation. It was insulting but not terribly so. And perhaps it would not have stuck if Damien had objected to it strongly and put a stop to his peers calling him it by giving anyone who did a bash on the nose. But he hadn't, because deep down, almost at a subconscious level, he felt he deserved it. Disgrace summed up how he regarded himself and his life. He wore it like sackcloth and ashes; like tar and feathers. Even when juniors in the school knew him by it and used it to his face, he bore their jibes with a martyr's patience. Disgrace? Yes, that was him all right.

He had a father who scarcely spoke to anyone; a mother who was an avid, one might even say obsessive ClanFan; an older brother who had died aged seventeen, victim of a hit-and-run drunk-driving incident, and who was never mentioned; an older sister who had moved out to live with her boyfriend but spent as much time back home as she did at her boyfriend's flat because when he was out of work, as he often was, he became morosely depressed and then became too free with his fists; and a younger sister with Down's syndrome who needed more looking after than they could cope with and so had been packed off to live in care but came back to stay for one weekend a month. He had, in short, a family only in the loosest sense of the word, and Damien, as a sensitive boy and then a sensitive young man, always believed at the back of his mind that in some way he was to blame. It was *his* fault that his father read the newspaper during mealtimes and whiled away all of his free hours down in the garden shed, allegedly fixing things but in fact quite evidently doing nothing. *He* was the one who forced his mother to lose herself in a fantasy world of Families, collecting magazines and books about them, clipping out newspaper articles about them to paste into scrapbooks, buying all manner of Family-related bric-a-brac and memorabilia, and building what was effectively a shrine to all things Familial in one corner of the lounge – the walls smothered with posters, the carpet heaped with cheaply-produced souvenir tat, Family members' faces peering out into the Scrases' lives all day every day. *He* was responsible for Jason being killed by that careering car and for Tanya hooking up with that godawful oaf Calvin. It was even possible that *he* had somehow brought about little Adele's birth defect.

As an adult, Damien would realise that he took all this unwarranted guilt on himself simply because no one thought to tell him otherwise. It didn't occur to anyone sit him down and explain that some things happen just because they happen. His parents never even noticed that he was in a state of almost constant torment, agonising over the reasons why his family was so blighted by misfortune and misery (it was something he had done, it must be). As far as Mr and Mrs Scrase were concerned, thank God one of their children had turned out quiet, undemanding, normal. It was a relief to be able to ignore him. They could forget about Damien, in the way they couldn't forget about Tanya and her latest black eye, Adele shrieking through her weekend visits, or the hurtful memory of Jason.

It was around the age of eighteen that Damien had a moment of revelation, an epiphany almost. He was shortly to leave school, and his teachers had assured him that a university place was his for the taking if he only applied himself in his exams. His reports routinely described him as highly intelligent but lacking in drive and motivation. The headmistress promised him that if he made the effort and gained the requisite grades, she would do her utmost to obtain one of the Family-funded university scholarships for him, which would see him through his degree course.

In the lounge at home, Damien knelt at his mother's Family shrine. He studied the clusters of happy faces, the elegant poses, the immaculately-groomed hair, the backdrops of palatial residences and unimaginably expensive furnishings. This privileged international elite who led such perfect, carefree, untroubled lives. Look at them with their arms round one another. Look at their clothes. Look at the way members of each Family, or part of Family, were able to stand together to have their pictures taken. Where was the missing brother, taken too soon? The sullen, uncommunicative father? The sister with the bruises? Oh sure, the Families must have their problems. Damien wasn't so naïve as to think that things didn't go wrong for them from time to time. But they had money, huge sums of it, and that made a difference. They also had unity.

Every image in front of him said so. Screamed it. Unity radiated from every item of his mother's collection. It shone like the sun.

All at once, Damien understood that he hated them. No, not just hated. That wasn't strong enough a word. He *despised* the Families. They were everything his family was not. They presented an ideal that it was impossible for others to live up to. Their capital F belittled every non-Family family in the world. Their wealth, even when they tried to disburse a tiny fraction of it as charity, mocked those who were poorer and less fortunate than themselves, which was everyone.

He knew, then, that he must dedicate his life to opposing the Families. He would fight them in whatever way he could. He would sacrifice himself to the task of damaging and perhaps even destroying them. It was his mission.

He flunked his exams abysmally. No hope of a Family scholarship then. He left home, moving from a small town just outside London's suburbs to the heart of the city. The night before he went, he did something which was appallingly mean and which he continued to regret but which at the time seemed like a necessity, even an act of generosity. He set fire to his mother's shrine. There were candles in front of it, which his mother would light occasionally to lend the shrine an even more votive air. They were aflame that evening, and Damien promised his mother when she went to bed that he would extinguish them when *he* went to bed. He didn't. He 'nodded off on the settee'. One of the candles must have 'accidentally fallen over'. When he awoke, the whole shrine 'was burning out of control'. He tried to put out the flames 'as fast as possible' but, obviously, 'not fast enough'.

The shrine was devastated. His mother was devastated. She was still in the lounge at dawn the next day, pawing distraughtly through the charred remnants of her collection, trying to salvage what she could of it. The last sounds Damien ever heard her make, as he sneaked out by the back door with a holdall containing all his clothes and possessions, were a series of helpless mewling sobs which degenerated into out-and-out lost-dog howling. The noise pursued him all the way down the street, onto the bus, into the city.

A decade on, if Mrs Scrase were by any chance to meet her younger son, she would almost certainly not recognise him. He was bulkier, thanks to a rigorous regime of body-building (in any mission, physical strength was a must). He was harder-looking (to survive as a resident of Needle Grove you had to be hard-looking). His face had taken on a leaner, meaner air (never let it be said that the outer person did not reflect the inner). If Mrs Scrase had ever hoped that Damien might find himself a nice, secure profession, settle down, marry and give her grandchildren, she would have been disappointed. His career, such as it was, consisted of intermittent menial jobs which earned him enough to pay the rent and keep body and soul together, with a little left over for book-buying. Whatever kind of work he did, he carried it out with no more competence or enthusiasm than was necessary to avoid being sacked, and when he got bored and wanted to be sacked, he simply lowered his effort level that little bit further until his employers took the hint. As for settling down, he had had a string of short-lived affairs, glorified one-night stands many of them, and his only relationship of any significance was the year he had spent with Is, which he now looked back on as the happiest and maybe the only happy year of his life.

He had met her while he was working as a porter at St Fiacre's Hospital. Not porter in the sense of pushing beds and bodies around. He had been under that misapprehension himself when applying for the job. In fact, the position had been for a porter in the hospital's kitchen, where it pretty much meant dogsbody. He had pictured himself racing desperately ill patients to the operating theatre and wheeling dead patients to the morgue, both of which tasks had a kind of dark, noble glamorousness, but in the event his duties were preparing and serving food. He would have quit after the first day had a nurse called Isis Necker not entered the cafeteria that lunchtime and taken a portion of shepherd's pie and mixed vegetables from him.

She scarcely noticed him. She was busy talking to a friend, a fellow-nurse. She glanced at him for no longer than the time it took for him to ask her what she would like and for her to tell him and for him to give it to her. Then she strode away from the serving counter with her tray, and although she would insist later that he *had* made an impression on her, he knew he hadn't. He was just the nonentity in the white smock and silly brimless cap who had slung some grub on a plate for her.

He stuck out the portering job for several months, just because of Is. Day after day he prepared and shovelled rank-smelling hospital meals, simply in hope of catching a glimpse of her. For long stretches of time he wouldn't see her. Her shifts changed; her hours and his didn't always overlap. Then she would be back, and he would have an opportunity to share a few words with her across the heat-lamps, maybe fire a quip at her, and always a smile. She made it all worthwhile. The smells of grease and boiled potato that seemed permanently suffused into his skin; the heat in the kitchen that left him dripping with sweat by day's end; the constant shouting of the chefs and the sullen bickering of the other porters; the numerous nicks in his fingers from knives and peelers; the dinning clatter of pots and pans – all worthwhile, all bearable, thanks to her.

What finally got them together was a chance remark about the Families. It was the day a new wing of the hospital was being opened, built with money endowed by one of the lesser British Families, the Graysons. The inauguration ceremony brought most of St Fiacre's to a standstill, with all the consultants and surgeons and registrars turning out in their best bib and tucker to applaud as Potiphar Grayson, the Family's head, made a lengthy speech about giving something back to the community and then applied scissors to ribbon. None of the nursing staff was invited to attend. Somebody, after all, had to carry on with the minor, inconvenient stuff like tending to patients and keeping the hospital ticking over. Is said as much to Damien as she took a helping of stew off him, and Damien nodded sympathetically and then said, 'You know, it surprises me that a Family member even knows how to use a pair of scissors. Don't servants normally do that sort of thing for them?'

To which Is, amused, replied, 'Lucky we have a casualty unit here, isn't it? Chances are he might give himself a nasty cut.'

It felt naughty, a little bit seditious. Each of them sensed immediately that here was someone who didn't kowtow to the Families the way almost everyone else did. Each of them recognised a kindred spirit.

And it had been so great to begin with, Damien thought as he left his flat and took the lift down to Block 26's mid-level. So perfect. Him and Is. He had taken it upon himself to educate her. He had shared with her the benefit of his years of reading about the Families, learning about them, going on anti-Family rallies, joining various anti-Family discussion groups. Having fostered and nurtured his own resentment of the Families, he had been given the opportunity to foster and nurture someone else's, and he made the most of it. Where Is was sometimes unclear on Family history, he enlightened her. Where her take on anti-Family ideology was perhaps somewhat wonky, he had straightened her out. Pygmalion to her Galatea, he had taken the raw material of her opinions and fashioned it into a fine and focused credo.

And then – ungratefully? – she had dumped him.

It still rankled. After all he had done for her. All he had given her.

She had come out with some guff about two different perspectives on life, two strong personalities not always meeting each other halfway. She had said she still wanted to be friends even if they couldn't be lovers any more. She had tried, he had to admit, to let him down gently. But it had hurt. Still did.

One thing he could console himself with, though. When he had come to her with his proposal for kidnapping Provender Gleed, she had needed little persuasion to join in. And the credit for that, he liked to think, lay with him. His patient indoctrination of her. He had changed her for the better, and the change was permanent. Pat on the back for Damien 'Disgrace' Scrase.

The lift bump-buffeted to a halt, and Damien stepped out into a murkily-lit shopping arcade. All of Needle Grove's indoor communal areas were bathed in the same low-wattage level of neon bulb, filtered through green plastic casings to cast everything in shades of that hue. The shopping arcade was no exception. The floors here were also green – lawn-coloured linoleum – and the walls, though not wholly green, sported a mural depicting a fir forest, the foliage of which was, of course, dark green. The mural was intended as a tribute to the expanse of coniferous woodland that had been present on this site prior to the estate being built. The name of the estate had been chosen with the same purpose in mind. But in the event, it all conspired to depress rather than uplift. It emphasised the kind of natural landscape that Needle Grove had erased and that its residents were unlikely ever to know.

Today being a Sunday, the majority of the arcade's shops were closed and had their protective shutters and grilles firmly up over their windows and doors, and even the premises that were open for business looked as if they were ready to shut at a moment's notice. Few shopkeepers put items of value on public display, for fear of smash-and-grab raids, so the windows were all but empty. Inside, likewise, care was taken not to offer too much in the way of temptation. Cash tills, for instance, were hidden away inside reinforced-glass kiosks, and shopkeepers more often than not served their customers from behind bars. Even with all these precautions, to work in retail in Needle Grove was to expose yourself to a certain level of risk, both fiscal and personal. Shrinkage ran at roughly thirty per cent. The mortality rate wasn't much lower.

Mr Ho's All-Day Emporium occupied a prime corner site and attracted, consequently, a higher than average share of theft and strife. Its proprietor nonetheless retained an almost touching level of faith in humanity, and that was partly why Damien was a regular customer. Optimists were few and far between on the estate and should be supported. The convenience of the shop's location was also a factor.

Loitering outside the All-Day Emporium now, as Damien approached, was a clutch of rag-clad kids who hunkered in various slovenly postures, each one apparently trying to out-slouch the rest. Damien recognised them as one of the more recent gang-tribes to emerge from Needle Grove's petri dish of youth culture, the Orphans. Their chosen theme was rejection of family in all its forms, including Family. They pretended their parents were dead. They squatted in vacant flats. They wore only what they could beg, borrow or steal. They considered themselves the absolute antithesis of everything to do with heredity, ancestry, consanguinity.

Damien, in that respect, could almost admire them.

In every other respect he abhorred them.

The Orphans bad-eyed him as he entered the shop. Damien didn't avert his gaze, neither did he stare back. He gave them a level, measured look that said they had nothing to fear from him as long as he had nothing to fear from them.

Mr Ho, behind his unbarred counter, greeted Damien with an ebullient wave.

'Mr Scrase.'

'Mr Ho.'

'How can I help you this fine day?'

'Just some cigarettes.'

'You've given up.'

'Not that I recall.'

'I could swear, last month you told me never to sell you another packet. You made me vow.'

'Well, I've changed my mind.'

'Don't tell me. You've failed to get back together with that lady of yours.'

'You can read me like a book.'

Mr Ho shrugged. 'She was the reason you took up smoking again the last time. You said the other day you had hopes of a reunion. Now you're buying cigarettes. It doesn't take a genius to work it out.'

'It's a tense time for me generally, Mr Ho,' Damien said, with a meaningful emphasis.

Mr Ho took the hint. 'Fair enough. Say no more. It's Pedigree Milds, isn't it?'

'Ho ho, Mr Ho.'

'No, of course not. Only Family-independent brands for you. Which narrows it down a bit.' Mr Ho reached round and took a pack off the shelf behind him. The carton was festooned with Cantonese ideograms. 'A twenty-pack of Parent Nation. China's finest. I'm afraid import duty has gone up again.'

Damien took the cigarettes off him. 'Can't be helped. Anyway, I don't mind. All in a good cause.'

'Yes, China,' said Mr Ho, with a sardonic glint in his eye. 'The only real democracy in the world. Family-free for fifteen years. A true paradise. I can't wait to return there.'

'Oh come on, it's not that bad.'

'Take it from me, Mr Scrase, China is a shit-hole. I know it offends your principles, but it's true. I couldn't wait to get out of there. Nothing works. Nothing gets done. Political corruption is off the scale.'

'And this country's better?'

'It's not worse.'

Damien remained resolutely unconvinced. He knew China wasn't perfect but it was trying its hardest. A decade and a half after ousting its Families, it was a country still struggling to find its feet. He was sure that, in time, it would succeed. China was an experiment. It was setting the pattern which, one day, the rest of the world would follow.

'Let's agree to differ,' he said.

'Fair enough,' said Mr Ho. 'Anything else I can get you?'

'Box of matches. Oh, and would you have latex gloves?'

'Latex gloves?' Mr Ho raised an insinuating eyebrow.

'Don't ask.'

'It just so happens that the All-Day Emporium does stock latex gloves. You mean the disposable type, I take it. They're down the household aisle. If you want, I can get them for you . . .'

'No, I can do it.'

'That's it. That's the aisle. A little bit further down. Yes, there you are, on your left. No, your other left. Look up now. Yes, there. Directly in front of your nose.'

On his way back to the counter with the box of gloves Damien heard the chime of the electric bell over the shop door. A moment later he saw Mr Ho's welcoming-shopkeeper expression curdle into distaste. He turned in the direction Mr Ho was looking.

Three of the Orphans had come in and were standing slumped, hands in pockets, each pretending to examine a different display of groceries. They could not have looked more like three would-be shoplifters if they had tried.

'Listen, you lot,' said Mr Ho. 'I know you're not here to buy anything. Scram.'

The Orphans peered at him from beneath their lank fringes. They all belonged to that category of teenager who was congenitally incapable of closing his mouth.

'Go on,' Mr Ho said, with a flick of his hand for emphasis. 'I mean it. Only good customers like Mr Scrase are welcome here.'

One of the Orphans grabbed a tin of frankfurters in brine and held it up. 'But I want this,' he said. 'I want to buy it off you. I want you to make a profit off of me with your enormous mark-up.'

'No, you don't. You have no money. Put it back and leave.'

The Orphan glared at Mr Ho. Mr Ho returned the glare.

Reluctantly, sullenly, the Orphan replaced the tin. He thought for a moment, then said, 'Fuckin' Chinkie tampon.'

Damien couldn't help himself. He snorted, half with laughter, half with derision. 'What was that? What did you just say? Was it "Chinkie tampon"?'

The Orphan, puzzled, nodded.

'Do you have any idea how asinine that sounds? "Chinkie tampon". It doesn't even make sense. It doesn't *mean* anything.'

'Yeah, it does,' said the Orphan, defensively.

'Does it? What?'

'It, um . . . it means he's a fuckin' slitty-eyed Chinese shit-wanker.'

'That doesn't mean anything either. For God's sake, if you're going to slag somebody off, at least make sure you do it coherently.'

Baffled now, the Orphan groped further into the limited recesses of his vocabulary, found nothing there that was going to be of any use, and so hawked up a wad of phlegm and gobbed it onto the floor. Then he spun on his heel and hunched out of the All-Day Emporium. His two cohorts followed.

'Sorry about that,' Damien said to Mr Ho.

'I'm used to it. I've been called worse. What gets me is that we went on that rent-strike two years ago to badger the Risen London Authority to improve conditions here, and when you see kids like those you have to wonder why we bothered. They don't deserve to have this place made better.'

'Maybe, but the rest of us certainly do. And if this place is made better, perhaps those kids won't behave the way they do.'

'Oh, I think they still will.'

'Yeah, you're right, but perhaps the next generation of gang-tribes won't emerge. If this estate was somewhere they could take pride in . . .'

'It's a nice dream. Doomed to failure, though, if our last experience was anything to go by.'

'Maybe,' said Damien. 'Maybe not. We'll see.'

Leaving the All-Day Emporium with his cigarettes, matches and box of latex gloves, Damien found the Orphans waiting for him outside. This wasn't exactly a surprise. It would have been foolish of him to think he could openly ridicule one of them and not be made to pay for it.

The Orphans had arranged themselves in a loose semicircle around the shop entrance. There were a dozen of them all told, and they were spaced out in such a way that Damien wouldn't be able to walk between any two of them without brushing at least one shoulder. The physical contact, however slight, would be construed as a shove. The shove, in turn, would be legitimate grounds for combat.

Damien halted in the shop doorway. He swivelled his head, taking in the Orphans one by one. Fully half of them had the reddened eye-whites and the receding gums of the habitual Tinct-user.

His face broke into a wide, fearsome grin. 'Trust me, lads,' he said. 'I will kill you all. Gladly. One of you so much as lays a finger on me, you're dead, the lot of you. You do not fuck with someone like me. So what do we say you just step out of my way and there's an end of it? Hey?'

The Orphans frowned. He was supposed to be intimidated. Why wasn't he? There were a dozen of them and only one of him. Why was *he* the one making the threats?

'Come on,' Damien said. 'I won't say it again. Do yourselves a favour. Get out of my way.'

All it took was one of the Orphans to shuffle his feet uneasily. Straight away, their pack mentality collapsed and their ranks broke. The semi-circle drifted apart and the various Orphans wandered off in twos and threes to regroup further down the arcade, where they began a fierce debate among themselves as to why and how it was that one man had managed to talk them out of kicking his head in. It was a mystery. Downright perplexing.

Meanwhile Damien, sauntering back to the lift, lit himself a Parent Nation. He dragged on the cigarette and felt the nicotine-hit scour through him. He had been on the cancer-stick wagon for far too long. Falling off it was like greeting an old, familiar friend.

Continuing to suck on the cigarette, his thoughts sharpening with every puff, he mused on his standoff with the Orphans. It was a truth not always universally acknowledged that in any confrontation with thugs your best weapon was your brain. Thugs were, almost by definition, thick. They were also, at heart, cowards. All you had to do was act more aggressively than them, state with utter conviction that this was a fight they couldn't win, browbeat them, and invariably they would back down.

Of course, it was crucial that you were prepared to enforce words with deeds if it came to that.

Damien could feel the pommel of his sheath knife pressing into the small of his back. The weight of the whole weapon was dragging down on his trouser belt. Cigarette in mouth, he reached behind him, slipped a hand under the fabric of his shirt and briefly stroked the knife's haft, his fingers tracing the ridged contours of deerhorn like a blind man reading Braille.

He was glad he hadn't been forced to use the knife.

And those Orphans should be thanking their lucky stars he hadn't.

20

Gangs of cheerfully whistling workmen dismantled Venice. With hammer and crowbar they clawed the city apart and loaded it section by section, shattered façade by shattered façade, onto the backs of flatbed lorries. What had taken days to construct was taking hours to deconstruct. The beautiful illusion of *La Serenissima* was being reduced, little by little, to paint-and-plywood reality.

Late in the afternoon, with Venice all but gone, Cynthia came out and exchanged a few words with the foreman overseeing the demolition. If the foreman thought she seemed wan and listless, her conversation not at all sparkling, he put it down to the effects of a hard night's partying.

Back indoors, her duty discharged, Cynthia debated whether to try taking a nap again. She was bone-deep weary. However, she had gone to bed earlier in the afternoon and not managed so much as a wink of sleep, her head a churning vortex of suppositions and fears. She didn't think she would have any better luck this time.

Keep moving. Keep busy.

She headed for the eastern end of the house, where Great's quarters were. On the way, she passed Triumph. The statue's ivory eyes, gazing down from its golden face, seemed to taunt her as she went by. Cynthia, by way of rebuke, reminded herself that Triumph's beauty was purely superficial. Such a weight of soft metal and brittle tusk could not support itself unaided. Within the statue lay an armature of thick iron bars, the crude, mundane truth behind the magisterial illusion.

Great lived in what had come to be called the Granny Flat – a self-contained ground-floor annexe with its own private patio outside and, inside, all the plush amenities you would expect. For Great's benefit, it was additionally kitted out with a panoply of medical and orthopaedic equipment, and there was a telephone hotline straight to the nearest hospital, in Reading, where the doctors were ready to drop everything and come running if an emergency arose. The annexe was a more than agreeable place in which to spend the last few years of your life, and back in another age, before the events of this morning, before her world collapsed, Cynthia had always foreseen herself retiring happily here, conceding full run of the house to the next generation and its progeny. Anticipating that she would outlive her husband, she had looked forward to being a resident grandmother, on hand but not in the way. Now, all at once, the prospect of such a future seemed an unrealisable dream.

Her knock on the Granny Flat's main door went unanswered. She knocked again, with still no response, and so opened the door and strode in. Sounds of splashing drew her to the bathroom, and she tendered a 'Hello?' as she neared it.

'One moment, ma'am.'

Not one but several moments later, Carver emerged from the bathroom. He had an apron on and his shirtsleeves rolled up, and he was drying off his forearms with a towel.

'Great offers his apologies but he is taking a bath and cannot see you right now. If you were to come back in half an hour . . . ?'

'As a matter of fact, Carver, it's you I want to talk to. Would that be possible?'

Carver glanced towards the bathroom doorway. 'I'm sure I can spare a minute or so. Great will summon me back if he needs me. How may I be of assistance?'

Cynthia marshalled her thoughts. Deprived of sleep, her brain seemed to be mired in mud.

'My husband has left for the Island,' she began.

'Indeed, ma'am. He and Master Fortune departed for the airfield an hour ago. I imagine the dirigible is taking to the sky even as we speak.'

'He's called an Extraordinary Congress.'

'That he has.'

'I'm afraid he's going to do something rash.'

'It's not my place to speculate on such matters.'

'He's blaming the Kuczynskis for Provender's disappearance.'

'The enmity between the two Families goes far back, ma'am.'

'Do you think he's right, then?'

'I couldn't say.'

'But you fought in the War.'

'I fought against the Pan-Slavic Confederation army. I fought Eastern European soldiers. I didn't fight the Kuczynskis directly. I was a mere infantryman, as was my master.'

'But war was sparked by a dispute between Gleeds and Kuczynskis.'

'A spat at a Family Congress – that, as I recall, was the catalyst, ma'am. Wojtek Kuczynski believed that Basil Gleed made an insulting reference to his albinism. Allegedly Master Basil called him a "white bastard" but in all probability what he said was "right bastard". Still an insult but not quite so personal. If only Master Basil had been able to overcome his speech impediment . . . It always flared up at moments of tension. But then it is said, isn't it, that the wheels of history turn on the tiniest of factors. Cleopatra's Nose and all that.'

'And I'm concerned that history is about to repeat itself, Carver. Prosper has gone completely off the deep end. I've never seen him like this. It's as if he's suddenly discovered a purpose in life, after fifty-odd years of significantly failing to do so. But the thing is, he's spent so long doing nothing, just idling along, that now that there's a crisis he doesn't know how to react. He's *over*reacted.'

'Again, ma'am, not my place to speculate.'

'I know. I know. I shouldn't really be burdening you with all this.'

'However, ma'am, *were* it my place, I would be expressing an opinion not entirely contrary to yours. I would add that it is good that Master Prosper's brother has gone with him. My hope would be that Master Fortune might act as a calming influence on Master Prosper. Perhaps, when they get to the Island, Master Fortune will be able to mitigate anything Master Prosper might say to the head of the Kuczynskis. Serve as a buffer between the two of them, perhaps.'

'I wish I shared your optimism.'

Carver gave a broad-shouldered shrug. 'Master Fortune's conviviality can be infectious. But I'm sensing, ma'am, that you're not here for just a sympathetic ear. You want something more from me. Perhaps some form of practical help . . . ?'

'Carver,' Cynthia said, nodding, 'practical help would be immensely welcome.'

'Specifically?'

'There has to be something we can do. *You* can do. To find out who has Provender.'

'Go to the police, perhaps.'

'Not the police. Not yet.'

'They have the resources. The manpower.'

'They also don't know how to keep their mouths shut. Gone are the days when you could be sure the police would act on a Family's behalf quietly and discreetly. Now, you call them in, and next thing you know, one of them's gone to the press or a TV station and told all, and it becomes a circus.'

'The modern media's interest in the Families is insatiable.'

'There's money to be made out of us, that's the trouble.'

'It's a debased age,' Carver said, with feeling.

Cynthia did not demur. 'So no, not the police. Not unless we absolutely have to. The longer we can keep this to ourselves, the better. What that leaves us with, however . . .'

Carver waited, then realised he was being asked to contribute. 'What that leaves us with, ma'am,' he said, 'is some kind of private avenue of investigation.'

'Yes.'

'Some independent organisation without authority ties, looking into the matter.'

'You sound,' Cynthia said, 'as though you may have something in mind.'

'Not necessarily.'

'Please say you do.'

'There is one possibility that occurs, ma'am. I cannot guarantee it will bear fruit, but I do believe discretion could be assured, which is a significant factor.'

'What is it? What do you have in mind?'

'I would require your permission to act in any way I see fit, and a substantial discretionary fund to draw on.'

'You have both.'

'I will not, however, be able to set anything in motion until tomorrow.'

'Why not?'

'Late on a Sunday afternoon, I fear that I would not be able to contact those whom I need to contact.'

'But you could first thing tomorrow?'

'I could, ma'am. First thing.'

There came a tapping from the bathroom, the familiar arrhythmic drumming of Great's signet ring. Against the bath's ceramic side the ring made a sharper and more resonant sound than it did when striking the frame of Great's wheelchair.

'My master calls,' Carver said. 'I must go to him. You'll excuse me.'

'Of course. Oh, but before you do, just one last thing. Fort mentioned something about an anomaly. Some kind of problem with the catering staff last night. He said you were looking into it.'

'That's correct. I have indeed looked into it.'

'And?'

'Master Prosper didn't inform you of my findings?'

'Obviously not.' Cynthia had had no contact with her husband since slapping him in his study. She and he had been scrupulously avoiding each other all day.

'It may be that two members of the catering staff left the party early last night,' Carver said. 'The head count at the end of the proceedings came up short. Now, it's by no means certain that the two were the kidnappers. They may simply have got fed up with working and decided to leave.'

'It's odd, though. They wouldn't have got paid.'

'Very odd. Unfortunately, we have little further information to go on.'

'We don't even have their names?'

'We have what appear to be false ones. It seems that the catering company is somewhat lackadaisical in its employment practices. It's very much a cash-in-hand, quick-turnover-of-staff type of business. I don't think a great amount of background vetting goes on.'

'But that's appalling. We hired these people! They were doing the catering for a Family event!'

'I suspect, if it proves they *were* at fault, they shan't be doing the catering for any kind of event ever again. But as I said, it's by no means certain this has any bearing on the situation whatever. There may even have been a miscount. I will continue to look into the matter and see what I can turn up.'

'Do.'

The tapping from the bathroom became louder and more insistent.

'And now, ma'am, if you don't mind, I really must attend to my master.' Carver leaned close, dropping his voice. 'Between you and me, Great isn't in the best of moods this evening. I'm due to give him his bimonthly prostate massage later – a procedure he seldom looks forward to. A procedure I can't say *I* look forward to much either.'

Cynthia wrinkled her nose. 'Who would? Off you go then. And Carver?'

'Yes, ma'am?'

'Thank you.'

She left the Granny Flat feeling comforted. She had been reluctant to go to Carver but was now pleased she had. He would do what he could. He hadn't held out any false hopes but he had at least given her *some* hope where before there had been none.

She ate a light supper with Gratitude and Extravagance, and retired to bed straight afterward.

There was a bottle of Oneirodam in the drawer of her nightstand which Cynthia usually had recourse to when she found herself in bed alone. Tonight, however, she didn't need to take any of the sleeping pills. No sooner had she lain down than oblivion engulfed her in a warm, welcome wave. Her night was empty of dreams.

Monday dawn came.

PART THREE

21

In an insalubrious borough of London, off an insalubrious street, down an insalubrious side-alley, you would come across the entrance to an insalubrious office building. Inside the building, if you mounted an insalubrious flight of stairs, through storeys that were of ever increasing insalubriousness, to a top floor that was the most insalubrious of all, you would find yourself on an in-no-way-salubrious landing. Passing along this landing, perhaps abandoning all hope of ever rediscovering salubrity, you would arrive at a door which may once have been tidy and shipshape, its paint not peeled, its mottled-glass windowpane not cracked, but which was now regrettably of a piece with its surroundings, a portal that was the epitome of insalubriousness. And on the windowpane you would see inscribed, in mostly intact transfer letters, the words:

MILNER & MOORE
ANAGRAMMATIC DETECTIVES

accompanied by the slogan:

'Honestly? Or on the Sly?
We can tell you which!'

And if, during usual office hours, you were to pass through this door, you would almost inevitably discover two men sitting in the room within. Two besuited, unassuming-looking men whom you might, if you didn't know otherwise, take for accounts clerks or bank tellers. That punctiliousness in their faces. That air of needing everything to be exact and due. That sharply side-parted hair. Those analysing eyes.

Their full names were Merlin Milner and Romeo Moore, but their parents could hardly have christened them less appositely, since neither man lived up to his forename. There was nothing wildly wizardrous about Milner, nor anything dashingly romantic about Moore. Then again, both possessed abilities which some might say were magical, and both were passionate about words and wordplay to a degree that might be called amorous.

Their names, at any rate, had played a significant role in determining their choice of career. Born and brought up in different parts of the capital, at an early age Milner and Moore separately came to the same realisation. Each noticed that his forename and surname consisted of the same letters jumbled up. This led to an interest in anagrams and in word games generally, and, as time went by, interest blossomed into an overwhelming compulsion. Acrostics, telestichs, pangrams, chronograms, codes – all grist to the mill for Milner and Moore. But anagrams were their first love, and though they might dally for a while with palindromes, say, or rebuses, or even lipograms, to anagrams they would always faithfully return.

There was, it seemed to them, something almost mystical about the way one word or phrase could be reconstituted to form another word or phrase. It felt as if one were playing with the stuff of existence, the very building blocks of life. To manipulate the letters, to randomise, to induce chaos and then reassert order, a new order – it was a heady thrill, and one they could not tire of. Research told them they were not alone in this. Anagrammatising had a long and noble tradition, going back to the medieval Jewish Cabbalists and even further to the Ancient Greeks. The use of anagrams as a tool of divination was common to those two races and to many others.

By their mid-twenties, Milner and Moore, still separately, had both arrived at the same conclusion: there was much more to words than met the eye. Words were not merely symbolic representations of abstract and concrete concepts. In some strange way words *were* the concepts. The two were indissolubly linked. When somebody spoke of a 'dog', for instance, they weren't merely using the noun which by common consensus had become attached to the wild or domestic animal of the genus *Canis*, they were also conjuring up the image of a dog in the mind of the listener. They were evoking the intrinsic notion of doggishness, the essence of dog with its attendant impressions of fur and slobber and devotion and implacable pursuit and cur-like cowardice, a whole raft of information compacted into that three-character monosyllable. It was impossible not to think of a dog when somebody said 'dog'. Everything you knew about dogs could be tapped into by mention of the word. It was the key to your entire mental archive on the subject, to your individual understanding of the nature of reality as far as dogs were concerned. If there was no word for dog, you might look at a dog and not know what it was. You might not even see it. It would be outside your sphere of comprehension. Without the appellation 'dog', it was possible that dogs would cease to be.

Such was the power of words.

And if words could be pulled apart and reorganised into new shapes, perhaps this pertained to the things the words stood for as well. By moulding and refashioning the letters, you could reveal meanings no one even knew were there. You could expose the hidden connections of the world, the patterns which people followed subconsciously, the secret interleavings of existence.

It was, in a way, like playing God.

Or, indeed, playing dog.

It should be pointed out that at this stage in their lives, when they formulated their individual but identical theories about anagrams, both Milner and Moore were exceedingly frustrated young men. Each was working in an unchallenging, dead-end job – respectively, town planning and hotel management. Each was unmarried, living alone, parentless, loveless. Each was coming to that midlife cusp where the dreams and aspirations of youth had nearly all fallen away and a sense of limitation was creeping in, along with feelings of disappointment and the first intimations of mortality. Each, at about the same time, arrived at the same conclusion: it was time to change tack. Try something else while he could. While he was still young enough to resume his old job if things didn't work out. It was now or never.

Each thought, *Why not put into practice, somehow, my theories about words? Why not make use of all those hours I've spent absorbed in my linguistic hobby? Turn a pastime into an occupation?*

Thus, simultaneously, synchronicitously, at opposite ends of the city, two Anagrammatic Detective agencies were set up.

Neither thrived.

Clients came, but hardly in their droves, and most departed without engaging the services of Milner or Moore. Once their initial curiosity about how an Anagrammatic Detective actually worked had been satisfied, they laughed and left. Those who didn't laugh and leave were surprised to discover just how effective that particular system of investigation could be.

They were in such a small minority, however, that it made no difference. The money wasn't coming in. Overheads were not being met. Bills began to pile up. After a year, both Milner and Moore were finding that (a) self-employment was not all it was cracked up to be, and (b) being a private detective was not all it was cracked up to be either. Each man knew he was staring failure in the face. The prospect of re-entering the job market, dispiriting though it was, was beginning to look like the only course of action available.

That was when each learned about the other. Neither could quite believe there was another Anagrammatic Detective out there. They communicated, they met up at a vertiginously high rooftop bar in central London, the Old Hyde Park Tavern on Kensington Heights, and, in the space of one drunken evening, they compared notes, got on, and decided to pool their resources.

By sharing an office, each cut his overheads in half at a stroke. At the same time, neither was in competition with the other for the same jobs. Work began to pick up. The trickle of clients became . . . well, not a flood, but a slightly faster trickle. And the agency scored some notable successes. Not the sort that garnered headlines, nor the sort that won awards and honours, but still, achievements to be proud of, all of them adding to a lengthening backlist of Cases Solved.

There was, for example, the time they tracked down a missing person, a certain Andrew Riding who had vanished from his home in Portslade, near Brighton, taking all the family savings and leaving behind two small children and a wife who was beside herself with worry. It turned out that Riding had for many years been harbouring a repressed transexualism. The woman in him had been trying to force her way out, until eventually he could keep her contained no longer. Having used the family savings to pay for a sex-change operation overseas, Riding had then settled down in a small town in Gloucestershire, which was where Milner and Moore unearthed him, or rather her. ANDREW RIDING of PORTSLADE was now INGRID WARDEN of ADLESTROP, and although Ingrid was unhappy at first to have been located, the Anagrammatic Detectives were able to coax her into rejoining her family on the South Coast. Regular letters from both Ingrid and his/her wife kept Milner and Moore updated on the progress of this somewhat unorthodox household. Neighbours had got used to them. The children quite enjoyed having two mothers.

Then there was the case of the taxi firm whose owner was alarmed and baffled by a sudden, substantial drop in his profits. Milner and Moore, inspired by the equivalence of TAXIMETER to EXTRA TIME, took several rides anonymously in the firm's cabs, then compared the drivers' journey records to their own receipts. It was straightforward enough. A number of the drivers were fiddling their records and diddling their boss. Sackings ensued, and the grateful owner rewarded the Anagrammatic Detectives with a bonus on top of the agreed fee: a year's free use of his cabs.

There was the complicated affair of the SHORTCAKE and the TRACK SHOE. There was the THRENETICAL CHAIN-LETTER. There was the case of the restaurateur who was POISONED, although not lethally, by a rival, the proprietor of a seafood eaterie called the POSEIDON. There was the unusual job involving a group of south-east Londoners who had taken it upon themselves to find mates for lonely-hearts in the vicinity, bringing them together by surreptitious means so that they did not know they were being matched up – it became known as the SIDCUP CUPIDS case.

But such exciting and intellectually demanding investigations were, alas, the exception rather than the rule, and sometimes in order to make ends meet the Anagrammatic Detectives were obliged to take on assignments which did not call on their powers of wordplay at all – run-of-the-mill stuff that any private investigator could do. More often than not this meant snooping on errant husbands and wives, and to console themselves that there was some sort of wordplay involved, however tangentially, Milner and Moore filed such cases under the heading of

BEDROOM BOREDOM. They argued, too, that adultery commonly took place within marriages where the APHRODITE had ATROPHIED or where an unmarried individual had got together with a MARRIED ADMIRER. Quite often the end-result of their evidence-gathering was a messy and combative divorce. That was when it became clear why the word MARITAL was just a letter-swap away from the word MARTIAL.

On this particular morning, the Monday after the Gleed Summer Ball, Milner and Moore had no work on, not even a BEDROOM BOREDOM case. There were no assignments pending, no invoices to be sent out. Their in-trays and out-trays were empty. Their bank accounts were starting to get that way too.

And so, as was their wont, they were sitting at their desks competing to see who could finish a cryptic crossword first. Each had a copy of the nation's highest-brow daily broadsheet and each was bent over its back page, forehead furrowed, pen poised, filling in the lights as fast as he could. Beating each other was part of the attraction, but devoting attention to the crossword meant, also, that for a few minutes they didn't have to think about their lack of work and the parlous state of their finances.

Milner was within a hair's breadth of solving the final clue when there was a rap at the door which not only shattered his concentration but came as such a shock that he half leapt out of his chair. Moore, lagging two clues behind, was no less startled. Each of the Anagrammatic Detectives looked over at the other, waiting for him to say something. Then each, in unison, stammered out an invitation to enter.

The tall, elderly man who walked into their office was a perturbing sight. Hulkingly large, bent like a lamp-post, and wearing a suit that would have set Milner or Moore back a year's salary, he strode in with a disdainful air, as though he begrudged every step of the journey that had taken him here to these tatty premises in this low-rent part of town. Having closed the door behind him, he rubbed fingers against thumb as if the doorknob left some kind of greasy residue. Then he cast an eye around the office, taking in the cracks in the ceiling plaster, the collection of dead flies inside the hemispherical light fixture, the shelves of old books bought by the yard to lend an air of respectability to the place, the arthritic electric fan flailing this way and that as it tried to lower the room temperature, the cheap metal-frame desks the Anagrammatic Detectives sat at, the clearance-sale typist's chairs they sat on, and finally the Anagrammatic Detectives themselves, with their shiny-kneed trousers, their nylon shirts, their fake leather slip-ons. Apparently none of what he saw met with his approval. Nevertheless he nodded in greeting to both men, and even attempted a smile, which caused the scar on his cheek to pucker and deepen in a very unwinning way.

'Gentlemen,' he said, 'the name is Carver.'

This was news to Milner, but Moore had already recognised the Gleeds' major-domo. Milner had little interest in Family affairs, whereas Moore, who affected indifference on the subject, was often to be found leafing furtively through the Family pages of the newspapers.

'And you'll be pleased to know that I'm here,' Carver continued, 'to offer you gainful employment.'

22

At around the same time that Carver stepped into the Anagrammatic Detectives' office, the dirigible carrying Prosper and Fortune was beginning its final approach to the Island. In the control car the captain barked out orders. 'Pitch Helmsman, rear elevator up two degrees! Trim Helmsman, keep her steady! Engineer, reduce thrust on starboard fore prop by a quarter! That's it, boys. Nice and easy. Gently does it.' The control car's atmosphere of apparent agitation belied a steely professional calm. There was noise and commotion but the captain had everything firmly in hand.

By contrast, in the dirigible's passenger lounge there was no discernible anxiety or urgency. Within both Prosper and Fortune, however, there was, to varying degrees, ferment. The day ahead promised to be eventful. Extraordinary Family Congresses seldom were not.

Fortune, breakfast Bloody Mary in hand, was leaning on the handrail of the for'ard-facing viewing gallery. Roughly five miles ahead, and getting closer by the minute, lay the Island. Set in a shimmer of Atlantic, it was an unprepossessing upthrust of volcanic rock, the kind that appeared virtually overnight, welling out of the waves during an eruption and hardening into a crack-contoured cone which was then colonised by only the hardiest and ugliest of vegetation – scrubby bushes with shallow roots and thorny stems, razor-edged grasses that could go for months without rain. Too small and too sheer-sloped to invite human occupation, for centuries the Island had sat at the far end of an archipelagic chain, unwanted, uninhabited, unnamed, an afterthought, an appendix, a full stop at the end of a sentence . . . until the Families came along and decided it was exactly what they were looking for.

In the wake of the First European War, it had seemed wise that there should be a place, neutral territory, where Family matters could be discussed, inter-Familial complaints worked out, and pan-Familial problems resolved. The Island fit the bill perfectly. Nobody else wanted it, it was centrally located, and it was going cheap. Every Family chipped in to have it built on and landscaped. In next to no time the Island had a Congress Chamber with several sets of living quarters attached, along with gardens, a beach, a harbour, and an aerodrome. The place served as a useful talking-shop, and everyone agreed that some potentially disastrous confrontations had been defused there. Everyone also agreed that the seeds of the *Second* European War had been sown there, but it seemed better not to mention this. The Island's successes far outnumbered its failures. That was good enough.

It was on the aerodrome that Fortune's attention was presently focused. Situated on a southern peninsula which had been dynamited flat to accommodate it, the aerodrome offered mooring spaces for up to fifty dirigibles as well as hangars and a runway for the security planes that were even now patrolling the skies around the Island, protecting the arriving Family members against attack. For any normal Congress this was sufficient. Many Family heads preferred to travel by sea rather than by air, and the Island's harbour afforded ample room for yachts and cruisers. A hundred boats could berth there comfortably. With an Extraordinary Congress, however, time was of the essence. Summoned at short notice, you went by the fastest mode of transport available. This meant flying boat, which could dock at the harbour, but more usually it meant dirigible.

'I count about five gaps still free,' Fortune commented. 'We made it before they start having to do turnaround.'

When spaces ran short at the aerodrome, the last few were utilised on a rota basis, each dirigible mooring for as long as was necessary for its passengers to debark, then taking off again. On the next island along in the chain, some ten miles away, there was a public aerodrome large enough to accommodate the overspill. Nobody was best pleased if their dirigible was one of those that couldn't get a permanent parking place. Therefore it was imperative to be punctual.

'Who's here already?' Prosper asked. He was reclining in an armchair with a steaming cup of coffee.

'Umm . . . I can see the von Wäldchenliebs' dirigible, I think. Theirs is the crest with the black eagle, right? And the Savages'. They've got the eagle that isn't black. What is it with some people and eagles? What's wrong with having something small and unpretentious as your Family symbol? A piece of fruit, for instance. Speaking of which, there's the Maketsis' pineapple. And that looks to me like the al-Harouns' crossed date-palms. The Borgia de'Medicis have made it, of course. Nobody beats *them* to the Island.'

'They get a head start. They're always the first to be told.'

'Being the ur-Family does have its privileges, doesn't it. Oh, and look. The Pongs. How the hell did *they* get here so quickly, I wonder.'

'Their dirigible has that new jet-propulsion system.'

'Even so. How far away is Thailand?'

'I expect they were visiting someone at the time. My guess would be the Savages.'

'Ah yes. What with all their marital and business links. The Savages and the Pongs. Imagine if they went the whole hog and merged. D'you think they'd call themselves the Savage-Pongs?' Fortune chuckled heartily.

'You're not the first to crack that joke, Fort,' said Prosper, 'and I seriously doubt you'll be the last.'

'It's still funny.' Fortune's expression abruptly turned sombre. 'Oh-ho, what have we here? Can it be the famous Black Dirigible?'

Prosper sprang to his feet and joined his brother at the viewing gallery.

Halfway along the line of tethered dirigibles, almost all of which were the standard silvery-grey in colour, was one whose canvas shell was the deepest, darkest, most night-like shade of black conceivable. The crest on its flank was picked out in blood red and was a simplified silhouette representation of a bat in flight.

'The Kuczynskis,' Prosper said, coldly, crisply.

'And to judge by the angle we're coming in at, I'd say we've been assigned the space next to them,' said Fortune. 'Luck of the draw? Or maybe someone down there in the control tower has a nasty sense of humour.'

The Kuczynski dirigible loomed like a thundercloud. Its rudder fins continued the bat motif – they were scallop-edged, like a bat's wing. Also unusual about the aircraft were its windows. All, with the exception of those in the control car, were blacked out. The Kuczynskis found it necessary, and preferable, to travel in constant darkness.

'They seem to have made it here in very good time,' Prosper observed. 'Perhaps they knew they'd be coming.'

'Steady on,' Fortune warned. 'Innocent until proven.'

The Gleed dirigible nudged in alongside the Kuczynskis' and, with a whine of reverse propulsion, came rocking and bumping to a standstill. Ropes unfurled from the mooring cones at the nose and tail, and were gathered up by ground crew and secured to motor-driven winches. The dirigible's engines cut, bringing a sudden sonorous silence, and the winches took over and slowly hauled the aircraft down to earth.

Once the dirigible was secured and stabilised, a gangplank was extruded from its belly. Crewmen descended first, lining up in two rows, fingers slapping to foreheads in salute. Prosper and Fortune emerged, passing between the crewmen. The heat was sudden and ferocious, and became more so as they stepped out from the dirigible's shadow into the full flare of the subtropical sun. At a brisk march, the two Family members set off along the peninsula, heading for the Congress Chamber and the ancillary buildings clustered around it.

23

Somewhat to his own surprise, Provender had slept. He had woken up several times during the night and been obliged to ease out a kink in his spine or a cramp in his calf. He had never managed to get anywhere near comfortable, there on the bare bathroom floor, blindfolded, bound hand and foot. All the same, he had slept.

He knew it was morning because the building around him, having been silent for several hours, was now making noises again. They were dim sounds, and all bathroom-related: water gurgling, a badly-fixed pipe rattling. The bathroom he was in shared its plumbing system with countless others. He pictured people going about their ablutions, their ordinary Monday-morning routine. Shaving. Bathing. Brushing their teeth. Using the lavatory. Thinking about work, or school, or the duties of the day, or perhaps trying their best *not* to think about any of these things. And all the while not having a clue, any of them, about the man being held captive in their midst, the man who could hear the results of what they were up to in their bathrooms, the man who would have given anything just to be able to stand up and wash his face as they were doing, perhaps check his chin for spots in the basin mirror, and then straddle the lavatory and partake of a long and blissfully unaided piss. How many flats were there in this building? How many bathrooms? From impressions he had collected, Provender guessed he was in a populous urban high-rise. There could be anything up to two thousand souls sharing this block with him, and each of them had a bathroom which was linked to this one by pipes and ducts. A connective maze of copper and ceramic tubing. The building's venous system. Clean water one way, waste water the other. It was, in some hard-to-describe way, reassuring. He was isolated but not wholly alone.

And then, very definitely, he was not alone. The door opened, the light switch clicked, the extractor fan started its bronchitic rattling again, and someone entered the room.

Straight away Provender knew it was Is's accomplice. The man had a heavy presence. He seemed to displace more air than most people.

Provender kept still, pretending he was asleep.

The man shuffled up to him barefoot and stood over him. His breathing was slow and steady. He jabbed a toe into Provender's midriff.

Provender flinched and braced himself, thinking the jab must be the prelude to a kick.

No kick came.

' 'Morning, Provvie,' the man said. 'Wakey-wakey, rise and shine. Sleep well? I expect not.'

Provender had decided on a policy of not talking to the man. The man seemed the sort you could antagonise without meaning to.

'Not at all what you're used to, eh?' the man said. 'Nothing fancy about the accommodation here. I bet even boarding school wasn't as bad. Still, it's good for you. This way you get to experience how the rest of us live, the ordinary people your Family craps on all the time. Speaking of which . . .'

Provender heard the lavatory seat being flipped up and the sound of the man seating himself. What came next he wished he didn't have to listen to: the squeak and grunt of someone defecating just inches away from him. Even worse was the smell, so ripe he almost gagged.

'How's that then?' the man asked, to the accompaniment of unravelling toilet paper. 'My partner's using a bucket out there in the main room. Says she couldn't "go" with you right next to her. Me? I'm not so squeamish. You could say I don't give a shit.'

Provender couldn't restrain himself. He was too revolted. The retort sprang out of him. 'That's because Is is a decent person and you're not.'

There was a moment of deadly quiet, then the man said, 'She told you her name. Stupid cow. I suppose it doesn't make a lot of difference, but even so . . . I told her not to. Oh, that's annoying.'

Provender braced himself again, fearing that he would be taking the punishment for Is's slip-up.

As before, though, the man did not lay into him. Instead he said, 'Well, I was going to do the decent thing and flush, but now I think I'll just leave it to marinade for a while. Nice chatting with you, Provvie.'

The door closed, and soon afterwards Provender heard raised voices coming from the other side of it. Is and the man arguing. He didn't catch everything that was said but the odd phrase came through, giving him the overall gist. Is was accused of treating their captive too leniently, not keeping a distance from him like she should. She defended herself by saying that the point of kidnapping him wasn't to torture him. She gave as good as she got but in the end the man's aggression won through. Provender heard Is's voice take on a conciliatory tone, and the volume of the conversation dwindled to inaudibility. Meanwhile the extractor fan churned away, toiling to cleanse the air in the bathroom, with little success. Eventually it timed out and lapsed into silence, as if exhausted from its efforts. The smell of the man's bowel movement lingered noxiously on.

Provender, taking care to breathe through his mouth, deliberated over what had just happened. At a stroke, two suspicions had been confirmed.

One was that the man was a confirmed anti-Family type, close to pathological in his hatred of all things Familial. The other was that the relationship between the man and Is was strained and that Is was helping him, if not under duress exactly, then against her better judgement.

It came as something of a surprise to Provender that he was heartened by these two pieces of information. He realised he could, if he chose to, use them to his advantage. Through them he could maybe even engineer his escape.

Then again, if he didn't play his hand just right, he risked making an already bad situation worse.

What it hinged on, really, was whether or not he had the guts to try.

That, and his captors' reading habits.

24

'Why us?'

It was a question that had to be asked, and Milner asked it with as much nonchalance as he could muster. He didn't want to sound as if he and Moore were unwilling to take on the case of Provender's disappearance, but at the same time it was a case of such magnitude, such awesome importance, that he felt obliged to voice a note of reservation.

'Why you indeed,' Carver said. 'First of all, you aren't the police.'

'That's for sure,' Moore said. 'COP LIE.'

Carver shot him a quizzical look.

'We haven't had much luck in our dealings with the police,' Milner explained. 'They've taken the credit for a couple of cases *we* cracked, and on the whole they've not been very cooperative. So we've anagrammatised POLICE to COP LIE. It's what we do.'

'It's what *they* do,' Moore grumbled.

'I see,' Carver said. 'Then that's a further point in your favour. Not only are you not the police, but you'll have no qualms about keeping the police out of the equation.'

'None whatever,' said Milner.

'The other reason I chose to come to you,' Carver went on, 'is that you have scored a number of notable successes while still managing to maintain a low profile.'

'You mean no one's heard of us.'

'If you like. I'd rather see it as you have everything to prove and nothing to lose, which in this instance is a highly desirable combination. It means I can be assured of your utter loyalty and your wholehearted attention.'

'So how did *you* hear of us?' Milner said.

'You may recall you applied to the Gleeds for patronage last year.'

'Did we? I don't think so.'

'Um,' said Moore, 'as a matter of fact we did. Or at least, I did.'

'What?'

'I didn't mention it at the time. We were going through one of our lean patches, and I thought, I'll put in an application for patronage, see if we can get the Gleeds to support us, no harm done if we can't, all it'll cost is the price of a stamp.'

'And you didn't tell me?'

'I was going to, Merlin, if anything came of it. But nothing did. I got a pro forma reply acknowledging the application had been received, and that was that. Nothing else.'

'Oh.' Milner looked askance at his fellow Anagrammatic Detective, unable to decide if what he had done constituted a betrayal or not. He felt, on balance, that it didn't.

'I apologise that you didn't get any more than that,' Carver said, 'but as you can imagine, the Gleeds receive hundreds of requests for patronage every week. Sorting through them is a Herculean task and sometimes some of them, I regret to say, slip through the net. Yours, however, was given due consideration, believe me. I was on hand when the Family discussed it, and while Prosper Gleed was minded not to accept it, I myself made a mental note to remember you. Something told me I might have need of your services sometime.' Again, he flashed that unenchanting smile of his. 'And here I am. I cannot, of course, offer you patronage. That is solely within the Family's power to decide. But I can guarantee you this. If you help us, if you do manage to find young Master Provender, you will never have to worry about finding work again. No question about it. There won't be anyone in the world who won't have heard of Milner and Moore, the Anagrammatic Detectives. Your reputation will have been made. Your future prosperity will have been secured.'

Milner and Moore avoided each other's glances. Neither wanted to see the look of wild avarice he knew was in his own eyes.

'Now,' said Carver, 'I take it you are going to accept the case.'

What could either of the Anagrammatic Detectives do except say yes?

'I'm most pleased. A couple more points, then, before I leave you to get on with it. You will liaise with the Gleeds solely through me. I am going to give you a private phone number to contact me on. Any information you uncover, you report to me. Is that understood? The Gleeds have entrusted me with their full authority in this matter. You are to treat me as if I am the Family.'

'Fine,' said Milner.

'Also, you will doubtless be needing funds to cover your start-up costs, incidental expenses and the like.' Carver reached into his inside jacket pocket and produced a thick wad of banknotes which he placed on the desk in front of Milner, just out of the Anagrammatic Detective's reach. 'More, much more, is available should you require.'

Milner and Moore stared at the money, agog. They estimated they were looking at the equivalent of an average year's income for the agency. Milner immediately thought about moving to more upmarket premises, while Moore entertained the idea of hiring a receptionist-cum-secretary. He had always fancied having a receptionist-cum-secretary in the office, someone young and attractive, with a trim figure and nice legs. She didn't even have to be particularly good at the job. Just sit there within his view, call him Mr Moore, make him coffee, dress smartly and sexily – that was all.

Carver butted in on his little reverie. 'And naturally, should you succeed in bringing about a satisfactory resolution to the situation, the financial rewards will be great indeed.'

A fiftieth-floor office, Milner thought, *with commanding views of the city.*

Not just one but two receptionist-cum-secretaries, thought Moore, *so there's one for each of us and no squabbling over which of us she likes better.*

'But.' Carver clamped a hand over the money, as if about to scoop it away. 'Just to make matters absolutely clear, gentlemen.' He looked at Milner, then at Moore. 'No one else is to know about this. You are to do what you do in absolute isolation. Your lips are to stay hermetically sealed. For the duration of your investigation, you are to avoid mentioning to anyone what you are up to and why. The consequences of failing to comply with this stipulation . . . Well, I don't need to paint you a picture, do I?'

Milner and Moore both shook their heads.

'Though if I did,' Carver continued, 'it would be a picture not unlike the wilder imaginings of Bosch or Breughel. A canvas filled from corner to corner with suffering and hellfire and brimstone. Do I make myself clear?'

Milner and Moore both nodded.

'Crystal,' said Milner, in a faint voice.

'Very well then.' Carver let go of the money. 'I look forward to hearing from you as and when you have made any progress. The very best of luck to you, gentlemen. Let us hope your endeavours bear fruit, and quickly.'

25

For several minutes after Carver left, a thunderstruck silence hung over the Anagrammatic Detectives' office. The money sat on Milner's desk, note stacked on note to an impressive, almost inconceivable height. Neither man dared touch it in case, like a conjuror's illusion, it vanished. Both just stared.

Finally Milner said, 'I don't know which I'm more intimidated by – what he's asked us to do, or him himself.'

'He didn't scare you, did he?' said Moore.

'Me? Oh no. You?'

'Not a bit.'

Each looked the other in the eye and gave a shuddery laugh.

'Just out of curiosity,' said Milner, 'what's his first name?'

'Carver's? How should I know?'

'Oh come on. You're into the Families. You know.'

'I am *not* into the Families. I just . . . I like to keep up with current affairs, that's all. It's important in our line of work to have a healthy interest in everything that goes on in the world. And the Families definitely count as current affairs.'

'So?'

'Neal. I'm pretty sure his first name is Neal.'

'En, ee, eye, el?'

'En, ee, *a*, el.'

'NEAL CARVER.' Milner tapped his lip contemplatively.

'LEAN CRAVER,' Moore offered.

'I think we can do better than a simple metallage,' his partner said.

'LANCE RAVER.'

'Doesn't feel right. No, I've got it.' Milner clapped his hands together. 'CLAN REAVER. Quod erat demonstrandum.'

Moore half-smiled. 'CLAN REAVER. Yes, he's certainly the Gleeds' enforcer, isn't he. Their tame thug. Even at eighty-something years old.'

'He's that old?'

'And a veteran of the last war.'

'Really? God, no wonder we won.'

'That's where this came from.' Moore mimed a scar on his cheek. 'He got it during the Siege of Prague. Bayonet in the face. Carried on fighting anyway.'

'And you say you're not into the Families.'

Moore blushed. 'I have a retentive memory. Anyway, don't mock. We wouldn't have this case at all if it wasn't for me and my . . . interest.'

'Actually, true,' said Milner, nodding. 'Full credit to you, Romeo.'

Moore accepted the compliment magnanimously.

'And with that in mind,' Milner said, 'perhaps we should get cracking. Time, after all, as Mr Carver indicated, is of the essence.'

Both men opened drawers in their desks. Milner took out a ringbound pad of unruled paper and a pen, while Moore produced a green felt bag tied with a drawstring. The bag contained dozens of square plastic tiles, each with a capital letter on it, taken from a well-known boardgame. He poured them onto the desktop, spread them out and began flipping the ones that were face-down face-up.

This was perhaps the most significant dissimilarity between the two men: the technique by which each generated anagrams. Milner preferred what he called 'the old-fashioned method', the crossword solver's tried-and-trusted trick of writing the letters out in a jumble. Moore, on the other hand, found it easier and more convenient to use Scrabble tiles. All you had to do was keep swapping them around and swapping them around in various combinations. No wasting paper. No having to jot the letters down all over again if one jumble failed to yield a result. Milner thought Moore's technique noisy and untraditional. Moore thought Milner's crude and labour-intensive. Each had long since given up trying to persuade the other of the rightness of *his* system.

And here was where the art began. Here was where Milner and Moore showed that there was more to being an Anagrammatic Detective than simply the ability to muck around with letters.

Because it wasn't just about making new words from old. Instinct was involved. A certain name or phrase could be rearranged into dozens of possible permutations. Knowing which was the correct permutation, which of all of them was the one you were looking for – that took a special talent. It was almost preternatural. Neither Milner nor Moore could easily explain it. Certain results just felt right. You saw them and you knew. Couldn't be put any more precisely than that. A tingle in the belly. A prickling at the back of the neck. The answer leapt out at you. You knew.

The sheer enormity of the case – a Family member, kidnapped – seemed to fall away as they set to work. It quickly became a matter of words. The words were what counted. The words would reveal the truth. Milner scribbled, pondered, tore off a sheet, scribbled again. Moore lined up tiles, frowned, slid them around with his fingertips, lined them up afresh. An hour passed. Each man looked at names. People's names, the names of places. Every relevant reference he could think of. At one point Moore went scurrying off to retrieve Friday's newspaper from the waste-paper basket. He leafed through it, located the article he was looking for, and returned to the Scrabble tiles with renewed vigour. Milner, meanwhile, consulted a local London telephone directory and noted down with keenness what he found there.

They broke for coffee at eleven o'clock and briefly compared notes. To their surprise, they discovered they were at odds with their conclusions. Moore was becoming convinced that the kidnapping was an inside job, while Milner was of the view that some outside agency must be responsible. They seldom, if ever, disagreed over a case, and so they were perturbed. Each decided to follow up the other's line of approach to see if it had merit. Pen scratched. Tiles click-clacked. Another hour passed, and still neither man could descry how the other could possibly be correct.

'Look,' said Moore, 'it's obvious. Provender and his cousin Arthur – they don't get on. I've read about it. Arthur's this upstart from the wrong side of the bed. He's never made any secret of the fact that he thinks he'd be a better heir than Provender. Big chip on his shoulder about that.'

'Big enough for him to kidnap his own cousin?'

'Why ever not? And for God's sake, his name screams it out. REGALED HURT. REAL RED THUG. RED LAUGHTER. HATRED GRUEL. 'E GLARED RUTH.'

'Bit of a reach, that last one.'

'I know, but still. For me, Arthur Gleed's your man. His name is a guilty party's name ten times over.'

'Wasn't he at the ball when Provender was taken?'

'Yes, he was. I checked the invitee-acceptance list in the paper. But that doesn't mean he couldn't have masterminded the whole thing. Perfect alibi. He was there all along, in plain sight, partying away, while henchmen carried out the dirty deed. And look. Here's the clincher. He's an actor, right, and he's appearing in a play. There's a preview tonight and the premiere's tomorrow night. Guess where it's on at?'

Milner shrugged.

'The Shortborn Theatre.'

'OK. SHORTBORN THEATRE. Let me think.'

'I'll save you the trouble. BROTHER SON THREAT. Arthur is the son of Prosper Gleed's black-sheep brother Acquire. It all hangs together.'

'Tenuously,' said Milner. 'I don't buy it. I don't buy the whole "inside" angle at all. I've gone through the Gleeds, all of Provender's immediate kin, and they've all come up innocent. I've not got a "hit" off any of them. Like his dad. PROSPER GLEED. GREED PROPELS. Now, no question, greed and Family go together. You can't have one without the other.'

'And you're always likely to get GREED if there's GLEED involved.'

'Quite. Practically an open goal. But greed, if you're Family, is hardly a motive to commit crime. It's more a way of life with them. Then there's Provender's mother. CYNTHIA GLEED. THE NICE G LADY. I even threw her maiden name into the mix. CYNTHIA LAMAS GLEED. Know what I got? CHEATING MALE'S LADY. Straightforward enough. Nothing sinister there. Her husband's famed for his extramarital affairs. Even I know about that. And THE LADY'S ANGELIC MA, that was my other one. Again, that would seem to sum her up, wouldn't it? And exonerate her.'

Moore conceded the point, reluctantly.

'As for the oldest member of the Family,' Milner went on, 'GREAT GLEED got me AGED GELTER. He's certainly aged, I think you'd agree. And "gelter"? Gelt is what a Family's all about. But as before, hardly a motive. I mean, if Provender's been kidnapped in order to be held to ransom, it *can't* be an inside job. The Gleeds are filthy rich. They don't need to make money, and more to the point why would they try and hold *themselves* to ransom?'

'Carver said there hadn't been a ransom note yet.'

'Yet.'

'But if Arthur's the culprit, maybe ransom isn't what he's after. Maybe it's recognition, or to get rid of his rival.'

'You think this might be murder?'

'If it isn't already, it could become. Provender could just, you know, *disappear*. Forever.'

Milner looked doubtful. 'Somewhat extreme.'

'We're talking about Families. Nothing's too extreme where they're concerned. With Provender out of the picture, Arthur stands to become the next head of the Family. Admittedly he'll have a hard task ahead of him. The chain of descendancy will have been broken. The Gleeds'll plummet in the Family ratings. But he'll be head all the same. And if the only thing that stands between him and that is Provender . . . Well, in his shoes, wouldn't you be tempted?'

'To kill my own cousin?'

'Arrange to have him killed. Keeping your own hands as clean as possible.'

'I don't know. I'd like to think not.' Milner tapped his ring-bound pad. 'I still think you're barking up the wrong tree, though. I'm getting a definite reading from Provender himself. His name—'

'His name,' Moore interjected, 'doesn't ring any of *my* bells. Look at it. PROVEN GREED-LED. You yourself said it. Greed and Family – virtually synonymous. And even with his middle name, Oregano, thrown into the mix . . .'

'Hold on, his middle name is Oregano?'

'It's something of a tradition with the Gleeds. They had their origins in the spice trade.'

'I know that, but *Oregano*?'

Moore shrugged. 'Provender itself isn't exactly normal, is it? Anyway, as I was saying, you throw Oregano into the mix . . .'

'For added flavour.'

'Thank you. And you get GREEN ROAD DEVELOPER, with the letters G, O and N left over. Which sprang out at me, but I have to say, what the hell does it mean? I can't think of a context in which it would apply.'

'And those left-over letters.'

'Yes. Messy.'

'Well, Romeo, to get back to what *I* was saying – his name by itself isn't terribly productive, as you have just shown, but splice it together with his predicament . . .'

'As in?'

'As in PROVENDER GLEED STOLEN.'

'And?'

Milner sucked on the cap of his pen. 'And you get confirmation that this was an outside job. You even get where he's being held and a clue to the identity of the person holding him.'

'Elucidate, please.'

'You don't believe me.'

'I'm a little sceptical.'

'Then let me propose this, Romeo. As we each appear to have our own theory about the case, why don't we pursue our leads separately?'

'What?'

'I know. A radical departure for us but, as things stand, a sensible one. Clearly we're not going to see eye-to-eye over this, so let's make it a competition. Not unlike our morning crossword.'

'Winner takes the dosh? Is that what you're saying?'

'Christ no. I'd never be that mercenary.'

'Glad to hear it.'

'No, just a gentlemanly challenge between friends. Your investigative skills against mine. We'll split this' – he pointed to the money – 'so neither of us will be out of pocket. By the way – cash. We're not telling the accountant. Agreed?'

'Agreed.'

'Good. So we split it, we go our separate ways, we work independently. It is a major case, after all.'

'It's not just major, Merlin. It's the biggest case we've ever had. It's the one that'll make us.'

'All the more reason, then, that we divide our forces. We can cover twice as much ground that way and double our chances of finding Provender. What d'you say?'

Moore couldn't fault his partner's logic. 'And whichever of us cracks the case, we both share the fee? Equally?'

'Of course. Like I said, this isn't about the money. It's about intellectual satisfaction.'

'And bragging rights.'

'They might come into it.'

Moore sat back in his chair. Milner, on the other side of the room, mirrored the action.

'All right,' Moore said. 'You're on.'

Milner grinned. He would not have thrown down the gauntlet if he hadn't been so confident that he was on the right track and his colleague on completely the wrong one. By the same token, Moore would not have picked the gauntlet up if he hadn't thought his take on the case was correct and Milner's hopelessly misguided.

The main thing was, personal rivalry aside, they were going to crack the case. Both of them were confident that, one way or another, the Anagrammatic Detective Agency was going to win the day.

They were forgetting that in such SELF-ASSURANCE lay the potential for A CARELESS SNAFU.

26

Massimiliano Borgia de'Medici, dapper little gent, comfortable with the weight of history and precedent that resided in his slender frame, a Family man to the marrow, called the Congress to order.

'*Signori, signore.*' His voice, though slight, was clear and carried far thanks to the Congress Chamber's impressive acoustics – the domed ceiling and the suspended disc-shaped baffles that bounced sound around. 'Gentlemen, ladies. I bid you all good afternoon and pray your attention.'

Gradually conversation dwindled around the concentric hoop-shaped tables, silence spreading from innermost to outermost, from premier Family to lowest-ranked. The hundred-or-so Family representatives at the edge of the room, in the proverbial cheap seats, were the last to go quiet. They seldom did as they were told straight away. They liked to remind everyone else they were there.

'Thank you,' said Borgia de'Medici. 'You will see that we have a number of absentees. The missing Family heads have all tendered formal regrets. They have prior commitments. However, we exceed the three-quarters quorum, so business may be conducted.'

He took care to keep his sentences short and leave gaps between them, for the benefit of the translators who accompanied several of the Family heads. A kind of massed whisper attended his statements, a Babel echo, as the translators did their job, leaning forward and murmuring in their employers' ears. Those Family heads who were conversant in English, the great majority, were allowed to bring along a companion in place of a translator, as moral support. By the rules of Congress, the companions were forbidden from speaking while the Congress was in session.

Fortune, who habitually fulfilled this function for his brother, found the no-speaking constraint almost unendurable. To compensate, he had devised a simple system of coughs and throat-clearings by which he could let Prosper know if he agreed or disagreed with the line Prosper was taking, and how vehemently. In extreme instances, when the system failed, he had been known to kick his brother in the leg, which usually achieved the desired effect.

He hoped that, today, no such drastic measures would be called for. He feared they would, though.

'An Extraordinary Congress is not lightly invoked,' said Borgia de'Medici. 'To ask the heads of Families to drop everything and come running is no mean thing. I say so not to undermine the reason for this meeting but to under*line* it. We are here to give audience to an accusation of the utmost gravity. We must devote our fullest attention to it and discuss it as honestly and frankly as we can. I have no need to remind you that anything said in the Chamber goes no further than the Chamber. You may speak your minds freely.'

Borgia de'Medici turned toward Prosper, who was three seats away from him on the central table.

'Signor Gleed,' he said. 'It is you who have summoned us here. Permit me to ask you to air your grievance.'

'Of course.' Prosper took a sip of water from the glass in front of him and stood up. Fortune, in the chair just behind him, reached forward to the table and grabbed his own glass, which contained a clear liquid which was not water. He took a sip and softly smacked his lips. Who said you had to be Russian to enjoy neat vodka?

Prosper ran his gaze around the central table till it came to rest on Stanisław Kuczynski. For the space of several seconds he simply looked at his rival Family head, and Kuczynski simply looked back, red eyes fixed unwaveringly on Prosper's. Kuczynski was dressed in nothing but black, which set off the pallor of his skin and hair to extraordinary effect. Were it not for his eyes, and his rose-blush lips, he would have been devoid of all colour. He could have stepped straight out of a monochrome movie.

His companion, his twin sister Stanisława, was similarly two-tone. Her outfit consisted of a black worsted two-piece with a sable tippet around her shoulders and, on her head, a black velvet Robin Hood cap topped with a raven's feather. Stanisława shared with her brother the same sharp cheekbones, the same pointed chin, the same soft economy of gesture which in her was feline, in him effete. She also, if the rumours were to be believed, shared his bed. With the Kuczynskis, it wasn't just albinism that ran in the Family. There was a tradition of incest which earlier generations of Kuczynskis had definitely indulged in – there was documentary proof – and which Stanisław and Stanisława at least *appeared* to be perpetuating, if the gloved hand with which Stanisława was stroking her brother's neck right now was anything to go by.

Of course, it could merely have been for show. This was a Family, after all, which wished the world to believe they were vampires. They drank human blood (two glass goblets of the stuff sat before them now). They shunned sunlight. If they were prepared to go to those lengths to maintain a reputation, then incest, or even the feigning of incest, was nothing.

It was Prosper who broke the eye contact between him and Stanisław Kuczynski. He would have gladly carried on staring, but his distaste for Kuczynski, for the man's very appearance, was too great. It threatened to overwhelm him and make him incoherent with loathing. When he looked at Kuczynski he thought of all the times the Kuczynski Family had outsmarted the Gleeds – snatched away some juicy business proposition from under their noses, bankrupted a corporation they knew the Gleeds were eyeing up, triggered a stock-market plunge that always somehow left the Gleeds out of pocket, generally indulged in sharp practices with no other goal than to inconvenience their age-old enemies. Prosper invariably struck back, but he rarely seemed to give as good as he got. Stanisław Kuczynski had a far better business brain than he did. That, although Prosper hated to admit it, was another reason he despised him.

'My fellow Family heads,' Prosper said, and now it was his turn to be dogged by the susurrant translator echo. 'I stand before you today, not as a Family head myself, nor as a Gleed, but simply as a father. A worried father. A frightened father.'

So far so good, thought Fortune. Appealing to a common bond. There were more than a few fathers in the room.

'My son Provender has been . . .'

Prosper faltered. Theatrically, in Fortune's view – but whatever got the point across.

'My son has been kidnapped.'

Shock rippled out across the Chamber. The consternation was loudest around the outermost table, from where cries of outrage and sympathy resounded up to the sonic baffles.

'Please, please, everyone,' said Massimiliano Borgia de'Medici. 'Please, *silenzio*! Let Signor Gleed continue.'

Prosper waited for the ruckus to die down, meanwhile gauging Stanisław Kuczynski's reaction to his announcement. The white face did not perceptibly alter. The eyes perhaps widened a little, but that was all.

Which implied nothing. In the event that Kuczynski was innocent, he wouldn't know that he was about to be accused of the kidnapping. If he was guilty, he would register no surprise at what Prosper had just said. Either way, he was going to maintain that impassive expression. Why, before a quorum of assembled Family heads, was he going to show that he cared what had happened to his enemy's son?

'He was taken the night before last,' Prosper continued, 'during our annual ball. Provender, as you all well know, is the next Family head in line, and my only male offspring.'

There were nods around the tables, and murmurs of concern.

'And,' Prosper said, 'I am convinced that the individual responsible for his abduction is in this very room.'

That had the Family heads in ferment again. The Congress Chamber churned with shouts, demands, accusations, denials. Arms waved. Fists thumped tables. Prosper savoured the medley of uproar, and also the scowls that had manifested on the faces of both Kuczynski and his sister. They seemed well aware, the pair of them, what was coming next.

'*Prego! Prego! Silenzio!* Silence!' Borgia de'Medici had to yell at the top of his voice to be heard. 'Signor Gleed, you had better explain yourself. Such comments are highly inflammatory in this company.'

'Oh, I'm going to explain myself all right, Massimiliano,' said Prosper.

Fortune coughed gently, in a way which very clearly meant *Watch your step now, brother.*

'But,' Prosper said, 'I suspect most of you here have already guessed who I'm referring to.'

Heads began to turn.

'In fact, I wouldn't be surprised if the guilty party were to stand up right now and say—'

Stanisław Kuczynski was rising to his feet even as Prosper spoke. Halfway, he hesitated, realising he had been caught out. But it was too late. He straightened, drawing himself to his full height. His eyes flashed a baleful red glare at Prosper.

'Gleed,' he said.

Uttering the name meant his lips pulled back, and his lips pulling back meant his teeth were revealed in all their jagged, filed-to-points hideousness.

'How dare you. How *dare* you.' Kuczynski turned to Massimiliano Borgia de'Medici. 'This man is a liar. His accusation is groundless. Where is the proof? Let him show us his proof!'

'The proof,' said Prosper, also addressing Borgia de'Medici, 'is right in front of us. Kuczynski knew I was talking about him. By standing up, he was all but confessing his guilt.'

'Nonsense! Gleed was making insinuations. Obvious insinuations. I knew I had to refute them.'

'Do you deny you have my son?'

'I do. Emphatically. What would I have to gain by kidnapping him?'

'Oh, everything. Blackmail. Leverage over me. The humbling of my Family. An escalation in the long-standing feud between the Gleeds and the Kuczynskis. You name it.'

'But there are certain codes of behaviour. You know what I am talking about. Among the Families. Certain lines one does not cross.'

'Oh really?' said Prosper. 'How interesting that you, of all people, should mention codes of behaviour, Kuczynski. Standing there with a glass of blood in front of you and your sister next to you. "Sister", of course, being the least part of the intimate role she plays in your life.'

'*Kurwy syn!*' Stanisława snarled, while, behind Prosper, Fortune let loose another of those cautionary coughs.

'Mr Borgia de'Medici!' Kuczynski said, with a beseeching gesture. 'Are you going to let him get away with this? First he falsely accuses me of a heinous deed, now he insults my Family and draws attention to our condition.'

Prosper leapt in before Borgia de'Medici could say anything. 'Your "condition"? Well, I suppose you could call it that, in that it's a psychological delusion you all share. Vampires! You really get off on it, don't you? Makes you feel dangerous and different. Why not just admit it? You're not "creatures of the night". You don't drink blood to survive, it's simply an affectation. And sunlight will give you a nasty burn, what with that lack of skin pigmentation of yours, but it won't make you explode into flames. Oh, but if you didn't play at being vampires, you'd have nothing going for you, would you? You'd just be an ordinary Family with an unfortunate hereditary complaint. Call yourselves vampires and we won't all look at you and think, "Now there's a perfect example of what inbreeding can – inbreeding can do to people."'

The break and repetition in that last sentence was the result of Prosper being kicked in the calf by his brother, once, sharply. As soon as Fortune heard the word *inbreeding* he knew Prosper had overstepped the mark. It was the one real taboo among Families, the one subject you did not raise under any circumstances. It was too close to home, too near the knuckle. In every Family represented in the Chamber there was at least one branch that had petered out into insanity, impotence, physical deformity, or any combination of the three. It was the risk you inevitably ran with a carefully cultivated bloodline. No one wished to be reminded of that fact.

Stanisław and Stanisława Kuczynski least of all.

Stanisława bristled. Her hands became claws. As for her brother, he shot Prosper a look that would have curdled milk.

'Prosper Gleed.' His voice was a feral hiss. 'Is there nothing you will not stoop to?'

'I'm not the one who goes around abducting other people's sons.'

'For the last time, I do not have your son. I do not know where your son is. Why say these things?'

'I don't believe you. I look at you and see a man acting very much like someone with something to hide. If you were truly innocent, you wouldn't be protesting your innocence so strongly.'

'What chance does that give me, then? I might as well be guilty, if you're telling me I cannot even claim I am innocent.'

'Don't claim you're innocent. Prove it. Prove it by returning Provender to me.'

'How can I? I don't *have* him.'

This exchange was conducted to the backdrop of a rumble of voices, which grew louder with each back-and-forth of the argument, becoming a thunder. It was the sort of noise you might hear from the audience at a boxing match as the two fighters slugged their way toward the knockout blow. The Family heads on the outermost table were almost baying in their excitement. A climax was looming. One or other of the combatants, Prosper Gleed or Stanisław Kuczynski, was about to deliver some sort of devastating killer punch. The Family heads partly didn't want to see it land; partly they did. This dispute had been a long time brewing. The Gleed–Kuczynski antagonism, a constant of Family life, was particularly heartfelt between the representatives of the current generation, and yet before now had never exploded in quite such a manner. For everyone, not just the two men directly involved, there was a sense of release. That which had been pent-up was now in the open. The years of continual sniping and needling across the centre of the Congress Chamber were at last giving way to something more forthright and fierce. A long-swollen pustule was being lanced.

Massimiliano Borgia de'Medici was duty-bound to intervene. Even as he did, however, he understood it was futile. Gleed and Kuczynski were on the warpath. Whatever he said, neither man was likely to back down.

'*Signori*, I beg you, let us sit down and think this through coolly. Prosper, you say he has kidnapped your son. Stanisław, you say you have not. Either it is that one of you is lying, or one of you is mistaken. Now, as you are both men of honour—'

'Honour?' Prosper snapped. 'That *thing* over there wouldn't recognise honour if it came up and bit him on the neck.'

'Thing! He calls me a thing! On top of all the other abuse he has heaped on me this day.'

'Oh pipe down, Count Dracula. You can't have it both ways. Either you're a human being or you're one of the undead, and if it's undead than by definition you're a thing. Live with it. Or unlive with it, or whatever it is you do.'

Stanisława Kuczynski was on her feet now. 'I cannot keep quiet any longer. I cannot sit here and say nothing while my brother's reputation and mine are – are *besmirched* by this person.'

'Signorina Kuczynski, I must ask you to resume your seat,' said Borgia de'Medici. There were growls of agreement from other quarters. 'The rules quite clearly state that—'

'To hell with the rules! The effrontery of Prosper Gleed knows no bounds. He has been breaking all sorts of rules. Moral rules. And not just today at this Congress. My brother and I are simply to accept all these insults from him without retaliating? No! How can we, when they come from a man who is a lifelong gambler, and a very bad one by all accounts. A notorious womaniser, too. A man who mocks the devotion of his loyal and trusting wife, to go around fucking any woman that moves. A man who cannot keep his *chuj* in his pants!'

'With respect to Miss Kuczynski,' said Prosper, 'I can think of one woman who I would definitely keep my *chuj* in my pants for. Assuming in the first place she was interested in any man other than the one she spent nine months in the womb with.'

'*Psia krew! Kurwa mać! Spierdalej!*'

You didn't have to be fluent in Polish to know that the words pouring from Stanisława Kuczynski's mouth were not exactly a hallowing paean of praise. But in case the tone in which she said them and the look of sheer venom on her face were not enough, she followed them up with an action that put the matter entirely beyond doubt. Snatching up her half-drunk goblet of blood, she drew back her arm to throw it.

'Stasia! No!' cried her brother.

But too late. The goblet hurtled across the room. It missed Prosper, shattering against the edge of the table instead, but the result was almost as good as if it had been dead on-target. Blood sprayed everywhere. Some droplets hit Fortune in the face, and the Family heads to either side of the Gleeds, Desmond Maketsi and John-Paul Savage III, didn't escape a spattering. It was Prosper, though, who caught the lion's share. His shirtfront was covered in crimson. His face was a ghastly red-stippled mask. But even as the blood began to dribble down his forehead and cheeks in runnels, he was smiling. Taking a silk handkerchief from the breast pocket of his jacket, he began dabbing himself dry. Meanwhile, there was aghast silence in the Chamber. Around each of the concentric tables, jaws hung open.

'Well now,' said Prosper, when he had cleaned the worst off. 'First blood to you, Kuczynskis. It seems you've shown your true colours. Expect a response. Expect it swiftly. Expect it to be total and utter and overwhelming. You started this. Now you're going to pay for it. Dearly.'

27

'Does he hit you?'

Is was taken aback. Provender hadn't said a word since she entered the bathroom and started giving him his lunch. He seemed to have sunk into a mood of sullen resentment. Then, between mouthfuls of tinned tomato soup, this.

'Him out there,' Provender said. 'Your accomplice.'

'I know who you meant. No. God, no. He doesn't hit me.'

'He seems the type.'

'Da—' She checked herself. She had nearly said Damien's name. 'He has a temper. He's a very passionate person. What he feels, he feels strongly. But he's not violent. He never has been to me. For one thing, he wouldn't dare. If he'd so much as laid a finger on me, he'd have been walking funny for a week.'

'He'd.'

'Eh?'

'You said, "If he'd so much as laid a finger on me". Past tense.'

'So?'

'So that implies not present tense. You and he aren't . . . you know. Any more.'

Is busied herself with tipping another spoonful of soup between Provender's lips. 'We shouldn't be talking like this.'

'I know. He doesn't like it. Gets shirty about it. Was he this jealous when you *were* going out?'

Yes, Is thought. *Very much so*. Damien couldn't bear her even speaking to another man. Whenever she came in after a shift at St Fiacre's, he would quiz her about the patients she had tended to, with the emphasis on the male ones. What had she said to them? They to her? It reached the point where she would have to give every male patient she mentioned a qualifying tag, such as 'He's only sixteen years old' or 'He's in cardio, can barely raise an arm', so that Damien would know the person in question wasn't a potential rival. And on social occasions . . . ! The hospital Christmas party, for instance. Damien had stuck next to her all evening, glowering at every man who approached her and scaring off most of the less intrepid ones. These were her friends, work colleagues, doctors and fellow nurses she'd known for years, and they were reluctant to come and chat because of the boyfriend-slash-bodyguard hovering at her shoulder.

Jealous? Oh yes, you could safely say that was among Damien's less appealing character traits.

'I'll take your lack of answer as a yes,' Provender said.

'He's not a bad person,' Is offered.

'He kidnapped me forcibly from my own home and he's holding me here against my will, and he's not a bad person? Forgive me if I give a little snort of incredulity.'

'He's doing it for a reason.'

'What reason?'

'I can't say. But it's all in a good cause.'

'Oh well. Marvellous. That makes it all right then.'

'He's altruistic.'

'If by that you mean he hates the Families, then yes he is. What about you, though? Do you hate the Families?'

'I . . . I used to think I did.'

'And now?'

'I'm not sure. I hate the way people worship you, but that's not the same thing. Maybe you should discourage them from doing that. But then why would you want to? It serves you well. You're the paragons, the ideal we're all supposed to aspire to. Wealth, power, a strong sense of kinship, rooted in heritage. As long as that's how people see you, you'll have their trust and keep your position.'

'But nowadays everyone knows we're human and fallible. We used to have mystique, but then came all the magazines and the TV programmes. They love to show us up. Warts and all.'

'And yet somehow that just makes the public love you even more. Probably because they feel they can identify with you. You have problems like they do. And yet still: wealth, power, kinship . . . It's the best of both worlds. You can slip up and yet you can still do no wrong.'

'Lucky us.'

'You *are* lucky, Provender. Really, you have no idea how lucky you are.'

'Remind me of that again, the next time I have to ask you to help me take a dump.'

Is fed him the last morsel of soup. 'This isn't for ever. This'll be over eventually.'

'When?'

'Honestly, I have no idea. But it will be over.'

'Is?'

'Yes?'

'This may sound like an odd question . . .'

'Try me.'

'Would you believe me if I said *I* hated the Families?'

She laughed, albeit softly, in case Damien overheard. 'No.'

'Why not?'

'Why would you? I could believe it, I suppose, if you were a surly adolescent and at that stage of your life where you just hated everything. Usually surly adolescents direct most of their rage against their own family. It's the most convenient target. But you should be past all that. You're a grown man.'

'Try telling my sisters that. But actually, you misunderstood. I said the Families. Meaning the lot of them, not just my own. The whole institution.'

'Then I really wouldn't believe you, no.'

'What if I could prove it?'

'How?'

'Would it make you feel differently about me?'

'You answer my question first. How?'

Is crossed the main room to the kitchen nook. Damien was slumped in front of the television, idly dialling between channels using the wired-in remote control. A cigarette smouldered between the first two fingers of his other hand. She had chastised him mildly about taking up smoking again. He had pretty much ignored her, although he had mumbled something about giving up for good after all this was over.

She deposited Provender's soup bowl in the sink with a clank and ran some water into it. Then, after a pause, she said, 'Damien.'

'Yup?'

'You know your copy of *The Meritocrats*?'

'Yeah. What about it? Oh, hold on.' Damien sat up, twisting round in his chair. 'You want to give it another go?'

He looked delighted, almost pathetically so. The strayed sheep Is, showing signs that she might be interested in returning to the fold.

Is felt vaguely ashamed of herself. 'I thought I might try.'

'It's hard work, I know,' Damien said, 'but my God, it's worth it. You just have to persevere. Everything that's wrong about the Families – it's in that book.' He started to climb out of the chair. 'I'll go fetch it.'

'No, no, it's all right. I know where it is.'

'Help yourself then.' Damien settled back. 'Enjoy. That Anonymous – he certainly nailed it. I'd love to meet him someday. Shake him by the hand. What a guy.'

Is headed for the bedroom, thinking that if Provender was telling the truth, Anonymous was the last person Damien would have wanted to meet.

And she couldn't see it, to begin with. *Read the first four paragraphs*, Provender had said. *Study them carefully.* She sat on Damien's bed with the tattily-bound book open in front of her and she scanned through the first four paragraphs of Chapter One and she simply couldn't see what Provender was getting at. The clue to the novel's true authorship. The subtle little give-away woven into the text.

She was, of course, familiar with the opening passage of *The Merito-crats* from her previous unsuccessful assaults on the book:

> Providence saw to it that Guy Godwin was born and brought up in a house at the confluence of three types of transportation. Road ran alongside the house. Overhead a railway viaduct arched. Very close to the end of the garden, a canal flowed. Every minute of every day, almost, Guy could look out of a window and see voyagers go by. Never did he not think of the world beyond his neighbourhood. Down on the canal, stately barges passed carrying rivermen and cargo to elsewhere. Electric trains thrummed on high, freighted with commuters. Rumbling traffic outside his front door ferried drivers and passengers to innumerable unknown destinations.
>
> Guy Godwin, you would say, was fated to become a traveller himself. Late in life, looking back, he would perceive that it had been his destiny. Ever since birth there had been a restlessness in him. Ever since birth he had been conscious that journeying was man's natural state of being. Definitely, the urge to move outward and onward was inherent in all humans, and in him more than most.
>
> When he was of an age to leave home, he did. Rolling up his belongings in a single small backpack, he began his wanderings on foot. Out into the world he went, to find what it had to offer. There could be no turning back. Even as he closed his parents' front door behind him, he knew this.
>
> The very first person he encountered on his travels was the tramp Jack Holloway. Holloway was to become Guy's boon companion during his adventures. It could be said that without Holloway Guy would not have seen and experienced half the things he did. Sancho Panza to Guy's Don Quixote, Holloway was guide, governor, guardian and goad all rolled into one.

Reading the lines now, and rereading them, she recognised nothing other than the qualities she habitually divined and derided in the novel: the lugubriousness of the prose and the shallowness with which the two central characters were sketched. Perhaps in the parts of the book she had never got to, Guy Godwin and Jack Holloway were better fleshed out and became more believable, but she doubted it. Holloway, in particular, she found a hopelessly far-fetched figure, an idea of a tramp dreamed up by someone who had never actually met a tramp. Is knew tramps. They turned up in Accident and Emergency all the time. Not one of them was anything like Holloway. Holloway wasn't mad or methylated or both. He didn't reek of piss. He didn't mutter constantly and profanely. He wasn't prone to dropping his trousers and aggressively masturbating. He was an untarnished angel-of-the-road, there to steer the hero through his exploration of the book's fictional Family-less world, offering tips and sage observations along the way.

Is was close to resenting Provender for making her re-immerse herself in *The Meritocrats*. It really was – and she was surer than ever about this now – a bad book.

Then she saw it. On perhaps her seventh perusal of the four paragraphs, the answer suddenly blossomed. There it was, plain as day. She was stunned by the overtness, the sheer nerve of it.

It must be a hoax, she thought. *Somebody having a laugh*.

But it wasn't. It was as clear and unambiguous a statement of copyright as could be imagined.

The first letter of each sentence.

Each paragraph denoting a separate word.

PROVENDER

GLEED

WROTE

THIS

28

The journey to the Island had been made under favourable conditions, a smooth flight. The journey home saw the Gleed dirigible bumping and buffeting through the air. It didn't help that the captain was under orders to make all speed and that they were running into a headwind. Instead of letting itself be buoyed and caressed by the air currents, the dirigible was hammering through. It also didn't help – at least in Prosper's view – that for the first couple of hundred miles they were following hard on the tail of the Black Dirigible.

'The Kuczynskis have something,' he insisted, gripping the viewing gallery handrail. 'Some kind of device that makes their wake choppier than normal.'

'Don't be ridiculous,' said Fortune. 'It's just bad weather.'

'Then why do they keep veering in front of us? Every time we turn to port, they turn to port. Every time starboard, the same.'

'They're mucking around with us, that's why, Prosp. Don't you remember when we were lads, you, me and Acquire, and we'd take the cars out on the speedway circuit and Ack would always pull ahead and then stay dead in front, cutting us up so neither of us could overtake him?'

'Bloody annoying it was.'

'Same principle here. Dog-in-the-manger tactics. They're angry and they're showing it.'

Tutting in disgust, Prosper trod a staggering, swaying course aftward to the armchairs. His brother joined him, moving carefully so as not to spill a drop of his glass of single malt.

'So, you picked a fight,' he said. 'And you got one. What now? Wait for them to make the next move?'

'Hell no. Keep the pressure on. Turn it up, if possible.'

'Prosp, has it occurred to you that Kuczynski might not have been lying? He might have been on the level when he said he didn't know anything about Provender?'

'*Et tu*, Fort?'

'Whoa, hold on there, big bro. Don't get all "Judas!" with me. Someone has to say these things to you.'

'Someone already did.' Prosper rubbed his cheek. 'My face still hurts from it.'

'Yes, well, hell hath no fury, blah-di-blah. That slap was long overdue, if you ask me.' Fortune swilled his whisky around and drank a slug of it. 'No, what I'm getting at is, it could be that your loathing of the Kuczynskis is muddying your thought processes. You might not be seeing quite straight here. You want them to be the villains of the piece so badly, you refuse even to consider the possibility that they aren't.'

'You saw how they behaved. He blustered. She chucked blood at me. Blood!' The first thing Prosper had done after returning to the dirigible was go to his cabin, scrub his face clean and dig out a new shirt. He had rid himself of all physical traces of the blood, but he could not so easily erase the memory of having the wine goblet hurled at him and feeling the warm wet spatter of someone else's lifestuff on his skin. Even to think about it now left him nauseated.

'It might be argued that you provoked them.'

'Or it might be argued that I called their bluff and they tipped their hand.'

'Poker analogies don't seem proper somehow, under the circumstances.'

'Why not? Life is a gamble.'

'Oh what rot! Gambling's a gamble. Everything else is a matter of careful analysis and proportionate response.'

'Says the man who nearly ended up with a spire up his arse the night before last. Says the man whose idea of proportion is "one part vermouth, three parts gin, that's how you make a martini".'

Fortune gave a slow, forbearing blink. 'You know I love and respect you, big bro. You know also that I'm one of the few people who can talk straight with you.'

'Straight? You haven't been straight since you were seventeen.'

'You know what I mean. I'm the one who can tell you to your face when I think you might be on the wrong track, and I'm doing so now. Tread cautiously, Prosp. It's probably a bit late for that, but do it anyway. I dislike the Kuczynskis as much as you. But just because they're white-skinned blood-sucking bastards, that doesn't automatically make them evil. Remember that.'

A few hours later, the Black Dirigible changed tack, heading off due east while the Gleed vessel continued on its north-eastward course. Progress was no calmer, even with the Black Dirigible gone. Objects rattled in the passenger lounge. The whole aircraft shuddered and strained. The bracing wires between the gas cells within the balloon sang and twanged distantly, like an Aeolian harp.

Alone, Fortune having retired to his cabin for a nap, Prosper brooded.

His brother did not understand. Could not. He had no children of his own. Provender was not *his* son. Fortune didn't see that a father must do certain things when the life of an offspring was at stake. It was primal. An alpha-male instinct. An enemy threatened; one must bark and snap back.

And Prosper was right about the Kuczynskis. He knew it in his bones. Fortune would soon be eating several helpings of humble pie. He would concede with good grace, Prosper was sure. When the Kuczynskis surrendered Provender up. When, as the screws were tightened on them, those ersatz vampires caved in. Fortune would admit his older brother had played a masterful game. His strategy had been flawless. Well done. Bravo.

Prosper looked forward to that. More, he looked forward to seeing Cynthia grovel in apology. He loved his wife but knew she didn't think much of him as a husband and father. Well, he'd be showing *her*, wouldn't he?

Ahead, through the windows of the viewing gallery, the coast of Spain was now visible on the far horizon, a faint brown blur beneath the misty purple of oncoming dusk. The dirigible was close enough to the landmass of Europe for Prosper to start making phonecalls, via radio relay. He picked up the handset of the private line and began dialling.

It did not take long. A handful of calls, each as brief as the next. A word or two in the right ears – ears belonging to people who owed the Gleeds for their positions, who were in some way indebted or obligated to the Family. It wasn't so much what was said as what was left unsaid. His implication was quite clear. *Do this for me. I am Prosper Gleed.*

That, when you were Family, was how easy it was to spark off a war.

29

Is waited till Damien next went out. He hated to be housebound for too long. He said he began to feel like a caged tiger, and like a caged tiger he would pace and pace, endlessly circling. Is herself was feeling cooped-up and claustrophobic. The flat was not large, and seemed smaller still with one room effectively off-limits. But she was reluctant to leave. In Needle Grove a woman out on her own had to be careful, especially after dark. She also wasn't happy at the thought of Damien alone with Provender. And she herself wanted to be alone with Provender. So when Damien said he couldn't stand it in here any more, he *had* to stretch his legs, she encouraged him to. She watched him strap on his sheath knife – his 'necessary precaution', he called it. She chivvied him out of the door. He told her he wouldn't be gone long and threw a meaningful glance towards the bathroom. 'Don't let him give you any bullshit.'

'I won't go near him, I swear.'

'Family try and twist people around their fingers. They can't help it.'

'I'm going to sit and read.' She pointed to *The Meritocrats*, on the table.

'Good. That's fine by me.'

No sooner had his footsteps faded down the hallway than Is grabbed the book and strode into the bathroom.

'Tell me this isn't true.'

Provender raised his head to peer at her, as if there were no blindfold. 'I take it you mean—'

'This.' She waggled the book so that he could hear the pages flopping against one another. 'You're not the author.'

'I think pretty clearly I am. Who else would do that? Stick *my* name and a claim of authorship right at the beginning?'

'It could be, I don't know, someone's idea of a joke.'

'Kind of a pointless joke, if you ask me. Especially as no one is likely even to notice it.'

'But how?'

'Don't you mean why?'

'No, I mean how. We'll come to why later. How did you write it? Get it out there?'

'I wrote it the way I imagine anyone writes a book: one word at a time. It took the best part of two years. I started when I was nineteen. I finished when I was just gone twenty-one. I have a lot of spare time. A lot of privacy too, if I want it. All in all, it was reasonably straightforward. Those first four paragraphs were the tricky part. The rest just sort of came out. Do you like it?'

'As a matter of fact, since you ask, no.'

'Oh.'

'It's almost unreadable.'

'Ah.'

'But I'm in a minority. I can think of one person who treats it pretty much like the Bible.'

'Him.'

'Him.'

Provender almost laughed. 'That's almost funny.'

'No, it isn't,' Is snapped. 'It's sick. It's twisted. Where do you get off doing that? What kind of perverted pleasure do you get from fooling all those people?'

'Fooling? I didn't write *The Meritocrats* to fool anyone. I wrote it because I had to, and I sent it out because I wanted to. It wasn't something I did on a whim. I printed off three manuscript copies and posted them to three radical anti-Family groups. Anonymously, of course. The addresses weren't hard to find. They're listed in the phone book under Political Organisations. I went for the three with the most colourful names. Kin Dread, that was my favourite. And then I just left it to them to do what they liked with the book. I thought, I hoped, it would get circulated. There was no copyright indicia, so they'd realise, if they had any sense, that they could run off pirated editions without getting sued. It was in the lap of the gods. The manuscripts might well have ended up being tossed in the bin. Instead . . .'

'Instead, anti-Family activists have taken the book to their hearts, little suspecting it was written by a Family member.'

'Actually, I did worry that I'd be rumbled. Sticking my imprimatur in at the beginning like that – it was an arrogant thing to do. But I couldn't help myself. And nobody's spotted it so far, it seems.'

'Unless you know to look for it, you'd never see it.'

'I suppose. Or else, if somebody did spot it, they'd assume it was a joke, just as you did.'

Is lowered the toilet lid and slumped down onto it. 'So now the why.'

'Why write it? I told you. I had to.'

'It was some sort of posh-boy challenge you set yourself, then. You were bored so you thought you'd write a subversive novel, see how well it did.'

'No.' Provender sounded offended. 'It wasn't like that at all.'

'But no one in your Family knows.'

'Is, as far as I'm aware only two people in the world know I wrote it – you and me.'

'So it's your amusing little secret. You've staked a claim on a little bit of independence from your upbringing.'

'You've got me there,' he conceded. 'That is why I did it, partly. Late-teen rebellion.'

'Not much of a rebellion, if nobody knows about it.'

'Well, quite. Then again, the book's out there, I hope inspiring people to imagine a world without the Families. What do they say – a million copies doing the rounds? That's a pretty effective piece of propaganda, by anyone's standards. So why should I worry that my own blood-relations think I'm just lazy old Provender, loner, oddball, dragging his feet about getting married, confirmed dilettante? Doesn't bother me when I know my magnum opus is a success. It's worming its way through the public consciousness. It's gnawing away at the foundations of Family-run society. It's doing its bit to help bring about the Families' downfall.'

'I don't believe I'm hearing this,' Is said. 'Provender Gleed, talking like an ardent anti-Familial.'

'And meaning it. Every word.'

Is stared at *The Meritocrats* in her lap with its monochrome cover and its dog-eared, thumb-marked pages – Damien's holy text. If only Damien knew. If only everyone knew.

She returned her gaze to Provender. Something about his posture had altered, although perhaps she was imagining it. He seemed to be sitting up straighter, looking less hunched and humbled.

'If the Families were overthrown, and I don't think it very likely, but if—'

'They did it in China,' Provender pointed out.

'Yes, and everybody looks at the mess *they're* in now and says, "Let's pray it never happens here."'

'But it's possible.'

'Anything's possible. But if it did happen, what about you? What would you do? The Chinese Families, after all, the Wings, the Cheungs, the Lees, they were either killed in the uprising or they had to go into exile with barely any of their wealth left.'

'I know. I think most of the Wings are in Australia now, living on handouts from the Jacksons and the McIntyres. Rather ignominious. And the Lees, haven't they set up a restaurant chain in San Francisco or something?'

'Could you do that?'

'Go into catering? Doubt it. I'm a lousy cook.'

'No, go from having everything to having next to nothing. What I'm saying is, have you really thought this through? You might want an end to the Families, but do you want an end to your lifestyle? The luxury. The not needing a job. The parties, for heaven's sake.'

'The parties I could happily do without. You saw me the other night. Did I look like I was having fun? As for the rest – it depends.'

'On?'

'The Families wouldn't have to be got rid of as violently as they were in China. That was mob hysteria. It needn't be like that anywhere else. There could be a quiet transition. We could be slowly edged out. We'd have our assets stripped from us bit by bit but we'd be allowed to hang on to the rump of our money. We'd have enough to keep going. We just wouldn't have the power and influence any more. Politicians wouldn't jump through hoops for us. We wouldn't be able to make or break a career with a single word. Lives wouldn't depend on our whims and whimsies.'

'You want to get rid of your cake and eat it, that's what you mean.'

'You make it sound like I'm being unrealistic. I think I'm being ultra-realistic. There's that bit in Chapter Thirty-Nine of *The Meritocrats* where I talk about, or rather Jack Holloway talks about, capitalism and responsibility. Basically, are they mutually exclusive. You know the section I'm talking about?'

'Provender, I've never got beyond Chapter Six.'

'You really hate my book, don't you.'

'Don't be hurt.'

'I'm not hurt. Well, yes I am. You have to understand, you're the first person I've met with a copy of it and you don't like it. That's not good for my author's ego. But I guess I can live with it. Your friend, after all, he loves it. Which is ironic, as I get the impression he'd happily stove my head in if I wasn't so valuable to him financially. That reminds me – how is the ransoming going? Have my Family agreed to cough up yet? How much am I worth?'

'I can't really talk about that.'

'Can't or won't?'

'Can't. There's a lot to do with this business that I'm being kept in the dark about.'

'What on earth for?'

'To protect me. The less I know, the safer I'll be if things go wrong.'

'Your friend's idea? How chivalrous of him. Or maybe he doesn't trust you. Maybe he has an inferiority complex and can't bear the thought of you, a woman, being on an equal footing with him.'

'Clumsy, Provender.'

'What?'

Is stood up. 'You were doing OK. This *Meritocrats* thing. That was working. A trump card, and you played it nicely. You almost had me on your side. But then you overstepped the mark. I can't blame you for that. You're Family, and Family members don't know when enough's enough. But if you're going to win me over completely, you'll have to be a whole lot subtler and a whole lot smarter.'

She exited the bathroom, slamming the door harder than she intended to. In the main room, she flung *The Meritocrats* down and stomped over to the window. It was a full-length window that gave onto a small balcony. To open it took some effort; the runners were warped and rusty; it rolled grudgingly. Is forced it sideways till there was a gap large enough for her to slide through. On the balcony she stood and gazed down on Needle Grove. In the twilight, the shadows were growing. The hum of the surrounding city was abating and the estate's own cacophony was becoming more audible. Shouts echoed, ricocheting upwards between walls. Music blared from windows. Televisions jabbered. Down at the lowest, most lightless levels the gang-tribes were starting to gather for their after-dark wilding. Is could see them at their regular meeting-places, tiny figures. She knew they would be sharing bottles of cheap strong cider, shots of Tinct, and pugnacious jokes. Soon Needle Grove would be theirs again. All decent folk would stay locked in their flats till daybreak.

It could be better than this. Damien had promised her that. With money extorted from the Gleeds, Needle Grove could be brightened up, smartened, cleaned, made more liveable. There could be green areas – foliage-green, not paint-and-neon green. There could be improved lighting, and some kind of system of security patrols, maybe, to keep the kids off the streets until the kids got the message and stayed off the streets voluntarily. There could be new drains installed to replace the old ones which got clogged up during rainstorms and meant certain squares and underpasses flooded and were unusable for days. There could be playgrounds, safe zones that weren't vandalised or commandeered by the gang-tribes for their fights, places where the smaller children could actually *play*. Needle Grove could become an estate people wanted to live in, as opposed to an estate people ended up living in when there was nowhere else available, or were stuck living in because they didn't have the wherewithal to bribe someone high up in the Risen London Authority to get them out.

Is wanted to believe Damien when he said this. She wanted to think it was a vision that could become a reality. It was how he had sold her on the whole kidnapping plan. He had painted a picture of Gleed millions – money the Family could easily spare – being siphoned off into Needle Grove. He had described, in beguiling terms, a reversal of the usual model: money going from the rich to the poor, rather than the other way around. He had so enraptured her with this noble design of his that it was nearly, *nearly*, like the old days, when they were first going out, before she got to know him too well. When he used to seem principled, rather than priggish; focused, rather than fanatical. When what he and she had in common was a bond of conviction and not, as it became, a bone of contention.

And now she was no longer sure. About anything. She was angry with Damien. Angry with Provender. Angry with herself. She was less and less happy about being a part of Damien's scheme. But if she backed out, she would be leaving Provender alone with Damien and she wasn't happy about that idea either. Perhaps Provender deserved whatever came to him. Then again, for all his faults, he wasn't a bad person. He was attempting, in his fumbling way, to be a good person. She wanted to hold *The Meritocrats* against him but, damn it, she just couldn't. Terrible though it was as literature, at least it was a gesture in the right direction. And the more she saw him, trussed up and helpless in the bathroom, the more she felt that he was a hapless victim in all this, and the more she pitied him.

Is simply didn't know what to do any more. A dusky haze settled over Needle Grove, the tower blocks clustered against the darkening sky, lights flickered on, the estate's nightly nocturne of yelps and yammering swelled – and she didn't know what to do any more.

PART FOUR

30

Overnight, it began.

Shortly after eleven p.m. GMT a battle group of British warships – three frigates and a destroyer – put out from Hull. Ostensibly on hastily-scheduled manoeuvres, they ploughed into the North Sea bearing due east on a course which soon took their radio transmissions within range of the listening post at Kolobrzeg in Poland.

Less than an hour later the German radar station at Zinnowitz detected ship activity at the naval yards at Gdansk and Köningsberg. Not just a battle group but fully half a division had begun steaming out into the Baltic. Polish military high command had not publicly announced any such deployment of vessels in advance. Messages flashed from Zinnowitz to Berlin, and thence to Stockholm, thanks to the intelligence-sharing pact between Germany and the Scandinavian countries instituted in the after-math of the last war. Stockholm contacted Helsinki and Copenhagen, and all German and Scandinavian armed forces went from green alert con-dition to yellow.

Around three a.m., watchtowers to the west of the border between Germany and Poland were submitting reports of armoured brigades trundling along local roads on the Polish side. Similar reports came in from watchtowers along the German/Czech border and the Austrian/Hungarian. The German and Austrian armies responded in kind, sending out tanks from bases near Dresden, Passau and Güssing. To either side of the line dividing West Europe from East, the night air was shaken by the rumble of diesel engines and the clank of segmented steel tread on tarmac.

As dawn approached, troops were brought into play. On both sides, whole battalions had been roused from their billets and were marching eastward or westward to take up position a few miles from enemy territory. By this stage the premiers, presidents and prime ministers of every country in Europe were out of their beds and on the phone. For most, the events unfolding came as a surprise. They had believed the continent to be in a relatively stable state, everyone rubbing along con-tentedly enough, the odd dispute here and there, nothing that couldn't be solved through diplomatic means. They had had no idea that the peace that had endured these past five decades was, in the event, quite so fragile.

While the political hotlines from capital to capital crackled, the sun rose. Light moved east to west across the face of Europe, and with it came warplanes. Aerial visibility enabled take-off. Reconnaissance craft, with fighter escorts, criss-crossed their own countries' airspace, coming near to but never quite entering enemy airspace. Strato-Class dirigibles also took flight, easing ponderously into positions of readiness in the upper atmosphere, at altitudes too great for fixed-wing aircraft and ground-based artillery to reach. These were huge creations, leviathans of the skies which made ordinary passenger dirigibles look like minnows, and they carried immense payloads of ordnance. City Smashers, they were colloquially called. Pregnant with death.

The national leaders, still on the phones, debated, soothed, squabbled, accused, objected, hectored, harangued, weaselled, wheedled, vilified, mollified, blustered, filibustered, postured, pontificated – and that was just with colleagues they knew to be allies. Within the bloc of West European states, a consensus started to form. Within the Pan-Slavic Federation, the same. Pledges of assistance were made to those countries on the front line of any potential conflict. *They invade you, they invade us*, was what it boiled down to. England in particular was keen to form a part of any western military coalition. Troop carriers were placed on standby at airbases in Aldershot, Colchester and Peterborough, poised to take to the skies at a moment's notice.

It all happened fast, as if it had been waiting to happen, as if some fault-line was suddenly starting to flex and tremble once more, a political seismic fissure long thought dormant, largely forgotten. From Lisbon to Lugansk, from Hammerfest to Syracuse, people awoke to discover the Europe they had gone to bed in was not the same Europe in which they were yawning and stretching and blearily blinking. A shift had occurred. An old rupture was reopening. As they picked up their newspapers, as they switched on their radios and TVs, they felt a vague dread settle in their bones, strange yet familiar, new yet known. A sense shared by millions of civilian souls across the continent: *Here we go again*.

31

As with any creative profession, being an Anagrammatic Detective entailed a highly disproportionate ratio of perspiration to inspiration. It was all very well shuffling letters around, making new words out of old. That was the fun part. But it was only the preliminary. The casting of the verbal runes, the reading of the orthographic tea leaves, the (in more than one sense) spelling – this was to lay the groundwork. Afterwards came the hard part, the standard gumshoe stuff, the gathering of proof, the amassing of evidence. The legwork.

For Romeo Moore, legwork had meant eighteen straight hours of covert pursuit and stakeout, with little to show for it except sore feet, the jitters from drinking too much coffee, and a notebook containing a breakdown of the movements of Arthur Gleed during the past afternoon, evening and night – a breakdown which, though meticulously detailed, was also sadly unenlightening.

Moore, stationed on a bench in the park at the centre of the Regency-era square where Arthur lived, was reviewing his notes now, by the early light of Tuesday morning. Birds were shrieking their aubade from the treetops. Traffic was beginning to move, London stirring from its rest. In the old parts of the city you heard and felt everything more clearly than you did in the metropolis's high-rise canyons. You got a glimpse of what London had been like before the aerial bombardments of the last war wiped seventy per cent of it from the face of the map. These were little pockets of the past, miraculously preserved, history nestling in the shadows of the newer, upthrusting London. Porched and palinged, the housefronts spoke of genteeler, more sensitive times. As property, however, the houses themselves fetched premium prices and never changed hands without cut-throat haggling and gazumping. Gentility cost. A hunger for sensitivity brought out the worst in people.

Moore had written comments to this effect in his notebook entry headed 3.40 a.m., after the words 'Still no apparent activity within the premises'. During the small hours, when all Arthur seemed to be doing was sleeping, Moore's notebook entries had taken on an increasingly personal and ruminative bent, becoming less an account of his suspect's behaviour (or lack of it) and more an internal monologue, Moore addressing Moore. 'I'll never be as rich as a Gleed' was a frequent refrain throughout the pages, along with 'Merlin's going to be laughing on the other side of his face' and other similar affirmations that he, Romeo Moore, was on the right track and his partner wasn't. Then there were the lists he had made of possessions he might like to buy with some of the fee from the investigation. A new record player and a more comfortable armchair for his flat were the common features of all the lists, and were probably the only things he *would* buy. He was somewhat saddened by his lack of material ambition. In the notebook's margins he had made several attempts to divine Milner's approach to the investigation, of necessity using Milner's own anagrammatising technique. Nothing useful had resulted. There were, in addition, a few doodles, scrawled by lamp-light.

It had been a long night.

He had picked up Arthur Gleed's trail yesterday shortly after two p.m. Arthur was returning to the Shortborn Theatre to resume rehearsals, following lunch at a nearby bistro with a couple of his fellow-actors. Moore's first note relayed his impression of Arthur's mood: 'Seems up-beat. Confident. Makes his companions laugh with a joke. About nuns and soap(?).'

Later, Moore tried to gain access into the theatre via the lobby but was prevented from doing so by an usher. 'Told I could buy a ticket from the box office for performance if wanted but not allowed to enter auditor-ium.' His next entry, fifteen minutes on, read: 'Stage door located in alley alongside theatre. Knocked on. Opened by large man. Bodyguard/doorman type. Tried to get on good side of. Claimed to be ClanFan autograph hunter. Bodyguard/doorman's good side not got on of. Claim believed but not effective. Told that Mr Gleed did not sign autographs. Persisted. Invited to "f*** off".'

Arthur re-emerged from the theatre shortly after five, this time with a gaggle of people. Together they wended their way back along New Aldwych to the bistro and shared an early supper. Moore sat at a table within earshot and nursed several coffees in a row while Arthur and company raucously discussed the preview performance that was due to begin in a couple of hours' time. Moore noticed their affectation of addressing one another by their stage characters' names. Arthur took it one step further by referring to himself in the third person, as the Prince and the Dane, as in 'Pass the Dane the salt please, Polonius, there's a good chap'. Moore's notes, which he jotted surreptitiously, using a menu as a screen, included the comment: 'Actors like nothing better than for other people in the vicinity to know they are actors.' He also observed that their reactions and mannerisms were never normal, always exaggerated, as if they lived life at a higher pitch of intensity than everyone else. ' "Laertes", describing event of trifling annoyance. Face aghast. Pinching bridge of nose. "I was incan*des*cent with rage!" '

The cast trooped back to the Shortborn. Moore followed in their wake.

From then till eleven, all he did was stand across the street from the theatre and wait. A few people went in to watch the preview. Critics, he assumed, judging by the fact that most were carrying pads of paper. As a point of interest he noted that on the marquee outside the theatre, the name which appeared largest was that of the star of the show. The play's title and the playwright were both subordinate. Arthur Gleed merited as many yards of neon tubing as Hamlet and William Shakespeare combined.

The critics emerged three hours later, some looking pleased, some not. However mixed the reviews were, Arthur's performance would be singled out for praise. He invariably got a gentle ride. Moore could never forget how one TV critic had striven manfully to say something good about Arthur's execrable *Cabaret Cop* series and come up with 'Gleed's torch-singing is astonishing enough to stop any burglar in his tracks', which veered just the safe side of ambiguous. Arthur's Hamlet, in that spirit, would very likely be acclaimed a great Dane.

Roughly half an hour later Arthur himself came out. He did not look best pleased. 'Stomping' was how Moore's notes put it. 'Thundercloud above head. Not happy with perf? Or other reason?'

At a safe distance, Moore tailed the disgruntled Arthur to a Family tram stop. Arthur spoke his name into the microphone funnel by the gate. The gate rolled open and he proceeded through onto the platform to await the next tram.

Moore, at this point, was in an ecstasy of dismay. Arthur had stepped onto Family-only territory. He could be headed anywhere on the tram network. Moore was about to lose him – and if Arthur was holding Provender captive, now was exactly the time when he might visit his hostage cousin, to check on him, perhaps crow over him.

As luck would have it, a taxi happened along, For Hire light shining like a beacon. Moore hailed it, and once a tram arrived and Arthur got on board, Moore instructed the taxi driver to trail the tram wherever it went.

'I can't do that,' said the driver. 'There's laws against that sort of thing.'

There weren't. At least, not proper laws. But there was the aura of untouchability that surrounded the Families, as good as a law to some folk.

Moore fished out a hefty wedge of his half of Carver's start-up money. 'Are you sure about that?'

The taxi driver eyed the cash. Looked to the tram. Back to the cash.

'Wife's got a birthday coming up,' he said, snatching the banknotes out of Moore's hand.

The pursuit was shorter-lived than Moore anticipated, and only once did the taxi driver seem in danger of losing the tram, when it plunged through a tunnel at the base of a building and he had to run a red light and screech around a couple of corners in order to catch up with it again. There was a near-miss with another car, as the driver's concentration on the tram momentarily eclipsed his concentration on the road. Other than that, the chase was problem-free. The tram lines, though hived off from the rest of the world by lofty chain link fences, stuck close to the public highways, piggybacking on the existing transport infrastructure. Keeping up with a tram in another vehicle was, if due care and attention were paid, a relatively painless affair.

'Disappointment,' read Moore's note, written after the taxi had deposited him near Arthur's destination. 'A.G. alights at tram stop closest to his house.' Appended to the note was a record of his outlay on the taxi ride, which he could not help commenting on with a large exclamation mark.

Outside his house, Arthur paused on his way to the front door to run a hand lovingly over the bodywork of a Dagenham Rapier convertible parked at the kerbside. The car was a sleek thing, low to the ground, with whitewall tyres, a bull-nosed radiator grille, and chrome headlamps that looked astonished at their own good fortune to be perched atop the front mudguards of so wondrous an automobile. Moore couldn't blame Arthur for stroking it like a pet. He would have done so too, had it been his.

Arthur paused again as a pair of ClanFans who were stationed near the house plucked up the courage to approach him, autograph books in hand. He spent a gracious five minutes with them, signing his name and letting them tell him how wonderful they thought he was. He parted from them with a show of great unwillingness, saying how tired he was. Then he went indoors, the ClanFans departed, thrilled, and Moore's midnight-to-dawn vigil in the park began.

He didn't think he slept. His handwriting was slightly slurred on a couple of entries but the very act of making regular notes kept him awake and alert. He left his post on the park bench only once, in order to find an all-night café where he had a torrential pee and then gulped down a pot's worth of coffee. He was gone for less than twenty minutes, and Arthur's house looked no different when he returned. Still darkened. Still nothing occurring within.

With the arrival of morning, Moore was disheartened but not de-spondent. He remained convinced that Arthur had Provender. Perhaps not here, though, at his house. That was too obvious a location. Cronies of his were keeping Provender somewhere else, somewhere remoter, isolated. Sometime today, before the first night of *Hamlet* this evening, Arthur would undoubtedly pay a call on his cousin. And Moore would be dogging his steps all the way. His plan was to flag down a taxi perhaps an hour or so from now and have it sit idling at the kerbside, near Arthur's house. When Arthur left, whether he went by car or tram, Moore would follow him in the taxi, just like last night.

One of Moore's private mantras was that to maintain HOPEFULNESS one must PUSH ONESELF. When things looked unpromising, when you were tired and fed up, that was when you had to try harder.

He repeated the mantra to himself, as he huddled, stiff and bleary, on the park bench and waited for Arthur to wake.

To maintain HOPEFULNESS one must PUSH ONESELF.

Moore's partner, meanwhile, was enjoying a pleasant breakfast after a good night's sleep, well earned after a long but profitable day's work. One thing troubled Merlin Milner this morning, and it had, as far as he could tell, no connection with the Gleed case. The news headlines were distinctly worrisome. Without warning, with shocking abruptness, Europe was lurching towards war. Politicians were talking about trade disagreements and about breaches of clauses of international convention so obscure that even legislative experts claimed not to have heard of them before. Live TV feeds from around the continent showed ambassadors shuttling between embassies on urgent rounds of negotiation. The military build-up, however, hogged the greatest amount of airtime, since tanks, troops and warplanes in motion were far more rivetingly photogenic than middle-aged men in suits speaking into microphones or stepping out of limousines.

Milner chose to believe that the matter would resolve itself peacefully. Something which had blown up so quickly could not, ipso facto, be that serious. The louder the heads of state on either side rattled their sabres, the more probable it was that they weren't going to draw them. It was an elaborate charade of bluff, double-bluff and counter-double-bluff. You couldn't ignore that something bad was happening, just as you couldn't ignore the commonality of the words ANGERED, DERANGE, EN GARDE, ENRAGED, GRANDEE and GRENADE, all of which seemed applicable here. At the same time, LEADERS were also DEALERS. WARMONGERING could be broken down into three component parts, GAME, WORN and GRIN, which in almost any order pointed to a *realpolitik* truth. What seemed MAD POLICY could in fact be DIPLOMACY. Those doing the SABRE RATTLING might equally be ARBITRAL GENTS.

More to the point, Milner was not prepared to let himself be distracted by outside events. The political situation was beyond his control. The Provender Gleed case was not, and needed his full attention.

Yesterday afternoon Milner had paid a visit to the Central London Library to check through the newspaper archives on microfiche. After an hour of scrolling he had found the article he was looking for, a short piece about tenant unrest on one of the capital's municipal housing estates. Next, he had gone to the Risen London Authority's records office, asked to see a list of tenants in a certain block on that estate, and been told by the registrar that thirty days' notice and a stamped endorsement from the RLA were required before such documents could be examined by a member of the public. In response, Milner had slipped the registrar a fifty, asked again, and shortly had the relevant paperwork in front of him and was busy jotting down the names of all those tenants whose initials were either D.S. or S.D.

The resulting list was long – some thirty individuals – and had to be winnowed down somehow. Back at his flat, Milner had spent the evening anagrammatising the names one after another. A bottle of wine was gradually emptied as the floor of the living room gradually filled up with discarded crumples of paper. Near midnight, Milner had reduced the list to seven. Each name, in one way or another, gave him a hit. Each could be refashioned into a phrase that sounded sinister, untrustworthy, or downright criminal.

Today, he planned to visit the estate and knock on the door of each of these seven tenants' flats. One of them would be the person he was looking for. Instinct, he was sure, would tell him which one. He would recognise the kidnapper straight away. He had seen enough guilt over the years to know the tell-tale signs. Over-friendliness. A tendency to talk too much. Distractedness. An underlying, ill-disguised aggression. One glance, and Milner would have his man.

Needle Grove was not a place he looked forward to visiting. It had a reputation. Teenage tearaways. Vandalism. Violence. Drugs. The joke went that the only needles you found there nowadays were on the tips of Tinct syringes.

Still, there was nothing he could do about that. The anagrams had spoken. The letters pointed just one way.

PROVENDER GLEED contained NEEDLE GROVE, and that had inspired Milner to try various phrases using Provender's name to see what they yielded. PROVENDER GLEED KIDNAPPED. PROVENDER GLEED TAKEN. PROVENDER GLEED CAPTURED.

It was PROVENDER GLEED STOLEN that worked. Stirred, mixed, muddled, reordered, the letters came out as NEEDLE GROVE RENT LOP D.S. or NEEDLE GROVE RENT LOP S.D.

The RENT LOP part had pricked a memory. A couple of years back residents of one block in Needle Grove had staged a protest about their living conditions, refusing to cough up their monthly dues unless their landlord, the Risen London Authority, acceded to a list of demands. The tenants barricaded themselves in the building, promising they would stay there for as long as it took, and were sternly, stalwartly militant right up until the moment the RLA offered them a small reduction in rent, at which point they caved in. It seemed they had had no real stomach for the fight, and the first excuse they got to back down, they took. The idea of a little more money in their pockets made everything else seem bearable. Of course all the other blocks on the estate demanded, and were given, the same rent reduction, but the Authority still won, in as much as the drop in its letting income was less than the amount it would have had to spend sprucing up Needle Grove to the standards the original protestors had been hoping for. Not only that but, if the RLA's track record elsewhere was anything to go by, rents at Needle Grove would have gradually, almost imperceptibly crept up over the past two years till they were back at the previous level. It wasn't just the Families who bled the common people dry. The common people were pretty good at doing it to each other too.

Block 26 was the one that had attempted and failed to persuade the Authority to clean up the estate, and so Block 26 was Milner's destination this morning. He finished breakfast, showered, shaved, dressed, and, with his short-list of seven names in his pocket, sallied forth from his flat and caught a bus that ferried him cross-town to a stop within ten minutes' walk of Needle Grove.

The walk, in the event, took more like twenty minutes. Milner's pace was that slow, that trepidatious. At last, however, he reached the entrance to the estate. Standing before the arc of iron letters, he nerved himself with a deep breath, squared his shoulders, straightened his neck, and, like Theseus about to enter the labyrinth in pursuit of the Minotaur, stepped forward.

32

Provender was home. He was lying in his bed, sleeved in sheets of Egyptian cotton. He could hear the rumble-hiss of the cascades outside his window. There was a vague memory of unpleasantness. Something bad. He had been . . . held prisoner? Something like that. But it was in the past, long ago. He was home again, and warm in bed, and it was bliss. He could stay here for ever, lying here, free to loll and luxuriate. He could straighten his legs—

—his feet hit an obstruction—

—and he could stretch out his arms—

—his knuckles cracked against a hard surface—

—and he could wallow in the depression his body made in the mattress—

—only there was no mattress.

There was just the bathroom floor that had been under him for more than forty-eight hours now. The blindfold was still fastened around his head. His wrists and ankles were still bound with electrical flex.

It was not as heart-sinking an experience as it might have been, awaking from a dream of home to find himself, as before, in captivity. Bathroom and blindfold and bindings had, in the course of the two days, become the norm. A kind of tired passivity had settled in him. He could, with a strange calmness, foresee spending the rest of his life like this, sightless and helpless, never to look on another human face again, dying an old man on this very spot. There was a contentment in believing that that would be his fate. He was rid of the tormenting hope that somehow, at some point, he was going to be freed. To be back in his bed at Dash-lands? Yes, that was truly a dream.

He lay and listened to the building's morning gush of water, the pipes, the ducts, the inner purging, till eventually Is arrived with something for him to eat and drink.

He realised immediately that there was something different about her this morning. A tremor in her voice, a tautness.

'What's up?'

'On the news. The TV. It's incredible. Dreadful.'

'What is?'

'I think . . . They're all saying we could be going to war.'

'Eh?'

'War, Provender. As in everyone kills everyone else.'

'Where did that come from? I mean, who's going to war with whom?'

'The Pan-Slavic Federation. The western European countries. Just like last time and the time before. It's happening all over again.'

'But that's bonkers! We're at peace with the Pan-Slavic Federation. Europe's all one big happy family. Why would . . . ?'

'Why would what, Provender?'

One big happy family.

But not one big happy Family.

Had Provender's hands not been tied, he would have slapped his forehead with one of them.

'Has anyone said what the reason for war is?'

'There's some sort of mumbling about treaties that haven't been honoured and other stuff like that, but the main thing is the Federation have started moving troops and warships around in a threatening way and we've had to respond in kind.'

'So nobody's invaded anywhere yet?'

'Not as far as I can tell.'

'You realise what this is, don't you?'

Is paused to ponder. 'You think *you*—'

'I don't think. I know.'

'Your Family.'

'My father, to be precise.'

'Your father's starting a war because of you? How is that going to help?'

'It isn't. At least, he thinks it's going to help but that's because he's clearly grasped the wrong end of the stick.'

'What do you mean?'

It didn't take Provender long to sketch out the state of antagonism that existed between the Gleeds and the Kuczynskis. Is knew about the feud. Most people did. What she and most people didn't know was just how deep the mutual hatred ran. Provender was certain that his father had pinned the blame for his kidnapping on the Kuczynskis and was taking steps to force them to hand him back. The Kuczynskis, in return, were responding in the only way they could. They didn't have Provender, and they had no doubt told his father that in no uncertain terms. They couldn't, though, simply sit back and let western Europe mobilise for war against eastern Europe. They had no choice but to meet the threat of aggression with the threat of aggression.

'Families can do that? They can throw a whole continent into chaos just because one of them doesn't much like another of them?'

'Is, think about it. There isn't a politician in office who doesn't owe his or her position to Family influence, or else wants to get on a Family's good side. They're like chess-pieces to the Families. Or, no, like trading cards.

To be bought, sold, swapped, trumped, disposed of. Politicians, in a sense, are the biggest ClanFans of all. The Families' power just mesmerises them. Being a politician is the closest they can get to being Family.'

'Well, yes, I know all that. What I meant is, Families are *prepared* to do that? They'll start wars over nothing?'

'I think I'm a little bit more than nothing, at least to my dad, but still, I take your point. And the answer's yes. My father's been itching for an excuse to get back at the Kuczynskis. I'm it. Tell me, was there by any chance an Extraordinary Family Congress yesterday?'

It had been mentioned on the news. 'Yes.'

'My dad,' said Provender, nodding. 'He called it. And I bet it didn't go well. I bet he and Stanisław Kuczynski got right up each other's noses.'

'But the Congress resolves Family disputes. That's the whole point of it.'

'In theory. In practice, when it's not just all the Family heads getting together and having a "we're so wonderful" knees-up, it's a massive bitch-fest. Everyone yells at everyone else, there's a lot of nasty name-calling, then they all go home again. Cathartic, I suppose, but otherwise essentially useless.'

'So it wouldn't stop a potential war.'

'The opposite. Any Family worth its salt, after all, has a munitions-manufacturing plant somewhere in its business portfolio, and an aeronautical engineering firm, and a shipwright's. War brings profits. It's an old maxim but still true. Those air forces will need new planes when their existing ones get shot down. Those navies will need new ships when their existing ones are sunk. And then of course there's the rebuilding. My Family made a killing from the reconstruction of London after the last war. We razed the old Dashlands House and built a brand new one just to celebrate how much profit we'd made.'

'It's about money.'

'It's always about money, Is. Not for my father right now, maybe, or for the Kuczynskis, but for the rest of them. They might have made disapproving noises at the Extraordinary Congress, some of them, but really each and every Family head was rubbing his hands and totting up the potential revenue.'

'That's disgusting.'

'Tell me about it.'

'But no one on the television mentioned anything about your Family or the Kuczynskis.'

'Why would they? Who, ultimately, owns those TV stations?'

'The Families.'

'Exactly. You won't get TV reporters reporting things the Families don't want them to, not the things that really matter.'

Provender heard Is let out a sharp hiss of contempt. For a minute after that she spooned breakfast cereal into his mouth, saying nothing. He could almost hear her thinking, the motor of her brain as troubled but as stoic as that of the extractor fan. Then she said, 'If we got you back to your Family, would that mean—'

The sentence was cut short by the sound of the door being flung open. There was a moment when everything seemed to stop, even the extractor fan. Provender pictured Is, startled, peering round. In the doorway: her accomplice. Provender had built up a mental impression of how the man looked. He imagined, now, a face that was cruel to begin with, further uglified, contorted with rage. The man had been eavesdropping at the door. He had overheard what Is just said. For all Is's protestations that he wouldn't dare lay a finger on her, Provender felt that, if pushed far enough, he would. And surely her unfinished question, what it implied, was 'far enough'.

Absurd notions flashed through Provender's mind. Leaping, somehow, to Is's defence. Interposing himself between her and the man. Taking, on her behalf, whatever the man dished out.

It was easy to be heroic when there was, in fact, little he could do.

Then the man spoke, and Provender was surprised at how even his voice was. Not the fusillade of fury he was expecting at all.

'You done here yet?'

'Nearly.'

'Only I need the bog.'

'Use the bucket.'

'Fuck that.'

'I'll be a couple minutes more.'

'OK. Hurry.'

No sooner had the door closed than Is let out a long, breathless 'Oh God.'

'Did he hear what you said?' Provender whispered.

'I don't think so. Christ, I hope not.'

'Did you . . . ?' Provender hesitated. 'Did you mean what you said?'

'I don't know. Maybe. Shit, no, it's madness. What am I thinking?'

'You're thinking that if you help me, you may just be able to prevent the whole of Europe turning into a bloodbath.'

'Yes, but – I don't know. I don't know how I could do it. I might not get the chance.'

'Does he go out ever? Leave you alone here?'

'Yes. But I never know how long he's going to be gone for. If he caught us trying to . . .'

'Is. Look at me.'

'I already am.'

'OK. Good. You see me? You see I'm not the inbred Family cretin you thought I was? You see what getting me out of here, getting me back to Dashlands, is worth? This isn't about ransom any more, or whatever the hell the reason is you kidnapped me. The stakes are much higher. This is a whole different business now.'

'Maybe I could talk to him. Explain what you said. About the war and the Kuczynskis and all that. It might change his mind.'

'You honestly think it would?'

'Honestly, no.'

'Me too. And you talk like that to him, it could rouse his suspicions. He could decide not to go out at all. Best not say anything. Act normal. Wait for an opportunity. It'll come.'

'I'm not sure, Provender.'

'Is, please. You know it's what's right.'

'It's crazy.'

'Often the same as what's right, unfortunately.'

33

It was known as the Chapel, but that was a misnomer and something of a bitter joke. It was no House of God. It was a folly built on a rise about half a mile west of Dashlands House, close to the site of the original house before the original house was flattened and replaced with the newer one. A cylindrical structure capped with a dome, it mirrored the observatory which stood on another, higher rise a mile due south-east. Externally, the sole difference between the two edifices was that one had a high-powered refractor telescope protruding from its roof.

The superficial similarity was no accident. Both Chapel and observatory had been erected in the mid-1800s by Prosper's great-grandfather, Cardamom, amateur astronomer and ardent atheist. The observatory peered up into the universe and saw only stars and space. No God up there. Plenty of beauty and scientific wonderment, but no God.

The Chapel, by contrast, was blind. It didn't have an eye on the heavens. It was deliberately purposeless. Inside, there was a flagstone floor, a low circular dais at the centre, and, set equidistantly around the wall, alcoves of the kind that could have held idols, statues of saints, representations of gods, something like that, but here were left ostentatiously empty. The message was clear. Deities had no place in the Gleed scheme of things. The Chapel was a parody of a church, a mock temple, blasphemous in its bareness. There was nothing within it to genuflect before, not even an effigy of Mammon.

This, nevertheless, was where Cynthia came when she needed to pray. There was nowhere else to go, nowhere else where she could be guaranteed solitude and silence and stillness, nowhere else on the estate that even vaguely resembled a place of worship. The cool air, the damp smell of stone, and the hollow, hushed echoes, all reminded her of the cathedrals of her childhood. The Lamases were rare among Families in that they had not wholly dispensed with religion. Perhaps it was because the trappings of Catholicism, especially Roman Catholicism, were reassuringly gilded and grandiose. Equally it might be because, as Cynthia's father often said, it was wise not to reject the Almighty altogether, on the off-chance that He did exist. Confession, too, and the taking of the Sacrament, and general prostration before a higher power, did much to shrive the wealthy of their guilt about being wealthy (assuming they felt such guilt in the first place). Attending a two-hour Mass every Sunday was a small investment of time, given the psychological and spiritual dividends one stood to gain from it.

As a girl Cynthia used to love going to Mass: the otherworldly elegance of the Latin catechisms, the fragrant fume trails left in the air by the huge swinging silver censers, and the fact that everyone in the congregation, not least herself, was decked out in their very best clothes – the men in crisp blazers and trousers, the women a froth of underskirts and mantillas, black cloth everywhere, wave upon wave of it in the pews, a sea of dark, solemn self-effacement. She had been Confirmed. She had learned her *Ave Maria* and was given a jade rosary by her parents on which to tell it, all 150 times, to expiate her sins. She had believed everything the Church claimed, implicitly, perfectly. She was so devout, her mother even began to ask her, half jokingly, if she was thinking of becoming a nun.

But Faith had ebbed from her as she reached adulthood. Faith, it seemed, was for children, who were innocent enough to accept it at face value, and for very old people, who had to have something to cling to as the shadow of extinction loomed ever larger. The world was infinitely more complicated than religion could account for. Life had shades and hues that the Church's broad primary-colour statements simply could not match.

Cynthia was not lapsed. A belief, of some sort, persisted, like a high-tide mark in her soul. She returned to Faith whenever she needed it, and was always somewhat surprised to find it there where she had left it, more or less intact, a little rusty but still serviceable. The Chapel, which she was just about the only person ever to visit, had become a sanctuary for her when things got difficult – and being married to Prosper Gleed, not to mention being mother to Provender Gleed, meant things often got difficult for Cynthia. She still had her jade rosary too, and to sit for an hour in the Chapel's emptiness, thumbing the beads one by one about their silk thread and murmuring the words of the *Ave* till they lost all meaning, brought solace in even her darkest moods. The unadorned walls and vacant alcoves were a far cry from the stained-glass splendour and seething iconography she had known in her youth, but such plainness was, in a way, better. It was a closer reflection of how she felt inside.

Perhaps, after all, she should have taken the veil. A part of her still seemed to yearn for a life of nun-like simplicity and contemplation.

As a nun, for instance, Cynthia would not be sitting here this morning in the Chapel, consumed with anger and despair; would not be telling a very unusual rosary, a substitute for her jade beads; and would not be considering an act of awful, soul-imperilling sinfulness.

She had heard the reports on the radio as she ate her breakfast – the cogs of the machinery of war, starting to turn. She had known, though, when Prosper arrived home in the small hours of last night, what he had done. He had crashed around their bedroom for a while, clumsily undressing in darkness, then headed off to one of the spare rooms to sleep. He had been unwilling to get into bed with her. He had been afraid to talk to her. She, for her part, had pretended to sleep, afraid in her own way to talk to him, not wanting to hear what he had to say. She had known. He had done everything he had threatened to. The news on the radio only confirmed it. Things had gone so far. So badly out of control.

Now, in the middle of the Chapel dais, Cynthia knelt. She was no longer young. It hurt her knees to kneel on bare stone. Nonetheless she did.

She was cold. Even in summer, the Chapel retained the chill of night through to midday at the earliest. The sun took that long to warm it. She had on an ash-coloured vicuña sweater but still she was shivering. Her breath emerged in pale wisps.

Her rosary consisted of little yellow pills – Oneirodam tablets from the bottle by her bedside.

With a trembling fingertip she shifted them across the floor, one by one, left to right.

'*Ave Maria, gratia plena; Dominus tecum . . .*'

Another pill was shunted across.

'*Ave Maria, gratia plena; Dominus tecum . . .*'

And another pill.

Could she? Should she? Dare she?

'*Ave Maria, gratia plena; Dominus tecum . . .*'

And another.

34

Is watched Damien watching the news. She wondered if he was going to make the connection. The war. Provender. She prayed he would. She prayed it would dawn on him that *he* was the root cause of all this. His conscience would do the rest. He was still, all said and done, a man of conscience.

But, although Damien voiced concern about the situation, which was getting steadily graver, he didn't appear to care that much. He was preoccupied. Once or twice he mentioned getting the ransom demand out, saying it was long past due. He was expecting his Family insider to call soon and give him the go-ahead. That call, too, was long past due. Is could see he was chafing, champing at the bit. Less and less was he liking the fact that he was not in sole charge of the Provender kidnapping and that he had to be accountable to someone else. She still could not fathom his relationship with this unknown Family member. She understood only that in order to get what he was after, the money to renovate Needle Grove, Damien had entered into a pact with a representative of his very worst enemy. He had done a deal with, if not the Devil, then one of the Devil's minions. To Damien, this was not a compromise but an alliance forged by necessity. He remained, however, not best pleased about it.

On the television, the politicians kept talking about a diplomatic resolution, even as the military build-up continued. Whether they were genuinely hopeful of a peaceful outcome or just saying what an alarmed populace needed to hear, Is couldn't tell, but she felt that at the very least they were going to take things right to the brink. Like Damien, they too were at the behest of unseen masters, in this case Stanisław Kuczynski and Prosper Gleed. Is found it bizarre to think that just two days ago she had been serving drinks to the latter, had stood within a few inches of him, had suffered him to ogle her boobs. A lecherous middle-aged man, similar to countless others she had come across, all too easily captivated by the sight of a generous chest – and yet he had the wherewithal to trigger a continent-wide conflict, almost without effort. Serially unfaithful to his wife, by all accounts, and addicted to gambling – and yet, with just a word, he could set one half of Europe against the other. That was wrong. That should not be. So much responsibility should not reside in the hands of someone so irresponsible.

The phone rang.

Damien snapped the TV off and picked up the receiver.

'Yeah? . . . Oh good. About time you got in touch again. I was beginning to think— Right, right. Yes, I've been watching it. Not good . . . Uh-
huh. Yes . . . Really? Jesus! . . . You think so? It won't make matters
worse? . . . So the one I've already written is no good any more . . . No, I
told you, I don't own a videotyper. Can't afford one. I use the public-use
one at the local library . . . All right then . . . I know, keep it simple, don't
say too much . . . Fine. And then the drop-off plan as before? . . . Well,
that's something . . . OK. Nice one. 'Bye.'

He replaced the receiver and looked at Is with a broad, almost boyish
smirk.

'Remarkable,' he said.

'What is?'

'Well, I had a feeling that all that stuff' – he jerked a thumb at the
television – 'might have something to do with him.' The thumb jabbed in
the direction of the bathroom. 'It was too much of a coincidence otherwise. But I couldn't think how the one joined up with the other till that
person' – now the thumb indicated the telephone – 'said the Gleeds think
the Kuczynskis are behind the kidnapping.'

'Oh,' said Is, trying to pretend this was news to her.

'Yeah, so now we've got an even bigger stick to beat the Gleeds with.
We can ask for twice as much as we were going to.'

'How do you get that?'

'Because, Is, the Gleeds are desperate. They think their arch-enemies
have Provender, and when they find out they don't, they'll be so damn
relieved they'll cough up any amount of cash.'

'I hate to say this, but isn't that a bit greedy, Damien? And isn't it
wrong to use what's going on to your own advantage? An international
crisis—'

'No, Is,' said Damien, very firmly. 'No, it's not wrong. The end justifies
the means. The end damn well justifies the means. We were going to ask
for five million for Provender, weren't we? We could do a lot for the estate
with five million, but think what we could do with ten. Fuck it, with
fifteen. Transform this place beyond recognition. Make thousands of lives
better.'

'At the risk of making hundreds of thousands of lives worse if this war
goes ahead.'

'But it won't go ahead. Once the ransom note's delivered, the Gleeds
will know it isn't the Kuczynskis who have their precious boy and they'll
call off the dogs.'

'What if it's too late?'

'It won't be too late.'

'You can't know that for sure. If the momentum keeps building the way
it is, events could spin out of control. Something could start that just can't

be stopped. Whereas all you have to do is phone the Gleeds now, tell them everything's all right, you're the one holding Provender and not the Kuczynskis . . .'

'The money, Is. *More* money.'

'At what point, Damien, does blackmail become extortion?'

'At what point, Is, does disagreement become mutiny?'

'That's ridiculous. All I'm doing is telling you—'

Two swift strides took Damien to within arm's reach of Is. She didn't, to her surprise, shrink away from him, though every instinct she had was ordering her to. Somehow her spine stayed straight, her head remained defiantly high.

'All you're doing is telling me you haven't the guts to do this any more,' he spat. 'Telling me Rich Kid has got to you. Telling me you'd rather hand him back for nothing than try and get the most we can out of him. Is that it, Is? Is he more important to you than us?'

'Us?' she replied, more calmly than she could have thought possible. 'You're talking about everyone on the estate, I take it.'

Damien blinked. 'Yes. Exactly. Yes, I am. Is he more important than everyone on the estate?'

'No. I'm just saying I think you've lost sight of what this is supposed to be about. And – and I think this war thing has gone to your head. Suddenly you've got a tremendous amount of power, suddenly you have the capacity to prevent something truly terrible from happening, and what do you do? First thing you think of is "What can I, Damien Scrase, get out of this? How can *I* benefit?" Which, in my book, makes you no better than the people you've been fighting against all your adult life. It makes you no better than Family, Damien.'

She wished, as soon as she uttered the last sentence, that she could take it back. To compare Damien to Family was the worst insult imaginable for him. She might as well have called him a vivisectionist or a child-molester.

'Oh, Is,' he said. His tone was deadly smooth. His eyes had gone dull and hard. 'Oh, that's not kind of you at all.'

Is didn't see it coming. She heard it coming, a whirr of displaced air, a sound she had no way of recognising, but she didn't actually see Damien's hand swinging at her, knuckles first. It blindsided her. It came at her too fast.

Then there was lightning.

Then there was the feel of carpet under one side of her face, and a ringing, droning hum in her skull, and her eyes were watering and the floor was pulsing up and down woozily, as though she were at sea, and Damien, from some deep distant cavern, miles away, was lecturing her, telling her she had asked for it, she had deserved it, and he was sorry – he didn't sound sorry but he said he was – and he was heading out in a mo and she could lie there if she wanted to, that was fine by him, but she should remember she had deserved it, and he wasn't that sort of bloke, he hated that sort of bloke, the type that hit women, but she had provoked him, it was her fault, she should think about that, she could think about it while he was gone, all right?

All right?

And then he was gone. Is heard him leave. The door slammed. A key turned in the lock. The floor oozed around her. The entire flat warped and distended, as though testing its own cubic dimensions.

Faintly, from far away, Provender was calling out her name: 'Is? Is? Are you there, Is? Are you OK?'

35

A car started, stuttering, then belching out a great four-cylinder roar. The driver revved the engine a few times, to get its juices flowing, then shifted out of neutral. The engine note changed from a growl to a purposeful purr.

Romeo Moore heard these sounds, identified them straight away as belonging to a sports-model vehicle, and mused happily on the fact that well-engineered automobiles always had such nice voices. In addition to looking good, a car had to sound good. There was no point in owning a Dagenham Rapier, say, if what lay under its bonnet produced a pathetic little fart of noise. You needed the whole package, aural as well as visual. Otherwise—

A Dagenham Rapier!

Moore's eyes flashed open. He started from the park bench. He was on his feet and running almost before he knew what he was doing.

He reached the park railings just in time to see Arthur Gleed's Rapier pull out from its space, Arthur at the wheel. He watched Arthur ease into the roadway then accelerate. Tyres pained tarmac. With a squeal and a roar and a burst of blue fumes, the Rapier shot away. A moment later, it was at one of the exits from the square. A moment after that, it was gone.

Asleep!

Damn and blast it, he had fallen asleep!

Moore checked his watch. Gone eleven. The last time he remembered looking, it had been nine.

Nodded off. Hadn't hired a taxi as he had planned to.

Stupid. Careless. Unprofessional.

He had lost his suspect's trail. Arthur was doubtless on his way to look in on Provender. Moore, through his own incompetence, had fluffed his chance of following him.

He cast around, hoping against hope to see a taxi cruising by through the square. There was none. It would have been a miracle if there had been.

With a groan, he lowered his head till his brow came to rest on the tip of a railing spike.

It hurt.

That was good.

HULKING CLEF!

36

Provender crawled for the bathroom door. It wasn't easy. He had to move like a caterpillar, sliding his arms forward, following with his torso, then arching his back and bringing his legs in behind. It also wasn't easy because he wasn't sure of the door's precise location. In the end, though, he did find it. Through sheer good luck, he crawled in exactly the right direction. Through sheer bad luck, he didn't know that until after he made one of his torso lunges and banged the door with his head.

When the pain faded, he called out to Is again. As before, there was no answer. He had listened to her arguing with her accomplice. He had heard their voices rise and then that final, climactic *thwack*, followed by the sound of someone falling. A short while later, a door had slammed shut. He hoped that meant that the man had stormed out of the flat. He hoped that what had gone before signified that Is had been struck but nothing more serious.

But if it *was* nothing more serious, how come she wasn't answering? And had the man actually stormed out? The door which had slammed might not necessarily be the front one.

Provender decided it didn't matter. He thought his interpretation of the sounds was correct, and if it wasn't, he would simply have to take the consequences.

Hunkering back on his knees, he raised his hands and hooked his thumbs under the blindfold. Lately the urge to do this had become all but unbearable. In spite of Is's warning he had been desperate to take a peek at his surroundings, just to be able to use his eyes again, see *something*. He had resisted. Now, he put such considerations aside.

Up the blindfold went.

The bathroom was dim. What light there was came in from under the door. Nevertheless Provender, having been sightless for two whole days, was dazzled. He winced. He screwed his eyes shut. After several moments he prised his eyelids apart again. The line of light under the door was a strip of pure supernova. It razored his retinas. He forced himself to keep looking at it, despite the agony. The sooner his vision adjusted, the sooner he could get out there and find out what had become of Is.

Gradually supernova became magnesium flare, which became white-hot metal, which became bright sunlight, then filtered sunlight, and finally cloudy sunlight. Provender looked around at the glimmering outlines of the bathroom's fixtures and fittings, shapes he had till now known only by feel. The bathroom was not large but it was bigger than he had thought. In the utter darkness of his captivity, it had seemed tiny and close-confining.

His eyesight was blurry but good enough, he thought, for him to venture out. He reached for the door handle and yanked it down.

Brilliance flooded in, a world of glare and shine. Provender thrust the door wide and groped his way over the threshold. Blinking hard, he tried to take stock of where he was. The main room of a smallish flat. Over there, a galley kitchen. Over there, the door to a bedroom, ajar. That was a relief. It couldn't, then, be the door that had slammed shut. The man *was* out.

His eyes watered and began to sting. He rubbed them and reopened them.

The flat was shabby, cheaply furnished, low-rent. He saw a couple of plywood bookcases crammed with paperbacks and a pine table with spindly legs and a set of chairs to match. The table was just that bit too large for the place, occupying more than its fair share of floor. A tall window afforded a view of . . . It was too bright out there. Provender couldn't look directly at the view. He turned his gaze to the TV set and armchairs adjacent to the window. Just past them, poking out, he spied a pair of legs. Woman's legs.

He caterpillar-crawled over as fast as he could.

The legs belonged to Is. She was lying supine, with her head turned. Her eyes were glazed. A large red welt had formed on her left cheek. The swelling was spreading to her lower left eyelid.

'Is?'

Her eyes flicked, a minuscule movement, the irises shifting a degree or so. 'Is, it's Provender. I'm here. Are you all right?'

What an absurd question! Of course she wasn't all right. What was he thinking?

'Listen, I don't know what to do. I can't do anything. I'm still tied up. You've got shock or concussion or something, I don't know what. You're the one with the medical training, not me. But you've got to come round. You've got to help me. Then I can help you. Is! Please!'

Her eyes moved again.

'He could be coming back any minute, couldn't he. This is our chance. Come on!'

Her head rolled. She let out a murmur. Provender thought what she said was *water*.

He crossed the floor to the kitchen in his ungainly caterpillar style. Rising to his knees, he planted his elbows on the worktop and hauled himself to standing. He took a glass tumbler from the sink draining basket, filled it at the tap, then made his way back to Is in a series of small hops, cradling the tumbler in both hands. By the time he got to her at least half the water had slopped out over his fingers. More was lost as he lowered himself thumpingly down into sitting position. Still, there was some left. He brought the tumbler to Is's lips and tipped it carefully. A dribble went into her mouth, while the rest splashed onto the carpet. It wasn't the water itself that counted so much as the act of drinking. Slowly Is's eyes gained focus. She stirred, moving her arms, shifting her legs. Her hand went to her injured cheek and explored the swelling there. She was as gentle and tentative as she could be but still made herself hiss a few times. Finally, she made to sit up. Provender did what he could to assist, propping his hands beneath her back and lifting. Is, though, did most of the work. She moaned as her head came up. The colour drained from her face and she looked, to Provender, as though she might pass out. A clenching of teeth, a furrowing of brow, sheer willpower, kept her conscious.

'More water?' Provender asked.

'No,' she said, thickly. 'Just give me a second. Wait for . . . I just need to . . .'

Deep breaths. A gingerly turning of the head to one side then the other. A flexing of the fingers. Little by little she steadied herself, re-establishing her equilibrium.

'OK,' she said at last. 'Now.' She looked at the knots that bound Provender. 'In the kitchen. Drawer by the hob. Big carving knife.'

Provender found the knife and hopped back with it, holding it out at arm's length in case he stumbled. Is took it from him, he knelt down beside her, she told him to stick out his wrists, he did so, and she inserted the knife blade between his forearms and began sawing at the innermost loop of the electrical flex.

Provender thought about telling her to be careful but then thought it was better to say nothing. Time was of the essence, and he would rather she worked swiftly and he received the odd nick than she sacrificed speed for precision.

The rubber insulation on the flex parted easily. The copper wire inside put up more resistance. Is worked the knife up and down, and Provender did his bit by keeping his arms rigid so that the flex was taut against the blade's cutting edge. He wondered if Is had any idea how long her accomplice was going to be absent. He was reluctant to ask. He wasn't sure he wanted to know.

The blade was through the copper wire. The last bit of insulation split apart. The loop of flex sprang open, and rapidly the other loops loosened and unspooled. Provender parted his hands. Never had such a straightforward action brought such joy. He felt like waving his arms around all over the place, just because he could. He managed to refrain from doing so, and instead kept himself perfectly still as Is set to work on the flex at his ankles. The knife cleaved. His feet were free. Kicking off the sundered flex, Provender extended each leg in turn and rotated each foot. His hands and feet tingled as full circulation returned to them. Provender felt, for the first time in two days, whole.

He flipped the blindfold off his head, stood shakily, then reached down and helped Is up.

'Thank you,' he said, simply and, he hoped, humbly.

'Welcome,' said Is.

'I take it the, er . . .' He gestured at her cheek. 'The romance is over.'

'Don't push it,' she shot back.

'Sorry.'

'But I suppose I have been put straight on a couple of things.'

Provender was indignant, ' "Put straight"! Like a woman needs the sense knocked into her from time to time.'

'Not what I meant. I meant I don't have any illusions about Damien any more.'

'Damien.'

'No call for secrecy now. Yes. Damien Scrase is his name. And this is Needle Grove. And we're getting the hell out of here while we can.'

'I like the sound of that.' Provender didn't know much about Needle Grove and what little he did know hardly filled him with delight. Getting out of there seemed, on every level, a good idea. 'Oh, and by the way, Is? Today's my birthday. Were you aware of that? My twenty-fifth. And I have to say you've just given me the best present I've ever received.'

'Happy birthday, Provender,' Is said tightly. 'But how about you save the gratitude till we're far away and out of trouble?'

37

The trust between her and Damien was well and truly breached. As if the throbbing great haematoma on her cheek wasn't already enough of an indication, Is quickly discovered that Damien now regarded her as no less of a prisoner than Provender. The front door was locked, and her own door key was gone – Damien had pilfered it from her shoulder-bag. The emergency spare key Damien kept in a drawer in the kitchen was also gone. The door itself was sturdy, a common feature of Needle Grove flats. The original doors on the estate had been thin and skimpy, little better than sheets of plywood, easy to break down. Rather than keep replacing them all the time, the Risen London Authority had seen the economic advantage in installing heavier, more solid versions so that would-be thieves could not simply barge their way in. The corollary of this, unfortunate in the present circumstances, was that would-be escapees could not simply barge their way out.

Damien had also taken the precaution of rendering the telephone inoperable. He had removed the coiled cable which connected the receiver to the body of the phone. Is and Provender could not summon help.

'What about that way?' Provender pointed towards the windows, squinting.

'We're forty-five storeys up.'

'Even so. Isn't there a balcony out there?'

'Yeah. So what?' Is thought for a moment. 'Hang on, you might have something.'

'I might?'

Is grappled with the sliding window and managed to haul it open. The exertion brought on a wave of light-headedness, which she did her best to ignore. She stepped out onto the balcony and looked left.

Each flat in each block had one of these balconies, a little square protrusion of outdoor space. Each flat was also a mirror image of its next-door neighbour, an architectural feature intended to make the residents feel marginally less like convicts in identical cells or battery hens in matching cages. This meant that the balconies were positioned alternately close together and far apart. The balcony to Is's right was a good thirty feet away. The balcony to the left, however, was much nearer, no more than six feet.

Provender appeared behind her, shielding his eyes against the daylight.

'Who lives there?' he asked, nodding to the left-hand balcony.

'Mrs Philcox. Those are her pot plants, or the dead remains of.' There was a range of clay pots on the balcony in which nothing sprouted except clumps of moss. 'She's getting on a bit, and not quite all there any more. The good news is, she'll definitely be in. Housebound, pretty much.'

'But do you think you can jump that far?'

Is studied the gap. 'Maybe, with a run-up, but not from a standing start. And not with that kind of drop below. You think *you* can?'

Provender took a look over the balcony parapet and jerked back. 'Even if I thought I could, I wouldn't want to try.'

Is's shoulders sagged. 'Then it's hopeless.'

Provender seemed to agree. He looked indoors, surveying the layout of the flat. 'How about if we ambush him – Damien – when he returns? We could lie in wait behind the door, in the kitchen bit, leap out, bring him down. There's two of us and only one of him.'

'Have you seen him, Provender?'

'Rhetorical question, right?'

'Right.'

'I got a glimpse of him, before you stuck that needle in me, but . . .'

'He's more than a match for both of us. Trust me.'

'Even with the element of surprise?'

'Even with.'

'There's that carving knife.'

'Have you ever stabbed anyone?'

'No, but if I was ever going to, it'd be him.'

'Big talk, but it's far easier said than done. Besides, Damien carries a knife. Sheath knife. Big one. Nine-inch blade. And he knows how to use it, and would, too.'

'On me? His precious ransom cheque?'

'He doesn't have to kill you with it. He could do worse than simply kill you.'

'Good point. Or he could use it on *you*.' Provender frowned unhappily, then brightened. 'I don't suppose you've any of that stuff left?'

'Stuff?'

'What you injected me with.'

'As a matter of fact I do. There's an extra dose lying around somewhere. I kept it ready as a precaution.'

'We could inject Damien, couldn't we, then. I grab him, hold him, you shoot him full of sedative or whatever.'

'Well, it's a nice idea, but again we have the problem – don't take this the wrong way, Provender, but he's twice your size and you're hardly the big bad fighting type, are you? You could grab him but I don't think you could hold him. Not even for a moment.'

She could see Provender trying hard not to look crestfallen. She hated to be the one to prick the bubble of his male pride, but it was best to be honest. Physically, in terms of sheer aptitude for violence, Damien was several leagues above Provender. In a straight contest between the two of them, Provender would not have a prayer.

'So we're stuck.' He let out an angry gasp. 'Unless we can somehow find something to bridge a six-foot gap between— Hold on.'

Is had the idea almost at the same time he did.

'The table.'

They manhandled the table out through the window, which was just wide enough to accommodate it sideways, legs horizontal; they manoeuvred the table onto its back; they manipulated it onto the balcony parapet. Then they had to shove it straight out, swing it around and slide it across to the other balcony. All this they accomplished with much effort and grunting and the occasional curse. They were hurrying and at the same time trying not to hurry, a recipe for grazed knuckles and squashed fingers if ever there was one.

The table, as its leading edge neared the lip of the other balcony, became increasingly heavy and difficult to control. It dipped down and wanted to slip out of their grasp and fall. Is and Provender hauled on a leg each, using it like a lever. Both heard ominous creaks coming from where the legs were screwed into place.

'Don't break,' Is begged.

'Cheap piece of *mierda*,' Provender muttered under his breath.

Finally, with a thumping scrape of wood on concrete, the far end of the table made contact with the side of Mrs Philcox's balcony. With a little further straining, Is and Provender got the table surface to overlap the parapet. They let go of the legs. The table stayed put. They had done it. The gap was bridged.

'Only one problem,' Provender observed.

Is nodded. The overlap at either end was barely an inch. Not, under the circumstances, much of a margin for error.

Provender peered out over the edge of the balcony again. 'Look on the bright side. You might not fall all the way.'

'No?'

'No, there's an overpass about halfway down. You'd hit that first, most likely.'

His bravado would have been more convincing if his face hadn't been so pale.

'Is,' he said. 'You don't have to do this. I do. You can stay. Tell Damien I got away. Pretend I overpowered you or something.'

Is snorted. 'He's really going to believe that!'

Again, that crestfallen expression, badly disguised.

'The point is, Provender,' she went on, apologetically, 'this whole thing has been a mistake. I should never have got involved in the first place. Somehow I've got to make amends.'

'You already have.'

'Then, also, I've no great urge to be here when Damien gets back.'

'Fair enough,' Provender surveyed the table, precariously poised, a slender traverse, all that stood between the person crossing it and a drop of several hundred feet. Just a few thin planks. Certain death below.

He turned to Is. 'Ladies first?'

38

Gratitude Gleed went in search of her father and found him where he had been all morning, in the television room, sitting on a sofa, transfixed by the images being projected over his head via a system of magnifying lenses onto the bare white wall in front of him. The Phone was waiting in a corner of the room – there, clearly, for when the Kuczynskis rang to talk terms.

Hearing his daughter enter, Prosper Gleed patted the space next to him on the sofa. Gratitude declined the invitation.

'I just came to say we're about to have lunch, Dad. In the solarium.'

'Have someone bring something through for me.'

'Also, Arthur's dropped by. What are we supposed to tell him? About Provender.'

'Tell him whatever you like. Might as well tell him the truth. He is Family.'

Not exactly, Gratitude thought. *Step-Family perhaps. If you wanted to be totally, brutally accurate: halfling bastard.*

'If you say so,' she said. 'Dad?'

She waited for him to look round.

On the wall, a reporter with an enormous microphone was addressing the camera from beside a road. *Lower Saxony* read the caption below him. Behind him, a convoy of armoured personnel carriers was rolling past, against a background of flat green plains. Dust clouds and engine thunder were making it difficult for the reporter to do his job. He kept half ducking and swatting the air in front of his nose. About one in every three words he said was intelligible.

The glow of the epidiascoped image on the wall lit up Prosper Gleed's face. It flickered and moved there, throwing his features into shifting relief. His expression, though, beneath the changing light, stayed firm. Resolute. His eyes, bright-wide, drank in all they were seeing.

'Dad?'

Again he did not look round, and Gratitude wondered if he realised she was still there. All she wanted from him was a word of reassurance. All he had to do was turn and say, *This will get your brother back.*

He continued to gaze straight ahead.

Silently, Gratitude slipped out of the room.

Uncle Fortune was in the solarium, as were Extravagance, Arthur, Great and Carver. They were ranged around the circular glass table with glass flatware and glass-handled cutlery set before them, all of them in glass chairs except Great who was in his wheelchair. Sunshine drenched the room and permeated its many transparent surfaces, some of which refracted the light prismatically and sent lozenges of rainbow-pattern brilliance scattering in a dozen different directions.

Gratitude arrived just as the first course, gazpacho soup, was being served. Everyone tucked in apart from Arthur, who was halfway through a thespian anecdote and would not be diverted from finishing it. When he was done with his tale of a faulty camera and the perfect take that was never captured on film, he paused and looked around, expecting some display of appreciation from his audience. He was taken aback when none came.

'I'm sorry, am I missing something here?'

The others exchanged glances.

'Only, I've played to livelier crowds of old-age pensioners.' He bowed to Great. 'Begging your pardon, of course, Coriander.'

Great glared glitteringly back at him, as if to say, *Why are you using my first name? Why are you even here?*

'Good soup,' said Fortune, slurping. 'Prosp not joining us, Gratitude?'

'Busy.'

'And Cynthia?'

'Still up at the Chapel, I think,' said Extravagance.

Gratitude shot her sister a look.

'What?' Extravagance demanded.

In spite of her father's edict, Gratitude was loath to let Arthur in on the situation. It was none of his business. He took liberties as it was – for instance, turning up at Dashlands whenever he felt like it, uninvited. He behaved like he was one of the Family, this cuckoo-cousin, and he wasn't, not really, and Gratitude, whenever she could, did what she could to remind him of that fact.

'The Chapel, eh?' Arthur said. 'So what's wrong?'

'Nothing,' Gratitude replied, quickly. Too quickly.

'Oh, come off it. Aunt Cynth retreating to the Chapel? That's a sure sign all's not well. Has your dad made another conquest? Carved another notch on someone else's bedpost?'

'No.'

'What, then?'

'Perhaps,' said Carver, turning round from feeding Great, 'Mrs Gleed is simply concerned about the rather tense state of affairs in Europe.'

'Yeah, could be,' Arthur said. 'Bad business, that. You know, my director actually phoned me this morning, wondering if we shouldn't cancel tonight's performance because of it. I told him, "Never." I said, "In troubled times, people need the solace of art more, not less." I said, "Even if only one ticket-holder turns up tonight and all the rest stay home, frightened, we will play to that person as if to a full house. We will bring that courageous soul the Shakespearian consolation he is seeking." That pretty much settled it. Anyway, I'm sure it'll all blow over. I imagine that's what Uncle Prosper is busy doing right now. Trying to calm things down. Smoothing ruffled feathers. What else is a Family head for? Correct?'

He looked round the table. Silence and sombre faces told him he was way off the mark.

'Not correct. Oh dear. Oh yes, how obvious. The Poles. Our blood-guzzling chums the Kuczynskis. What's happened? They must have made some serious blunder.'

'You may as well know,' said Fortune, and explained.

The news that Provender had been abducted, possibly by the Kuczynski Family, had Arthur going through paroxysms of incredulity and anguish. He waved his hands about; he shook his head; he gasped 'No!' loud enough to be heard in the back row of the stalls. It was all very histrionic, Gratitude thought, but then with Arthur the boundary between profession and life had long since become blurred. Drama was his natural state of being. Everything was an act.

'My God, and there we were at the party just the other night,' he said, 'me and Provender, having a lovely time. Rubbing along like we always do. And then – somebody nabbed him. Right from under our noses. I can't believe it.'

'None of us can,' said Extravagance.

'I even invited him to the show tonight. All of you, too. I insisted he come. That feels so – so *trivial* now.'

'So perhaps you will cancel tonight's performance after all,' Gratitude suggested. She said it with just a soupçon of viciousness, hoping Arthur's answer would confirm her low opinion of him.

It did.

'Hell, no.' Arthur bent over his soup and dipped his spoon in. 'Show must go on and all that.' He glanced up. 'I mean, it's what Provender would want, isn't it? Surely?'

39

What Provender would have wanted, right then, was not to have to crawl across an upturned pine table, forty-five storeys up, with no guarantee whether that the table would support his weight or that it would remain securely perched on the two balcony parapets while he was on it. He would have wanted anything but this sickened feeling in the pit of his stomach, this sense that every last drop of moisture in his mouth had somehow transferred itself to the palms of his hands, above all this fear that if fate was going to choose any day for him to meet a messy, spectacular death, why not today, the twenty-fifth anniversary of his birth? Fate had a nasty sense of humour, after all. This was not the day for him to be inviting it to play one of its grim practical jokes.

Then again, he had no desire to remain in Damien Scrase's flat, and the table was his only viable means of escape.

The opportunity for Provender to entertain these thoughts arose because Is had left him alone on the balcony. Saying she had just remembered something, she had ducked back into the flat, and Provender was waiting for her to come out again. He wasn't crossing the table without her holding one end of it down as they had planned. What she was actually doing in the flat, he had no idea. A part of him wished she would get on with it. A part of him didn't.

Finally she emerged. She had with her the hypodermic syringe and a medical ampoule containing a fluid. She showed them to Provender, then bundled them up in a cloth and stuck the bundle in her shoulder-bag.

'Just in case,' she said.

'Not for me, then.'

'Not this time.'

'Funny. I could do with being unconscious right now.'

'Me too.'

Provender gestured at the table and looked plaintive. 'Are you sure you don't want to go first?'

'You're heavier than me. If it can take you, it'll take me.'

'What if it can't take me?'

'It will.'

'You know that for certain?'

'Stop fannying about and get on the table, Provender.'

Is placed her hands close together on the end of the table and pressed down with all her might. Provender, feeling his heart start to pound, slid himself into the gap between her left arm and the table leg nearest the building. He eased himself out across the table's underside, lying flat, braced on his forearms. His feet were still on the balcony floor, taking most of his weight. Cautiously he lifted one leg, then the other. His weight was transferred to his torso.

The table creaked. Provender froze, his legs sticking straight out behind him.

'Can't do this,' he breathed. 'It's going to break.'

'It's not. Keep going.'

Little encouraged, Provender wriggled a few inches further forward.

The table creaked again, a deeper, sadder sound this time – the sound of resignation, almost, as if the table accepted it wasn't going to survive this ordeal.

Provender thought of the drop beneath him. He thought of the thickness of the wood that was keeping him from falling, or rather the thinness of it. An inch at most. Closer on three-quarters of an inch.

Three-quarters of an inch of cheap pine. It was nothing. Nothing. He might as well be lying on a sheet of balsa.

'Provender.'

Is's voice. Urging.

But what Provender was listening to was the sound of space around him. The faint breeze thrumming through Needle Grove's canyons. Distant shouts that echoed nebulously. The height – and depth – of the world he had now ventured into. Air. Immensity.

He quailed inside. He clenched his eyes shut. He wanted to slide back onto the balcony where Is was, where safety was, but he couldn't. He couldn't move.

A table. A few screwed-together planks.

He was going to die.

'Provender, listen to me. You've just got to go forward. There's nothing else you can do. You'll be fine.'

'Is . . .'

'I mean it. I promise.'

She meant it. She promised.

How could she promise something like that? That he would be fine? She couldn't.

But what mattered was that she said she could.

Provender took a breath; held it. He clamped his teeth together. Eyes still tight shut, he threw himself fully onto the table. He slithered forward. He did it fast. Knees, elbows, scrambling, and there was a noise coming out of him, a fusion of expelled breath and battle cry, low-pitched, rising.

The table flexed beneath him. The table jumped. The table juddered and groaned. He heard a yelp from Is. He fell.

Forward.

A short plunge.

Landed hands first on Mrs Philcox's balcony.

Tumbled.

Rolled.

Fetched up with his head between two plant pots.

He lay dazed, glad, numb, exultant. Alive.

Then he levered himself up onto his elbows and craned his neck to peer over the parapet at Is. He was about to say something blithe and plucky like 'Nothing to it' or 'Hop on over then', until he saw Is's face . . . and realised that the table was no longer there, suspended between the two balconies.

At that precise instant, from far below there came a faint but fierce *crash*.

40

Merlin Milner had had a busy but so far fruitless morning in Needle Grove. He had crossed off five names on his list of seven. He had not yet found the person he was after.

Still, he refused to be discouraged.

Even when a pine table plunged from the sky and almost killed him.

Shortly before this incident occurred, Milner had decided to take a breather, grab a bite to eat, and assess the state of his investigations. It never hurt to take time out to regroup and retrench – especially after having come across five of the least savoury individuals he had ever had the misfortune to encounter, in surroundings that were not, anyway, conducive to feelings of goodwill toward one's fellow-men. Moreover, Milner wasn't looking forward to tackling the last two names on the list, and certainly didn't want to do it on an empty stomach.

Midway up Block 26 there was a mezzanine area which boasted a shopping arcade, along with a café and various other communal amenities. Milner had glimpsed it a couple of times on his way between different flats, as the lift had a tendency to stop at that floor to let people in or out. At the café he purchased a ham sandwich and a bottle of orange juice. The sandwich was so dry as to be near inedible, the juice so sharp as to be near undrinkable. He persevered with both while sitting at a cigarette-singed plastic table and perusing his list of suspects and the notes he had appended to the names of the ones he had already approached.

First in line, alphabetically, came Sable di Santis, who lived at Flat 37J. She had opened her door circumspectly – it proved to be a common habit among the denizens of Needle Grove – and had glared at Milner with an unnerving mixture of aggression and dismissal. She was taller than him by nearly a foot and had short spiky hair that matched the short-spiked dog collar she was wearing. The towelling bathrobe she had on revealed a glimpse of leather corsetry. While greeting her and introducing himself, Milner glanced past her and noticed an array of implements mounted on one wall of the main room – whips, manacles, ball-gags, and some large, long, nobbly devices the sight of which, frankly, alarmed him. He was still speaking when a muffled female voice called out from an adjoining room in the flat, asking Sable if she was coming back. Sable snapped a reply: 'Shut your mouth, bitch!' Then, not much more pleasantly, she told

Milner she was busy with a client, he should state his business, otherwise fuck off. Milner apologised, said he'd made a mistake, got the wrong flat, sorry for bothering her, goodbye.

So much for SABLE DI SANTIS – LESBIAN SADIST.

Next up was Serena Drummer, down on the fourth floor, flat number 4P. Milner had arrived just in time to find her locking her door, on her way out with a group of snivelling, clamouring children around her legs. 'Miss Drummer?' he had asked, and had been firmly and tartly corrected: 'Mrs.' She wasn't any more warm or agreeable a woman than Sable di Santis, and during her conversation with Milner broke off to scold each of her children at least once. She had dull, grainy skin, lank hair, a chipped front tooth, an all-over air of harassment. She was, however, surprisingly forthcoming. She was just off with the kids to visit her husband, she explained. Went every Tuesday. He was inside, she said. Been banged up for killing someone eight years ago. Brixton Towers jail. He didn't do it, though. Well, he did. But the bastard had it coming. Fiddled with one of the kids, didn't he. 'Anyway,' she said, 'if yer another journalist after me story, I in't talkin' to yer. Not till we've discussed terms.' Milner informed her he wasn't a journalist. 'Why you wastin' my fuckin' time then?' she snorted, and strode off with her brood in tow. Milner couldn't help but wonder if her husband, after all this time in clink, found it curious that at least three of her offspring were under eight years old. Did he ask himself how she kept getting pregnant? Or were conjugal visits less well supervised than Milner had been led to believe?

Not his problem, though. And SERENA DRUMMER, MURDER MAN SEER, wasn't his problem either.

Sherman Dungate, of Flat 19C, answered his door in vest and underpants but appeared fully clothed thanks to the tattoos that covered his torso to the neck, his arms to the wrists and his legs to the ankles. There were skulls, roses, angels and naked women on his body but the majority of the tattoos were non-representational, zigzags and swirls and interlocking knots, like a kind of animal marking, blue-ink camouflage. He was liberally pierced, too, with a dozen earrings, a nose stud, a lip ring, and a nipple ring prominent through the fabric of his vest. He was skeletal-skinny, with rodent eyes, and the moment he caught sight of Milner his expression turned peevish and sullen. 'You're new, aintcha,' he said. 'All right, I'll give you your bung. But tell your Super I can't keep paying off every fucking one of you who turns up at my door. I got a business to run here, you know.' Before Milner could say anything, Dungate disappeared into the flat and returned with a wad of greasy, crumpled banknotes. 'Fifty usually covers it,' he said, licking a finger and peeling off five tenners. 'Cop tax,' he sneered, holding out the money. At last it dawned on Milner what was going on, and he assured Dungate that he wasn't a policeman, at which the other man brightened. 'Oh, you're here for some stuff then, are you?' Milner said no, not that either. Now

Dungate became resentful. 'So why you fucking bothering me? There's half a dozen buyers probably been scared off by seeing you here. You're costing me money, man.' Milner tried to apologise but Dungate launched into a volley of invective, using all sorts of unflattering terms to describe Milner, *time-waster* being the least offensive. Milner beat a retreat.

SHERMAN DUNGATE was many things, including a MEAN DRUGS THANE, but he was not, Milner was quite sure, Provender Gleed's kidnapper.

Fourth on the list came Dudley St Barstow, and although Milner did not actually meet the man face to face, what he heard through the door to Flat 48F was enough to convince him that St Barstow was not holding Provender on the premises. He seemed to have plenty of livestock in there, however, to judge by the clucks and squawks and woofs and oinks that emanated from within, and he seemed to be enjoying an unnatural relationship with several of them. Milner, ear pressed to the door, heard a crooning male voice compliment a bird on its alluring tail feathers, refer admiringly to some mammal's shanks, and entice another mammal to come over and snuffle around for a treat he had hidden somewhere in his lap. St Barstow cracked jokes with the animals. He sounded a lot like an Arab sheik immersed in his harem, doting on his many concubines. Milner did not knock on the door. Nothing on earth would have persuaded him to meet the man inside.

And so DUDLEY ST BARSTOW, exponent of WRY ODD BEAST LUST, was eliminated from Milner's enquiries.

It was with some haste that Milner had moved on to Dennis Sandringham, who proved to be the best of a bad bunch. Sandringham looked, dressed, was coiffed, above all *smelled*, like the perfect lothario. As the flat door opened, a waft of cologne greeted Milner, then Sandringham did too. Immaculate in blazer and cravat, late-middle-aged but not looking it, he invited Milner in, offered him a nip of sherry, behaved like the most beneficent of hosts, and did not bat an eyelid when Milner asked to use his bathroom, a pretext for taking a sneaky peek around the entire flat. The phone rang while he was doing so, and when he returned to the main room, satisfied that Provender was not here, he found Sandringham cradling the receiver and chatting in such a way that Milner had no doubt the person on the other end of the line was a favoured female. 'One of my ladyfriends,' Sandringham explained after he hung up. 'Wants me to drop round and see her. Can't say no, can I? She'll want me to stick my todger in that dried-up crack of hers, worse luck, but a chap has to earn a living somehow. Speaking of which,' he added, insinuatingly, 'I could fit you in if you like.' Milner made his excuses. 'I do men as well, you know,' said Sandringham. Milner made more excuses, vehement ones this time, and left.

DENNIS SANDRINGHAM, DAMN DASHING SINNER, had not been the likeliest candidate for the role of Provender's kidnapper. Milner had felt obliged to check him out anyway, just to be sure. He rather wished he hadn't.

So, five down, two to go; and the final two were the ones Milner was most hopeful about, and most dreading meeting. Their names had given him the strongest hits out of all the seven. Last in alphabetical order was Demetrius Silver, who lived at the very top of the block in Flat 60M. DEMETRIUS SILVER, the anagrams said, IS DEVIL MUSTERER. Milner envisaged a goateed Satanist in a flat adorned with pentacles and inverted crucifixes, black candles guttering everywhere, the curtains permanently drawn.

It was an unappetising image, but the question was whether or not it was preferable to the impression Milner had built up of the resident of Flat 45L, one Damien Scrase.

From DAMIEN SCRASE Milner had extracted a plethora of anagrams, none of which was exactly a source of great comfort: SCARES MAIDEN, CRANIA MESSED, MEAN CAD RISES, INCREASES MAD, I END MAS-SACRE . . . The anagrams spake sooth. This Scrase fellow was not some-one to be taken with a pinch of salt. He was, if not unhinged, then close to it. Potentially very dangerous. I END MASSACRE could, Milner supposed, be regarded as a good attribute rather than a bad. Then again, a person who ended a massacre might well be the very same person who started it, and in the light of the other anagrams Milner was more inclined towards the negative interpretation of the phrase rather than the positive.

The Satanist or the madman? It was a tough call, and in order to defer the decision, Milner found an exit from the shopping arcade and went outdoors.

He was on an overpass. The sun, now at its zenith, sent a hard white light straight down on his head. He shaded his eyes and basked in the brilliance, thinking that in these slivers of space between buildings the presence of direct sunshine must be a rarity and a blessing. He wondered if areas of Needle Grove ever even saw the sun during winter, when it was low and usually behind cloud.

He decided he would amble the length of the overpass, to the adjacent block, and come back. Idly he mused on Romeo Moore. How was he getting on? How far had he got in his quest to nail Arthur Gleed as the culprit? Not far at all, Milner suspected. Moore was a good anagram-matic detective but not, to be perfectly honest, as good an anagrammatic detective as Milner. Often Milner felt he was carrying Moore, doing a greater than fair share of the work. In any partnership, however much of a meeting of equals it appeared to be, there was inevitably one person who was superior to the other. An unwelcome truth but it had to be acknow-ledged. And if the current divergence of investigative paths proved any-thing, it would prove that.

On this uncharitable note, Milner sallied forth along the overpass . . . and that was when the table, like a divine judgement, came hurtling down from heaven.

It missed him by inches. It landed slap bang in front of his right toecap. If he had been half a stride further on, if he had started walking a split second sooner, Milner would have been right under it. He would have been killed instantly.

He watched the table, as if in slow motion, hit the concrete in front of him. It seemed to dismantle itself, shrugging into its component parts, the planks of its top separating, its legs splaying, its bracing timbers splintering in all directions. The impact made an almighty *whump* but was also somehow soundless, too stunningly loud for Milner's ears to comprehend. Fragments and flinders flew. The bulk of the table collapsed, plank bouncing off plank, shard off shard, slithering, spreading, coming to rest. Milner found himself staring at a heap of firewood at his feet, and he thought, *That used to be a table*, and then he thought, *Was that a table?* It seemed inconceivable that the wreckage just seconds ago had had shape, had been functional, had been a Thing and not merely Stuff.

Reflexively he anagrammed the word *table*.

TABLE – BLEAT

That was all. Only BLEAT.

Then sense returned. His scattered wits came thronging back. He glanced up where the table had come from, not really looking. He saw tower blocks, balconies, windows, sky, sun. An impression of Needle Grove bearing down angrily upon him. He spun on his heel. He headed for the exit he had come out of. He plunged back into the shopping arcade, back into apparent safety, into a place where tables did not, could not, fall on you from a great height. He fetched up against a shopfront. He leaned into it for support, panting. Adrenalin surged through him like jolts of electricity. His legs went weak. He slumped. His heart rat-a-tat-tatted. He stayed there, shellshocked, for he didn't know how long.

Death. Death had come within a hair's breadth of getting him.

Gradually Milner began to realise how lucky he had been. How fortunate he was to be alive still. With that realisation a calm began to descend on him, and his breathing slowed and so did his heart rate.

What he would never know was that the falling table incident was a near-miss in more ways than one.

Had he remained outdoors a moment longer, had he kept looking up, Milner would have seen two heads appear, looking down from adjacent balconies directly overhead, fifteen storeys above the overpass. He would, if he had been in full possession of his faculties, surely have recognised one of the heads as belonging to none other than Provender Gleed.

That was how close Merlin Milner came to cracking the Provender Gleed case, and in the process winning his gentlemen's bet with Romeo Moore.

Painfully close.

Lamentably close.

Tragically close.

41

Is felt many things when the table dropped away. The first was annoyance. If Provender hadn't scuttled across in such a frantic hurry, the table
would not have started bouncing and the end she was holding down
would not have slipped out of her grasp. The next thing she felt was
chagrin. She should have held on tighter. She was to blame for the table
falling, not Provender. Then came exasperation, as an old, familiar
thought-routine welled to the surface: *Typical Family, taking everything,
leaving nothing for anyone else*. Finally there was a peculiar kind of guilt,
as she recalled the real reason she had gone back into the flat before
Provender set off across the table – not to fetch the hypodermic, as she had
claimed, but to leave a kind of time-bomb for Damien. She had committed
an act of petty vengeance, and already karma had caught up with her. She
had done something she should never have stooped to doing, and here was
her reward, to be stranded on the balcony with her means of escape well
and truly gone.

All these emotions came and went in a flash. It then occurred to her that
there might have been somebody below when the table fell. She poked her
head out over the parapet. Provender, on Mrs Philcox's balcony, did the
same.

The table had struck the overpass. It was in about a thousand pieces
but none of those pieces, thank God, was embedded in the anatomy of
a human being. There was no one on the overpass. The only person
adversely affected by the table's fall was Is herself.

'Shit,' she sighed. She looked across at Provender. His body language
said *puzzled* and also *sheepish*. 'Well, that's that, then. What the hell am I
going to do now?'

'Erm . . .' Provender scratched his head. 'No idea. Bugger. I'm sorry, Is.
I don't even know how it happened.' His expression turned hopeful.
'Look, I could go into Mrs What's-her-name's flat and asked to use her
phone. Call the police.'

'We've no idea how quickly they'll get here.'

'If they hear my name, pretty quickly.'

'They might think it's a hoax call.'

'I didn't think of that. Still, it's our best chance.'

'But if Damien gets back from the library before the police arrive . . .'

Provender nodded. 'Then you just have to jump.'

'Are you joking?'

'Nope. Deadly serious.'

'I can't jump that distance. We already established that.'

'Why not? You could if we were on the ground.'

'Maybe. But we're not on the ground. If we were it wouldn't matter, I could jump and miss. Here, I can't.'

'But you won't miss. You'll make it.'

'Says who?'

'Says me. Is, a moment ago you promised me I'd get across that table safely. Lo and behold I did. Now I'm making you the same promise. You *will* jump across. You *will* reach this side. And I'll be here to catch you. Just do it.'

There was complete earnestness in his face and voice. He believed implicitly what he was saying. He was trying to make her believe it implicitly too.

To her surprise, Is found herself clambering up onto the parapet.

The building swooped away beneath her. Her entire body went numb. Her head became as empty as a balloon.

She lurched back down onto the balcony and stood there clutching the parapet and trying not to vomit. She wasn't scared of heights, but that meant nothing when you were teetering five hundred feet above the earth, contemplating a six-foot jump onto a foot-wide concrete wall. Then, the natural terror of falling took hold and overrode all else. It wasn't even a tussle between instinct and logic. There simply was no logic in what Provender was encouraging her to do.

'Is,' he said, 'get up there again and jump.'

'Fuck off, rich boy. You do it, if it's so easy.'

'Just spring forward. Throw yourself. I'll be here. I'll grab you, cushion your landing.'

'You won't cushion my landing because I'll be landing right fucking down there and unless you plan to be standing under me like a one-man fireman's blanket . . .'

'Do you want to be there when Damien gets home?'

'I don't have a choice, do I.'

'Yes, you do, and it's jump.'

Is thought of Damien coming home and finding her alone in the flat. She could undo her 'time-bomb', that wasn't a problem, but there would be no getting around the fact that Provender had absconded. That was something she could not undo, and there was just no predicting how Damien would react. The lump on her cheek was testament to that, not to mention the way her left eye was starting to puff shut.

She heaved herself, trembling, back up onto the parapet. There, she clutched the side of the building, shuffled her feet forward till the tips of her toes were at the parapet's outermost edge, and waited for an upsurge of courage.

And waited.

And waited.

Courage didn't seem to want to arrive. Every nerve in her was telling her to step back. Every cell in her recoiled from the drop in front of her.

If she leapt, for a moment she would be in flight between the balconies, nothing below her, greedy gravity eager to gets its hands on her and drag her down.

She could not see herself doing it.

Then she was doing it.

She did not know how or why. She had no idea what impelled her. All at once, obeying some subconscious command, she crouched, tensed her legs, put everything she had into it, and sprang.

There was no sense of transition. No notion of flight. One moment she was on Damien's balcony, the next she was on Mrs Philcox's.

Or *almost* on Mrs Philcox's.

One foot scraped the parapet. Then the lip of the parapet jarred into her knee. Then she was sliding, flailing, tumbling. She knew she had failed. She was going to fall.

Then Provender had her. His arms were around her torso, his hands scrabbling for purchase, finding it in her clothing, in the strap of her shoulder-bag. She dangled, clinging onto him, he clinging onto her, and then she began kicking against the parapet, pushing herself up against it with her toes, mad, panicked, desperate to get onto the balcony, not caring what it took, screaming, yelling, clawing, fighting, and Provender hauled backwards, and the parapet was under her belly and then the balcony was beneath her and Provender was spreadeagled next to her, and Is caressed the solidity of the balcony's concrete floor, loved it like she had loved nothing before.

A long time later, still sprawled flat out, Is said, 'Did you honestly believe I'd manage it?'

'Not for a second,' Provender replied.

'You absolute fucking bastard.'

'I know.'

'When all this is over, I'm going to kill you. You know that, don't you?'

Provender grinned. 'It will be a sweet death.'

She punched him. It was the least he deserved.

42

Lunch was done and Arthur took his leave. Threading his way through the house, he got a little lost. He was still not totally familiar with the layout – really, the place was a maze – but with time and a few further visits he would, he felt, have it solved.

He emerged into one of the drawing rooms, expecting it to be an entrance hall. There he came upon his aunt, Cynthia, who was sitting with several string-bound stacks of post in front of her. She looked – and it was hardly surprising – desolate.

'Arthur?'

'I know all about it,' Arthur said, going over to her. 'I am so, so sorry.'

She made a vague gesture of acknowledgement which turned into a trembling caress of her forehead. 'Birthday cards,' she said, indicating the letters. 'For Provender. Most arrived today. From well-wishers out there. You do know it's his birthday?'

'He mentioned it the other night.'

'Twenty-five. Not a special age, like twenty-one or forty. Not a milestone. But still, a quarter of a century.'

Arthur laid a hand on Cynthia's shoulder.

His own mother he loved. She was outspoken, forthright in her feelings, handsome in a rough-hewn Hebridean way, and she had defended him throughout his boyhood against the taunts and jibes that were frequently flung at him, while also encouraging him to stand up for himself (it had not been easy, growing up a Gleed in a small island community). For all that, she was not a woman like Cynthia Gleed. Arthur was in awe of his aunt. She was glamorous, ethereal, saintly, compassionate, forgiving . . . In a word, perfect. The kind of mother every son should have. The kind of mother he, in furtive, wistful moments, wished *he* had had.

His heart went out to her now, and at the same time he inwardly damned Provender for any and all of the distress he had caused Cynthia over the years, the long litany of upsets and disappointments he had brought to this fine, upstanding, blameless woman.

'If there's anything I can do to help . . .'

Cynthia patted his hand. 'Thank you, Arthur, no. I can't think of anything.'

'If you like, I could go back to the Chapel with you. We could pray together.' Arthur had never prayed for anything in his life, but for Cynthia he would. Happily.

'No need, Arthur. That's kind, but it's all under control. I know what I have to do.'

'Oh. Well. If you're sure . . .'

She nodded, sure.

'I'll be getting back to town, then,' Arthur said. 'We're having a full-dress run-through this afternoon. Clear up a few snags that happened last night. The director said it isn't necessary, but I wasn't completely happy with the performance, and when a Gleed's not completely happy there's no rest until he or she is. Isn't that right?'

'I agree,' said Cynthia, with definiteness.

'Anything and everything must be done to bring about the right conclusion.'

'Absolutely.'

She seemed cheered, and all through the drive back to London Arthur was pleased to think he had brought her comfort with his words. A better son than her own son, he opined. Far more deserving of her maternal affections than Provender would ever be.

43

Winifred Philcox was surprised to see her son Barry standing on her balcony, tapping on the window. He hadn't rung to tell her he was visiting. Come to think of it, he hadn't called in ages, and she couldn't remember when he had last dropped round. A month ago? A year? Time was strange, wasn't it. Sometimes it shot by and sometimes it didn't seem to pass at all.

Winifred made her way to the window as fast as her trick hip would allow. She signalled to Barry that she would need his help sliding it open. Oh, and look, Barry had brought his girlfriend with him. Andrea, Angela, something like that. Winifred had met her twice previously. They hadn't got on. Not good enough for Barry, that was the trouble. Barry was a prize and that Andrea/Angela girl simply didn't deserve him.

Still, Winifred was impeccably polite as she greeted them. She told them to come in, come in. She went to hug Barry and he seemed startled, but he returned the hug. Winifred then held out her hand to Andrea/Angela and said it was nice to see her again.

'I'm sorry,' she added, 'you'll have to remind me. Is it Andrea or Angela?'

'Neither,' said the girl. 'Don't you recognise me, Mrs Philcox?'

'Of course I do,' Winifred said with a sniff. 'You're Barry's Andrea. Or Angela.'

'No, I'm Is. I used to live next door, sort of. With Damien.'

'Don't be daft. You're Andrea or Angela. I remember that Is. She looked nothing like you. Lovely girl, though.' Winifred turned to Barry. 'Now then, young man, why have I seen so little of you lately?'

'Erm . . . Because I've been holed up in an ashram in the Himalayas for the past decade, pondering on *koans*?'

Andrea/Angela hissed at him sharply, which Winifred chose not to comment on. Really, though, a girl should never backchat her man like that. No wonder she had that big bruise on her cheek and that swollen eye. Probably asked for it.

'Mrs Philcox,' Andrea/Angela said, 'actually we haven't got time to stop and talk. Could we use your phone?'

Winifred turned round again. 'All right, I've been very patient with you, young lady, but even I have my limits. I was speaking to my son and I'll thank you not to interrupt. When and if you want to ask me something, you can jolly well wait until the right moment arises. Otherwise keep yourself to yourself.' She clucked her tongue, uttered a little snarl, and shook her head. Honestly!

'As a matter of fact, er, Mum,' said Barry, 'we do rather need to use the phone.'

'Go on then,' Winifred said, somewhat irritably. That girl had put her in a bad mood. Completely ruined what should have been a happy reunion. It hadn't escaped Winifred's notice that Barry appeared not to have shaved for three days. The blame for this clearly lay with Andrea/Angela. She was a bad influence on him in so many ways. He used to be such a clean and tidy lad.

'Dead,' Barry said, with his ear to the phone receiver. 'No dial tone. Nothing.'

'Are you sure, Prov—Barry?' said Andrea/Angela.

'If Barry says it's dead, it's dead,' said Winifred. 'Is it really, Barry?'

'As a dodo. When did you last pay your bill, Ma?'

'I don't know. Can't remember. I'm sure it was recently.'

'Well, I'm afraid you've been cut off.'

A light dawned in Winifred's head. 'That'll be why you haven't rung in a while. I bet you've been trying and trying to get through.'

'Yes. Quite. That's it.'

'Payphone, then,' said Andrea/Angela. 'That's our best chance.'

Barry agreed, and together the two of them made for the door.

'You're going?' said Winifred, not even trying to hide her dismay. 'Already?'

'I'm sorry, we have to,' Barry said. 'It's been great to see you. I'll call again soon, I promise.'

'You won't even stay for a cup of tea?'

'We'd love to but we just can't. Next time.'

'Well, take care then. Look after yourself.'

'Thanks, I fully intend to.'

It might be argued that Mrs Philcox, mild senile dementia notwithstanding, was not in fact wrong to mistake Provender for her own son. After all, Family members were in some sense members of everyone's family. People knew them as well as, and sometimes better than, their own kin. And people often preferred them, or the idea of them, to their own kin.

Certainly Barry's visit, brief though it was, left Mrs Philcox with a warm glow of happiness that lasted the remainder of the day. Her son, whom it so happened she had not seen in nearly four years, still loved her. Her son, who in fact couldn't stand the sight of her any more, still cared.

44

Anxiety dogged their steps as they headed along the corridor towards the lift bank. It seemed that at any moment Damien might appear. He might be riding a lift up to this floor right now. The lift car would stop, the door would roll open, he would step out – and there would be Provender and Is straight in front of him, not where they were supposed to be, and with nowhere to hide.

Reaching the lift bank, Is stabbed the call button urgently. Nothing appeared to happen, but the lifts in this block, as in all of them, were notoriously sluggish and sometimes simply refused point-blank to work, for reasons no repairmen could fathom. If lifts had souls, the ones in Needle Grove were as downtrodden and surly as those of long-abused slaves. They bore a grudge about their lives of constant hard labour and all the times they had been pissed in and shat in and the fact that the legal minimum of maintenance work was done to keep them going. They resented their own existences, and it showed.

Is couldn't bear to be out here in the corridor, exposed, waiting for a lift to deign to come. She tried the button a couple more times, then jerked her thumb towards a nearby access door and said, 'The stairs.'

45

'May I be of assistance?'

The voice was mildly accented and polite but with an undertow of quiet warning. It belonged to an Asian man – Chinese, Milner thought – with a soft round face, hair that had receded to the crown, and eyes that were deep-set and yellowed and, at this moment, wary.

'Only,' the man continued, 'you're leaning against my shop window, and I'm always a bit concerned when people lean against my shop window.' He gave a wry grimace. 'It often precedes people breaking my shop window.'

Milner immediately straightened up, to prove that he was not the type of person who did that type of thing.

'Sorry. Wasn't really thinking. I was taking a rest. I've just had a bit of a sort of close shave, you see.'

The shopkeeper nodded, understanding only too well. 'Ah yes. You're not a resident, are you? I can tell. Needle Grovers have a certain look about them, and you don't have it. Though you seem to be well on your way to having it. What happened? Run into one of the gangs? Get stuck in a lift for an hour?'

'No, I just grabbed a bite to eat from that café over there—'

'Say no more. The food there is a traumatic experience.'

'No, it wasn't that. Then I stepped outside for a breath of what passes for fresh air in this city, and somebody went and dropped a table on me.'

The shopkeeper shrugged, as if such an event was a daily occurrence in Needle Grove. 'They missed, though.'

'Just barely. I swear to God, an extra layer of skin and I'd have been a dead man.'

'You're lucky.'

'Don't I know it.'

'Lyman Ho,' said the shopkeeper, extending a hand.

'Merlin Milner,' said Milner, shaking it.

'I am, as you might have guessed, the proprietor of this establishment.' Mr Ho rapped an affectionate knuckle on the shop window. 'Mr Ho's All-Day Emporium. Robbed and/or vandalised a grand total of seventy-eight times since I took over the lease, and still in business.'

'That's a record to be proud of.'

'I like to think so. Would it be rude of me to ask why you've come to the Grove? It's simply that we get very few outsiders here and you seem, if I might say so, not the typical visitor. A cut above that.'

Milner was only too happy to accept the compliment. 'I'm here on business. I can't really tell you much more than that. It's confidential and rather serious.'

'Forgive my enquiry. I'm famously nosy. I like to know everything that's going on. It's a useful trait for a shopkeeper, to be interested in the lives of all his customers and potential customers, but sometimes, I realise, I go too far. I cross the boundary of good manners. You English and your good manners – it's very confusing for a foreigner like me. You all know where the lines are drawn but you're damned if you're going to let anyone else in on the secret.'

Milner smiled. Already he liked Mr Ho, and Milner wasn't someone who warmed to people easily. Then there was Mr Ho's name, his full name, Lyman Ho. It hardly even needed anagrammatising. Just swap forename and surname around, and hey presto, instant trustworthiness.

'You must be from Hong Kong, correct? Anglo-Saxon first name like that.'

'Indeed. Son of very prestigious banking family. Not Family, not quite, though we had aspirations to be. Perhaps a couple more generations and we'd have made it. But it wasn't to be.'

'The Shanghai Uprising.'

'The great revolution.' Mr Ho sneered. 'When the Four Acquaintances took power and the people of China became a single, billion-strong Family. And my own family, like many others, was obliged to . . . "pool our assets", the phrase was. "Had our assets stolen by the government", more like. We were truly Shanghaied. No more rich, no more poor. Everyone equal. No Families lording it over everyone else. And look how well it turned out.'

'And naturally you emigrated, and you ended up here. Running this place.'

'It's not glamorous, it's not lucrative, but it's a living. And, if all goes well, it's a start. Three, four generations from now, maybe there'll be All-Day Emporiums across the entire country, and maybe a couple of generations after that the Hos will be a Family. It's possible. Anything's possible.'

Milner looked from Mr Ho's modest retail enterprise to Mr Ho's dreamy expression, and saw a gulf between the two that all the ambition in the world could not bridge.

Time to change the subject. It was obvious to Milner that Mr Ho was an unparalleled source of local knowledge and might be able to help him with the dilemma he presently faced. Chances were Mr Ho knew at least one of the two names remaining on his list, if not both. Some inside info on Damien Scrase and Demetrius Silver would come in handy.

As Milner opened his mouth to speak, there was a commotion at the far end of the shopping arcade. Turning, Milner saw a bustling group of about thirty people come into view. They were a mixed lot: elderly women, overweight middle-aged males, some teenagers, a smattering of children. What they had in common was an air of eager excitement and the fact that each was carrying a candle.

The group passed by Mr Ho's shop and headed out into daylight.

'ClanFans,' observed Mr Ho. 'If I'm not mistaken, the official Needle Grove Block Twenty-Six ClanFan Society.'

'Where are they off to? What are the candles for?'

'To hold a vigil. Didn't you know? It's Provender Gleed's birthday today.'

'Oh. Ah.' Milner hadn't known. But then, unlike his partner, he didn't follow the Families.

'Yes, they'll stand in a ring, sing "Happy Birthday". It's a ritual they have.'

Little do they realise, Milner thought to himself, *that the person whose birthday they're celebrating is actually here. Provender might even be able to hear them singing.*

'Mr Ho,' he said, trying his best to make it sound as if what he was about to say had no connection with the foregoing exchange, 'a short while ago you asked if you could be of assistance. As it happens, you can.'

'You'd like to buy something?' Mr Ho started to usher him towards the shop entrance. 'Be my guest.'

'No, it's not that. It's more to do with . . . I'm looking for someone. Two people, to be exact. One's called Demetrius Silver, and he's—'

Mr Ho's expression turned sour. 'Don't. Don't mention that person. A wicked, wicked man. They say he sacrifices babies. I don't believe it myself, but I do know that he's involved in some very dark practices. He keeps coming in and asking if I could get a goat's skull in stock. A goat's skull! As if I can just ring up my wholesaler and order half a dozen. He offers to pay me handsomely for it, but that makes no difference. I'd rather not help a Black Magician if I can avoid it. He does have a fondness for tinned apricots, however. Don't ask me why.'

'The other person is Damien Scrase,' said Milner. 'Would you by any chance know him too?'

'Damien? I know him well.'

'What's he like?'

'Damien . . . Thoroughly decent. A prince among men.'

Milner frowned. That didn't seem right. It didn't tally with the anagrams. Maybe Silver was the perpetrator of the kidnapping after all.

'Yes,' Mr Ho went on, 'a good man who's quite out of place in this rat-hole. He wants a better world. He wants to get rid of the Families. I try to explain to him that that might not be a good thing, but he never listens. You have to admire altruism like his even if you don't agree with it.'

'He doesn't like the Families?'

'Didn't you hear what I said? He detests them.'

Milner was feeling a quickening of the blood. 'Why is that, do you think?'

'Who can say? He just believes we'd be better off without them. And he can't stand people like that lot who went past just now, those ClanFans. If he'd been standing here with us, he'd have laid into them verbally. Called them suckers and slaves and morons and sheep. I've seen him do it. It doesn't win him friends, but then with beliefs like his you can't expect to be popular. There was a rent protest a couple of years back. Maybe you read about it.'

'I did.'

'Damien was one of the prime movers of that. Helped organise it. Rallied tenants to the cause. But because he's such an anti-Familial he didn't have everyone's full respect, and when it came to the crunch, when the RLA tried to fob us off with a minor rent reduction which we knew they wouldn't keep to for long, Damien advised against accepting it. He told everyone to hold out for better terms. And no one listened. The rebels rebelled against one of their ringleaders and the protest fell apart. *That's* the drawback with hating the Families. You get hated in turn.'

Milner was beyond excited now. He knew – *knew* – that he had his man.

'Have you, um, have you seen him lately?' he enquired.

'Yesterday. No, I tell a lie, the day before yesterday. He came in for cigarettes. He'd given up smoking for a couple of months but he was back on the fags again. Which is usually a sign that he's under strain of some sort. In this case it's a woman. He's been in an on-off relationship for a while. More off than on. For all his apparent self-assurance, Damien is sensitive when it comes to things that matter to him.' Mr Ho thumped himself in the chest, over the heart. 'Matter to him here. He also,' Mr Ho added, 'needed latex gloves for some reason.'

That clinched it, as far as Milner was concerned. The smoking might be connected to a woman but the likelier reason for it was the kidnapping and holding captive of a certain Family member, which would surely put anyone on-edge. And the latex gloves – to prevent leaving fingerprints, obviously.

'And at this point,' Mr Ho said, 'I suppose I should ask what your interest in Damien is, why you're looking for him. I've told you a great deal about him. Now you tell me about *you*.'

'That's easier said than done.'

'You aren't plain-clothes police. You look a bit like it but you aren't. But you're here in some kind of official capacity. What?'

'Would it be all right if I said you'll know in a day's time?'

Mr Ho chuckled. 'It would be fine. I don't much care. I'm just a natural gossip. I'd tell you anything you wanted to know. Also, Damien's an idiot, really.'

'I thought you said—'

'I said I admire him. I said he's a good, decent man. I never said I *like* him. I don't. Not a bit. And if he's done something wrong, committed some offence, then more fool him. He deserves to be caught.' Mr Ho clapped Milner on the back. 'Now, if I really can't tempt you to make a purchase, I'd better be getting back inside. Off you go. Hunt him down. Good luck. And watch out for any more falling tables!'

With that, Mr Ho disappeared into his shop, leaving Milner bemused, enlightened, but, above all else, elated.

Damien Scrase.

The intimidating anagrams were all at once unimportant. They were relegated to a position way down on the list of considerations, ousted by the sheer rapture Milner felt at knowing that his detective work had paid off and that the biggest case-bust of his career, probably ever, was now mere minutes away. He almost didn't need to pay a visit to Flat 45L, so confident was he that Damien Scrase was the guilty party. Caution, however, not to mention thoroughness, dictated that he should. As well as a location for the kidnapper, he wanted to be able to supply a first-hand physical description of the man before he picked up a phone and called the CLAN REAVER.

The lifts beckoned. Milner sauntered towards them with his head held high and a spring in his step.

PART FIVE

46

For the Block 26 ClanFan Society, it was a special day, and about to get even more special.

They didn't hold a candle vigil on just anyone's birthday. Like most ClanFan groups they had their favourites, the Family members they liked above all others. By common consent, the Block 26 Society held Cynthia Gleed in the highest regard. Plenty of societies did. But they also greatly admired Llewellyn Madoc, head of Wales's pre-eminent Family; Detver von Wäldchenlieb, that most Anglophile of Germans, who with tweeds and monocle and mutton chop whiskers and cries of 'Toodle-pip old chap!' was a living parody of a country squire (and perhaps the whole thing was a sly dig at the English, although given the impenetrability of the Teutonic sense of humour, who knew?); Siobhan Beauchamp-Dalziel-Featherstonehaugh, a tangential relative of one of the lesser British Families, who possessed the hardest-to-pronounce name known to man and who made up in camp outrageousness what she lacked in lineage; J.B. Bannerjee, hailed throughout the world for his philanthropic works, the most good-hearted spendthrift the planet had ever known; and last but not least, Provender.

They liked Provender largely because they liked his mother, but also because he was an unknown quantity. There was something wilfully romantic about a Family member who shunned the limelight, who kept his privacy while all around him were squandering theirs, who was handsome and intelligent yet chose neither to flaunt nor to exploit these attributes. Provender was a blank slate on which the Block 26 ClanFans could write their own dreams, a cloud whose shape they could interpret any way they wanted.

For some of the Society's female constituents, and a couple of the male, he was a heart-throb, the one they would fantasise about during their erotic daydreams or perhaps think about while making love with someone else. For the Society's junior contingent, he was just still young enough to be considered cool. For the older ladies among their number – and the Block 26 ClanFan Society was predominantly made up of women of mature years – he was the son they wished they'd had. He brought out the maternal instinct in them far more strongly than their own offspring ever had.

The Society assembled, as was its wont, on the shopping level of Block 26, then trooped outdoors, because it was a nice day and why not make the most of it? They skirted around the remains of a smashed table. As resident Needle Grovers it scarcely occurred to them to wonder what *that* was doing there. You came across displaced objects all the time on the estate. They crossed the overpass to Block 31 and descended to an outdoor plaza some ten storeys lower, a recreation area protruding platform-like from Block 31's western flank.

This was where they habitually went. It was a recreation area in name only. The tennis court there had no nets, the netball court likewise. In the children's section, the climbing frame was a hazard to life and limb – the RLA had posted KEEP OFF signs on it and kept promising to have it dismantled. The sandpit had become a litter tray used by every cat in the neighbourhood, and no self-respecting parent let their kids go anywhere near it. As for the seesaw and the merry-go-round, there were concrete stumps where those once sat. Magically, mysteriously stolen.

Today, a handful of Young Moderns had gathered on the site, but they cleared off, conceding it to the ClanFan Society. One kind of gang-tribe recognised another kind, and the Moderns saw in the ClanFans a degree of fanaticism that in their view was not healthy. It was one thing to base your lives around a mode of fashion, quite another to base your lives around certain people – people, moreover, you had never met and would never meet. The Moderns didn't even think about picking a fight. They just upped and left, wanting to put distance between themselves and the candle-toting nut-jobs.

The Block 26 ClanFan Society spread themselves out in a circle on the netball court. In an atmosphere of joyous fervour, a match was struck, a candle lit, and then the flame was passed from wick to wick both ways around the circle until some thirty-odd candle-tongues were flickering in the breeze. Laughing and chattering, the ClanFans stood like a human birthday cake. They were waiting for one of them to start the singing. They were, at heart, a shy lot. En masse they had a robust strength but individually none liked to stand out.

At last one brave soul overcame her reticence and began the song in a warbling contralto:

'Happy birthday to you . . .'

Swiftly the rest joined in, at various different tempos, in a range of keys. The first two lines were a complete cats' chorus, but by 'dear Provender' everything came together and the final line was delivered in rousing, gusto-filled unison. Then there were hip-hip-hoorays and someone embarked on 'For He's A Jolly Good Fellow', which the others sang along to with relish.

Traditionally what came next was a series of personal testimonials.

Each ClanFan in turn uttered a statement about the birthday boy or girl, which could take the form of a paean of praise, a humble confession of admiration, a direct personal address as if the Family member were actually there, or perhaps a story, anecdotal or fictional, about what he or she meant to the storyteller.

The ClanFans had come prepared, each with speech notes set out on slips of paper. The statements were made in halting voices, stammered out, stumbled over. Each was listened to in respectful silence.

'. . . I wish he would make up his mind and marry, make his mother happy . . .'

'. . . know that if only we met, he would see straight away that I was the one for him . . .'

'. . . yeah, so if I had all that money like he does, I'd, like, build this enormous house with all games and that in it, and all my friends could come and live there, and if he did that I'd be one of his friends and we could . . .'

'. . . if royalty meant anything any more, he'd make a great king . . .'

'. . . and Provender, please, if you can, don't let there be a war, in fact I have faith you're doing everything you can to stop there being one . . .'

'. . . and he said to me, "Of course, what a great idea, why don't you come and live at Dashlands and be the official Gleed biographer?" . . .'

'. . . I'm not asking for much, just enough to keep me going till I'm back on my feet and have a job again, and he's got so much cash to spare he wouldn't even notice, I mean we're talking pocket change for him, and oh. My. God. Oh my sweet Jesus. He's right over there. It's him. He's coming right this way. I swear. I don't believe it. He's there!'

The ClanFan speaking, a man who had been out of work and living on benefit handouts for the past sixteen years, raised a trembling finger and pointed. The other ClanFans at first weren't sure what to make of this. What was he jabbering on about, Provender here? None of them wanted to turn and look in case it was just a practical joke, as when somebody yelled 'Behind you!' and there wasn't anyone behind you.

But the man kept urging his fellow ClanFans to look. His face had gone white. His eyes were out on stalks. He could barely draw breath.

So the other ClanFans did eventually look, and rapidly their faces went the way of the pointing man's. A couple of them dropped their candles. One woman spilled molten wax on her hand and didn't feel a thing. Another, unnoticed by the rest, fainted.

Like some miracle, like some visitation from on high, like a sighting of the Blessed Virgin Mary or an alien from a spacecraft, the impossible made real, over the recreation area at a fast lick he came.

Loping, stubble-bearded.

Provender Gleed.

47

On the twentieth floor of Block 26, Is and Provender were beginning to tire. They had lost count of the number of flights of stairs they had descended. They seemed to have become lost in a continuum of downward clockwise winding, their future an endless set of concrete risers coming up to meet them. The twentieth-floor landing offered release. There was a glass door leading out to a kind of cloister, which led in turn to a covered, colonnaded overpass, which terminated at the apex of a spiral staircase, which helter-skeltered all the way to the ground with overpasses radiating off from it at intervals. Still overdosed on stairs, the two fugitives exited at the first opportunity, heading across to Block 31. Is had calculated that there was little likelihood now of their and Damien's paths crossing. The estate library was on the other side of 26. He had no reason to be coming through 31. Still she wouldn't be wholly happy until she and Provender had found a phone, in fact until they had got clear of Needle Grove and were somewhere, *any*where else.

The overpass decanted them onto a recreation area attached to 31, and finding their way into the block itself seemed a simple matter. A recreation area invariably had easy access to and from the block it belonged to. The gathering of people on the netball court scarcely gave Is pause. They weren't a gang-tribe, just a bunch of ordinary Needle Grovers having a chat in a circle. Some kind of residents' discussion group? Probably. Is did not give them a second glance as she and Provender passed along the netball court's perimeter.

Then the residents started shouting Provender's name.

It was something that Is hadn't thought about, something that hadn't even fleetingly entered her mind. She was out in public with a Family member. Provender's might not be the best-known Family face but it was famous nonetheless. A coating of stubble didn't do much to disguise it.

Then she noticed that the people on the netball court had lit candles in their hands, and the penny dropped. ClanFans. She and Provender had had the awesome misfortune to stumble across a crowd of ClanFans who were out celebrating Provender's birthday.

'Fuck my luck.' Is seized Provender by the arm. 'Come on, we need to get moving.'

She said this because the ClanFans were themselves getting moving. A handful of them had broken away from the group and were stalking towards Provender, hesitant but with mounting confidence. They and the ones who remained rooted to the spot all had loose, inane grins on their faces and kept looking at one another – that was, when they could tear their eyes off Provender for a second – to seek reassurance that this was really happening, the person in front of them really was who they thought. They continued to call out to him, repeating the three syllables of his name in high, querulous voices like hatchlings in the nest vying for mother bird's attention. Then, all at once, the entire group surged forward, apart from the one they had left behind, who lay prone on the ground, insensible. With their hands outstretched, the ClanFans beelined for the object of their adoration . . .

. . . who stood immobile, uncomprehending. Is yanked on his arm. His body sagged in her direction but his feet stayed where they were.

'ClanFans, Provender,' she said.

Her words had no meaning to him. He didn't seem to know what he was looking at, why these people were calling to him. He was as mesmerised by them as they were by him.

Is's medical training kicked in. Procedures for rousing or getting attention of semi-conscious patients. Either: pinch the earlobe. Or: rub knuckles up and down median line of sternum.

The latter worked only if the patient was lying down. Otherwise you couldn't get any leverage. There was nothing to push against.

Is reached up and dug the nails of thumb and forefinger into Provender's earlobe.

'Oww!'

'Run. Now. Us. Fast.'

The ClanFans were a dozen paces away as Provender, galvanised, finally began to move.

It was love, pure and simple.

It was the need to touch, to grab hold of, to be sure of.

It was wanting to know if the person before them was flesh and not some figment of their imaginations.

It was the desire to lay hands on.

It was a form of lust.

It was worship.

It was greed.

It was all these things, and yet to the ClanFans it felt like nothing. A blinding urge. Indefinable. Primal.

When Provender was standing still, they had to home in on him.

When Provender took flight, they had to give chase.

Across the recreation area.

A square cavity in the side of Block 31.

A concrete tunnel burrowing into the building.

A narrower tunnel that jinked off to the side.

Stairs.

Is ran, pulling Provender after her. She ran in the knowledge that this was absurd, ridiculous. They were fleeing from a bunch of people who, by rights, were harmless. Ordinary individuals who normally wouldn't hurt a fly. Yet, in their devotion, their love for Provender, they might well tear him to pieces if they caught up with him. If nothing else, they were drawing attention to him, and that was exactly what he and Is did not need.

So she kept running, even as hilarity bubbled inside her, threatening to become hysteria. Had there been a moment to pause, had the ClanFans not been pressing hard on her and Provender's heels, she would have stopped and given in and laughed herself hoarse. But the ClanFans were right behind, yelping and imploring, a mass of needy arms, a rumble of desperate footfalls. 'Provender!' they cried. 'Provender, please! Please!'

She hit a landing, Provender still in tow, and barged through a doorway, which a woman with an armful of groceries was trying to negotiate from the opposite direction. Is shouldered her out of the way and the woman swore at her ripely and profusely. Next moment, the stampeding ClanFans burst through the doorway, and the woman and her groceries were sent flying.

Into an arcade, similar to the one in Block 26. Shops blurred by on either side. Ahead: a defunct indoor fountain, which a cluster of Orphans had commandeered – *our spot*. The Orphans, loaded to the gills with Tinct, chortled to see two adults come sprinting by, and laughed even harder at the sight of their pursuers, an assortment of grown-ups and children, all huffing and puffing frantically.

Beyond the fountain, a ramp. Down that, out onto a plaza, diagonally across to its only exit point, down another ramp to a disused swimming pool that had a residue of grimy water at the bottom in which car tyres and a rusty bicycle frame formed a reef. Around the pool, onward, till there were stairs, and more stairs, and yet more stairs, and suddenly, just like that, the ground.

They paused, Is and Provender, to take stock. They had managed to put some distance between themselves and the ClanFan pack, not much but enough to allow a brief respite from running. Compared with the majority of the ClanFans, they were young and relatively fit. Indeed, although they couldn't know it, there had been attrition among their pursuers. A few of the older and fatter ClanFans had had to abandon the chase and were strung out at intervals along the route, bent double, wheezing, experiencing all sorts of unpleasant palpitations to accompany the ache of anguish and frustration in their bellies. The rest, however, were still coming, undeterred by the fact that their quarry appeared to be getting away from them. They were relentless. They would keep after Provender as long as they were able to. Their lives had condensed down to a single objective: catch up with Provender, be with him, unite with him, embrace and cling to this avatar of Family, for ever. And as for that girl who was with him – what girl?

Is, panting hard, cast her gaze around. She didn't know Needle Grove all that well anyway, and down here on the ground it was another country, a gloom-hung, alien place, hostile territory. There were few map diagrams that hadn't had graffiti slapped over them and few signposts that hadn't been torn down, and the only other landmarks were car husks, which looked virtually identical, and trenches which the gang-tribes had dug out and fortified with rubble in the course of their perpetual turf-wars. The roads that wound through led somewhere but not necessarily out into London. Is could have navigated her way out of the estate if they had been standing at the foot of Block 26, somewhere near the parking garage entrance, since she knew that route reasonably well. But they were standing at the foot of 31, on the far side of the block from 26. She had only the vaguest notion of which way to go.

Above, on the staircase, the ClanFan clamour was growing louder. The front-runners of the group were closing in.

'Where now?' Provender gasped.

'There,' said Is, pointing along a road that ran to the right, and added, 'I think.'

'You think.'

She rounded on him. 'Would you like me to leave you here?' She nodded upwards. 'To meet your adoring public?'

'Uh, no.'

'Then shut up and follow me.'

48

Walking back from the library, videotyped ransom demand in hand, Damien reflected on what he had done to Is. He felt terrible about it, even if he hadn't hit her that hard, just a backhand swipe, barely even a tap. It wasn't right. He should have been able to control his temper. Whatever the provocation – and boy, had he been provoked – he shouldn't have lashed out like that. He had probably ruined any chance he had of getting back together with her. She wasn't going to forgive him in a hurry, that much was certain. Yet he remained hopeful that he could make it up to her somehow and that he and she could be reconciled. Perhaps once this kidnap business was over, when Provender wasn't there any more in the flat, when the money had arrived and the regeneration of Needle Grove commenced – then Damien could say to her, 'Look. See? It was worth it. All we went through, all the hassle and strife – all worth it.'

Is didn't know true love when she saw it. That was her problem. That and getting a bit too chummy with Provender fucking Gleed. But Damien couldn't even fault her there, not really. It was Is's nature to be kind, to see the best in people. That was one of the things he loved about her.

As the lift hauled him up to the forty-fifth floor, Damien contemplated stopping off at Mr Ho's along the way and buying some flowers. It would, however, be too corny and obvious a gesture. Is might even take it the wrong way: as if a bunch of flowers could just wave everything away like a magic wand. No, humility would be best. Honest, sincere contrition.

He was formulating his apology as he stepped out of the lift. He was still working on it as he unlocked the door to the flat. Composing himself, he swung the door open and began, 'Is, I've just got to tell you . . .'

She wasn't there.

She wasn't on the floor. She wasn't sitting in a chair. A glance through the bedroom doorway told him she wasn't in there either.

The flat was silent. Shockingly, tellingly silent.

What was the balcony window doing open?

Where the fuck was the table?

Then Damien caught sight of the loops of severed flex on the floor not far from where Is had been lying when he left. That was when he knew what had happened, but he strode over to the bathroom and flung the door wide, because he had to be sure, he had to see it with his own eyes . . .

And when he did, when the bathroom's emptiness gaped at him, he felt a tremendous downward rush, as though the building had vanished and he was plummeting to earth, five hundred feet straight down. Weak, he grabbed the door frame for support. He croaked, 'No,' and then 'No', again, as though by denying it he could somehow make it not have occurred. He lowered his head, closed his eyes, reopened them and looked up, hoping against hope that Provender would be there again, bound and helpless on the floor.

Of course he was not. The bathroom remained empty.

But not completely empty. Something was there which should not be there. Something had been placed there for him to find.

Bending forward, Damien reached out a numb hand and picked up his copy of *The Meritocrats*, which was on the floor next to the bath in the exact spot where Provender should have been.

There was handwriting on the front cover. Damien held the book up to the light and read:

Look on page 1.
This is how misguided and gullible you are.

He knew the handwriting was Is's, and although he resented being called misguided and gullible he resented even more that she had defaced his copy of the book. It wasn't in the best of condition to start with, admittedly, but to scribble on the front like that was just plain vandalism. Sacrilege, even.

Look on page 1.

Damien's fingers felt thick and clumsy as he obeyed the instruction. He leafed the book open to the start of the story, wondering what Is had done there. More defacing, he reckoned. That bitch.

He knew he should be out looking for her and Provender. He should be scouring the estate for them. He couldn't let them get away.

But first this. He had to see what was on page one. Why he was allegedly so misguided, so gullible?

Here was the page. Initially Damien couldn't discern anything different about it. What was he meant to be looking at?

Then he noticed that certain letters had been underlined – the first letter of each sentence of the first four paragraphs.

<u>P</u>rovidence saw to it that Guy Godwin was born and brought up in a house at the confluence of three types of transportation. <u>R</u>oad ran alongside the house. <u>O</u>verhead a railway viaduct arched. <u>V</u>ery close to the end of the garden, a canal flowed. <u>E</u>very minute of every day, almost, Guy could look out of a window and see voyagers go by . . .

And as he read, and as he perceived, and as he understood, there came that downrush again, that giddying sense of freefall, but worse this time, as though all certainties were collapsing, as though support columns were giving way and the structure of Damien's life was crumbling to pieces beneath him.

Now he couldn't hold himself up. He buckled to his knees. He began moaning, rocking his head from side to side, not willing to believe that such a huge, monstrous trick could have been perpetrated on him. Not just on him but on thousands of others. The magnitude of it. The evil of it!

How long he knelt there, he couldn't say. Abject in his misery, he went into a state of withdrawal, distant from the world, outside time. There was no meaning. There was no fairness. Everything was a hoax, a cruel prank. He seriously considered ending it all, there and then. Draw his knife from its sheath, plunge it into his guts like a dishonoured samurai. But his arms were nerveless. He couldn't reach behind him. He lacked the strength.

What finally roused him from his stupor was a rap at the door and a quiet voice saying, 'Excuse me.'

He had left the door open.

A man he didn't recognise was peering into the flat.

The man rapped again on the door, a formality, looking directly at Damien as he did so. Puzzled that Damien was crouched there in the bathroom doorway. Nervous.

'Yeah?' Damien intoned, bleakly, wearily.

'I'm, umm . . . I'm looking for Damien Scrase,' said the man. 'Would you be he?'

49

Milner fully expected the answer to his enquiry to be no. He had the correct flat, 45L, but the man slumped in the bathroom doorway could not have corresponded less with his vision of Damien Scrase. He looked confused, helpless, broken, lost. He looked like someone who couldn't, at this moment and maybe at any moment, tell his BOWEL from his ELBOW, or for that matter his ARSE from his EARS. No way could he be Provender Gleed's kidnapper. And no way could this flat, with its front door wide open, be where Provender was being held captive. As far as Milner was able to see, it was empty, the slumped man its sole occupant.

Provender, he concluded, was elsewhere, and so was Scrase.

Maybe with Demetrius Silver? Were Scrase and Silver in it together, co-conspirators?

Such a prospect was not at all comforting, and Milner felt it was time to cut his losses and run. He would get a call out to Carver. Carver would do the rest.

'My mistake,' he said. 'Didn't mean to bother you. I'll just—'

'Who are you?' the man demanded.

'Uh, nobody.'

'No, you said my name. You came to see me. Who the fuck are you?'

Milner was lost for words – a rare occurrence for him, a dereliction of duty, almost anathema. His mouth opened and shut soundlessly, even as his mind raced to come up with some sort of excuse for his being there and knowing Scrase's name. He grasped the enormity of the blunder he had made. He had assumed the man was not his suspect, and he had been wrong.

'I, um, I thought . . .'

Scrase moved fast – shockingly fast. He sprang to his feet and lunged. Milner barely had time to flinch, let alone take evasive action. All at once Scrase had grabbed him by the shirtfront and was hauling him into the flat. Scrase kicked the door shut, slammed Milner backwards against the wall, and thrust his face so close to Milner's that the Anagrammatic Detective could hear the breath whistling in and out of his nostrils.

Milner knew then that the anagrams had not lied. The furious, staring eyes that filled his field of vision were all the proof he needed. MEAN CAD RISES. INCREASES MAD.

SCARES MAIDEN? he thought, remotely. *SCARES ME AND I!*

'What do you know?' Scrase snarled. His breath reeked of tobacco. 'Where is he? What have you done with him?'

'I have no idea what you're—'

With a soft *zing*, just like that, a knife appeared. Scrase held it up in his right hand while his left continued to grip Milner's shirtfront in a tight knot at his throat. Milner's stomach went hollow, and for a moment he thought he was going to soil himself. Everything seemed to have turned upside down. Reality was gone and there was only an insane nightmare: the knife poised in front of him, its blade about a foot long or so it seemed, light playing along honed steel, Scrase's eyes behind the weapon looking hard and lifeless and pitiless, knifelike themselves.

'I'll ask again,' Scrase said with bitten-lip patience, 'and you will answer in a straightforward and completely truthful manner. I'm not in the mood for mucking around. First off, who are you?'

'Merlin Milner.'

'And you're here because . . . ?'

Milner didn't dare tell Scrase the truth: *I'm here because I've found the person who kidnapped Provender Gleed – you.* That would be nothing short of suicidal. He struggled to come up with some sort of cover story, and did. It wasn't much of one but it would have to do.

'Authority,' he said. 'I'm from the Risen London Authority. We, er, we're following up on that rent business a while back. You know, the protest. We're canvassing residents' views. How are we going, have things improved, and so forth.'

Scrase took the information on board and, with a nod, appeared to accept it as an explanation. The knife wavered in the air, then drew away from Milner's face. Milner allowed himself to relax. There. A nice piece of lying. A plausible tale plausibly told.

Then, almost a sigh, he heard Scrase say, 'Rubbish.'

There was a flash of metal, and a faint ripping sound, and a feeling like an icicle being drawn sideways across his cheek, and a moment later a sensation of warmth, of wetness, and then a sudden sharp sting of pain which opened up into something fiercer, fierier, more deep-seated.

Milner moaned, and his hand flew to his cheek to clutch the wound. At the same time Scrase relinquished his grip on him and stepped back a couple of paces, like an artist wishing to observe his handiwork.

'You're not RLA,' he said. 'The RLA doesn't do follow-ups. The RLA couldn't give a big fat hairy shit about this place. Authority officials come here once in a blue moon, and when they do it's always in groups, never alone. They're not stupid. *You* are, thinking I'd fall for that load of bollocks.'

Milner wanted to say something indignant. Through the pain, through the sight of his blood on his fingers, he wanted to tell Scrase he had no right to do that – cut him like that. He felt violated. It was an outrage for this man to have slashed his face, split his skin, simply as punishment for not being honest. It was disproportionate and spiteful and unjust.

Sensibly, however, Milner kept his opinion to himself. Instead, in humble, faltering tones, he said, 'Please, let me go. I won't tell anyone anything. I'll leave and not come back. You'll never see me again. Just . . . don't hurt me.'

Scrase studied him sidelong. 'Well now, that depends. I'm having a pretty shitty day, as you can probably tell. Things that were supposed to be . . . working, haven't. I find out I've been lied to and cheated on in all sorts of ways. And then you come waltzing up to my door and I reckon you know something about what's going on here, you're involved in this somehow, and you won't give me any straight answers, so . . .' He shrugged. 'So you've paid the price for that. And I don't think you'd be so daft as to try it on with me a second time. Right?'

Milner nodded eagerly.

'Right. What I think would be best is if you come over and sit down and you and I have a nice little chat. Discuss a couple of things.'

Scrase motioned to a chair, and Milner, on weak, wobbly legs, tottered over to it and sat down. Scrase pulled up another chair and seated himself opposite, laying the knife across his lap. The knife was angled towards Milner but not pointing directly at him. Milner chose to regard this as a positive sign, cause for optimism.

'That's, erm, an impressive-looking utensil you've got there,' he said. Admiring the knife seemed a good way of defusing its dangerousness. A compliment about the knife was a compliment about its owner.

'Bought it at an army-surplus shop,' Scrase said. 'See that?' He indicated the haft, which was gnarled and muddy brown for the most part, shading to white near the pommel, colours like an Irish coffee. ' "Stag-handled" is the technical term for it, but it's deerhorn to you and me. Kind of ironic, since it's a knife designed specifically for gutting and skinning deer. Talk about adding insult to injury. See those serrations along the top edge of the blade? That's to prevent it slipping out too easily when you're using it. And now that we've established that my knife is a handsome, well-made piece of kit, let's get down to business, Mr Milner. Because I think we're past the pleasantries stage, and I think if you're trying to delay me for some reason, that would be very unwise of you.'

Milner nodded to show he was in complete agreement with that last remark. 'It would be, and I'm not trying to delay you.'

'Good to hear. So now you're going to come clean about everything. Who, when, what, why.'

Honesty, Milner told himself. SAY TRUTH and STAY HURT – *stay* as in *prevent*.

He started speaking, and what he said elicited head-shakes from Scrase, and a hardening grimace, and eventually a hiss of dismay. And when he was done – when he had explained who he was, what an Anagrammatic

Detective did, who had employed him, and how he had found Scrase – there was a long silence from the other man. Scrase's eyes were narrowed, calculating. The silence stretched on, and Milner began to believe that he had won himself his life and liberty. Just as his lying had been punished, his candour would be rewarded.

'You have no idea where Gleed is then?' Scrase said at last.

'None whatsoever. He should have been here.'

'Well, he isn't, is he. The fucker escaped. I don't know how but I know he had help. She helped him.'

'She?'

Scrase flicked a hand. 'Not important. You don't need to know. You mentioned you have a partner, another Anagrammatic Detective. You said he's pursuing a different line of enquiry. He thinks the kidnapping is an inside job.'

'When it so obviously isn't.'

'So obviously.'

'Yes. Poor old Romeo.' Milner was keen to continue to be helpful. He had gained Scrase's trust, he was certain of that, but it wasn't a bad idea to ingratiate himself further if he could, so as to ensure his safety beyond all doubt. 'He's barking up totally the wrong tree. He's convinced one of the Gleeds is behind everything. Absurd, really. I mean, why?'

'Which Gleed?'

'Provender's cousin. The actor. What's his name . . . Arthur. Romeo bases that conclusion – he's a bit of a closet ClanFan, not like me, I'm not that way at all, if anything I'm anti-Familial – but Romeo, he says there's no love lost between the two of them, Provender and Arthur. If anyone had something to gain by Provender being out of the picture, it would be Arthur.' Milner spread out his hands and pulled a face to show what he thought of Family in-fighting. 'But there you have it. Romeo's down on New Aldwych, hanging around outside the Shortborn Theatre, and wasting his time there, all because he thinks this is a spat between cousins. Whereas I know, and you know, Mr Scrase, that this is a political act, isn't it? A show of strength. Us versus them. Right?'

Scrase did not reply. He was thinking again – that calculating look.

Then he took hold of the knife, and Milner knew he was going to sheathe it. Scrase stood up, and Milner knew he was going to put the knife away and was then going to thank the Anagrammatic Detective for being so cooperative and invite him to depart. Milner knew he had just talked his way out of the stickiest predicament he had ever been in (literally sticky, in that the blood from the gash in his cheek had started to congeal – he could feel the dribbles of it tightening the skin on his face and neck), Milner knew he had just been through one of those life-threatening, life-changing experiences which only ever seemed to happen to others. It was an anecdote he would be able to regale people with for years to come. The near-miss with the table was nothing. *This* – being held at knifepoint by a stone-eyed psycho and actively winning his freedom through words alone – you might almost call it playing CHARADES with a HARD-CASE – this was the stuff of heroism. A true adventure. And he was determined that he was going to be a better man for it. More patient, more tolerant, not as snooty as he knew he could sometimes be. What was the point in a brush with death if it didn't make you reassess your life and want to change?

Milner's moment of epiphany lasted right up until the knife plunged into his stomach.

He didn't understand.

What was this?

It felt as if he had been punched in the gut, but no mere fist-blow could go so deep and feel so wrong.

Scrase tugged the knife out and plunged it in again.

The blade grated against the bottom of Milner's ribcage. Milner felt it glance off the bone, angling upwards into his chest cavity.

He couldn't breathe. He wheezed for air. He choked, and there was liquid at the back of his throat and a taste like a nosebleed.

Scrase was crying.

Milner found that the oddest part of what was happening.

A third stab of the knife, and tears were spilling from Scrase's eyes and he was sobbing.

Dimly Milner thought, *I should be the one who's sad, not him.*

Then came an inrush of darkness.

An emptying-out.

A seizing-up.

And a final anagram, one last scattering and regathering.

DEATH.

HATED DEATH.

50

The baying of the ClanFans was a sad and distant sound and getting fainter by the minute. That, undeniably, was good. What was not so good was that Provender and Is had not reached an exit from Needle Grove. They didn't even seem to be near the edge of the estate. If anything, they were heading deeper into it. They moved from the shadow of one block to the shadow of another, hoping with every corner they turned that a way out would present itself. They were repeatedly disappointed. En route, they passed several payphones and, likewise, were repeatedly disappointed. Each had been wrecked beyond repair and the majority were nothing more than hollow shells, kiosk-shaped steel skeletons, glassless and scorch-marked.

'This,' Provender commented at one point, as they were hurrying across a patch of hummocky grey wasteground, 'is like Hell. No one should have to live in a place like this.'

'Welcome to the real world, Provender,' Is replied. 'There are dozens of estates like it, and that's just in London alone. This is the world you Family members never even get a glimpse of.'

'Estate,' Provender said with a dry chuckle. 'Funny how my understanding of the word is so different.'

'Hilarious. Now how about we do less of the talking and more of the getting us out of here?'

'I thought that was what we were doing. Or rather, *you* were doing.'

'I am. So shut up and let me concentrate.'

'And you're making such a fine job of it too.'

'Provender!'

'All right. Sorry.'

They roamed onward, and Is wondered whether Damien had returned to the flat yet and, if so, whether he had found her 'time-bomb'. How would he react to the discovery that his favourite book, his wellspring of inspiration, had been written by none other than Provender? Not calmly. If she knew Damien, it would cut the legs from under him. He would be livid. He deserved it, though. Perhaps she had overstepped the mark in accusing him of being misguided and gullible, perhaps it was an unnecessary twisting of the knife. But then he deserved that too. She was surprised, now, that she could once have been his girlfriend. It was strange to think she had loved him when she wasn't sure she had ever even liked him. It was stranger still to think that he had somehow been able to convince her that kidnapping Provender was a good idea. Six months after they had officially become Just Friends, his brooding charisma continued to be effective on her. She didn't know if that reflected well on him or badly on her. Probably a bit of both.

Is permitted herself this brief, introspective lull while still maintaining a level of alertness and apprehension. Daytime down here on the ground in Needle Grove wasn't as dangerous as night-time, but you nonetheless had to be careful. She and Provender had slowed to a walk now, both believing they had managed to give the ClanFans the slip. The ClanFans, however, had hardly been a threat. A nuisance, more than anything. On the ground, even in the early afternoon, genuine hazards lurked.

Such as a group of Changelings.

At first, Is had only a vague suspicion that she and Provender were being followed. She thought it might be the ClanFans again – somehow they had caught up – but she dismissed the notion immediately. The ClanFans would have been making plenty of noise; it would be impossible to miss them. Whereas, as far as she could see, there was nobody around. There was simply the feeling that someone was nearby, lurking, looking. This was a world of hiding places – doorways, the struts that held up overpasses, deep shadows everywhere. Eyes could be watching from any of them. From all of them.

Is's pace quickened. Provender, catching her mood, followed suit.

Somewhere over to their left, gravel crunched. No one there. Then, over to the right, what sounded like a cross between a giggle and a whisper. No one there either.

'Are we—?' Provender began.

'Look straight ahead,' Is said. 'Keep moving. If I give the word to run, run like fuck.'

If it was a gang-tribe, and it must be, Is doubted she and Provender would be able to outrace them. But what else could you do? Stop and reason with them? Not likely, especially not if they were off their heads on Tinct.

The first gang-member sauntered into view ahead. His Changeling garb consisted of a flock-pattern waistcoat, a denim shirt, a tartan kilt and sandals. He was grinning, and not in a friendly manner. A cudgel hung loosely from his hand.

Is did not need to turn round to know that there were other Changelings behind her, but she turned round regardless. Sure enough, two more of the gang-tribe had emerged from concealment. One was rag-clad like a scarecrow, while the other was like two people put together, his top half clad in dinner jacket and bowtie, his bottom half in stripy leggings and, bizarrely, a tutu.

Now four more Changelings came in from either side, and one of them,

Is noted, had a cricket jersey on and was carrying a cricket bat, and another sported a jockey's cap and his weapon of choice, appropriately enough, was a riding crop.

Her heart pulsed in her throat. No point in telling Provender to run. It was too late for that now.

The Changelings closed in.

And then Provender did something unbelievably foolhardy.

51

As far as Provender was concerned, of course, it was not unbelievably foolhardy. On the contrary, it was eminently sensible, even cunning.

He raised his arms. Hands aloft, high enough to be pacificatory but not quite a gesture of surrender, he took a step towards the Changeling in front. With as winning a smile as he could muster, he said, 'Do you know who I am?'

He knew they were not ClanFans. They were skinny, wiry youths, none older than nineteen, and they were armed and clearly out for trouble. They had the hunched, leering look of hyenas and the irises of their eyes swam in baths of blood-pinkened white. Anyone could tell they weren't the sort to be impressed by Family.

Nonetheless . . .

The Changeling in front gave Provender the once-over, head to toe, and something dawned in those feral eyes, a spark of recognition.

Provender pivoted through 360 degrees so that the others could get a clear look at him too. In the process he saw Is with a worried question in her eyes: *what the hell are you up to?* He tried, with a look, to reassure her that he knew what he was doing.

'Gleed,' said the front Changeling. 'The son. Weird name. Property?'

'It's Propeller,' another of the Changelings offered, and that triggered a bombardment of suggestions.

'Probable.'

'Providence.'

'Pronto.'

'Prostitute.'

This last got all the gang-members laughing.

Provender laughed along, complaisantly, then said: 'As a matter of fact it's Provender.'

'As a matter of fact,' the Changeling in front replied, 'we couldn't give a toss. Family? What the fuck's Family ever done for us?'

Murmurs of assent did the rounds.

'You think you being Family means you can just wander through our turf, bold as you like, and get away with it? I don't think so. Actually, what *are* you doing here? The Grove isn't the sort of place your kind hang out in.'

'Ah, thereby hangs a tale,' Provender said. 'Would you believe—'

The Changeling cut him off with a wave of the hand. 'Not interested. I only asked 'cause I thought I should. What I really want to know is how much of a fight are you going to put up.'

'I was hoping it wouldn't have to come to that.' There was just the slightest of wavers in Provender's voice, a hint of a tremble. 'I was hoping, instead, that we could come to some sort of accommodation.'

'Ooh, "accommodation",' the Changeling echoed. 'Hear that, everyone? Prompter here wants to come to an "accommodation". Whatever the fuck that is.'

'All I meant was—'

'You'd like to buy us off.'

'Yes.'

'With cold, hard cash.'

'Absolutely. See, the thing is, I'm lost.' Provender tipped his head in Is's direction. 'We're lost. We've been wandering around searching for an exit and we've got turned about and back-to-front and completely confused.'

'And you'd like us to escort you out maybe?'

'God, would you? That would be fantastic.'

The Changeling looked over at Is. 'And you're with this bloke? Yes? No? Bruise-face woman, I'm talking to you.'

Is, in spite of herself, was doing all she could to distance herself from Provender. She was angled away from him, her body language proclaiming that she and he were nothing to do with each other, he was just someone she'd happened to be walking beside. In truth, she was wondering what had come over him. All of a sudden he was behaving like an upper-class nitwit and she couldn't decide if this was bluff or, possibly, the real Provender coming to the surface at last.

Eventually, under the Changeling's continued scrutiny, she gave a cautious nod. 'Yes.'

'You Family too?'

'No.'

'He your boyfriend?'

With vehemence: 'No.'

'But you want to get out of the Grove as much as he does?'

'Yes, I suppose so. Yes.'

The Changeling turned back to Provender, cocked his head and scratched the underside of his chin. 'How much money are we talking here?'

'You tell me.'

'A grand?'

'Sounds fine to me.'

The Changeling barked a laugh. 'Seriously? No bullshit? One thousand notes?'

'Is that enough?'

'Oh, I'd say so. Wouldn't you, boys? Wouldn't you say a grand was enough to buy these people an escort off the estate?'

The Changelings bellowed in general agreement.

Is held her breath and braced herself. She was quite certain this was when the gang-tribe would weigh in. They were just toying with her and Provender. She was set to retaliate with everything she had – teeth, nails, knee to the groin, whatever it took. The Changelings would come at her expecting a pushover and find a hellion.

'Prognosis,' said their spokesman, 'you have yourself a deal.' He stuck out a hand. 'Shake on it.'

Provender, with manly forthrightness, pumped the proffered hand.

Moments later, he and Is were striding through the estate accompanied by their very own gang-tribe honour guard. As they walked the Changelings amused themselves by coming up with yet more words with a 'Pro-' prefix. Provender, meanwhile, kept darting jubilant glances at Is, which she refused to acknowledge. Her face was set in a scowl of frank incredulity. This couldn't be right. There must be some drawback here, some catch. The Changelings surely weren't going to see them to the gate and then just wave them off, were they? It couldn't be that simple. She and Provender couldn't have got that lucky.

52

The Changelings discharged their half of the bargain and deposited their two-person cargo safely at the perimeter of the estate. Then, in the middle of the road, beneath the arching entranceway sign, the members of the gang-tribe huddled together expectantly, waiting for Provender to hand over the agreed-on sum. It seemed reasonable to them that he must have the money on his person, and although it had crossed their minds more than once that if he was carrying that much cash on him they could simply take it off him by force, there was something oddly satisfying about earning it. Earning it so easily, as well. All that dosh in return for a stroll through their own backyard, ten minutes' work, nothing to it. Maybe their attitude towards Family needed reconsidering, if this experience with Provender Gleed was anything to go by. Maybe there was something to be said for people who were burdened with so much wealth that they could spill it around so casually, so liberally.

'This is so great of you,' Provender said, looking from one Changeling to the next. 'Thank you all, very much. We really appreciate this. What I need now is to take down your names. Or the name of just one of you, if you prefer. You.' He pointed to the Changeling with whom he had struck the deal. 'Why not you?'

'Huh?' said the Changeling, with a slow, nonplussed blink. 'What d'you want my name for?'

'So I can write you a cheque, of course. Which you can then take to a bank and cash and divvy up between all of you. Seven into a thousand goes . . . Well, I'm not sure. I'll leave it to you to do the maths.'

'No, see, that's not going to work,' said the Changeling. 'Not a bit. Cheque won't do. Cash or nothing.'

'Surely a Family cheque—'

'Cash or nothing.'

'Fine then. Cash. I can always send it registered delivery. But in that case I'll need an address as well as a name.'

'No,' said the Changeling. 'Now. Not later by post. Cash now.'

'But I don't have that much . . .' Provender's voice tailed off, as if only now was it dawning on him that he and the Changelings had got their wires hopelessly crossed.

'Tell me you're joking,' the Changelings' spokesman said to Provender.

'You're taking the piss, right?' The other gang-members were muttering in low voices to one another, and their various weapons, which had been lowered, began to rise, going from at-ease to port-arms.

'I wish I was,' Provender replied, feebly. With somewhat more force he added, 'But look, I swear you'll get it. First opportunity I have, I'll send it. In fact, let's make it two grand, shall we? Just to show there's no hard feelings.'

'Make it ten, it won't matter. You tricked us. Good as fucking lied to us.'

'I didn't. It was an honest misunder—'

'Get 'im,' the Changeling said, in a grim low growl.

At that selfsame instant, Provender grabbed Is's arm and started running.

It wasn't funny this time. There was no element of absurdity about it, as there had been when they were fleeing from the ClanFans. It was in earnest. It was sheer blind panic. It was a flat-out sprint in order to get away from a foe who was manifestly dangerous and whose reason for wanting to catch them was not, as the ClanFans' had been, overwhelming love but quite the opposite.

The Changelings, as it happened, were not as quick off the mark as they might have been. Provender had surprised them by taking action so abruptly. Catching them on the hop, he gained himself and Is a few seconds' head start.

Once they had roused themselves, though, the Changelings gave chase with a vengeance. Provender and Is heard the clatter of their footfalls behind him and both knew they weren't going to be able to stay ahead for long. As far as Provender could see, their only hope lay in finding some busy part of town, a street filled with passers-by, where either the Changelings would think twice before assaulting them in front of so many witnesses or they could lose themselves in the crowd. Being in a populous public place did not guarantee immunity from attack, of course, and it was by no means certain they would get to one before the Changelings caught up, but it was all Provender could think of to do. He was barely even conscious of thinking it. It was an instinct more than anything, the natural desire of pursued prey to seek refuge in numbers. In Is's brain much the same notion had formed.

Together they hurtled along pavements, turning left, turning right, into side streets, down alleyways, out into main streets again, weaving through the city's grid pattern but unable to shake off the Changelings at their heels. They soon found themselves beyond breath, beyond tiredness, in a world where the only thing that mattered was to carry on running, running, running. Both felt their lungs starting to rasp, their legs starting to ache. But these pains were far-off, ignorable, needing to be ignored.

On main roads, traffic roared past them. Occasionally a horn tooted, in mockery, in exhortation, who knew? The drivers in their vehicles were faceless entities, irrelevant. The vehicles themselves were irrelevant except when Provender and Is reached a junction and had to cross. Then they were moving metal obstacles to be darted in front of or around. Then, too, the horn beeps were rapid tattoos that more often than not came between a squeal of brakes and an angry out-of-the-window curse.

There were pedestrians around, but only a few, never enough to constitute a crowd, and invariably when they caught sight of Provender and Is running towards them they moved out of the way, not wanting to get involved; they even scurried over to the other side of the street if they had time to. It was early afternoon on a weekday in a more or less residential area. At this hour, this portion of London was hardly teeming.

And the Changelings were gaining. Hard as Provender and Is ran, the staccato slap of the Changelings' shoe soles was getting ever louder, ever closer, their shouts and panting likewise. Neither of the pursued dared look over their shoulders. They dashed onward, dragging each other along.

Then, up ahead, Provender caught a glimpse of something that was as good as a crowded space, if not far better.

He yanked on Is's arm and gesticulated. She peered and saw a chain link fence, a high-sided enclosure running parallel with the next street they were coming to. She looked harder, not understanding why Provender was so excited about this, and then she got it.

They rounded the corner, and Provender's spurt of hope became a full-blown flood of happiness.

It wasn't just that they had stumbled across the Family tram system.

About half a mile away, there was a break in the chain link fence. There was a gateway, and beyond it a platform.

He took a tighter hold on Is's arm, dug deep within himself, and gave his all in a final, fraught dash for sanctuary.

53

Tinct, like any street drug, did more harm than good. For a while after injection it brought euphoria, clarification of the senses, a feeling of near-invulnerability. The metabolism was sharpened, the pain receptors were dampened, and the synapses fired like machine-guns. On Tinct, you could accomplish extraordinary physical feats. Your body was on overdrive and refused to acknowledge fatigue. It was a warrior's drug and for that reason a favourite among the gang-tribes.

The downside? The effects were only temporary, and when they went, the drug's absence was felt like a sucking vacuum. Tinct's influence didn't fade, it vanished. One minute you were on top of the world, the next the world was on top of you.

Then there was the physical damage done during the periods when the drug was active. Muscles and joints could suffer excessive wear and tear which, if not allowed time to mend, became a cumulatively worsening problem. Habitual Tinct users invariably became stiff and arthritic in early middle age. And of course the metabolism adjusted. In order for the user to gain the same intensity of result, larger and larger doses were necessary, and in high concentrations Tinct could kill. Hardened Tinct-heads had been known to drop dead from heart attack, pulmonary oedema, deep vein thrombosis, even brain haemorrhage.

None of which occurred with the Changelings who were chasing Provender and Is, for all that the latter pair might have wished it would.

What did occur, though, was that the exertion began to take its toll on the gang members. For a while the Changelings felt as if they could keep going for ever. They could run and never stop. Then, just as Provender and Is reached the street with the tram track beside it, the Changelings started to crash. They had shot up together, using the same needle, so the comedown was pretty much simultaneous. The Tinct had burned through their systems like wildfire, the flames fanned by the adrenal rush of the pursuit. Then, all at once, it snuffed itself out. There was no more.

The Changelings didn't come to a screeching halt but there was an abrupt and marked decline in their rate of progress. To them, it was as though their legs had hollowed out, all muscle gone. They carried on running but it was momentum more than anything that bore them along. Searing pain seeped into their lungs. Their heads went swimmy with oxygen deprivation. One of them, without breaking stride, puked bile down his chest.

A gap opened between them and their intended victims. A half-dozen yards became a dozen, a dozen a score.

Provender and Is failed to notice because they were concentrating on one thing only: the tram stop ahead. They didn't even notice that the racket made by their pursuers was dwindling. All they could hear was their own breathing, their own thumping hearts. Ears, eyes, everything they had was focused on the tram stop's gate, getting to the gate, the swiftly nearing gate . . .

The gate.

They arrived at it and almost shot straight past. It appeared beside them with such surprising suddenness that they could scarcely believe it was there. Belatedly their brains told them to halt, and they both skidded to a standstill. Provender then bent to the microphone funnel and tried to heave out the two words that would activate the gate opening mechanism: his name.

The first time, what came out of his mouth didn't sound like language, just a muddled mishmash of syllables. The voice recognition system didn't register it as an entry attempt. The small display screen mounted above the microphone funnel remained starkly blank.

Provender sucked in air and had another go.

The second time, what he said was recognisably *Provender Gleed* but it came out in a garbled splurge, as though a single word. The voice recognition system failed to accept it as valid. The display screen flashed up a curt response:

VOICE UNFAMILIAR
TRY AGAIN

While Provender collected himself for a third try, Is looked left and was astonished to see how far the Changelings had fallen behind. They were still coming, however, white-faced and gasping but still staggering on along the pavement. She shook Provender and told him to stop mucking around and get the ruddy gate *open*.

Provender ordered himself to be calm, to say the words slowly, clearly and audibly. At the back of his mind lurked the knowledge that the voice recognition system often did not work. The technology was reasonably new and therefore prone to glitches. The waveform-comparison generator was not sensitive to extreme fluctuations in the human voice and so didn't allow for a large margin of difference when matching a spoken name against the recorded version stored in its memory bank. Also, the company which owned the patent on and constructed the system was a Kuczynski holding, and it was believed that the Kuczynskis had arranged for a special design flaw to be installed with the express purpose of inconveniencing one other Family and one other Family alone. The jury was still out as to whether this was anything more than paranoia on the Gleeds' part. No statistical evidence existed to support the theory that the system failed more frequently for a Gleed than for anyone else. Then again, it seemed to certain members of Provender's Family that such sabotage was just the sort of thing the Kuczynskis would do, a suspicion given weight by the fact that, were the roles reversed, were the voice recognition system a technology owned by the Gleeds, then rigging it so that it gave the Kuczynskis trouble was just the sort of thing *they* would do.

Ignoring this thought as best he could, Provender brought his lips right up to the mouth of the microphone funnel, close enough for kissing, and uttered his name. He enunciated every syllable of it with an elocution master's precision. There was a pause, during which he could have sworn he heard a tiny mechanical giggle, the system snickering to itself, and the display screen cleared the extant message but seemed reluctant to put up anything in its stead, and he understood that the Kuczynskis had, if the belief about their mischief-making had a basis in fact, just condemned him and Is to a vicious beating and perhaps worse.

Then, like a prayer answered, a new message appeared:

VOICE FAMILIAR

PROVENDER GLEED

ACCESS PERMITTED

At the same instant, the gate unlocked itself. Bars retracted. Bolts were unshot. Pistons hissed. The gate eased inward.

Provender thrust Is through and followed right behind, then swung round and grabbed the gate. The gates on the tram network were notoriously slow in closing, which had never struck anyone as a problem till now. He leaned hard on this one to expedite the process. Out of the corner of his eye he could see the Changelings, the frontmost of them now within spitting distance. The gate would not be hurried. The hydraulics did not like to go at anything but their own speed. Is squeezed in beside him and pushed too. The gate groaned in protest. The Changeling, who was the one armed with a cricket bat, drew level and lunged exhaustedly.

The gate clanked shut at the very moment his hand grabbed it. Enraged, he drew back, brandishing his weapon. He swung the bat behind his head and brought it forward. The blow, which was aimed at Provender's fingers, missed, Provender having let go of the gate a split second earlier. The bat struck ironwork with a resonant, shivering *clanggg*. Provender and Is drew back as the Changeling dropped the bat and threw himself at the gate, thrusting an arm through and grabbing for them. The other Changelings joined him, reaching through the bars and pawing at the air.

Their movements were feeble, desperate, a last flailing effort to get at their quarry. They knew Provender Gleed and the girl with him had escaped, but they could not yet admit it to themselves. One of them made an attempt to clamber up the fence but did not get far, unable to find a decent toehold in the chain link. Another tugged on the gate as if he truly believed he had the wherewithal to rip it loose from its frame, but there was little strength left in his arms. Eventually all of them were reduced to cursing and hawking gobs of sputum at Provender and Is, and soon they didn't even have the energy for that as the post-Tinct lethargy took a firm hold.

Provender and Is retreated to the tram platform, from where they watched their pursuers succumb to lassitude. Some of the Changelings sagged against the fence and gate while others sank to the ground, looking for all the world like marionettes whose puppeteer had grown bored of conducting the show. It seemed an ignominious finish to such a frantic chase, but Provender and Is weren't complaining. Exhausted themselves, though nowhere near as depleted as the gang-tribe, they settled down on the platform and got comfortable. For a while neither could speak and so they simply looked at the Changelings, who stared stuporously back with eyes that suggested they had forgotten why they were there and who the people on the platform were. During this curious stalemate one of the Changelings even managed to fall asleep, nodding off where he stood, kept upright solely by virtue of his fingers being hooked through the chain link.

Provender, when his face was no longer such a hectic shade of scarlet, said, 'I never thought we'd manage that. I thought they had us for sure.'

'Tinct crash,' Is replied.

'Oh. What?'

She outlined the pathology of the drug.

'Ah. Still, good for us that we ran so fast, eh?'

'Tell me that when I've stopped feeling so ill. How long till a tram comes?'

Provender glanced both ways along the track. 'Should be soon. The most anyone's ever waited is half an hour. It depends on where the nearest one is when you activate the gate.'

Just as he said this, as if on cue the overhead cables started to crackle and the steel rails began to hum.

54

The tram arrived, coasting to a halt alongside the platform. Accordion doors hissed open, and Provender, with a gentlemanly gesture, invited Is to step aboard, then hopped in after her.

Depressing a brass handle triggered the door-closing mechanism. Provender then ambled to the front of the car where the control console was situated, a sloping bank of switches, levers and lightbulbs. He frowned at it, hesitant.

'Tell me you know how to drive this thing,' Is said.

'To be honest, this is the first time I've travelled in one on my own. Not on my own exactly, but you know. Without another Family member.'

'Don't get out much, do you.'

'Not till lately. However . . .' Provender toggled a switch and several bulbs lit up on the console. 'It isn't that difficult, I think. If Extravagance can manage it, I can. All you have to do is – yes.' Another switch brought illumination to a display window marked DESTINATION. 'Then you just dial in the place you want to . . .' He manipulated a pair of knurled knobs, one of which caused the display window above it to scroll through a list of regions throughout the country, the other of which summoned up a sub-list of tram stops located within each of those regions. Finding BERKSHIRE with the first knob led him to find DASHLANDS easily with the second. 'And then,' he said, 'with just a press of this button – *voilà*. We are on our way.'

The tram car gave a lurch and began to roll, pulling away from the platform, the stop and the inert Changelings. It picked up speed and in no time was cruising at a steady twenty m.p.h. through west London. The city trundled by outside; the wires above gave off enthusiastic fizzes and sparks; the wheels drummed. Provender ensconced Is in an armchair, then went to the bar at the rear and fixed them both a whisky, adding ice from an ice-cube maker. They sipped the drinks facing each other, and Provender felt the weight of his recent travails begin, at last, to lift. He was truly out of harm's way now. In little over an hour, he would be back home. The whole horrible escapade was over.

'You, er, you didn't think that was really me back there, did you?' he said.

'What?'

'When I was talking to those kids. Offering them a bribe. Acting like a twit. I was just putting it on.'

'Could have fooled me.'

'No, really, I was – Oh, I see. You're mocking.'

'Frankly, Provender, at the time I wasn't sure what to think. I thought you might have gone mad. I also thought there was no way they were going to fall for it.'

'Neither did I, but I reckoned it was worth a shot. They were going to beat us up anyway, but I thought if I could persuade them to take us out of the estate first, we'd have a better chance of getting away from them before they started. It worked. I'm stunned that it did, but it did.'

'Must be the Family mystique.'

'Must be. Also, there is a kind of magic in behaving like a blithe, posh nincompoop. It protects you like a charm. People are disarmed by it. I don't do it myself as a rule, but I've seen it work for others. My uncle Fort, for instance. He does it all the time. Acts the buffoon and get away with murder. Mind you, with him I'm not sure it's an act.'

Provender drained his whisky tumbler at a gulp, much as his uncle might have done, and asked Is if she wanted hers refreshed. She shook her head, then changed her mind and said yes.

Second whiskies in hand, they gazed out of the tram's windows as the turrets of Acton and then the tenements of Old Ealing passed by.

'I have to ask now,' Provender said. 'I can't not. What was it all about? Why was I kidnapped? What did your friend Damien want with me?'

'Money.'

'That's it? Just the money?'

'Isn't that enough of a reason? He wanted several million from your Family, money he would put to use renovating Needle Grove, to make it a nicer place, not the sort of place that breeds gangs like that lot back there.'

'But . . . he wouldn't expect to get away with it, surely. It's hardly subtle or covert. He gets the money, hands me over, next thing we know someone's spending a fortune doing up a slum housing estate. If he wanted to draw attention to himself, if he wanted everyone to know who the kidnap culprit was, he couldn't do much better than that. My Family would be on it like a shot. We'd have him. He'd be in jail faster than you can breathe.'

'Don't think Damien didn't realise that.'

'But he was still prepared to take the risk. D'you know, I'm almost starting to admire him.'

'No, because there was no risk.' Is studied her tumbler, swilling the liquor around inside it and making the ice cubes clink. 'Look, I suppose you ought to know. It's only fair. Damien wasn't acting alone.'

'He had you with him, yes. And if you're worried about that, don't be. My Family will go after him, have no fear, but you are going to be absolutely safe. I'll see to that. You'll have complete protection. No one's going to prosecute you or anything.'

'Do you actually listen to me when I'm talking, Provender? Sometimes I think you only hear what you want to hear. I'm not referring to me when I say he wasn't acting alone. Clearly I was an accomplice. That's pretty bloody obvious.'

'There was someone else? A third party?'

'Genius! And they say Family inbreeding lowers the IQ.'

'Hey!'

He looked genuinely wounded. Isis waved a hand at him in apology. 'You're right, that was uncalled-for. It's just – I don't like to have to be the one to break this to you.'

'Go on.'

'Because you're not going to like it.'

'I'll be the judge of that.'

'He had help. Damien. Inside help.'

'Help.'

'From Family. From someone in your Family.'

'No!'

'And before you ask, I have no idea who. He wouldn't tell me. Said I was safer off not knowing.'

'Oh, but that's preposterous. No one in my Family would do anything like this. He must have been having a joke with you.'

'Believe me, he wasn't. I saw him have phone conversations with this person. He didn't like having to rely on a Family member, it didn't sit well with him at all, but he did it anyway. He – we – couldn't have pulled off your kidnap otherwise. Somebody had to buy off the security guard so that he wouldn't be at his post when we were leaving Dashlands, and Damien didn't have access to those sort of funds. And of course another part of the arrangement was that when Damien got the ransom money, he'd be guaranteed immunity from prosecution and from anything else the Gleeds might have in mind for him. He could spend the money how he wanted and not get caught for it.'

'And this is somebody in my immediate Family?'

'I don't know. I suppose so.'

Provender wagged his head wonderingly. 'It can't be. I mean, who? My mother? Never. My father? Unlikely. Gratitude or Extravagance? It wouldn't be Grat, no way, and 'Strav, she and I don't get on but she'd hardly stoop to something like this, not even as a practical joke. Far too much like effort. Then there's Great, but he wouldn't. He *couldn't*. And Uncle Fort . . . He's a troublemaker, a piss-head, fond of himself, no question, but not – it's just isn't him. What would he gain from it? What would any of them gain from it? No, I don't accept this. I refuse to.'

'Provender, you have to. It's the truth.'

'It's someone in my Family?'

Impatiently: 'Yes,'

'My immediate Family?'

'I told you, I don't know. How immediate is immediate?'

'Well, a cousin . . . Oh.'

'What?'

Provender rubbed his temples, his brain churning. 'A cousin. Oh *mierda*, yes. Arthur. That little *pendejo* rat-bastard.'

'This obviously sounds like one of your favourite relatives.'

'Hmm? Arthur? Oh no, far from it.'

'Sarcasm, Provender.'

But even Is's admission of sarcasm was wasted on him. He was pondering too hard, too deep in concentration.

'Arthur,' he said, 'Arthur doesn't like me, and that's fine, no problem, the feeling's reciprocated, but would he go so far as to . . . ? He might. He definitely might. Just to fuck up my life. And maybe, maybe . . . To annoy my father? To get him to resent me for costing him a chunk of money? That's like Arthur. And then, while I'm off the scene, tucked away in a Family-hater's bathroom, Arthur could always swan over to Dashlands and pretend to be all concerned, show sympathy, come across as the perfect cousin. Jockeying for position. Reminding everyone who he is, how wonderful he is, isn't he better than Provender?'

'I'll just join in the conversation when you're ready.'

'And then at the party . . . Good God yes. That tirade of his about actors. His attempt at the world record for the most uses of the word "bloody" in a single sentence. And, no, before that, when he was talking about his play. Offering me tickets. He said – he said I should come if I wasn't doing anything else.'

'Any time you want some input, you only have to ask.'

'No, he didn't say that, it was more specific than that. What the hell was it? If I'm not . . . otherwise detained! *Detained*. Christ, that cocky little *cabrón*, he was telling me, he was just about giving it away. This was what was going to happen to me. I wouldn't be going to his *Hamlet* first night because I'd be fucking being held hostage!'

'I'll sit here quietly minding my own busi—'

Provender sprang to his feet and hurried over to the control console.

'What are you doing?' Is asked.

'What's it look like?' He grabbed one of the destination knobs. 'I'm diverting us.'

'We're not going to Dashlands?'

'Nope.'

'But we have to.'

'No, we don't.'

'Yes, we do. Your father. If your father sees you, if he knows you're safe, he can get the politicians to back down. There won't be a war.'

'It can wait.'

'It damn well can't.' Is stormed up to the front of the car and seized Provender's arm. 'What's more important, Provender? Going after your cousin or pulling a continent back from the brink of conflict?'

'Going after Arthur.'

'You don't mean that.'

'I do. I want to catch him unawares. I want to see his face when I turn up on his doorstep, free. I want to watch him gape and gulp like a stranded goldfish.'

'Fine, then do that, but leave it till after we've been to Dashlands.'

'No way. If all of a sudden everyone starts suing for peace, Arthur will know the game's up. Whereas if everything remains as it is, just for now, I can walk right up to him and he won't be expecting it. It's the only way I'll ever know if he's involved in the kidnapping.'

'No, it isn't. Damien could rat him out. To the police. If he was arrested and being interrogated.'

'Arthur would deny it. There's no proof of a connection between them, I bet. No physical evidence. Just phonecalls. Just Damien's word against a Gleed's. Guess who everyone'll believe. Especially,' he added, with an ironic leer, 'when one of them's a much-loved star of stage and screen.'

'But what if everything goes wrong? What if war is declared? For all we know it could already have been. We haven't exactly been keeping up with current events this past couple of hours.'

'There's an entertainment system somewhere in the tram, with a radio. You could turn it on and listen.'

'That isn't the point.'

'An hour, Is. All I need. One measly hour.'

55

Romeo Moore – now, although he was as yet blissfully unaware of the fact, the world's only remaining Anagrammatic Detective – was at his post outside Arthur Gleed's house. He couldn't think of anywhere else to be. The shame of letting Arthur slip through his fingers that morning had abated, but he still couldn't think about what he had done without feeling a smart of self-recrimination. Determined not to repeat the mistake, he had contacted the cab firm whose owner he and Milner had once helped – the TAXIMETER/EXTRA TIME case – and had hired the exclusive use of one of his cars for the entire day. The year-long free-travel offer had expired a while ago but the owner still held Moore in enough esteem that he was able to negotiate a decent rate. The taxi was now sitting at a corner of the square, engine running. Moore would have been in the back, in a far more comfortable seat than the park bench he was on, but for the fact that the driver was one of those garrulous types who not only couldn't stop talking but couldn't seem to take the hint that his passenger was in no mood for trivial chit-chat. After half an hour of listening to the driver bang on about any subject that crossed his mind, a torrent-of-consciousness rant, apparently unstoppable, Moore had excused himself, saying the park was the better vantage point, with a more direct view of the house. The driver had carried on talking even as Moore exited the taxi. For all Moore knew, he was still talking now.

The newspaper crossword was done-and-dusted a long time ago, Moore winning his battle of wits with the setter in just six minutes. The newspaper itself, with its disturbing reports of potential armed conflict, had been perused from cover to cover. Moore was pleased to note that the review of last night's performance of *Hamlet* was more or less as he had predicted: the paper's theatre critic was ho-hum about the production itself but Arthur Gleed had 'essayed a unique Hamlet, inhabiting the role of arch-vacillator as though born to it'. The comment had more edges than an icosahedron.

As for the threat of war, Moore had seen little evidence that people were unduly concerned. Everybody seemed to be going about their business as normal. Shops were open and there was no panic-buying as one might have expected, nor was there any sign of an imminent exodus into the countryside. London was proceeding at its customary pace, hectic but no more so than usual. Doubtless things would change if war was declared. Then again, *Homo sapiens* was on the whole a phlegmatic species, and sometimes events were so momentous that they simply had to be ignored. Unless bombs were actually raining down on the capital, life would go on with the minimum of disruption. The taxi driver had touched on this, when flitting from one unrelated topic to the possible war to another unrelated topic. 'Not a sod I can do about it,' he had said. 'I just drive a cab. Unless it's stopping me driving my cab, I'll just carry on doing that.'

And Moore was an Anagrammatic Detective and it wasn't stopping him doing *his* job, so he was carrying on too.

Needing something to occupy his thoughts till Arthur returned, Moore set himself the task of devising a word game. It was what he often did during idle moments, a way of pressure-valving his philologically hyperactive brain. Initially he came up with the idea of forming words from the letter sequences on vehicle licence plates. He tried it out with the cars parked in the square and it was satisfactorily entertaining but not much of a challenge. Looking for something a bit more taxing, he hit on the notion of finding words in which you could substitute one vowel with any of the other four vowels and create a valid new word each time. This was altogether more intellectually demanding, and Moore put his brain to work on it, mindful not to get too wrapped up in case Arthur reappeared and he didn't notice. He thought Milner would be pleased by the game, and wondered what he might call it. A Latinate or Hellenic name was conventional. Varivocalis? Pentalogue?

Before the astonishing event occurred – before the resolution to the Provender Gleed case all but fell into his lap – Moore managed to identify two strings of words which fulfilled the game's criterion. One was pack, peck, pick, pock, puck. The other was mate, mete, mite, mote, mute. He was racking his brains to find a third, preferably something more than four letters long, when two people walked into the square via its eastern end, emerging from the street which led to the nearest Family tram stop. Moore registered them, thought them of no significance – a young man and a young woman, perhaps a couple but, if so, they were in the throes of a lovers' squabble, not getting along, because he was a few paces ahead of her and she had her arms folded across her stomach in a manner that reeked of discontent – and then Moore blinked, hard, then rubbed his eyes as if to wipe them clean and start afresh, because his eyes were faulty, surely, some defect was causing them to tell him he was looking at the kidnappee, the Gleed heir-apparent, the reason for his vigil outside Arthur's house, Provender, who was now striding round the square's perimeter, heading for that selfsame residence, and it must be a vision problem, brought on perhaps by lack of sleep, a hallucination, and further blinking and rubbing would get rid of it, but this didn't work, not even banging a hand on the side of his head would do the trick, Moore tried it, a few hefty knocks with an open palm, but what would usually fix a television set when the picture wasn't right did not have the same effect on the mechanism of the human cranium and the Provender apparition did not correct itself, there he still was, with his companion a few steps behind him, climbing the steps to his cousin's front door and prodding the doorbell button with a forthright forefinger . . .

Finally Moore galvanised himself to move. It was the faint ringing of the doorbell within the house that did it, that proved he wasn't imagining what he saw. Hallucinations, he reasoned, couldn't make doorbells ring, could they? Leaping to his feet, he hastened feverishly out of the park and arrowed towards Provender.

I was right, Merlin, he thought. *I don't know why it's turned out the way it has, I didn't think this was how I would find him, but I have, I've done it, I've won our bet, dammit I was right!*

56

'He's not home.'

Provender wheeled round.

The man who had spoken was a timid-looking individual, slight of stature and dressed in a cheap, rumpled suit. He stood on the pavement clutching the bottom of his jacket and rocking on his heels like a nervous schoolboy. Is was peering at him quizzically, and Provender couldn't help but do the same.

'And you are . . . ?'

'Oh, yes, forgive me. Romeo Moore, Anagrammatic Detective.'

'Whatsis detective?' said Is.

'I have a card.' The man reached inside his jacket and rummaged. 'They're in here somewhere. I'm a private investigator. A special sort of private investigator. Oh dear, can't find them. I've been charged with the duty of— A-ha!' He produced a sheaf of business cards and handed one to Is, then climbed the front steps and proffered another of the cards to Provender, who took it, glanced at it, saw that it said *Milner and Moore, Anagrammatic Detectives* together with an address and phone number, and tucked it away in a pocket.

'Charged with the duty of . . . ?' Provender prompted.

'Uh, well, you, I suppose.'

'Me.'

'Yes,' said Moore, and added, 'Sir.'

'No need for "sir". What about me? What duty?'

'Finding you.'

'Right. Which you appear to have done.'

'I know.'

'Congratulations.'

'Thank you. Your Family, you see, hired my colleague and myself to locate you after you . . . er, went missing. They had reason to believe you'd been taken against your will, but now . . . umm.' Moore threw a look at Is. 'Perhaps they were mistaken and it wasn't involuntary after all.'

Provender saw what the Anagrammatic Detective was implying. 'Trust me, it was. Very much so. My Family hired you?'

'Along with my colleague, yes. Courtesy of the Clan Reav— Of a certain

Mr Carver. And so here I am.' Moore's mouth flirted with the idea of a smile. 'Case successfully solved. I can call Mr Carver and inform him that Provender Gleed is alive and well and no longer a captive. I can, can't I?'

Provender was frowning. 'But you're here. Outside Arthur's pad. Which means you think Arthur . . .'

'. . . kidnapped you? I did think that. Current evidence would appear to indicate otherwise.'

'Not necessarily. What reason do you have for thinking it was Arthur?'

'The anagrams.'

'The anagrams?'

'The anagrams.'

'What anagrams?'

'Of Arthur Gleed. There were all sorts. His name positively dripped guilt. My colleague had a different theory about your disappearance, but me, I had your cousin in the frame from the very start. Turns out I was wrong, but my roundabout route brought me to the right destination in the end. That's how it is with the anagrams sometimes. They move in mysterious ways, their wonders to perform.'

'Let me get this straight. You're a private investigator who uses *anagrams* to solve crimes?'

Moore beamed proudly. 'I am.'

Provender shook his head in mild disbelief. 'And my Family took you on to find me. Just you?'

'And my colleague, Merlin Milner.'

'Of course, your colleague. But no one else.'

'Not that I know of.'

Provender let out a hollow laugh. 'Thanks for trying, everyone. No disrespect to you, Mr Moore, but you're hardly the thorough search party I'd have hoped for. A small army of private investigators I could understand, but two people who use anagrams . . . ?'

'We were told that discretion was paramount.' Moore was trying not to look as though his feelings were hurt. 'A low-key approach. Obviously not good enough for some people, but I would submit that the results speak for themselves.'

'Yes, yes, they do,' Provender said, mollifying. 'I really wasn't trying to cause offence.'

'Though you did,' Is chipped in.

'And,' Provender went on, 'it so happens, Mr Moore, that I believe you're on the right track. Arthur *is* involved. He arranged for me to be kidnapped. He's the brains behind the operation.'

'*Yes*,' said Moore under his breath. 'But you've escaped.'

'I have, and I'm here to confront the little creep and get him to 'fess up.'

'And he's not home, as I told you. He's elsewhere.'

'Where?'

'I wish I knew.'

'You don't have any idea? There isn't anywhere else he could be?'

'Well,' said Moore, cautiously, 'there is one place I've been staking out apart from here.'

'Which is?'

'The theatre where his play's on. On New Aldwych. The Shortborn.'

'Could he be there now?'

'I doubt it.' Moore consulted his watch. 'Curtain doesn't go up for another four hours. I don't think make-up and costuming takes that long.'

'What do you say, Is? You think we should try there?'

'Don't ask my opinion. My opinion apparently doesn't count for anything.'

'Well, I think we should. Back to the trams. Mr Moore, thanks for your help. It will be remembered.'

'Very kind. Might I just say, though, that I have a taxi waiting. It might be quicker, more convenient.'

'A taxi?' Provender pondered. 'Yeah, good idea. A taxi. Why not?'

57

The television room stank of sweat, of body odour, of manly musk, of maleness. Prosper had infused it with himself over the course of the day. Just by being there he had scent-marked it as his, a section of Dashlands House that was now Prosper Gleed's exclusive territory.

Or so Cynthia felt as she cracked the door open and tentatively entered. The smell might have been in her imagination, her senses confirming what she wanted to believe. She wanted the television room to have an offensive aroma, thus it did.

Prosper was on the sofa, fixated as ever on the projected TV image on the wall. The Phone was in the corner, dozing where he stood, poor fellow. Prosper ought at least to have instructed the man to sit – it wasn't against the rules – but no, he was too preoccupied, too absorbed in his own fermenting megalomania, too drunk with amazement at the turmoil he had instigated, to think of anyone but himself.

The glint in Prosper's eyes, as he watched a report being transmitted from a forward command post somewhere in the Sudetenland, was all but indistinguishable from the one that appeared when he was making a move on some nubile young creature. There was the same avarice in it, the same thrill in exerting his influence. Girls fell at Prosper's feet because he was handsome, certainly, but also because of who he was, his surname, his status. Cynthia understood this all too well, since she herself had been one of those girls, a long time ago. He had been utterly captivating back then, youth giving his charm a freshness, an innocence almost. Although Cynthia had been Family too, and therefore in theory his equal, looks coupled with the aura that hung around the word *Gleed* had made Prosper an irresistible package. Naïve as she had been, she had found him endlessly, fascinatingly sophisticated, and when it became clear that he was courting her, wooing her, she could scarcely believe her luck. Nor could her parents. For the Lamases, a union with the Gleeds was several steps up. Their Family status would be immensely enhanced by the association. It was a match made in heaven. How could she not have been happy about it?

After almost thirty years – and countless infidelities – the question now was, how could she be happy about it any more? And the answer was, she had adapted. She had adjusted. Incrementally, as time went by, she had hardened herself to the disappointment and the betrayal. She hardly felt his indifference to her.

And then this. On top of her son being gone, her only boy, his absence like one of her own organs having been torn out of her, she was confronted with a husband who was no longer content with fucking his way through the women of the world and was now trying to fuck the world itself. Cynthia despised coarseness but there it was. Fucking. That was what Prosper was doing, there was no other word for it. Fucking like some maddened rapist, not caring who got hurt so long as he exerted his power.

Well, no more. Enough. It was time she put a stop to it. After hours of soul-searching, Cynthia knew what she must do. As her nephew had said: *Anything and everything must be done to bring about the right conclusion.* God help her but she had no choice.

The Phone's eyelids flickered, then snapped open. He came to attention and nodded to her. 'Ma'am,' he said briskly, hoping to sound like someone who had not just been half-asleep.

Cynthia smiled at him and kept the smile in place as she turned to her husband.

'Prosper. Dear. You've been sitting there for ages. You've barely touched your lunch. Might I get you something to eat?'

'Hmm? Oh, no. I'm fine.'

'Drink, then?'

'Again, fine. Don't need to fuss over me.'

'I take it the Kuczynskis haven't called yet.'

'Only a matter of time. Only a matter of time. The Pan-Slavic Federation's demanded that America step in and play peace-broker. That's a definite sign. They're cracking. Can't take the pressure.'

'If you say so. You're sure about that drink? How about some coffee? Strong coffee? You look worn out. You need something to help keep you going.'

The solicitous, ever sympathetic wife. How often had she pretended to play that role? It came to her easily now, second nature.

'Some coffee?' said Prosper. 'Yes, all right. Why not? Have a servant bring some.'

'Better yet,' Cynthia said, 'I'll make it for you and bring it myself.'

58

The taxi driver was tongue-tied throughout the journey to New Aldwych, repeatedly trying to formulate a sentence and failing. Frequent checks in his rear view mirror confirmed that none other than Provender Gleed was sitting in the back of his cab, but he simply could not work out a way of remarking on the fact that wouldn't come across as glib or grovelsome, nor did he feel he could opt for some innocuous comment – about the weather, say – for fear of sounding disrespectfully trite. He was torn between excitement and the desire to appear unflustered, as if driving a Family member across London was something he did every day. He knew that at the first available opportunity he would call his wife and anyone else he could think of and tell them about this, and the prospect somewhat mitigated his present state of speechlessness. In his account of this episode, he and Provender would be chatting like old pals and the Gleed heir would declare himself impressed by the taxi driver's opinions and observations on life. It wouldn't be a lie so much as an embellishment of the truth: had the driver not been dumbstruck, Provender would surely have been delighted to hear what he thought about things.

As far as Moore was concerned, the driver's silence was golden. He'd been worried that the man would talk them all to death before they reached the Notting Hill Skyway or even the Shepherd's Bush Tunnel. Provender's presence, however, was talismanic. It granted an unexpressed wish.

It did the same at the Shortborn Theatre. The building which Moore had been unable to penetrate, this seemingly impregnable fortress of Thespis, raised its portcullis and lowered its drawbridge and surrendered without a siege. All that was needed was for Provender to enter the lobby, and within seconds there were members of the front-of-house staff rushing around madly, and the manager appeared, and there was much hand-wringing and kowtowing, and the three visitors – Provender, Moore, the girl called Is – were given free rein to venture anywhere they wanted. Provender asked the manager where he might find his cousin, and was told, 'On stage.' It transpired that an unscheduled extra rehearsal was going on, the show's star dissatisfied with the previous night's perform-ance and wanting to give the play that last little extra polish to make it just so.

'A consummate perfectionist, our leading man,' said the manager.

'A complete pain in the arse, more like,' Provender muttered. 'So we can go into the auditorium, then? Have a look at what's happening?'

'But of course,' said the manager with an unctuous writhe. 'Allow me to escort you.'

'No. If you don't mind, I'd prefer it if we slipped quietly in. So as not to cause a fuss.'

'Very well.' The manager bit his lip with disappointment. 'Perhaps later, though, I could take you on a tour of the theatre. The Shortborn is one of London's most historic venues, substantially rebuilt after the war with funds from the Bannerjee Foundation, but still retaining—'

'Yes, maybe.' Provender turned to Moore and Is. 'Public place. Lots of witnesses around to see. This should be good.'

Rubbing his hands, he headed for the doors that led from the lobby to the stalls. Moore and Is filed after him.

Outside, at a bus stop across the street from the theatre, a figure who had been lying in wait made his move.

Damien had been standing at the bus stop for nigh on an hour. Buses had come and gone, passengers had stepped on and off, and Damien had stayed put, making it look each time as if the bus he was waiting for wasn't this one but the next. His air of long-suffering, barely-contained impatience was readily recognisable to anyone with experience of the vagaries of London's public transport system. His huffs and grimaces were taken by others to mean he was being badly let down by the RLA and its inability to run a bus service which was even on nodding acquaintance with the word efficiency.

It wasn't completely an act, but the real source of Damien's discontent was not, of course, buses. Every minute he spent at the stop had been a minute in which it seemed even more implausible that Provender Gleed and Is were going to turn up at the theatre. As long shots went, this one was inordinately, inconceivably long. It was, however, his only shot. He had no alternative, other than to sit at home and stew in his own frustration. Which he couldn't anyway do because there was the small matter of the body of a dead detective cluttering up his flat. His only option had been to come here and hope.

Hope that the detective had not lied.

Hope that Is had conferred with Provender and told him that Damien had collaborated with a Family insider.

Hope that Provender put two and two together and came to the same conclusion as the dead detective's partner.

Hope that Provender would choose to visit the Shortborn Theatre and confront his cousin.

A ragged patchwork quilt of hopes, threadbare and full of holes, but it was all Damien had to draw around him and take comfort from. Where else could he go to look for Provender? What other chance did he have of getting his hands on his hostage again? Circumstances forced him to be at the theatre. His choices were narrowed down to this tiny, mote-like, infinitesimal scrap of possibility.

And he had been close to giving up, on the point of going back to his parked Dragon Wind and driving dismally back to Needle Grove, when remarkably, astonishingly, his against-all-odds gamble paid off. A taxi pulled up in front of the theatre and three passengers disembarked from it: Provender Gleed, then Is, then a little man Damien did not recognise but, were he to hazard a guess, would have said was Merlin Milner's partner-in-crimebusting.

There was no time for Damien to catch them in the few seconds it took them to cross the pavement and disappear into the theatre lobby. The traffic was flowing thick and fast in the roadway and he wasn't able to reach the other side of the street for a full minute. When he got there, a glance through the lobby's glassed doors showed Provender surrounded by people and speaking to someone who was obviously the theatre manager. Damien considered barging in, but the lobby was too public a place. What with all the theatre employees, there were too many eye-witnesses, too many potential have-a-go heroes who could make his life difficult. Then Provender left the lobby, heading deeper into the building, and Damien knew he would have to find another way into the theatre.

Easily done. All theatres had stage doors, and the Shortborn's wasn't difficult to find. It was situated down an alley at the side. Damien walked up to it and jabbed the buzzer-button marked ENQUIRIES.

The person who answered the buzzer was not some wispy theatrical type as Damien had anticipated, but rather a stocky, thick-necked, short-back-and-sided individual whose bad suit and matching attitude said, unmistakably, bouncer. Which made sense, what with a Gleed in the play's cast.

Damien was unfazed. Not pausing, he shunted the man backwards with an outstretched hand, unsheathing his knife with the other hand. The bouncer, taken by surprise, staggered and collided with a plastic chair, sending it and the nudie mag that was lying on it skidding across the floor. He recovered his balance expertly and came back at Damien, adopting a boxer's stance, weight on the rear foot, fists loosely clasped at jaw height. The knife was still concealed behind Damien's back, so the bouncer had no reason not to feel confident that the fight would be his. This bloke who had pushed him was big but not that big, and a venue-security profes-sional feared no one. A venue-security professional was trained for moments like this, *lived* for moments like this.

He swung. Damien parried. Huge equalled slow. The bouncer might as well have stopped and told him when the punch was coming and where he intended it to land.

He swung again, another hefty, lumbering roundhouse. Damien ducked in under it and brought the knife into play, whipping it in from the side and sinking it hilt-deep into the bouncer's flank.

By rights the knife-thrust ought to have settled the scuffle then and there. It was a mortal blow and the shock alone should have toppled the bouncer. Damien gave the deerhorn handle an extra twist, further ruining whichever vital organs the blade was embedded in, then stepped back, as if inviting his opponent to do the decent thing now and fall.

The bouncer teetered, looking down, exploring the knife handle with inquisitive fingers, feeling the shape of it, fathoming what it meant to have this thing protruding from his abdomen, this wetness leaking out. Then, to Damien's surprise, instead of having the good grace to keel over, he grunted and lunged, arms spread wide.

The strength with which the arms pincered around Damien's chest and began to squeeze was, literally, breathtaking. Damien's ribcage constricted; he all but heard bones creak. His lungs were suddenly straining for air but he could get none into them. Meanwhile the bouncer's own breath was gusting in his face, a series of rapid, meaty-smelling exhalations that added to the torture of being suffocated: even if he could inhale, there was nothing to inhale but *this*. Damien writhed and gasped but could not wrestle free. The pressure of the bouncer's bear-hug intensified. Damien's head woozed. His backbone groaned. Something, surely, was on the point of snapping.

Then, at last, the knife-wound took effect. The bear-hug relaxed. The bouncer seemed to crumble away. Suddenly he was supine on the floor. His heels were kicking the linoleum. His teeth were bared in a rictus of anguish and dismay. He started to choke, gagging gutturally.

Damien, reeling somewhat, bent down and yanked out the knife. He raised it and plunged it into the bouncer's chest, doing this much as he would have if the man had been a suffering animal – matter-of-factly, out of necessity, putting the creature out of its misery. The bouncer shuddered, spasmed, and went still. His eyes rolled and settled. A croak escaped his slack, gaping mouth. Gone.

Damien swabbed the blade clean on the bouncer's trouser-leg, then re-sheathed the knife. He stood up carefully. His chest throbbed, tender to the touch, and his head was swimmy, but otherwise he was unharmed.

He took stock of his surroundings. He was in a short corridor which terminated in a pair of swing doors inset with frosted-glass panes. A notice drew attention to the fact that no unauthorised persons were permitted beyond this point.

Damien barged both doors open and strode past dressing rooms, into the Shortborn's backstage area.

59

Arthur had not only demanded the additional rehearsal, he had insisted on it being conducted in full costume, props and all, with the lighting and sound technicians on hand to supply the necessary effects, the stagehands at work behind the scenes . . . basically the entire cast and crew giving up their afternoon to put on a matinée to an empty house, for no extra pay.

Naturally there was disgruntlement, mutinous mutterings backstage, threats to sabotage the proceedings, but none of it amounted to anything. The scenery humpers and the follow-spot jockeys knew better than to put their jobs at risk by offending a Gleed. As for the actors, they were too jealous of Arthur's fame and renown to mind, truly, doing as he asked. Besides, if he remembered this favour, he might be inclined to invite them to take part in some future production. In the acting world you always had to think about your next job, and open resentment of somebody higher up the ladder than you was never a wise career move. Cross Arthur Gleed, and it would be a lifetime of amateur dramatics from hereon after. *Another* rehearsal? Well, if Arthur wanted it . . . And come to think of it, last night's show hadn't been *that* great.

The director, Seán Lockwood, was trapped somewhere between these two categories, as cowed as the backstage people and as career-covetous as the people onstage. He wasn't happy about the rehearsal, but what could he do? Lockwood, in fact, had all but surrendered control of the production to his leading man and was feeling much as the captain of a pirated ship must do, watching helpless as his vessel was steered on a course he never plotted.

And it had all started so well.

At the outset Lockwood and Arthur had been of one mind: this would be a traditional *Hamlet*, a *Hamlet* Shakespeare himself would not have been surprised to see. Period dress and setting? Absolutely. None of your needless updating. And no gratuitous nudity or excessive bloodletting either, nothing like that, nothing that would bait the critics and earn shock-value kudos. A classic, conventional production, free of tricks and shenanigans.

How that had changed. First of all, a fortnight into rehearsals, Arthur suggested they cut the text by a quarter, in particular trimming Hamlet's soliloquies, which he said were very long and difficult to memorise.

Lockwood nearly asked why Arthur wanted to play Hamlet if he didn't fancy handling the soliloquies, but he held his tongue and did as requested.

It was the compromise which paved the way for a hundred further compromises. Most of them were relatively minor, but one wasn't, namely Arthur's sudden decision that the original Ophelia should be sacked. He had had a brief, torrid fling with her, it had got messy, he had broken her heart and now was running scared of her. You couldn't have a Hamlet who was afraid to look his Ophelia in the eye. Reluctantly Lockwood did the deed, braved a flood of weeping from the distraught actress, and then endured several long late-night phonecalls from her as she tried to come to terms with the emotional and professional rejection. The new Ophelia was not as right for the part as the old one but had the advantage of being a lesbian and therefore immune to Arthur's amorous approaches.

Through it all Lockwood thought of just one thing: Gleed patronage. He was young, twenty-two, and this was only his second professional directing gig. If it did well, the Gleeds would look kindly on him, put their name behind him, and he would be set up for life.

Then came the biggest blow of all. With the sets designed, scale models constructed, parts of Elsinore Castle already built, not to mention the costumes measured for and in the process of being sewn, Arthur had a change of heart. He came to Lockwood and said he had decided he didn't want a traditional *Hamlet* any more, he wanted a bold one, a ground-breaking one, a *Hamlet* that would startle (but still please) the Bard and would enliven modern audiences who were jaded, he felt, by stuffy old renditions of Shakespeare and were seeking something different, some-thing that was exciting and spoke directly to the modern-day theatregoer. He had roughed out some drawings of how he wanted Elsinore and the dramatis personae to look. Lockwood stared at the drawings, and stared at them some more, and calculated how much it would cost to abandon the existing designs and begin afresh, and came the closest he had ever got to punching someone. This thoughtless, this *arrogant* little fuckwit . . . ! How dare he turn up with a few clumsy ballpoint sketches and expect the set designer, the costumier, the property master, *everyone* to scrap every-thing they'd already done – work they had sweated over – and start again from scratch.

But, as ever, Lockwood capitulated. *Gleed patronage*, he told himself. *Gleed patronage, Gleed patronage, Gleed patronage.* He tried to talk Arthur into sticking with the original concept but Arthur's mind was made up and no amount of friendly persuasion could get him to budge. There was a near-riot as Lockwood announced the change of plan to the assembled design crew. For some reason not wishing to make Arthur a scapegoat, he took half of the responsibility onto himself, claiming it was a joint decision by the pair of them. He also promised to meet any overtime costs out of his own salary, an offer which meant that by the end of the play's run Lockwood would have earned a grand total of nothing, his income as director entirely eliminated by the expense of implementing Arthur's alterations.

It was around this time that Lockwood developed insomnia and, on his GP's advice, went on a course of antidepressants. Ever since, he had stopped caring about the production nearly as much and was even content to let Arthur assume some of his directorial duties. Arthur made suggestions about blocking and stage business which Lockwood rarely disagreed with. If he objected strongly, all he would do was say yes and then later have a private word with the players concerned and tell them to keep to the original way of doing the scene. They ignored him, invariably going along with Arthur's idea instead, but at least Lockwood had made the effort to look like he was still in charge. Nor was he in a position to be upset now if the reviews castigated the style and quality of the production, as some of them this morning had. He wasn't to blame. He had tried his best. He could do no more.

Arthur's re-envisioning of the play had turned it into something Lockwood barely recognised any more. The setting was now not a thirteenth-century Danish castle but a latterday English mansion, expensively decorated and furnished. The characters were kitted out in the latest fashions and had been advised by Arthur to declaim their lines in a free-form manner, ignoring the rhythms of Shakespeare's iambic pentameter. The play-within-a-play in Act II, scene ii, had been supplanted by a film-within-a-play, a prerecorded one-reeler projected onto a backdrop screen while Hamlet and family sat in cinema seats and, would you believe it, munched popcorn. The arras behind which Polonius meets his doom in IV, iii, had become a tinted-glass picture window, and Polonius himself was wheelchair-bound, though no less crotchety an old codger for that. There was no Ghost. Arthur preferred a modern psychological interpretation of the spectre – it was all in Hamlet's mind, a subjective manifestation of Oedipal leanings and madness – and so he taped Hamlet's Father's lines himself and had them played over the sound system. As a consequence, any of the other characters who see the Ghost in the course of the play were expected only to *pretend* to see it, as if humouring Hamlet, even if Hamlet didn't happen to be onstage at the time. It was absurd, but it was what Arthur wanted, and what Arthur wanted Arthur got.

Then there was Arthur's performance itself. He had chosen to essay the role naturalistically and with a set of tics and mannerisms clearly modelled on a real person, perhaps someone he knew or had once met. This lent it the air of an in-joke, but one so obscure that possibly only Arthur himself got it. Certainly Lockwood, as he observed the rehearsal at a dispassionate distance from the back row of the stalls, had no idea who Arthur was aping with those hesitancies of his, those inhibited gestures, those improvisational ums and ers, that whole peculiar blend of realistic underplaying and relentless mugging. Not forgetting that wig which was not a wig – a fine-furred latex cap which fit snugly over Arthur's own slicked-down hair and gave the impression of a close-shaven, downy scalp.

Provender, on the other hand, understood who it was straight away.

And was at first thunderstruck, then indignant beyond belief.

When Provender entered the auditorium, with Is and Moore not far behind him, the play was halfway done. Hamlet had just killed the figure lurking behind the arras – or rather the picture window, which he had shattered to spun-sugar smithereens by hurling a heavy potted shrub through it – and discovered that his victim, whose skull had been crushed by the pot plant, was not his uncle but Polonius. Gertrude was now soundly berating him, as well she might, and Hamlet was defending his actions at some length, though not, of course, at the length Shakespeare originally envisaged.

'Nay,' said Arthur, 'but to live / In the rank sweat of an enseamed bed, / Stew'd in corruption, honeying and making love / Over the nasty sty!'

'O, speak to me no more!' replied the actress playing his mother. 'These words like daggers enter in my ears./No more, sweet Hamlet!'

'A murtherer and a villain!' Arthur exclaimed.

'You bastard,' Provender hissed, almost simultaneously. His voice did not carry far but it did reach the ears of Sean Lockwood, who swivelled in his seat to see who had spoken. In the dimmed auditorium light he failed to identify Provender Gleed, but something about the person was naggingly familiar. The way he held himself. His cropped hair.

'You absolute and utter bastard,' Provender hissed again as, onstage, Arthur began a conversation with the unquiet spirit of his father. Much like a lunatic hearing voices in his head, Arthur twitched and twisted and frowned while he interpolated his own lines with the Ghost's booming taped tannoy pronouncements.

What Provender was looking at, however, was not acting. It was rank satire.

Is, standing at his shoulder, came to the same realisation. In a low whisper she said, 'He's doing you, isn't he?'

Provender hadn't needed it confirmed but to hear it from someone else was heartening. It meant he wasn't imagining things, this wasn't an instance of misplaced vanity; his cousin really was playing Hamlet in the guise of Provender Gleed, or perhaps Provender Gleed in the guise of Hamlet.

And the more Provender looked, the more grotesque and insulting it all became.

The set – it was highly reminiscent of Dashlands House. The décor, the furnishings. The slain Polonius was lying next to an overturned wheelchair and, although Provender didn't have a clear view of the actor's sprawled body, what he could see of him made him think of Great. As for Gertrude, the actress playing her did not physically resemble his own mother but she was smartly turned out, beautiful, coiffed, shapely, stately. The similarities were there.

Rage boiled up within him, so vast and fierce and all-consuming that he could barely think straight. Laying hands on Arthur was his one over-riding imperative. Wringing his cousin's scrawny little neck. He scanned the auditorium to see how he might get up onstage. The Shortborn, being an old-fashioned theatre, had an orchestra pit between stalls and foot-lights. It wasn't a gap that could be easily leapt (it was wider, indeed, than the gap between the closer pairs of adjacent balconies on a tower block in Needle Grove). As he cast around for some other means of reaching the stage, he noticed a man sitting in the back row. The man was staring at him in that manner Provender was fast becoming weary of: the I-know-you look. As their gazes met, the man got sharply to his feet.

'Sean Lockwood,' he said. 'Director. This is an honour, Mr Gleed. I'm sorry, it took me a moment to place you. Arthur mentioned some of his Family might be coming along at some point but I didn't expect—'

'There,' Provender snapped, pointing at the stage. 'How do I get there?'

'But the rehearsal is—'

'How?'

Lockwood collected himself. 'You can get backstage if you use that exit.' He indicated a door close to the stage, with a green sign glowing above it. 'Turn right, there's another door beyond which connects to the wings. It's locked during proper performances but I don't think it will be at the moment. You can . . .'

His voice trailed away. Provender was already off and running – running with the determination of a man who had business to finish and didn't care if he finished it with help or alone.

60

Backstage was traditionally a place of hush and caution, but the need to be discreet and avoid causing a disturbance was not, it must be said, uppermost in Provender's mind as he thrust open the door at the end of the passageway that ran alongside the auditorium. The only circumspection he showed was a brief pause, as the door swung shut behind him, to allow his eyes to adapt to the sudden gloom he found himself in. Gradually shapes made themselves apparent. He was on the side known as Opposite Prompt. Facing him was a short flight of steps, which you had to surmount in order to get level with the stage. Up there, in the wings, he could see a handful of motionless figures, various bulky props either waiting to be carried on or just recently taken off, black dropcloths hanging in swathes, and rows of sandbag-weighted ropes tethered to a complicated array of pulleys – people and objects in a state of suspension, all dimly limned by the light that filtered in sidelong from the stage.

No sooner had he got the lie of the land than he made for the steps, bounding up them two at a time. Heads turned. You weren't supposed to thump around like that back here. Move slowly, tread softly. Provender ignored their scowls. One man – big brawny chap, had to be a stagehand – did a double-take, evidently recognising him. Provender was by now heartily sick of being recognised by strangers. He was also, at this moment, too incensed by Arthur to care much about anything else. He breezed past the man, drawn towards the stage lights. Between two flies he caught a slivered glimpse of the set. There was Arthur-as-Hamlet, revealing to Gertrude his knowledge of Laertes's plot against him and his plans for foiling it:

> Let it work,
> For 'tis the sport to have the enginer
> Hoist with his own petar, an't shall go hard
> But I will delve one yard below their mines,
> And blow them to the moon.

By the time it took Arthur to deliver these lines, Provender was just a step away from entering stage right. His foot was inches from the white gaffer tape on the floor that marked the sightline.

Then he heard a heavy huff of breath behind him. Then hands seized him, one clutching his chest, the other clamping over his mouth.

> O, 'tis most sweet
> When in one line two crafts directly meet

The sense of déjà vu was sickening. Provender knew, in an instant, who had grabbed him. He knew these arms, their strength. *Him.* He was here. Damien Scrase. Is's accomplice. No, *Arthur's* accomplice.

> This man shall set me packing;

Immediately, he writhed. He struggled. He fought as he had before at the party but this time with even greater force and viciousness, with an absolute refusal to be taken captive again. Damien hauled him backwards . . .

> I'll lug his guts into the neighbour room

. . . but Provender continued to resist, jabbing behind him with both elbows, left, right, kicking with both heels, right, left. When that didn't work he thrust his head back, hoping to smash Damien's nose with a reverse head-butt. It didn't work either, but he did manage to dislodge his face partially from the other man's grip . . .

> Mother, good night indeed.

. . . so that now his mouth was level with the top of Damien's hand, his lips pressing against the ball of the thumb.

Nothing else for it. Provender opened wide and sank his teeth in. No squeamishness, no hesitation. Biting as hard as if he was tucking into a succulent chicken drumstick.

A gush of blood over his lips. The ghastly sensation of skin splitting, flesh parting. His incisors cleaving down into gristle and knucklebone.

> Come, sir, to draw toward an end with you.

And, from Damien, a scream. A shrill, unbridled howl of agony. Deliciously, deliriously wonderful to hear.

Everything onstage stopped. Backstage, pandemonium broke out. Shouts, cries from the stagehands and actors. Shh! What was this? What was going on?

The hands let go of Provender, Damien rearing back. Provender spun round, spitting out blood, spitting, spitting, and thinking he would never be able to forget the taste, never to his dying day forget how it felt to bite through the flesh of a living being. A retch reflex brought bile to the back of his throat. He spat that out too.

He looked at Damien. Damien was clutching his wounded hand under the other arm, pressing it against his ribs, and he was stamping, hissing, seething, like a stove kettle on the brink of boiling. His face was contorted, as ugly in this state as Provender had imagined it would be. His eyes, in the stage-light glow, were a pair of fireballs.

Then he had a knife. Damien's uninjured hand, his right hand, was holding a knife. The knife Is had mentioned. The sheath knife he knew how to use like an expert.

'I'm . . .' Damien said, and a fresh wave of pain hit him and he winced. 'I'm,' he said again, 'going to do humanity a favour. Fuck the money. Fuck Needle Grove. You' – a clench of teeth, a gasp – 'are going to pay for everything you've done. Everything your Family has done. All the Families have done. And I'm going to be a hero. The nation will thank me, the world will thank me. It starts now. The British Uprising. This is the first blow. Freedom begins today.'

The knife came up, quivering. Damien poised himself to attack. Provender knew he needed to run, or defend himself somehow, but he was overcome with the terrible certainty that it wouldn't make any difference. Whether he fled, whether he stood and fought, he would not win. The man had a knife. The man had vowed to kill him. The man was going to let nothing get in the way of achieving that goal. Provender had arrived at the last moments of his life, and he wished there wasn't this sense of impotence, of inevitability. He wished fear had not rendered him so pathetically helpless.

Then Damien let out yet another sharp yelp of pain, his face briefly creasing up. A look of curiosity crept over him, closely followed by a look of bewilderment. He half turned, groping behind his back with his empty hand, the bitten one. Fumbling exploration located something near the base of his spine, in the muscle above his hip. He plucked the foreign object out. His hand came round and it was holding a small transparent plastic tube, needle-tipped, empty. Damien peered at the tube, perplexed, trying to make sense of it. A hypodermic syringe. What was *that* doing stuck into his back?

The answer came to him at much the same time that it came to Provender.

'Is,' said Provender.

'Is?' said Damien.

Is was behind Damien, just out of his immediate reach. Her arm was still extended with the fingers of her hand loosely configured for depressing the syringe plunger, thumb behind middle and index. Her face showed fear, regret, determination, defiance, all at once.

'Shouldn't talk so much, Damien,' she said hoarsely. 'That's your trouble. Too much in love with the sound of your own voice.'

'Bitch!' Damien yelled, and turned and charged at her.

Provender, at the same time, charged at *him*.

Whether Damien would actually have reached Is was a moot point. Already the Comaphase was racing around his system, shutting faculties down like a janitor switching off lights in an office block. His legs were sluggish, his thoughts were slurred, and his blood was moving like molasses in his veins. After only one step he teetered, and then Provender collided with him in a rugby tackle and Damien fell. Floorboards rushed up to greet him. The last sensation he was aware of was his face smacking into wood and his nose breaking. He did not even feel Provender on top of him. There was a skull-shivering crunch, a burst of agony, and then the emptiness of the void – pure, pain-free, weightless oblivion.

Provender, for his part, felt it wise to remain on Damien's back, pressing him down, until he was one hundred per cent certain that the drug had taken effect. He had the presence of mind to bat the knife away from Damien's limp hand, sending it slithering across the floor. Thereafter, simply lying atop his fallen enemy was about all he could do. Even if he had wanted to get up, his trembling body didn't seem ready yet to accept the command to do so.

Finally he mustered the strength to raise his head. He looked for Is. He wanted to see her acknowledge what he had done, see her smile at him. When the threat had been to himself he had been paralysed, incapable of reacting, but the moment Is had been in danger he had known exactly what to do.

Just as his eyes met hers, however, an angry figure stepped in the way, obstructing his view.

'Provender?' exclaimed Arthur, glaring down, fists on hips. 'What in hell's name are you doing here?'

61

'Nonsense.' The denial was punctuated with a head-shake and a snort. 'I can't possibly be in league with that man. I've never seen him before in my life.'

'Never *seen* him, maybe, but you've talked with him on the phone.'

'Not that either.' Arthur nodded emphatically to where the prone, unconscious form of Damien Scrase lay in the wings. Two burly stage-hands had wrapped Scrase up in gaffer tape, all but mummifying him, and were standing watch over him self-consciously, like a pair of bit-part players – First and Second Guard. The hand Provender had bitten was wrapped in a towel, through which blood was already starting to seep darkly. 'I do not know him. I have no idea who he is. And as to conspiring with him to kidnap you, Provender . . . Now we're in the realm of utter bonkersness. Why, for God's sake? What could I hope to gain?'

'Disruption of my life, of my Family, which you could take advantage of. An opportunity to, well, upstage me. Usurp me. Who knows, it could be you even planned to come to my "rescue" at some point, finding out where I was and dramatically freeing me from my captors. The whole thing was an elaborate set-up designed so that you could play the hero and raise your standing in my Family's eyes.'

'Pah!'

'He said "Pah!",' Is said sidelong to Moore. 'I didn't know people actually said "Pah!".'

'Apparently they do,' Moore replied.

'Do you have any idea how far-fetched this sounds?' Arthur went on. 'As if I'd want to upset my relatives. Especially not Aunt Cynthia – who's worried sick about you, by the way.'

'I believe you'd risk upsetting them for a short while if it meant you could be saviour of the day later on. In fact, the more upset they were, the better it'd be for you. They'd be so relieved when you brought me back, they'd give you anything you asked. Your own room at Dashlands, even.'

'I don't want a room at Dashlands. All right, I'd take one if it was offered, but I don't want it *that* badly. And yes, I wouldn't mind a bit more acceptance from you lot, but I'd never go about getting it through something as contrived as a kidnap plot. That's too much like . . . I was going to say hard work but that's not what I mean. Too much like . . . a real thing. A thing that might happen.'

'I thought if it was all a sham, a pretend kidnap, that'd be right up your street. Like this.' Provender waved, indicating the stage set. By this point the house lights were up and the play's cast had gathered in the auditorium to view the unscripted events that were unfolding up there on the boards. The interruption to the performance had brought everyone out from the greenroom, so that now there was an inversion of the usual order of things, an audience of actors watching a group of people being themselves onstage. Nobody was quite sure what Arthur and Provender were arguing about or who the two supporting characters with them were, or for that matter who the unconscious man in the wings was. It was all, nevertheless, fascinating stuff and, like the best kind of entertainment, had them glued to their seats.

'This?' said Arthur. 'This is a whole different matter.'

'Is it?' said Provender. 'What is it anyway? What's it all for? Some kind of joke, I can see. But what's the point of it?'

Arthur scratched an itch beneath his velvety skullcap abstractly. Most of his fellow-troupers had been in on the game: Arthur, with this production, was gently guying his own Family. Few of them had realised, however, how explicitly his Hamlet parodied a certain member of the Gleeds till now, as Arthur and his cousin faced each other, dressed similarly, tonsured alike. Arthur, they saw, had borrowed heavily from Provender for his rendition of the lead role and it was clear that this to no small extent accounted for Provender's unhappy mood.

'The point . . .' Arthur said. 'Are you accepting, first of all, that I wasn't responsible for your kidnapping? I wasn't the evil-genius mastermind behind it?'

'No, I'm not.'

'Because I cannot stress enough that I wasn't. Apart from anything else, for the past three months I've been busy as hell putting this damn play together. I haven't had a moment's spare time, so there's no way I could have organised anything as complex as a kidnapping. No way.'

'For what it's worth,' Moore whispered to Is, 'I believe him.'

'Me too. I think Provender's beginning to as well, but if I know him he'll take his time admitting it.'

'And,' said Arthur, with a flicker of irritation, 'don't you see? Can't you tell? This play – that's why I was so keen for all of you to come and see it.'

'So we could watch you laughing at us.'

'No. I wanted you to watch yourselves. I wanted to "hold, as 'twere, the mirror up to nature". I was trying, in my way, to get the Gleeds to look outside themselves for once, see themselves as others see them.'

'With a play.'

' "The play's the thing",' Arthur said, ' "Wherein I'll catch the conscience of my kin." '

'He's practised that line,' Is muttered.

Moore concurred. 'Hours of work to come up with that misquotation.'

Arthur rounded on them and snapped, 'Would you two please stop with the asides! We're trying to settle some important stuff here and it's not easy with you two yammering on in the background. Why don't you go and do something useful? Has anyone called the police, for example? That flat-on-his-face person just tried to kill a Gleed. I think he should be put under arrest, don't you?'

Is and Moore exchanged looks, then Moore shrugged. 'I'll go and find a phone. Provender? May I just say, the PLAY-ACTOR seems like he's being authentically PLACATORY. You might want to consider his innocence.'

'I'll be the judge of that,' came the frosty reply.

'Just saying.' Hands patting the air, Moore exited stage left.

'And you?' Arthur said to Is.

'What about me?'

'Can you find something to do?'

'I'm staying put. You can't order me around.'

'I can.'

'No, you can't.' Is plumped herself down on a suede-sheathed ottoman that sat at an angle, close to the proscenium arch. 'Carry on.'

Arthur glared at her, then sighed and turned back to Provender. 'So, yes, I staged this *Hamlet* for your benefit. I didn't realise at first that there were parallels. All I knew was I wanted to play the Dane because every actor does. It's the peak, the Everest of theatrical roles. I had to do it, a challenge to myself, to prove I had what it takes, I had the chops. Once we began rehearsing, though, and I got more and more familiar with the text, I began to see that the play was about a powerful family, a Family, with all sorts of tensions within, and that Hamlet himself bore similarities to, well . . .'

'Me.'

'You. He doesn't quite know what to do with himself. He can't quite commit to any course of action. He procrastinates. He prevaricates.'

'You don't know me that well. I'm not like that at all.'

'Perhaps not, but that's how you appear. That's how you appeared to me when I first came south, when I was more of an outsider to the Family than I am now. I thought you a particularly ungrateful, snobbish sort of person.'

'Oh thanks.'

'Because you have so much going for you, Provender. You're privileged, fortunate beyond most people's wildest dreams, and what do you do with yourself? Nothing. You're miserable. You gloom around all day, your own private storm cloud hanging over your head. You can't even manage the one simple duty that's expected of you: finding a wife, carrying on the line.'

'It may seem simple to you.'

'It *is*. Others have done it. Your mother plonks these perfectly agreeable girls in front of you and you turn them down without even considering them. You claim you want to find someone under your own steam but you can't even be bothered to do that. You never make a decision, Provender. You live in your own world. You can't step out of it and engage with anyone else. It's just ridiculous!'

'And so you had me kidnapped—'

'No!' Arthur exclaimed, stamping his foot in exasperation. 'No, I told you, I staged a fucking play! I made it this way, I arranged it to be highly reminiscent of the Gleeds, I reorganised the whole production with one specific aim: so that you would see it. I hoped the Family would see it too and that they would understand what I was getting at even if a dunderhead like you couldn't. This was all, basically, for you, Provender. I was . . .' His voice lowered. 'In my way I was trying to help. To tell you a few home truths. To show you *you*.'

Provender was stalwartly keeping up a sceptical front but his eyes had begun to betray him. They had softened, no longer hard and angry and righteous. They were the eyes of someone who, in spite of himself, was starting to acknowledge that he might have been wrong.

'And why shouldn't I?' his cousin said. 'It's not as if you and I are close or anything. I'd have nothing to lose by being the one who got you to finally face up to your responsibilities. We could hardly fall out if we'd never been *in* to begin with. Really, it couldn't be anyone but me. My duty as a Gleed was to make you accept *your* duty as a Gleed, and I was doing that how I thought best. Maybe if you'd seen the play the whole way through . . . Hamlet's pretty dynamic in the final scene when he's lobbing "envenom'd" swords around. Maybe if you'd seen that bit you'd realise I was trying to be fair.'

'As I recall, Hamlet dies at the end.'

'So? Everyone dies at the end. It's a tragedy.'

'He also goes mad.'

'No, Ophelia goes mad, Hamlet only pretends to. Look, it wasn't intended to be some kind of direct metaphor. The resemblance isn't perfect. After all, Shakespeare didn't look into a crystal ball and see the Gleeds four centuries in the future and write a play that was exactly about them. I took a play that was written four centuries ago and saw how I could adapt it to fit what I wanted to say about you. A reasonably close match but not an absolute one.'

'Fine, but . . .'

'But what, Prov? I shouldn't have? How dare I? How could I have the nerve? Come on, out with it. I'm barely even proper Family, isn't that right? Wrong side of the blanket, possibly illegitimate. Only proper Family can criticise Family.' He shook his head. 'That wouldn't seem to work, though, would it? Not with the Gleeds. No one in your immediate Family is prepared to confront anyone about anything. Oh, you bicker, there are sideswipes across the dinner table, you think you're sorting things out, but you're not. All you're doing is dusting off a problem before sticking it into the back of the wardrobe again.'

Provender jerked a thumb towards the auditorium and lowered his voice. 'I don't think it's appropriate to talk like this in front of strangers.'

'Precisely!' said Arthur, shrill with triumph. 'Precisely! Don't talk. Don't mention anything. Keep it in the Family, or not even there if possible. Hide. Bury. Disguise. Deny.'

'Arthur . . .'

Arthur, who had puffed himself up like a bantam cock, deflated, relenting. 'All right. Fine. But I've made my point, haven't I?'

'Amply.'

'And you now know I didn't have anything to do with the kidnapping.'

Provender pondered, making it look as if he was only just coming to that conclusion. 'Probably you didn't. On balance, no. You can under-stand, though. I mean, the evidence was pretty incriminating.'

'Not me,' Arthur said, arms spread out. 'I'm guilty of machinations but not those ones.'

'Right then,' Is said, jumping to her feet. 'Now that that's all been established, it's time you kept your promise, Provender.'

'Promise?'

'To speak to your father and tell him you're OK.'

'I didn't promise that.'

'Yes, you did. You asked for an hour to confront Arthur here and then you'd call home. You've confronted Arthur, so . . .'

'It wasn't a promise as such.'

'As good as.'

'But we still don't know who the insider is.'

'Well, what are we going to do? Ask Damien?'

'When he wakes up, yes. Good idea.'

'You'll never get a straight answer out of him.'

'Maybe I won't, but the cops will, I'm sure, when they come.'

'It could take a while. He'll be groggy when he comes round. Remem-ber how you were? Could barely string a sentence together.'

'So we just leave it, is that what you're saying?'

'One phonecall, Provender.'

Arthur had been following the conversation like a spectator at a tennis match, eyes flicking back and forth. Now, with a wry grin, he said, 'Provender, have you managed to pick yourself up a girlfriend by any chance?'

Provender blushed, flushed, blustered, was flustered. 'No. I don't . . . We just . . . She . . .'

'Because she's talking to you a lot like a girlfriend would.'

'We've been through a lot together, that's all.'

'Well, whatever. But she has a point. I've been to Dashlands. I was there today. The place is a volcano, ready to erupt. Your dad is sitting like God on the eve of Judgement Day. Your mum is at her wits' end. War's brewing out there, and we all know why. You need to get in touch and defuse the situation. I'm amazed you haven't done so already.'

'There've been other . . . Oh, all right. Have it your way. The theatre manager's office. There'll be a phone there, right?'

'I imagine so.'

Provender strode offstage; Is, though not invited to, went with him; and Arthur was left alone, in the full glare of the house and stage lights. Like someone waking from a dream, he blinked, remembering himself – what he was, where he was. Out there in the auditorium was an audience. A small one, to be sure, and made up entirely of people he knew, fellow-thespians, but an audience all the same, and he could see them, they weren't lost in amorphous darkness beyond footlight dazzle, they were visible, each and every one, scattered among the raked, red-velvet tiers of seats, faces upturned and expectant, ready for the dénouement.

He could think of only one thing to say:

> I cannot live to hear the news from England,
> But I do prophesy th' election lights
> On Fortinbras, he has my dying voice.
> So tell him, with th' occurrents more and less
> Which have solicited – the rest is silence.

His voice cracked in the middle of the final line, as rehearsed, as it should. Then he flopped forward from the waist in a classic curtain-call bow, arms limp, head down, and the thirty-odd occupants of the auditorium set up such a tumult of clapping and cheering you would have thought them a full house. The applause echoed to the theatre's gilded ceiling, and Arthur remembered, as he always did when he heard this sound, why he loved his job.

62

Moore was just replacing the phone receiver when the theatre manager ushered Provender and Is in.

'Police are on their way,' he said, stepping back from the desk. 'I took the liberty of dropping the Gleed name, just to speed things along.'

Provender seated himself at the desk, and Is took up position at his elbow. He twisted round in the chair, frowning up at her. 'I'm going to do it, all right? You don't have to stand guard over me.'

Is, relenting, moved one pace back.

Provender *tsk*ed, picked up the receiver, and dialled the main private number for Dashlands House. As he listened to the ring tone, he surveyed the manager's office: a small room painted tobacco-brown, with framed posters, playbills and review cuttings on the walls and a pair of ungenerously-proportioned windows whose panes were browned with decades of London air-grime. The manager himself was hovering in the doorway, uncertain whether he should stay or leave. Provender invited him in with an inclusive gesture.

Then there was a click on the line and a deep, threnodic bass-baritone voice said, 'Dashlands House.'

'Carver? It's me.'

'Master Provender.'

'Yes.'

'Master Provender, what a relief. How good to hear you. Where are you? How are you?'

'I'm as well as can be expected, and I'm at the Shortborn Theatre on New Aldwych, of all places.'

'May I enquire how you came to be there?'

'Long story. Another time.'

'But you're not being held hostage.'

'Not any longer.'

'That's news indeed. You're safe. Out of danger.'

'Completely.'

'I shall alert the household.'

'Do that. My father specifically. Tell him the Kuczynskis aren't to blame. They've had nothing to do with this. Tell him to call off the dogs. I'm OK, everything's OK, let's not have a war. Is that clear?'

'Uncontestably.'

'I'm heading home right now. Should be there in an hour or so if the trams behave.'

'Your arrival will be eagerly awaited.'

'And Carver? That detective you hired to find me. Moore. Excellent choice. He did some brilliant work.'

'He found you? I am most impressed.'

'I'll tell him you said that. It'll make his day.'

Provender replaced the receiver and looked at Is, then Moore. 'Right, who's coming back to my place with me?'

Is looked doubtful, Moore flabbergasted.

'My Family'll be breaking out the champagne. I really think we all deserve a celebration. And it is still, officially, my birthday. More than one good excuse for a party, wouldn't you say?'

Is shook her head, while Moore was too astonished to do what he wanted, which was nod.

'Oh go on, Is. What harm will it do? Please?'

'We should stay till the police get here,' Is said. 'Someone should.'

'What for? It's open-and-shut. There's the bad guy lying on the floor, dead to the world. We've got eyewitnesses galore who'll say that he attacked me. And you can bet, with Mr Moore having mentioned my name to the cops, there'll be reporters and photographers on their way here too. This'll go berserk, and I'd rather not be around when it does. Look, soon as I get home I'll send Carver back here to deal with everything. In the meantime, I'm sure our friend' – he indicated the theatre manager – 'can handle the situation.'

The theatre manager professed himself only too happy to do so.

'There we are,' Provender said. 'I need to get back to Dashlands. I need to see everyone. I've had three days of hell and I just want to go home, and I want you two to come with me. What do you say?'

If he had spoken an ounce more commandingly, a smidgeon less imploringly, Is would have dug her heels in and refused. As it was, he gauged his appeal just right. To judge by her expression she had reservations but, with effort, she managed to set them aside. 'OK,' she said.

As for Moore, what else could he do but splutter out *yes*?

63

And so Romeo Moore, Anagrammatic Detective, wound up aboard a Family tram, sipping at a nip of Family brandy, on the afternoon of a day which without question was the most remarkable of his life.

They took the taxi to the tram stop, Moore tipped the driver, and soon they were trundling westward in a tram and Moore was urging himself to take this all in, remember it, savour it, record every detail in his memory because surely nothing like this would ever happen to him again. Dashlands! He was going to Dashlands House, for heaven's sake!

If there was a fleck on the lens of this moment, a wart besmirching its beauty, it was that Milner wasn't there to share it with him. Now that the case was solved, it would have been nice to enjoy the moment of success together. Then again, perhaps not. After all, Moore had been wrong: the kidnapper was a non-Family outsider, just as Milner had surmised. According to Provender an *in*sider had been involved as well, but they knew now that it was not Arthur Gleed. This meant that Moore had lost the bet with his partner. And Milner would doubtless be anything but magnanimous in victory. Moore knew him. Milner would preen and crow and take every opportunity to rub Moore's nose in it, whereas if the roles were reversed Moore would, he was sure, have been the model of a quiet, dignified winner.

So, on balance, Moore did not mind too much that the world's only other Anagrammatic Detective was somewhere else right now.

Still, within him there was a nagging, wormy sense of concern that would not go away. Where *was* Milner anyway? Having contacted the police from the theatre manager's office, Moore had then phoned work to see if his partner was there. This was the call he had been finishing when Provender, Is and the theatre manager walked in. No one had picked up, so he could only assume his partner was still out in the field pursuing his investigations. Which was all well and fine, but Moore now knew, from things gleaned over the past hour, all about Damien Scrase, the knife-wielding thug who had held Provender captive in Needle Grove and who would have killed him at the theatre if not for Is's timely intervention with the syringe full of sedative; and the unsettling thought that hunkered at the back of his mind was that Milner might have encountered the selfsame individual in the course of his enquiries and fallen foul of him. Nothing anyone had said had given Moore cause to believe his supposition had any grounding in fact, but the anxiety nonetheless remained. Had Milner gone to Needle Grove? If only he hadn't been so cagey and had revealed *something* about his line of approach to the case. Then Moore would have genuine reason to be fretful, or alternatively no reason at all, either of which would have been better than the nameless, nebulous unease he was feeling.

Thus, Moore's joy was not entirely unalloyed. It was sufficient, still, to fill him with a warm glow inside, which he nurtured and stoked with the brandy. As the tram raced on he thought of the money that would now, thanks to him, be coming the detective agency's way, and soon he was daydreaming again about the secretary he and Milner were going to employ. She would have to love words, of course. In fact she would, perforce, require a vocabulary far more extensive than most people's if she was going to cope with *their* paperwork. She would be pretty, presentable, demure, with nice legs – Moore liked a well-turned lady's leg as much as he liked a well-turned phrase – and with, perhaps, a soft spot for a softly-spoken man who would happily compose flattering anagrams of her name, pen pangrams for her filled with bouquet-bursts of consonants such as *waltz* and *nymph*, offer her acrostics that capitally expressed his Liking Of Verbal Engagement and his Laudably Orderly Valentine Esteem for her . . .

. . . and while at one end of the tram car a quiet, reflective Moore entertained this fantasy of the future, at the other end Provender and Is found themselves all too uncomfortably in the present moment, neither talking when both felt they ought to. The tram was almost at Heathrow before one of them spoke, and then it was only Provender saying, banally, 'I'm starving. I just realised. When we get to Dashlands, first thing I'm going to do is get someone to rustle me up a huge sandwich. Roast beef with pickle and horseradish. How about you? Sound good?'

Is nodded non-committally. 'It's a nice world where you can say the word sandwich and a moment later one appears.'

'It's not the only world, I realise that, Is. God, I realise that more than ever now.'

'Doesn't it worry you?'

'Does what worry me? The unfairness of life? You know the answer to that.'

'No, does it worry you that there's still a snake in this paradise of yours? That somebody in your household wanted you gone for some reason?'

Provender thought about it. 'Right now, no. Right now simply getting back there is all I'm concerned about. The rest I'll take care of in due course. Whoever it is will become clear pretty quickly, I reckon. I'm keen to know why they did it, what they've got against me, and when the time's right I'll find out and I'll respond accordingly. There will be payback.

There will be. I just don't know at the moment what form it'll take. What I do know is that I'm not going to be intimidated. I feel, now, that I can face anything. I feel that there's nothing so bad it can't be tackled head-on. Rather like I tackled Damien.'

Is laughed. 'After I'd pumped him full of sedative.'

'Well, yeah, but when he turned on you and attacked you . . .'

'Full of sedative. With about five seconds of consciousness left in him.'

'But he still attacked you, and I barrelled into him and he went down . . .'

Is understood what he was after from her and, feeling generous, gave it to him. 'Thank you, Provender. And thank you, too, for when we were on the balcony and you got me to make the jump. And for when we were surrounded by the Changelings and you got us out of there.'

He was pleased. 'It was nothing. Thank *you* for all you did for me.'

There was a brief, genial lull, then Is said, 'And now you're taking me to meet the Family.'

She tried not to chuckle at the way he squirmed in his seat. 'It's not like that.'

'Of course not. Anyway, I've met them already, haven't I?'

'Yes. You have. But not properly.' He added, as if as an afterthought, 'I think you and my mother will get on.'

There was no easy response to that, and Is pretended something out there in the passing countryside had distracted her, permitting her to turn away from him. It so happened that the only eye-catching thing on view was a pair of swans who were afloat on a pond by the trackside, nuzzling bills and forming a heart shape with their necks. Drat nature! Where was a gloomy omen when you needed one? Is stared at the birds anyway, and sniffed, as if unimpressed.

From then onward till arrival at Dashlands the awkward silence was back between her and Provender and neither of them could figure out a way of breaking it again, least of all Is, who sensed, with heart-sinking certainty, that at some point later today Provender was going to say something to her she didn't want to hear and she was going to have to say something back that *he* didn't want to hear. And Provender, she felt, sensed this too.

64

One of the kitchen staff had to show Cynthia where the coffee beans were stored and how the grinder worked. The staff member, a sous-chef, offered to make the coffee for her but she would have none of it. 'I really ought to be able to do this sort of thing for myself,' she said with an airy laugh, sounding just as a doyenne of Dashlands should, ashamed by but not apologising for her lack of practicality. 'I've never fixed coffee for my husband before. It strikes me it's about time I learned.'

The sous-chef looked on as she ground the beans, boiled the water, filled the cafetière, found cups and saucers and a milk jug and a sugar bowl and spoons, all with a halting determination, a keenness to get the procedure exactly right first time, and he didn't know whether to feel admiration or pity, but settled on admiration, for who could not, in the end, admire Cynthia Gleed?

She carried the tray with the coffee on it through the house, a six-minute journey that took her past Triumph. In the statue's shadow she paused, glanced about to make sure she was unobserved, set the tray down, and swiftly and deftly introduced Oneirodam pills into one of the cups. She tapped out a dozen of them all told, then returned the small brown bottle to her pocket and resumed walking. The pills were so tiny they didn't cover even half of the cup's bottom. They were potent, though. One alone was enough to ensure a deep night's sleep.

Entering the television room, she laid the tray on a teak chiffonier which was out of Prosper's direct line of sight and high enough that, as long as he remained seated, he could not see into the cups. She then turned to the Phone and told him to leave the room; she wished some privacy with her husband. As the Phone exited, Cynthia heard the far-off trilling of another phone, one of the house's standard landlines. Someone would get it, Carver most likely. It didn't matter. What was important now? Nothing. Nothing except what she was about to do.

She poured out the coffee, making sure she knew which cup was which. It was simple: Prosper took his white with sugar, she took hers black. She stirred the one with the pills thoroughly until she was sure they had dissolved. Would the taste of the Oneirodam be detectable? She thought not. She had made the coffee strong, and, from experience, the pills had only the merest flavour, a faint acrid tang which you were aware of, if at all, after rather than while swallowing them. They would slip down unnoticed.

She brought the two coffees over to the sofa, handed Prosper his, then sat down in an armchair cater-corner to her husband. She reached for the cabinet into which was set the control panel that operated everything in the room – curtains, lights, television – and rotated the TV volume dial down to zero. In silence, she waited for Prosper to look round at her. Eventually he did.

'What?' he demanded. He looked haggard, irritable, old, uncharming.

'Do you love me?' she asked.

'That's an extraordinary question.'

'Well?'

'Yes. Of course. What do you think?'

'I still mean something to you, even after all this time, even after all your . . . strayings.'

'Is that another question?'

'It is.'

'Same answer. Of course. You're my wife. It would be ridiculous if you didn't mean something to me.'

'You're sure about that?'

He stared at her levelly, sincerely, and said, 'I'm sure.'

Cynthia believed him. The eyes did not lie. Whatever feelings Prosper had for other women, they were fleeting, whereas what he felt for her was a constant in his life, a guy-rope which kept him tethered and which he could always count on. It was love. It wasn't passionate love, or lustful love, but a well-aged, weathered emotion he was so accustomed to and comfortable with he barely realised it was there any more. She had reminded him of it now. In the midst of all these tribulations, he knew once again where his heart and hope and health lay. His expression became almost fond. Years eased from his face.

'What's this about, Cynthia?'

'Nothing. I just wanted to hear it from you. Drink your coffee.'

'It's the strain, isn't it? I thought you'd stopped feeling it but I was wrong. Oh Lord, Cynthia, I love you, my daughters, my son, the whole of my Family. I may not show it as readily as you, but I do. You have to trust me on that. All the time, beneath it all, it's you. You I care about.' He was bordering on tears. Cynthia could not recall when she had last seen him that way. 'You want confirmation of it? Here it is. I'm saying so now. It's you.'

'Thank you, Prosper. Drink up.'

'Silly creature,' he said affectionately.

'It'll get cold.'

Prosper, smiling lifted the cup to his lips and took a sip. Cynthia, mirroring him, sipped too.

PART SIX

65

Is was on edge from the moment she stepped off the tram. Returning to Dashlands was in effect revisiting the scene of the crime, and although she was confident there would be no reprisals from the Gleeds, she suspected they would not take to her. Provender had assured her he would tout her as a heroine, the woman he owed his life to, but his life would never have been endangered in the first place had he not been kidnapped, and she had played a part in that, and his Family would learn that fact soon enough, and why would they not resent her then? All she had done for him after the kidnapping did not, in her mind, atone for the original offence.

That she cared at all what the Gleeds thought of her struck her as odd. She intended to stay at Dashlands for, what, a couple of hours? Enough time to join in the celebrations, drink a bit of the promised champagne, keep Provender company as he had asked – then she would demand a ride home. If she had to call a cab to come and take her back to London, so be it. Hang the expense. She didn't think she could cope with more than a couple of hours at the house, and setting herself a time limit was a sensible tactic. If things got uncomfortable for her, all she had to do was count the minutes till she could leave. The Gleeds could hate her if they wanted – they were welcome to – but they had only a fixed period in which to do so. Two hours, then she was gone.

The tram stop at Dashlands was roughly a mile from the house and set in a wooded glade where leaf shadows rippled and birdsong blared. As the tram car rolled away, Provender inhaled a deep, bracing breath – the sweet, sweet air of home – then struck off along an asphalted road that curved through a trunk-ribbed tunnel of deciduous forest. Is and Moore, of course, had no choice but to follow, and soon all three of them were out in the open, in the simmering flare of a summer afternoon, passing through the bowl of a shallow valley with parkland rising on either side; swathes of grass just starting to turn sere, dotted with oaks and chestnuts of venerable ancientness. Other than the drowse of insects, there was nothing but silence in the air. Moore encapsulated in two words what both he and Is, and perhaps Provender too, were feeling:

'Another world.'

'It is, isn't it,' she said.

'May I ask you something?'

'Go ahead.'

'Your full name.'

'Isis. Why?'

'And surname.'

'Necker.'

Provender glanced over his shoulder. 'I didn't know that.'

'Why should you? I never told you.'

'Isis Necker,' Provender said, trying it out.

'ISIS NECKER,' said Moore, and hummed. 'Oh yes.'

'Oh yes what?'

'Well, as you know, I anagrammatise. It's what I do. The truth of a person is encoded in their name. And yours came out as . . .'

'Oh God, I dread to think.'

'. . . NICE KISSER.'

'That's it? That's my truth?'

'If we take "kisser" in the American slang sense of "face", I would say yes, unquestionably.'

'Thanks. I think.'

'Not pleased?'

'I suppose I was hoping for something a bit more spectacular.'

'Well, give me time, I might be able to come up with another.'

'If you ask me, it's spot-on,' said Provender. 'And maybe you're a nice kisser in another sense, who knows?' He had one eyebrow raised. His gaze was hopeful.

'What about Provender?' Is said, laughing in order that her changing of the subject would not seem quite so obvious.

'Ah, Provender is a man of many anagrams,' said Moore. 'Believe me, my partner and I deciphered dozens. The one that hit me hardest was, in fact, the one I can least explain. I took his full name, including middle name, which is—'

'Stop right there,' said Provender, groaning. 'Don't. It's too embarrassing.'

'Go on,' said Is.

'I beg you, please.'

'It's not as if it's a state secret, Provender. I could easily look it up in Burke's Family Almanac.'

'Mr Moore, I will give you anything you ask, anything at all, just do not tell her.'

They were all laughing now, and Provender kept cajoling, offering Moore wilder and wilder bribes in return for his silence, and Is matched him by threatening Moore in increasingly elaborate ways, bidding against Provender's wealth with promises of violence, until the Anagrammatic Detective eventually blurted out 'Oregano', saying that he feared permanent physical disfigurement far more than he craved material goods, and Is began hooting hysterically and repeating the word Oregano over and over, and nothing Provender could say, no amount of feigned stroppiness, could get her to stop.

This happy scene was brought to a halt by the arrival of a three-strong welcoming committee from the house. Gratitude, Extravagance and Uncle Fortune appeared on the road, and no sooner did the two sisters catch sight of their brother than they broke into a run and fell on him in a flurry of shrieks and hugs and kisses. Extravagance gripped him so hard he had to push her arms off him in order to draw breath. When Fortune caught up, he too embraced Provender, then leaned back to examine him from top to toe.

'Intact. A bit rough around the edges but otherwise good as new.'

'I've been lucky,' Provender said. He submitted to another gratefully extravagant, extravagantly grateful display of affection from his sisters, then made introductions.

Is felt the weight of the Gleed sisters' gazes on her and saw the wary calculation in their eyes. Women always assessed one another on first meeting, but usually from a position of equality. There was no equality here. Gratitude and Extravagance scrutinised her from a viewpoint of implicit superiority, and saw that her clothes were inexpensive, her hair was simply and cheaply styled, her figure was not as diet-gaunt as theirs, and her looks and attitude nowhere near as refined as theirs. She refused to give them the satisfaction of looking cowed, though that was how she felt. She held her head high and, even when they frowned at her bruised cheek and puffy eye, didn't allow that to make her self-conscious. *You're no better than me.* She radiated nonchalance until, in the end, the sisters had their fill of looking and turned away. Possibly they had come to the conclusion that she was haughty, even impertinent. Is was not bothered. Let them think what they liked.

'Where's Mum?' Provender asked.

'Somewhere,' said Gratitude. 'Carver found us three first to tell us you were on your way home. He said he was going to look for Mum and for Dad. I bet they're not far behind us.'

'Now then, nephew,' said Fortune, 'I think you should tell us all about where you've been and what happened to you.'

'Can it wait till we get back to the house? I'm sorry but I haven't eaten since this morning and I'm . . .'

Provender's voice trailed off as he spied a figure hurrying along the road towards them. It was Carver, moving at a brisk jog-trot, fast as he could go, which was considerably faster than you would think likely for a man his age. In long, loping strides he reached the group, then braced his hands on his knees while he got his wind back. Finally, raising his head, he gasped, 'Quick. You must. Come quick. The house. Something's wrong. Mrs Gleed.'

66

In the television room, by the bright flicker of images of impending war, Prosper Gleed was in anguish. Medics were on their way. Carver had summoned them by using the emergency hotline in Great's apartment. But how long would they take? How soon could they get here? Soon enough?

He blamed himself. He should have noticed. His attention had been elsewhere. Cynthia had gone quiet and he thought she had simply drifted off to sleep. He had been sitting there, TV-absorbed, not realising – not even having an inkling – that something was wrong with his wife, until Carver walked in. Carver, clearing his throat, had been about to make an announcement of some sort, but one look at Cynthia and that was that. He had hurried over to her, felt for a pulse, tapped her cheek, asked how long she had been like this, then run off to the Granny Flat. Prosper had been alone with her ever since, alternately kneeling beside her and pacing the floor in circles. Her face was terrifyingly pale. When he touched her skin, she was cold. Her breaths were so shallow as to be all but imperceptible. To the casual observer she might have appeared to be asleep, but no one sleeping was quite so slumped, so slack-limbed, so motionless. Like a becalmed yacht, sails drooping, inert. How could he not have realised? It had happened right next to him, whatever it was. This silent, catastrophic collapse. Stroke? Heart failure? He had no idea. How could he have been so idiotically oblivious? His wife, slowly dying beside him! What kind of heedless moron was he?

And where the hell were those medics?

A commotion outside in the corridor brought Prosper's head snapping round and surge of hope to his heart. Here they were. At last.

But it wasn't a team of white-garbed ambulancemen who entered the television room. It was . . .

'Mum!'

Prosper's jaw dropped as first Provender, then a girl he faintly recognised, then Gratitude, burst in through the door. They were followed by a couple of other people but Prosper was too shocked at the sight of his son to register them. He stammered out Provender's name, but Provender scarcely spared him a glance. He rushed over to his mother with an awful keening wail. The girl was close behind him, and no sooner had she reached Cynthia's side than she began examining her, rather as Carver had but much more methodically. First the neck, two fingers pressed to it. Then lifting one eyelid, checking the eye, doing the same with the other one. Back of the hand to the forehead. The whole procedure was brisk and deft and unhesitating, and Prosper could not understand why he recognised her, but by God, what did it matter? She clearly had medical training. She knew what she was about.

'Poisoning of some kind,' the girl said.

'Poisoning?' said Provender. 'No. God, surely not.'

'Were you here when it happened? Mr Gleed?'

Prosper realised he was being spoken to. 'No. Yes. I mean, I was but I didn't see. She came in with coffee and we . . .'

'Coffee.' The girl looked around and saw the tray, the cafetière, the drained cups. She snatched up one of the cups, then the other. Something about the dregs in the second cup caused her to frown, then nod. 'OK. Provender, give me a hand. We're going to lift her and lay her out on the floor. Come on, move!'

When Cynthia was supine on the floor, the girl knelt, slipped Cynthia's nearside hand under one hip and began to pull her over. Cynthia was on her side when her body was wracked by a sudden convulsion. Dark vomit spurted from her mouth onto the girl's lap. The girl, without missing a beat, rolled her fully over while the vomit continued to pour. Someone, Gratitude probably, let out a piteous moan.

'No, it's good,' the girl said to nobody and everybody. 'Getting it out of her system.'

When the vomiting had run its course, she inserted a forefinger into Cynthia's mouth and wiped around inside, clearing out blobs of regurgitated matter. She began arranging Cynthia's limbs into the full Recovery Position, then halted. Something was not right. Swiftly she pushed Cynthia onto her back again.

'Not breathing,' she said.

Provender, kneeling the other side of his mother's body, gaped at the girl. 'What did you say?'

'I said she's stopped breathing. We're going to have to resuscitate.'

'We?'

'Yes, we. Works best if there's two of us.' She tilted Cynthia's head back, then placed both hands on her breastbone, ready to start compression. 'Put your mouth over hers and pinch her nose. When I tell you to blow, blow.'

'But she just—'

'Your mother, Provender. Do it!'

Provender winced. 'I can't.'

'Yes you bloody well can. It's only puke. It won't kill you.'

'I'll do the chest pumping thing.'

'You have to know how. Do you?'

He shook his head.

'Then you're on Kiss of Life. Quickly!'

Provender lowered his head and, with a brief creasing of face, brought his lips to his mother's.

The girl bore down on Cynthia's chest five times, then said, 'Blow.'

Provender blew.

Five times. 'Blow.'

He blew.

Five times. 'Blow.'

Blew.

Five. 'Blow.'

Blew.

Five. 'Blow.'

Blew.

Exactly eight minutes later an ambulance skidded to a halt outside Dashlands House with a spray of driveway gravel. Carver was waiting to greet it and hurried the ambulancemen indoors and through the house to the television room. There, the ambulancemen found Cynthia Gleed sitting up on the floor, supported on one side by her son and on the other by a girl who informed them that she was a nurse and that Mrs Gleed had taken an overdose of an unknown sedative or tranquilliser. She had vomited and had had to be given CPR. Her breathing had normalised but she remained listless and unreactive.

The ambulancemen unfolded their stretcher, declaring that Mrs Gleed required immediate hospitalisation. They were overruled by her husband, who told them point-blank that it was out of the question. Family did not go to hospital. Hospital, if anything, came to Family.

The ambulancemen objected but Prosper Gleed was adamant, and so in the end they had no choice. They stretchered the patient up to the master bedroom. Items of medical equipment were commandeered from the Granny Flat, most importantly Great's emergency oxygen cylinder and mask. Further equipment was brought over from Reading General, along with a couple of doctors. Cynthia Gleed was made comfortable, put on a saline drip, and hooked up to an ECG monitor, and the doctors then began giving her a blood transfusion using plasma from the exclusive, Family-donated blood reservoir which was kept at the hospital. Her condition was officially designated serious but stable. The next hour was, the Family were told, crucial. If she survived the next hour, then the prognosis was good. During that time it would also be possible to begin to establish whether any lasting damage had been done to her system. There was a possibility that organs such as the liver and kidneys could suffer failure as a result of the overdose. If that happened, the doctors said, she was going to hospital whether Prosper Gleed liked it or not.

A bedside vigil commenced. Prosper and his daughters kept watch over Cynthia, taking it in turns to hold her hand and trying not to get in the doctors' way. Fort, meanwhile, constantly harassed the medical professionals in order to make sure his sister-in-law was getting the very best attention and care. It was unlikely that the doctors would be neglectful when it came to looking after a critically ill Gleed, but Fort, at least, felt better for chasing them around. As for Provender, he wafted in and out of the room, never staying for long. He couldn't bear to see his mother lying there so weak and pallid, but more than that, he couldn't stand to be in the presence of his father, who he knew was the reason his mother had taken the overdose. It was obvious she had set out to prove a point to him, to shock him out of his belligerent stance against the Kuczynskis. In that respect she had succeeded, but if she were to die now . . . She was still enough of a Roman Catholic to believe that suicide was a mortal sin. If she were to die now, she had damned herself. For her husband's sake she was risking eternal hellfire. The disgust Provender felt for his father then meant he could barely look at the man. His sole consolation was that, to judge by his father's distraught manner, Prosper Gleed loathed himself almost as much.

It was while Cynthia Gleed hovered between life and death, surrounded by her Family, that the first shots were fired in what looked like becoming the Third European War.

67

Neither side, in hindsight, could say with any accuracy who started it. Arguably, neither side did. What had been simmering all day finally reached boiling point and seethed over into conflict. It was, in that sense, spontaneous, an inevitable outcome that the politicians couldn't have prevented even if they had tried. At a certain stage, events took over. The build-up to war, which had been achieved so speedily, just kept accelerating until it started helter-skeltering out of control. Men were involved – from nervous foot soldiers in the theatre of combat to calculating field marshals and rear admirals in their strategy rooms – and men could make mistakes, and did; but really war itself was to blame. War, one might say, was an organism. Once conceived, given a glimmering of existence, like any organism it wanted to survive, and thrive, and be strong, and spawn, and proliferate. Offered a chance to live, it took it.

Initial contact occurred in the Bohemian Forest, that section of the German/Czechoslovakian border where the dividing line was blurred, one country shading coniferously into the other. There, an advance detachment of Western Alliance troops encountered an advance detachment of Pan-Slavic Federation troops. Encountered? Stumbled upon would be closer to the truth, for the Federals were in a clearing, sitting on cushions of heaped pine needles, brewing themselves tea, and were as startled as the Allies were to find themselves all at once face-to-face with the enemy. There was a limited exchange of fire, before both detachments beat a retreat and radioed news of the skirmish to headquarters.

War twitched and stirred.

At approximately the same time, out in the Baltic there was a brief naval engagement, when a Swedish frigate dropped depth charges on a Federation submarine, or what it thought was a Federation submarine. Sonar had picked up a large moving object which could just as easily have been a grey whale, but the captain of the frigate was new to his command, lacking in experience and also in caution. Better to attack the thing, he felt, just to be on the safe side. If it was a submarine, then he would have done well in defending his ship against possible torpedo attack. If a whale – well, what was one less cetacean in the world? The depth charging proved nothing conclusively either way. The moving object went into a steep dive, hastening out of detection range. The captain dutifully reported in to his base at Karlskrona, ship-shaped models were shunted around on a table map of Europe, and support vessels were despatched to his location.

War flicked open its eyes and drew breath.

In the skies above north-eastern Germany, over the canal-fretted low-lands of Uckermark, a feinting sortie by six Luftwaffe fighters ended in disaster. Instrument failure in the group captain's aircraft, or possibly a misinterpretation of the dial readings, resulted in him leading his wing-men over the border into Polish airspace. By the time anyone realised the error, it was too late – a larger group of Polish fighters was zeroing in on them, guns blazing. The dogfight was nasty, brutish and short. One and one alone of the Luftwaffe pilots escaped, limping back across the border with his engine smoking and his tail rudder shot to pieces. He had to bail out over the Oder river, but alas his parachute failed and he hit the ground simultaneously with his plane and only slightly less explosively. The Polish pilots returned to base triumphant, and word flashed to Warsaw. An incursion. Roundly repulsed, but an incursion nonetheless.

War flexed its limbs and started to rise.

And so the news began zinging along the wires, journalists speaking, looking and sounding properly anxious, electronic footage and phoned-in reportage whirling through the ether to transmitters, to receivers, being pumped out again by the TV and radio stations, finding its way down aerials into homes and workplaces, the truth, the knowledge, the informa-tion, unfurling with deadly earnest now in million upon million of living rooms and office rec rooms, crisis becoming event, potential becoming fact, and nothing, it seemed, could halt the process, nothing could kill the nascent beast that was crawling out of the belly of the continent to spread carnage everywhere.

68

The name of the Gleeds' Phone, for he did have one, was Neville Quigley.

As a rule, Quigley enjoyed his job. It was an important job, perhaps the most important in the entire household. It had a cachet which elevated Quigley above the other domestic staff. He didn't flaunt that, he never put on airs and graces, but he knew it and they knew it: at Dashlands, Phone outranked butler, cook, housemaid, chauffeur . . . everyone except Carver. Phone sat in on Family meetings other staff members were excluded from. Phone was privy to Family secrets other staff members could only guess at. Sometimes Quigley wondered if he was, in fact, even more essential to the running of the Gleeds' daily lives than Carver. But no, that was not possible. It was madness even to think it.

To be a Phone demanded a knack for remembering numbers, a tolerance for standing still for long stretches of time, and discretion. Discretion was the real watchword. As a Phone you listened in on intimate, inter-Familial conversations. Admittedly you only got one side of them, but that was enough. The revelations Quigley had overheard, the details he had eavesdropped on . . . He could tell you a story or two. Only he wouldn't.

Some Families employed deaf-mutes as Phones for just that reason. What couldn't be heard or repeated remained safely within the Families. However, there were problems with the use of deaf-mutes, mainly the difficulty of summoning them when required and communicating your wishes to them, but also the fact that they couldn't necessarily detect when there was an incoming call, although that had been remedied by fitting their backpacks with a vibrating buzzer or even, unpopularly, with a node that emitted a mild electric jolt. A hearing-unimpaired Phone was better on all fronts, on condition that he was not a blabbermouth.

Quigley was not. Nor was he one to interfere in Family affairs. Ever. That was simply not his place. While he had his backpack on he was a Phone, a living implement, a technical device with legs on. He hung in the background till asked for. He did not speak unless spoken to and never spoke while his employers were speaking *into* him. He did nothing, when on duty, that a machine would not do. Often, indeed, during interminable periods of inactivity, Quigley fantasised that he actually was a machine, a telephone who dreamed he was a man. Circuits for veins, electricity for blood. It passed the time.

This afternoon, in the wake of the dreadful incident in the television room, Quigley was in a quandary. Prosper Gleed, being occupied with other matters, had not dismissed him from duty, but neither was there any call for a Phone to be loitering around upstairs, near his master, while Mrs Gleed lay in her sickbed. Quigley couldn't intrude on the Family's distress, not unless a call came in and perhaps not even then.

What he did was re-enter the television room and resume his position in the corner. It was sensible to be in the last place Mr Gleed had seen him, in case Mr Gleed should come looking for him.

As he stood there, however, watching the TV, he realised that the game of brinkmanship Prosper Gleed was playing with the Kuczynskis was edging out of control. Even with the sound down, it was clear that war was breaking out. Provender was back at Dashlands, which meant his father ought to have contacted the Kuczynskis and defused the situation. He had not done so, of course, and it appeared that Quigley was the only person in the house who had any idea what was happening out there in the rest of the world. The Family was worried about Mrs Gleed's well-being, and rightly so, but at the same time there was an equally if not more pressing emergency they should be concerned about.

What to do? Quigley was in two minds. On the one hand, someone in the Family must be informed that conflict had begun. On the other hand, it couldn't be him – he was only a Phone.

The solution was to find Carver, and Quigley set out from the television room with a view to doing just that. Carver was the interface between Family and staff. Carver would be able to decide if and how to carry the news to Prosper Gleed.

Not knowing where Carver was in the building, Quigley began his search in the vicinity of the master bedroom, reasoning that the Gleeds' major-domo was likely to want to be close at hand for the Family. In the event, Carver was not there, but Quigley did come across Provender instead, who was in a corridor, morosely tracing with one finger the dimples in the glass bricks which were inset into a section of the wall.

Quigley wavered, then made a decision which, had the circumstances not been so exceptional, he would have otherwise balked at.

'Sir?'

Provender either did not hear or refused to acknowledge that he was being addressed.

Undeterred, Quigley said, 'Sir?', more loudly this time, and added, 'Master Provender?'

'What?' said Provender. 'What do you want?'

Quigley quickly explained.

'If,' he said, by way of conclusion, 'you could somehow convey to your father the need for—'

'Dial,' said Provender.

Quigley gaped.

'Dial the Kuczynskis.'

'Master Provender, I can't do that. You know I can't. A Phone is for the exclusive use of the head of the Family.'

'The head of the Family is indisposed. The head of the Family can't come to the Phone right now. I'm the *de facto* head of the Family. Dial.'

'It's simply not—'

Provender grabbed Quigley by the shoulders, swung him round and snatched the handset off his back.

'Dial,' he said, with such firmness and finality that Quigley knew he had no alternative.

He flipped open the central section of his chestplate so that the rotary dial was exposed.

This isn't my fault, he thought. *I can't be held accountable. I'm just a machine.*

A machine, however, would not have got itself into such a dilemma in the first place. Nor would a machine's index finger have trembled as it began spooling in the digits of the Kuczynskis' Phone number.

69

'*Słucham*. Stanisław Kuczynski.'

'Mr Kuczynski, this is Provender Gleed.'

'Excuse me? There must be some interference on the line. I could have sworn you just said *Provender* Gleed.'

'I did.'

'I see. Yes, that would account, I suppose, for the Mr before my name. But your father, then . . . Has something unfortunate occurred?'

'It has, but not what you're thinking.' Hoping for, if Kuczynski's tone was anything to go by. 'Listen, Mr Kuczynski, I won't fanny about. We need to—'

'What is this "fanny about"? I don't know this phrase.'

'I won't waste time. We need to stop this thing immediately, while we can, before it gets any worse.'

'You're referring to . . .'

'You know what I'm referring to.'

'Provender, I'm not sure it can be stopped, not now. But look on the bright side. We all stand to make a bit of profit out of it.'

'People will get killed, Mr Kuczynski. You or I could get killed.'

'I doubt it. You live in the countryside. My castle has a bunker. A Family would never survive without a heightened sense of self-preservation, and that certainly is true of yours and mine. So sit back, Provender. Have fun. Enjoy the show. And may the best Family win. By the way, I may be wrong, but aren't you supposed to be my prisoner?'

'Yes, I know. Problem there. I'm trying to think of a good word for it. A misapprehension on my father's part.'

'A misapprehension.'

'He blundered, I'll admit it. Leapt to the wrong conclusion.'

'And did so in the most insulting fashion. Do you know what he said to me and my sister?'

'I don't, I'm afraid.'

'I'll tell you. He called us inbred. There were many other things he called us but that was far and away the worst. Inbred.'

'I'm sorry that he did.'

'You shouldn't be apologising to me. My sister was the one who truly took offence. Stasia has been cursing your father's name ever since.'

'I'm sorry to her too, then.'

'It would be better to hear it from your father than from you.'

'That's not possible at the moment. My father has other things to attend to. A Family crisis.'

'I see. You have assumed the duties of Family head, then.'

'Evidently.'

'Interesting. Does that, I wonder, give you the authority to speak for all of the Gleeds?'

'Under the circumstances, I'd say yes.'

'Hmm. I'm curious to know what those circumstances are.'

'Maybe another time. Let's stick to the matter at hand.'

'Ah, still keen not to "fanny about". Well then, Provender Gleed, son of my great enemy, tell me why exactly I should back down now. Especially when, as the fact that we're having this conversation at all proves, I am not and never was your kidnapper. Why should I, the wronged party in all of this, be the one to surrender?'

'I'm not asking you to. I'm conceding defeat.'

'Excuse me?'

'You win. You and my father were eye to eye. On his behalf, I'm saying he has blinked. You have successfully called his bluff. You are the victor.'

'I can't believe I'm hearing this. Are you sure you're a Gleed? You aren't some hoaxer who has tapped into the Family Phone network?'

'I'm a Gleed through and through. Just not the same kind of Gleed as my dad.'

'That would seem to be so. Undoubtedly you sound like him, your voice is just like his, though that is hardly surprising. But the words you're saying – they are completely different.'

'My father is a proud man, Mr Kuczynski, and for all his faults he feels the weight of history heavily. The feud between the Gleeds and the Kuczynskis is important to him. He defines his Family role, I think, by it. It is – has been – his one main way of feeling that he's doing right by his Family. Whereas me? I'm not sure I care. I mean, the feud is so old. It's been going on so long. It hasn't got anyone anywhere and it's brought so much misery generally. If it were up to me, I'd say just forget it. It isn't up to me, of course, but if it were . . . '

'Something so long-standing, so ingrained, cannot simply be swept away at a wish.'

'No, I agree. It's woven into our Families' lives. It can't be undone overnight.'

'But your implication is that we could make a start.'

'Possibly.'

'At least try.'

'Yes.'

Kuczynski said nothing for a while, but the sound of relay chatter and crackling atmospherics on the line was the sound of thoughts turning over.

'I would expect some concessions,' he said.

'What sort of concessions?'

'A gesture. A token of goodwill.'

'Money?'

'I was thinking a factory, maybe, or some other business concern. That's all. It doesn't even have to be an important one. A paper mill, a shipping contract. I'm not fussy. Something simply handed over freely, of your own will. It would be a show of . . . what's the word? Earnest?'

'Earnest, yes.'

'You would consider that?'

'I'm sure it could be arranged. I can't promise it because it would require my father's authorisation . . . but I could talk to him. Talk him into it. Is that really it? Is that all you want?'

'I would like a formal apology from your father, before a quorum of the Congress, but I realise I'm never going to get one.'

Provender half chuckled. 'You're right there. I can promise you almost anything but that.'

'Then a business concern will have to do.'

'You hear me when I say I can't guarantee it?'

'I do. But do you know what? Surprised though I am to say this, I trust you. I trust you to try.'

'I appreciate that trust. Very much.'

'And of course, if you fail, it wouldn't take much to put the wheels of war back into motion if I had to.'

'I don't want that. You can tell from my voice how much I don't want that.'

'Indeed I can. To be honest with you, I have had no stomach for this particular fight. My sister . . . Well, just be thankful she is not head of the Family, that's all I can say.' Kuczynski chuckled. 'Provender, it has been unusual and refreshing to talk with you like this. I feel strangely optimistic in my heart – and yes, I have one, whatever your father might have told you. I do not believe that the Gleeds and the Kuczynskis are going to settle all of their differences as of this moment, and anyway, what is wrong with a bit of healthy competition between Families? It adds savour to our lives. We might become dull and jaded otherwise. I do believe, however, that something has at last shifted. I could be wrong. I could be being foolish. Stasia will doubtless tell me that I am. But if what has happened today means that our Families are no longer butting heads quite so forcefully, that is surely a good thing. Perhaps, before long, you and I will be meeting in person?'

'You mean at the Congress table? My father's still got plenty of years left in him. I don't think I'm going to be Family head just yet.'

'Perhaps so. Nevertheless, you might go along as his second in place of your uncle? You are of an age when, as first-born son, you should.'

'I don't know. It remains to be seen.'

'Well, whatever. I should look forward to it, though, if it were to happen. And now I must go. Calls to make. Politicians to persuade. I think I shall even be speaking to your country's prime minister. I suspect, once he gets over the shock of hearing from a Kuczynski, he will prove as biddable as the rest of them are. It's wonderful, don't you think, how those in government, who give out orders so readily, are also so eager to take them?'

'It's . . . it has it uses,' Provender conceded. 'Mr Kuczynski, many thanks for this.'

'Stanisław, Provender. Please, I insist. Call me Stanisław.'

70

Diplomatic breakthrough.

Somehow, miraculously, within a couple of hours of the pendulum starting to swing towards war, all at once it lurched in the opposite direction. When all seemed lost, a resolution was found. Governments – impelled, it seemed, by the direness of Europe's predicament – redoubled their efforts, exhorted their ambassadors to try that bit harder, composed fresh formulae for peace, and even offered to stand down their forces unconditionally if that might convince the other side to do the same. One final, last-ditch round of negotiation seemed to produce a workable solution to the crisis. All of a sudden the grim high-ranking faces that had been a fixture of TV screens for the past few hours became relieved high-ranking faces. There was even, here and there, the odd hint of a smile.

Planes were recalled. Ships about-turned and cruised back to port. Soldiers decamped and marched back to base. City-Smashers vented hydrogen and commenced the long cumbersome descent to their hangars.

A continent sighed.

War, slain in infancy, died a swift and painless death.

71

A man could get lost in a house this size, thought Moore, before promptly doing just that.

It was late afternoon, edging into evening, and Moore wasn't sure if anyone even knew he was still there. He had been left behind in the rush of events, a piece of débris stranded after a dam-burst. Upstairs the Gleeds clustered and fussed around their stricken *materfamilias*. Even Is was up there, helping. Moore, however, was no use in such a situation; he had no pertinent skills to offer. All he could do was hang around downstairs and wait for developments, and the longer he did that, the more he started to feel he had outstayed his welcome. He was unwilling to slope off without saying goodbye, but increasingly, as time went on, that looked like being his only option. It was a disappointing outcome, a far cry from the hearty congratulation, the lavishment of praise, the acclaim he had been looking forward to. He understood entirely that Cynthia Gleed had to be the focus of the Family's attention for now, he was nothing compared to her in terms of importance . . . but still it would have been nice, wouldn't it, to have received just a little of the recognition he was due.

No, that was a selfish way to think, and Moore cursed himself for the lapse in empathy. If only there had been something he could do, some contribution he could make to ease the Gleeds' distress. But there wasn't.

Before departing, he decided to explore. After all, he remained a guest in the house until someone told him he wasn't, and that gave him the right to roam the premises, and when was he going to get an opportunity like this again? When was he next going to be an invited visitor to Dashlands, implicitly permitted the run of the house? Never, that was when. If someone asked him later to describe what Dashlands was like inside, he would be ashamed if he could tell them about a couple of rooms at most.

So he set off wandering, room to room, corridor to corridor, passing through lounge and library and hallway and gallery, pausing every so often when some *objet* or unusually opulent specimen of décor caught his eye. He lingered for some time in a windowless, humidity-controlled chamber whose sole purpose was to display oil portraits of every head of the Family going all the way back to Rufus Gleed. It was like a snapshot of three centuries of history of art, from murky Old Master to lurid, broad-brush Modernism and all points in-between. The styles changed, the frames grew simpler, but the features of the subjects stayed consistent throughout. Really what Moore found himself surrounded by was a dozen-plus studies of a nose. Wherever he looked, whichever way he turned, the prominent Gleed proboscis poked out at him from the walls. It, rather than any of the pairs of eyes in the portraits, was what followed him around the room. None of the artists had attempted to flatter or disguise the nose. Rather, they celebrated it, and the room itself seemed a shrine to it, and to heredity, and longevity. A monument to the nose's size and staying power, and also the Family's.

Moving on, Moore encountered a pair of servants who were going around switching on lamps. He avoided their stares, which subtly challenged him to account for his presence in the house, and continued his stroll. It was shortly after this that he realised he had roamed so far, he no longer had any clear sense of where he had set out from and how to get back there. He was the inexpert swimmer who had carelessly floated out of sight of land. Immediately, he about-faced and headed back to the spot where he had come across the two servants, but they were gone. He followed the trail of lit lamps, which by rights should have led him to them but somehow didn't. It petered out, and he was left cleaving his way through labyrinthine gloom.

Further meandering brought a by now slightly fretful Moore into the wing of the house which contained the Granny Flat, although he of course did not know this. What he did know was that all at once he could hear a voice – a profoundly deep voice that he recognised as Carver's. It muttered only a few words, but this was sufficient to enable him to pinpoint where it was coming from. Within moments he was face to face with the Gleeds' major-domo, and also with the fabled Great, whom Carver was pushing along in his wheelchair.

Moore could not believe how glad he was to see Carver. It was unclear whether the feeling was mutual, but Carver at least tried to soften his expression so that it looked marginally less unwelcoming than normal.

'Mr Moore,' he said. 'I assumed you left a long time ago.'

'I planned to. I've sort of been trying to. It's just . . . This place is very hard to find your way around in, let alone out of.'

The ring on Great's left hand rapped out a brief, agitated tattoo on the frame of the wheelchair. Great's moist blue eyes were fixed on Moore.

'You haven't met the senior member of the Family, have you,' Carver said.

'I haven't had that pleasure.'

Carver bent down, bringing his mouth near to Great's ear. 'This, sir, is one of the gentlemen I told you about. One of the detectives whom I hired to locate Master Provender and who, it would appear, succeeded beyond my wildest dreams.'

Moore nodded respectfully to Great. 'An honour.'

'The honour,' Carver replied, 'is all ours. Is that not so, sir?'

As if in response, Great's hand started tapping again.

'Great would, I'm sure, wish to extend his warmest thanks to you, Mr Moore. You have performed a remarkable service. Speaking for myself, I can scarcely express how gratified I am that I chose to employ you and your colleague. Where, by the way, is Mr Milner?'

'I'm not sure. Frankly, I wish I knew.'

'Oh well. The glory is all yours. It does strike me as almost uncanny how you knew where to look for Master Provender.'

'It was luck. Well, no, skill played a big part. The anagrams guided me to where I needed to be, even if the reason I was there wasn't the reason I *thought* I was there. If that makes any sense. SHORTBORN THEATRE, which I anagrammatised as BROTHER SON THREAT, I see now didn't actually refer to Arthur Gleed, at least not directly. It referred to his role as Hamlet, Claudius's brother's son, the nephew who opposes his uncle and ultimately proves his undoing. Which, however, got me to Arthur's house, which in turn brought me to Provender, or should I say Provender to me, and then—'

A sudden sharp rap from Great's signet ring shut him up as effectively as any words would have. Moore had to believe the timing was coincidental. He knew Great had no control over the only part of him that moved. All the same, it was hard not to feel he had been commanded to silence, and the balefulness of Great's gaze did nothing to vitiate that impression.

'Yes, yes,' said Carver, 'your methodology, most intriguing. But perhaps you can tell us about it some other time, when there are less pressing matters weighing on all our minds.'

'Of course. I'm sorry.'

'No need to be. I just happen to be conveying Great to pay a visit to Mrs Gleed. Come with us and I will direct you to a room where you can wait until such time as I can arrange transportation for you back to London. That young lady who was with you and Master Provender – I trust she would wish to return home too?'

'I have no idea. I expect so.'

'Very good. This way, then.'

They walked, the three of them, or rather one of them walked while one of them walked-and-pushed and one of them was pushed, and Moore was in a subdued mood, thinking again about how this hadn't turned out as he had hoped. Carver, for all that he had said complimentary things about Moore's work, didn't seem unduly impressed or full of admiration. That might simply be down to the way he was – Moore thought it would take a lot to impress Carver – but equally there was an inescapable sense that he was annoyed somehow.

Or was that just Moore's insecurity? His heightened sense of self-criticism getting the better of him?

As they journeyed onward, the only sound was that of the wheelchair tyres rumbling and the tapping of Great's signet ring, which was inter-mittent but unrelenting. Moore remained sunk in thought but not so deep that he didn't find the continual clack of gold against steel just that bit distracting, and after a while aggravating. How did Carver put up with it? No doubt over the years he had learned to tune it out. Didn't even notice it any more.

There was something about its arrhythmic insistence, though.

Something that demanded attention.

That would not be ignored.

If it had been just that bit less repetitive, just that bit more random . . .

Random? Moore was puzzled. The tapping was quite clearly random. Why would he have thought it was anything else?

He began listening to it, as opposed to simply hearing it, and yes, he could detect no obvious pattern. There were sequences of impacts, some louder than others, which came in clusters with short and sometimes long intervals between. Nothing regular about it other than that it kept happening. Random.

Some louder than others.

And Moore listened more closely to it, and then even more closely, and oh God, it couldn't be, it wasn't what he thought, it surely could not be . . .

And the pattern became apparent.

There *was* consistency.

'Great's real name,' he said, needing confirmation, 'his first name – what is it?'

'Why do you ask?'

Moore tried to sound casual. 'Uh, curiosity. Nothing else.'

Carver seemed to think there was no harm in telling him. 'It's Coriander.'

CORIANDER GLEED . . .

The letters whirled like wind-blown leaves, then settled again.

And Moore said, because he couldn't help blurting it out:

'Morse.'

And Carver halted, and swivelled his head, and pinned the Anagram-matic Detective with his gaze, and said, 'I beg your pardon?'

And Moore said again, because that gaze of Carver's brooked no lies or evasion:

'Morse.'

And Carver said, 'Ah.' And then said, 'Oh.' And then said, 'What a shame.'

'You didn't know,' said Moore. Hopefully.

'Know?' Carver replied. Evenly.

'You did,' said Moore. 'Of course. You communicate. Army. You understand him. He can ask for things. Give you orders . . .'

With that, Moore's voice trailed off into silence.

He saw it.

Saw everything.

Provender's insider. The brains behind the abduction.

Insiders, plural.

Why else was Carver glaring at him now? Why else was Moore not supposed to have spotted that the tapping was not as uncontrolled as it was claimed to be? It was obviously a secret shared by only Carver and Great. And why else would it be a secret if it wasn't being used for some kind of subterfuge?

With that revelation, the wider picture began to open up. Why had Carver hired Moore and Milner if it was against his own interests? Why else unless . . .

'Yes, a shame,' Carver said, nodding. 'I mean it sincerely. And I'm being just as sincere when I say that you're good at your job, Mr Moore. Exceedingly so. Far too good, indeed, for your own good.'

'We weren't supposed to find him,' Moore said, meekly, weakly. 'We were meant to fail.'

'With the greatest of respect: *Anagrammatic* Detectives? Jumbling up words in order to solve crimes? It's just plain silly. There's no earthly reason for it to work.'

'But it does.'

'It did. Or you just got lucky. You've just got lucky in every one of your few successful cases. Who knows?'

'But you took us on, threw money at us—'

'—so that I could be seen to be doing something. Within the remit I had, you were perfect. Private investigators, not police. Detectives but not, as far as I could see, especially effective ones. You'd tackle the case but had little chance of cracking it. Provender would remain a captive as long as was necessary.'

'Which was how long? What were you hoping to achieve?'

'You'll never understand,' Carver said. 'It's not your place to, anyway.'

Great had begun tapping furiously, and the difference between the dots and dashes was all too apparent now, soft for short, loud for long, and Moore knew the individual letters of the Morse alphabet but Great was going too fast for him to keep up. Words were pouring out. The wheelchair frame rang with speech.

'And,' Carver continued, 'I regret to say I cannot allow you to share this discovery of yours with anyone. Damage limitation is now my goal. Given the latest turn of events, Mrs Gleed's act of self-harm, it would reflect badly on Great and myself were we implicated in Master Provender's kidnap. I cannot allow that to happen.'

'Can't allow it?' said Moore, dry-mouthed. 'Or are you being told not to allow it?'

Carver appeared to smile. His scar, at any rate, puckered more deeply at the bottom and became curved like a hook.

'It amounts to the same thing,' he said, and lunged.

72

'It's a snug fit,' said Extravagance.

'Tight, you mean,' said Is, struggling with the zip at the side of the skirt. 'Do you have anything even a little bit looser?'

'That's the biggest-size thing I've got. I'm not sure why I bought it. Moment of madness. Perhaps I was a couple of pounds overweight that day. I've never worn it, anyway, because it hangs off me like a tent. I thought it would be fine on you, but . . .'

'But I have hips.'

'You're rounded.'

'And my bum is twice as large as yours.'

'Rounded.'

Is fought with the zip for a while longer, Extravagance assisting, but eventually both accepted that it was going up only so far and no further. An inch-long V of unmeshed teeth remained above the fastener. The skirt, however, stayed on, and when Is tugged the hem of her jumper down, the gap in the waistband was hidden. She did a couple of turns in front of Extravagance's dressing-room mirror. It was a lovely skirt, Italian silk screenprinted with a floral pattern and trimmed with lace which slithered pleasingly around her calves. Not the sort of item she herself would have bought, even if she could have afforded it. Too feminine-looking, too impractically delicate. But as a one-time-only deal, a substitute for the skirt Mrs Gleed had been sick over, she was happy to wear it.

'I'll get it back to you as soon as I can.'

'Oh God, no. It's yours. Keep it.'

'But I can barely breathe in it.'

'Well, I don't want it. Think of it as a thank-you gift.'

'Thank you for . . .'

'For Mum, of course. What you did.'

'I didn't do much.'

'You saved her life!'

'But—'

'Is, none of us had a clue how to help her. We all stood around like prunes, whereas you got straight in there and did all that chest-pushing and whatnot.'

'Provender pitched in.'

'Only because you told him to. You were amazing. A miracle-worker. A saint.'

Is could not look her in the eye. Extravagance didn't know yet about her role in the kidnapping. No one in the household did, apart from Provender.

Is felt she was still a long way from redeeming herself.

'Will she be all right, do you think?' Extravagance asked as she and Is left her room.

'I can't say. A full recovery is perfectly possible. Then again, worse comes to worst, she might lapse into a coma.' Seeing Extravagance's face fall, Is hurried on, 'But that's unlikely. On balance, if she's otherwise healthy, your mother ought to be fine. We got there reasonably soon after she took the pills, and she threw up, which helps.'

'I still have a hard time believing it. It's just not like Mum to do something so . . . extreme.'

'The circumstances were extreme. People respond unpredictably to pressure.' Is had offered such soothing bromides to patients' relatives in the past, but never before with an underlying sense of guilt. The guilt was starting to feel constricting – or maybe that was just Extravagance's skirt. Either way, getting away from Dashlands was now more imperative than ever as far as she was concerned. Worse than the Gleeds' enmity, she was finding their gratefulness hard to bear.

'Look, Extravagance . . .' She stumbled over the name. It was quite a mouthful.

''Strav,' said Extravagance. 'It's simpler.'

''Strav. I really think I should be getting back home.'

'Oh, you can't go! Mum—'

'—is in very good hands.'

'But then there's Provender.'

'What about Provender?'

'Well, don't you at least want to say goodbye to him?'

'Maybe another time. When he hasn't got so much else to worry about.'

'How did you and he meet anyway? There's still a lot I don't understand about all this. Come on, at least stay till tomorrow. We've plenty of spare rooms. You can even have the official guest suite. You'd love the guest suite. It has a Jacuzzi, a four-poster, a hell of a view . . . Normally only Family heads get to sleep there but I could swing it for you I'm sure. And in return, you can fill me in on what's been going on and you can tell me why my brother looks at you in that way.'

'He looks at me in a way?'

'Don't be daft, you know he does. When we were out there on the road to the tram stop, and even when you were bossing him about in the television room . . .'

'He doesn't look at me in a way.'

'Trust me, he does. He's smitten. You can see it a mile off.'

'Please, 'Strav, he doesn't.'

'You may not want him to but that's not the same thing. It's nothing to get alarmed about. I mean, you're not Family, but at this stage, frankly, we're past caring about that. It's just a relief that he's considering anyone at all.'

'"Considering".'

'Yes.'

'Implying *I* don't have any say in the matter.'

'Is,' said Extravagance, sweeping an enthusiastic arm around, 'what choice is there to make?'

They had arrived at the head of the staircase that curved down around the perimeter of the cylindrical atrium where Triumph stood, and Is had to admit that, if what you were after was a life lived amid splendour, Dashlands House was unquestionably the place for it. Extravagance's gesture took in the statue itself, the apexed glass roof, the staircase's ornate wrought-iron banister, and by implication the whole of the rest of the house. She was offering Is, in effect, a future as glittering as Triumph's gold accents.

Before Is could respond, there was a commotion down below, quickly followed by the appearance of Romeo Moore in the atrium, fleeing, and Carver, in hot pursuit. Moore took to the stairs, and Carver was right behind him, arm out, inches away from grabbing hold. Halfway up, Moore missed his footing and stumbled. Carver seized him by the jacket collar. Moore writhed, wriggled free from his jacket, and resumed running up the stairs. Carver tossed the item of clothing aside and carried on after. His face was set in a ferocious leer. Moore's expression was pure terror.

Near the top of the stairs Moore caught sight of Is and Extravagance and faltered. The pause was brief but enough to allow Carver to catch up with him again. This time he took a firm hold of the Anagrammatic Detective, swung him around with appalling ease, as if he weighed next to nothing, and slammed him against the banister. The air was driven from Moore's lungs. Carver then proceeded to bend him backwards over the banister's handrail, fist locked against the base of his throat. Moore's head was canted directly over Triumph's upraised left hand; her fingertips daggered up approximately four yards below the back of his skull. He grunted, he grimaced. Carver's contorted face, looming over his, was surely the worst thing anyone would want to see when in a position like this, and Moore's bulging eyes said exactly that.

'Carver!'

Extravagance's sharp cry had little effect on the manservant. He pushed Moore further over, until the detective was touching the stairs with just his toecaps.

'Carver, what are you doing? What is the meaning of this?'

'It doesn't concern you, Miss Extravagance,' Carver said from the side of his mouth. 'You should leave. You too,' he added, meaning Is. 'This is between me and this . . . thief.'

'Thief?'

'I caught him attempting to pilfer some small trinkets. Great and I both witnessed him getting ready to stuff his pockets with Family valuables. Naturally, when we came upon him *in flagrante*, he ran, and naturally I gave chase.'

Moore was whipping his head from side to side and would have denied the accusation out loud had Carver's knuckles not been sunk into his windpipe.

'You're hurting him,' said Extravagance. 'Let him go.'

'I can't do that, Miss Extravagance. Not without risk to yourself. He's a desperate, dangerous man.'

'He's half your size,' said Is, 'and from what I know of him he's no danger to anyone.'

'Nobody asked *your* opinion,' Carver growled.

'Let him go,' Extravagance said again. 'That's an order.'

Carver did not obey, nor did he openly disobey. What he did was shove Moore fully onto the banister, so that all that was supporting Moore and keeping him from falling was the banister itself and Carver. Moore's arms flailed and his eyes rolled, panic-stricken. The drop beneath him, assuming he missed Triumph on the way down, was far enough to kill a man.

Is took a step towards Carver, and at that same moment the banister groaned. A shudder ran through it from top to bottom and from somewhere along its length there came a resonant metallic *snap*. Moore let out a strangulated moan. Is took three more steps. Carver turned his head and shot her a look that would have scorched paint. The scar was a livid lightning flash against the thundercloud of his face. His lips were pulled back and Is could see that several back teeth were missing on the same side as the scar, presumably knocked out when the injury was inflicted.

'Do not interfere, girl,' he said, reverberantly low. 'Stand back or I will mess you up so badly your life will not be worth living.'

'You don't scare me,' Is said.

'I should and I do.'

'No, you don't.' She meant it, too. 'This man hasn't tried to steal anything. You're lying about that and I think I know why. He's rumbled you, hasn't he? And you want him out of the way, you want to silence him. I know who you are, Mr Carver. I know what you've done.'

'You know nothing.'

'*You're* Damien's insider.'

'Shut your mouth. You're talking nonsense.'

'Is, what do you mean?' said Extravagance. 'Who's Damien? What's going on here?'

'Gleeds not paying you enough, Mr Carver? Oh no, wait, all the money was going to Damien. So what was your angle? What were you after? Do you not like Provender much?'

'I have never,' Carver said, 'ever done anything to the detriment of the Gleeds, any of them, and never would. I have served this Family immaculately all my years. I am loyal to them to my core. You're speaking of things you have no way of understanding, girl. I reiterate: shut your mouth.'

'Will someone explain this to me immediately!' Extravagance shouted.

Is said, 'Put him down, Mr Carver. We'll sort it out without hurting anybody.'

The banister gave another groan and wobbled slightly beneath Moore's back. Moore yelped and clutched Carver's sleeve in fright.

'No one has to die over this,' she said. 'There's no point in killing the detective because I know your secret now and so does 'Strav.'

'I do not,' said Extravagance. 'Do I?'

'Carver masterminded the kidnapping. He's behind it all.'

'Carver? This can't be true. Is this true?'

'An abject falsehood, Miss Extravagance.'

Extravagance looked puzzled. 'Why don't I believe you?'

'Probably because he's holding a man suspended over a thirty-foot drop,' said Is. 'That puts a bit of a dent in his credibility.'

'But what's my brother ever done to you?' Extravagance wanted to know.

'And what about the war?' said Is. The truth was unfurling in her head like a roll of carpet. 'I bet you didn't count on that. And Mrs Gleed. Surely you didn't intend her to come to harm, did you? It was a consequence you just didn't foresee.'

Carver looked down. Oh so briefly, but the action was a giveaway nonetheless. It spoke of a conscience pricked – remorse felt, however fleetingly.

The banister gave a lurch.

Moore squawked.

Carver raised his head again and looked Is squarely in the eye.

'I only caught a glimpse of you at the ball,' he said, 'otherwise I'd have recognised you straight away when you came back today. I didn't even make the connection when you attended to Mrs Gleed, which was remiss of me. I thought you were an associate of his.' He nodded at Moore, who flinched in the mistaken belief that he was about to be head-butted. 'Had I been thinking more clearly at the time, I would have put two and two together. It came to me shortly afterwards. The nurse. Damien's helper. But of course I wasn't going to say anything even then, and thereby incriminate myself. I'd pay no attention to you, and then you'd leave and no one would be any the wiser.'

'Except it didn't work out that way. You realise, don't you, that Damien would – will – identify you as his accomplice.'

'Will he I wonder. And even if he does, I'll have protection. You really don't know as much about this as you think you do, young lady.'

'Maybe not. Still, we're discussing it rationally, it's out in the open – so perhaps, please, you can pull Mr Moore back. He doesn't need to be hanging over the edge like that now. He's not a threat to you any more.'

'I'm not accustomed to taking orders from a non-Family member.'

'Tell him, 'Strav,' Is said, turning. 'I don't like the sounds that banister's making. Tell him to—'

The sound the banister made next was like nothing Is had heard before. There was a long raspy shriek, punctuated by a series of deep pizzicato *plunks* as though some giant harpist was running her fingers along the uprights. Then came a warping, grinding *sprunnng* noise, and Is spun round in time to see the upper end of the banister detach itself from the staircase and twist outwards as fluidly as though it were cotton ribbon. It went flat, and Moore and Carver went flat with it, sprawling one on top of the other. The banister kept them there, suspended, for an instant of infinity. Then, with a squeal, it gave way.

Is threw herself forwards headlong, hand outstretched. She grabbed blindly, and more by instinct than aim seized hold of a forearm.

She hoped, she prayed, it was Moore's and not Carver's.

The banister peeled away, unspooling downward until its upper end hit the atrium floor with a clang. In the echoes of the impact Is heard a cry of pain followed by gurgling distress and then a sharp sigh. Her eyes were closed. She was lying flat on the stairs, with one arm hanging over the edge and supporting the weight of a grown man. Something had torn in her shoulder – a muscle wrench rather than a dislocation, she thought, but still it hurt like hell. She could not move. Dared not. She was gripping whoever's wrist as hard as she could. She would not let go, refused to. She was aware of Extravagance beside her. 'Come on,' Extravagance was saying. Not to Is. 'Help us help you up. Come on. Put your foot there. Yes, that's it.'

She would not let go, even after the man was safely on the stairs next to her. It took Extravagance pulling back hard on her fingers to get her to unclamp them from his wrist.

Then, at last opening her eyes, she looked and saw Romeo Moore, prone, panting frantically.

Alive.

Which meant . . .

She rolled her head round and looked over the edge.

It was a sight which Extravagance was trying desperately to avert her eyes from and which Moore was too traumatised to think about viewing just yet.

But Is looked. Stared. Had to see.

Triumph's upraised arm. Hand gloved to the wrist with blood. And below the hand, like some ghastly bracelet, a body. Carver. Limbs dangling. Head thrown back. Impaled through the abdomen. Twitching his last.

73

A gathering of the Clan.

The place: the fourth largest drawing room at Dashlands House, decorated with bamboo screens, tropical ferns in urns, an elephant's foot umbrella stand, and a plethora of animal pelts, from tiger throw rug to antelope wall-hanging to leopardskin upholstery – a great white hunter's paradise.

Present, seated left to right: Provender Gleed, Isis Necker, Prosper Gleed, Fortune Gleed, Gratitude Gleed, Extravagance Gleed, and Great.

Supervising the proceedings: Anagrammatic Detective Romeo Moore . . .

. . . who was acutely aware how this scene resembled the final chapter of one of those country-house murder mystery novels he used to devour as a child, the revelatory moment when the police inspector or the private investigator unmasked the villain, who was usually the person you least suspected until after you had read widely enough in the genre, whereupon he/she became the person you suspected from the start. Moore could not help thinking he ought to say something like, 'I expect you're wondering why I've called you all together.' The temptation was there, but resistible. He also had to fight the desire to crack a joke about the butler having *really* done it.

No, this was a sombre moment, not the time for clowning around. Nor was it the time for revelling in success. Moore's achievements as a detective, pleased with them as he was, meant little when he was confronted by a Family in a state of shock. The faces arrayed before him, Great's excepted, were bewildered and drawn and haggard. The Gleeds had a lot to come to terms with, and Moore's natural courtesy inclined him to downplay his role here as bringer of truth and exposer of foul play.

'I'm sorry I have to be the one to tell you what I have to tell you,' he began. It helped, from the point of view of sounding tactful, that his voice was reduced to a husky croak. His throat hurt if he spoke above a certain volume. Carver's fist had bruised his larynx and Is said it would probably be sore for the next few days but the only remedies were time and not talking too much. Talking, of course, was something he couldn't avoid right now.

'I didn't even know what I was doing,' he added modestly. 'It all just seemed to fall into place of its own accord. I suppose it's because I'm in the habit of looking for patterns. Patterns within words, patterns in everything. If not for that, I wouldn't have—'

'Why did Carver try to kill you?' said Prosper Gleed, curtly.

Moore was thrown by the interruption. He blinked, regrouped and restarted. 'Allegedly he wasn't trying to kill me. Allegedly he caught me stealing something and was tackling me as he would have any thief. But in fact I believe he *would* have killed me if he had had the opportunity to get away with it. Then he'd have planted some piece of incriminating evidence in my pocket and come to you with the whole terrible story. And my death would have been made to look like an accident, I'm sure, or less his fault, more mine. Your manservant was keen to cover his tracks, and I, as far as he was concerned, was in every way expendable.'

'But it's hard to conceive,' said Gratitude. 'Carver, willing to take a man's life.'

'An ex-soldier? And by all accounts a fearsome warrior in his day? Not so hard to conceive, Miss Gleed.'

'You weren't there, Grat,' said Extravagance. 'He was berserk. I think he really meant to do it.'

'But why?' said Prosper. 'What for?'

'To protect the Family,' said Moore.

'Protect us? From . . . ?'

'Er . . . Me. Or rather, what I had found out, a piece of information that was highly damaging to him.'

'Come on, man, talk straight. What information?'

'I'm getting to that.'

'Well, can't you hurry it up a bit?'

'Dad,' said Provender. 'Stop hassling him. Let him explain in his own time.'

'But he's—'

'*Dad.*'

Prosper fell silent, cowed by his son's forthrightness.

'Go on, Romeo,' said Provender.

'Right. So. Um. What it comes down to is the fact that the whole kidnap plot was orchestrated not by some outside agency but from right here, at Dashlands.'

Now it was Fortune's turn to expostulate indignantly, although he did so in a more muted manner than his brother. 'That's not right. Can't be right. Why would anyone . . . ?' Rather than complete the rhetorical question, he submerged it in a draught of gin and tonic.

'We can, I hope, get to the bottom of "why?" shortly,' Moore said, with a surreptitious glance towards Great. 'I myself had an inkling from the start that it might be an inside job. What I didn't realise was that the culprit was the very person who was employing me to investigate the crime.'

'Yes, why is that?' said Provender. 'Why would Carver have hired you unless he thought you . . . Oh.'

Moore nodded, with chagrin but also with a hint of vengeful satisfaction. 'He told me himself shortly before he attacked me. He honestly didn't think I or my partner had a hope of cracking the case. He took us on . . . well, principally so that he could appear to be doing something useful, but also because of all the trees he could have barked up, ours was the wrongest one. If you see what I mean. It was almost a joke to him, I feel. "Who's the least likely person I can find to send to look for Provender?" '

'We only have *your* word on any of this,' said Fortune. 'You could be spinning us some cock-and-bull story in order to . . .'

'In order to what? Get myself off the hook for supposedly stealing some trinket from you? Hardly likely. Besides, I have a Family witness here who'll attest to the fact that Carver was trying to silence me, don't I, Extravagance? He all but confessed his connection to the kidnapper, Damien Scrase, in the moments before he . . . we . . .'

Moore experienced again the terror of being bent over the banister, Carver's furious features filling his vision, the sense of the drop beneath him, the hard tiles below, his utter helplessness. His fingers, reflexively, went to his throat and explored the tender flesh there. It was weird to be alive after having been so close to death. It was at once exhilarating and deflating, an emotional alp from which the only route was down.

He became aware that he had faded out and Extravagance was speaking, filling the gap he had left. She told everyone that not only had Carver clearly been intent on murder but he had recognised Is, who also had some connection with this whole messy business.

'Don't you?' she concluded, with a frosty look at the person with whom, half an hour earlier, she had been going through her wardrobe, selecting skirts to try on, all girls together.

Before Is had a chance to reply, Provender stepped in. 'She was an unwilling accomplice, forced to take part against her will. She helped me escape, too, and in case you've forgotten, she saved our mother's life.'

Is shifted in her seat, exquisitely uncomfortable. She opened her mouth to say something before deciding that saying nothing was the better option.

'I can vouch for her as well,' said Moore. 'I saw her tackle Scrase at the Shortborn, when he was threatening Provender. She's definitely on the side of the angels.'

Is started gently massaging her wrenched shoulder, head down, avoiding all stares.

'But if we're looking to lay blame,' Moore continued, 'there is someone in this room deserving of our attention. Carver is guilty of a lot but there's someone who I'd say is even guiltier.'

He let the words hang in the air, allowing the Gleeds to draw the correct inference, which, gradually, they did. Heads turned, homing in on the one person present whose head could not turn.

Great's stare remained forward-fixed as ever, his eyes stony. His hand was not tapping. His whole body was statue-still. Then, little by little, his eyes began to move, sweeping across his assembled relatives, defiant, challenging. You could read anything into the way those glittering blue orbs looked, from an admission of culpability to astonished, out-and-out refutation.

'No,' said Fortune.

'Great?' said Gratitude.

'Too far,' said Prosper. 'You've gone too far now, Mr Detective.'

Even Provender looked dubious.

'I understand your scepticism,' said Moore, 'and no doubt I'll only add to it when I tell you that it was his full name, his proper name, which set the seal on it for me, bearing out my suspicion that Carver was just the brawn of the outfit and someone else was the brains.'

'What *is* Great's proper name?' asked Extravagance.

'Oh really, 'Strav!' said her older sister. 'You don't know?'

'I forget. No one ever calls him by it.'

'Arthur does.'

'Does he?'

'You are *so* unobservant sometimes. Coriander.'

'Oh yes. So it is.'

'Coriander,' said Moore. 'And CORIANDER GLEED happens to be an anagram of CODE RINGLEADER.'

Fortune snorted a laugh.

'It is.'

'I don't care if it is, Moore, I simply think you're taking the mickey. Anagram indeed!'

'It's what he does, uncle,' said Provender, 'and I hate to say it but it works. That was Carver's mistake. He thought it was ridiculous too.'

'So we're expected to believe, on the strength of an *anagram*, that a paralysed old man was capable of—'

'Forgive me,' Moore interjected, 'but Great is not paralysed.'

'Some bloody detective! Of course he is. Look at him. He's been in that chair for, Christ, over a decade. He's not faking it. What, suddenly he's going to get up and walk and tell us it was all a big sham?'

'No, no, not at all.'

'And I'll bet he speaks, too. Eh? He's just been pretending he can't all this time.'

'As it happens, he can speak. Not in the conventional sense, but—'

'Pure bollocks!' Fortune exclaimed. 'I can believe, I suppose, that Carver's a bad guy. Never much liked him, to be honest. But now you're telling us that the oldest member of the Family, for some reason that has yet to be established, went to the trouble of having the heir-apparent abducted and caused all this chaos. Why, for God's sake? Family doesn't harm its own. That's an unwritten law.'

'His motives I hope to find out. His methods? When I said he can speak, what I meant was he can communicate.'

'Oh, and how?'

'What isn't he doing right now?'

'Anything. He isn't doing anything. Because he's paralysed.' Fortune said this condescendingly, as if conversing with a simpleton.

Provender said, 'Tapping. He's not tapping.'

'Correct,' said Moore. 'But when he does . . .'

'Code.'

'Exactly.'

There was a pause, a collective intake of breath, a communal click of understanding.

'It's not possible,' said Gratitude. 'We'd have noticed. Surely we would have.'

'But we didn't,' said her brother. 'It happened slowly. He lost movement, he lost his speech, the tapping started . . . We just didn't think about it. We thought it was a symptom.'

'Right under our noses,' said their uncle, wonderingly.

'And Carver,' said Prosper, 'he knew.'

'They served together in the army,' said Moore. 'Both would have a working knowledge of Morse code.'

'Well, of course,' said Fortune. 'Carver always seemed to know exactly what Great wanted. We thought it was just because he was a good servant and had spent so much time in Great's company. What's that word when two different species of animal cooperate?'

'Symbiosis.'

'That's the one. That was their relationship. Kind of psychic, almost.'

'Only it wasn't,' said Provender. 'Carver knew what Great wanted all the time because Great was telling him.'

'Are we idiots not to have seen it?' said Extravagance.

No one else answered, so Moore felt honour-bound to. 'Not necessarily. Why would it occur to you that that's what was going on?'

'*You* spotted it.'

'Like I said, patterns. And the anagrams. It's how my brain is wired.'

'But you met them and saw it straight away. We *live* with them.'

'Sometimes, when a thing's right in front of you, you adjust to it. You take it into account and don't think anything of it. It's just *there*. Also, an elderly, disabled relative tends to fade into the background, especially when, as with this Family, everyone else has such a strong personality. The elderly relative becomes, with all due respect, part of the furniture.'

He anticipated protests, but there were only mute nods of assent.

Throughout the foregoing, Great's eyes flicked from speaker to speaker but his hand stayed resolutely still, denying by its very motionlessness the abilities Moore was asserting it had. Then, abruptly, it started shaking, twisting from the wrist to bring the finger with the signet ring into contact with the wheelchair armrest.

The assembled Family listened in silence, paying attention to a sound they had hitherto regarded as just so much meaningless reflex-movement drumming. Not one of them had any idea what Great was saying but they knew for the first time that he was saying *something*, and this, in itself, lent the tapping a strange articulacy. Great, dumb for a decade, was talking again. Speech – incomprehensible but speech nonetheless – was issuing forth from him.

'Can you understand him?' Prosper asked Moore.

'I know Morse. Sort of. I know how each letter is represented. But he's going too fast for me to follow.'

'Great,' Prosper said, 'you'll have to slow down. Mr Moore will be able to translate then.'

The rate of the tapping decreased, but Moore, try though he might, still could not make head or tail of it. The louds and softs, dashes and dots, all seemed to merge into one another.

'Slower still,' said Prosper.

The tapping became painstakingly protracted, Great leaving long gaps between letters and making the distinction between the dashes and dots as marked as possible. Moore was just about able to keep up now, although not without effort. He had memorised the Morse alphabet a long time ago, purely as an intellectual exercise, but he had never actually had to use it before. Adding to his difficulties was the fact that he was having to recall it under pressure. He made, therefore, several mistakes to start with, although gradually his ear attuned and his fluency improved.

'FAMILY GETTING WEAP,' he interpreted. 'WEAP? What's that?'

Great tapped out the last word again.

'Oh, WEAK. NEEDED SHAKING UP. BOY NEEDED . . . SHOCK? Is that it? SHOCK?'

Great tapped out dash-dot-dash-dash, dot, dot-dot-dot. YES.

'BOY NEEDED TO GET OFF . . . I'm not translating *that* word. AND DO SOMETHING.'

'Me?' said Provender.

'YES,' said Moore. 'USELESS LAZY . . . I'm sorry, could you run through that one again please?'

Dash-dot-dash-dot, dot-dot-dash, dash-dot, dash.

'SO-AND-SO.' This was not, strictly speaking, the term Great had used, but Moore had no wish to offend anyone by repeating the actual profanity.

'THEREFORE KIDNAP. RUDE AWAKENING. BRING TO SENSES. GLEEDS MUST SURVIVE.'

'A bit extreme, don't you think?' said Provender.

'DESPERATE TIMES DESPERATE MEASURES. IN MY DAY WAR

MADE MAN OF YOU. FACE FOE FACE SELF. LEARN COURAGE AND DUTY. NO WAR NOW THEREFORE OTHER CHALLENGE NECESSARY.'

'Only there nearly was a war. You didn't count on that, did you?'

'GOOD IF BOY TURNED SOLDIER.'

'Yes, like *that* was going to happen. And Mum. Another little drawback to your scheme, Great.'

'SAD. WRONG. CYNTHIA ONLY DECENT GLEED. PROSPER UNGRATEFUL . . . No, I won't say it.'

Great banged the word out again, forcefully, and Moore relented.

'All right. UNGRATEFUL BASTARD. I apologise, Mr Gleed, those aren't my sentiments of course. I'm simply the messenger.'

Prosper waved it aside, looking as if he knew he deserved the censure.

'And if I'd been killed?' said Provender to Great. 'Believe me, I came close. That would've scuppered you, wouldn't it? Talk about an own goal.'

'ACCEPTABLE RISK.'

'Oh, thanks.'

'CARVER MONITORING SITUATION.'

'Obviously not that closely.'

'ACCEPTABLE RISK,' Great reiterated, via Moore.

Provender sighed. 'You're quite mad, aren't you? I'm not saying I don't understand why. Sitting in that chair all day. Stuck inside your own body. Stewing in your own thoughts. Staring out at a world you can't directly affect. Year after year of that – it's not surprising a few of your marbles have gone astray. But that's no excuse for what you did. To me. To all of us. Do you regret it now? Do you feel even the slightest remorse?'

Great's hand stayed in his lap for almost a minute, until with solemn, precise emphasis it sounded out two letters: dash-dot, dash-dash-dash.

Translation was superfluous.

'Thought not,' said Provender.

'ACTED FOR FAMILY. DOING BEST FOR FAMILY. GETTING HOUSE IN ORDER. FAMILY EVERYTHING. FAMILY MUST NOT FADE. GLEEDS MUST SURVIVE. GLEEDS MUST . . . again, SUR-VIVE. GLEEDS. GLEEDS.' Moore listened as Great continued to tap out the same sequence over and over. In the end the Anagrammatic Detective shrugged. 'That's it. GLEEDS, GLEEDS, ad infinitum.'

The tapping quickened and grew louder. It was all Great had to say now. His gaze scanned left to right and back again, taking in each and all of his relatives. The pattern of dashes and dots became insistent, hypnotic, like a peal of church bells, a phrase from a song, a complex tom-tom polyrhythm, dinning itself into every skull in the room, until eventually Provender snapped to his feet, strode over, grabbed Great's hand and wrested off the signet ring. The ring came free with surprising ease, a little too large for the bony finger it encircled. Provender tossed it upwards and snatched it from the air at the start of its downward arc, stealing it from sight.

Great resumed tapping the wheelchair frame, but with his bare knuckle the sound was nowhere near as sharp and attention-getting. All he could manage was a dull, scarcely audible thud which the Gleeds could ignore without too much difficulty, and did. In a demonstration of contempt they began talking amongst themselves, huddling close, literally turning their backs on Great. Provender was asked to provide an account of his adventures of the past three days, and he duly fleshed out the sketchy details the others already knew and filled in some blanks. There were questions, prompts, interjections, and the volume of the conversation mounted until, quite deliberately, it was so loud that Great hadn't a hope of making himself heard above it. He soon gave up trying. His hand fell limply into his lap and all he could do was sit and glower, a picture of impotence and thwarted fury.

For Moore, it was hard to reconcile the frail-looking figure in the wheelchair with the force and recklessness of the scheme he had hatched, yet some clue as to the vigour of the mind trapped within that useless body lay in Great's eyes – their blue blaze radiated manic energy. Mad? Quite possibly. Bad? Not by his own reckoning. Great had been trying to save his Family. For him there was no nobler objective.

With his right-hand man gone, Great had lost his one sure link with the rest of the world, the conduit through which he channelled his wishes and desires. Moore felt little sorrow over Carver's demise, horrible though it had been. Carver would have happily visited the same fate on him, indeed had been trying to. Natural justice had in this instance been poetic justice too. Still, Great was bereft of his lifelong companion now, and it looked unlikely that the other Gleeds were going to forgive him any time soon for what he had done. If Cynthia Gleed did not recover, they might never forgive him. Moore predicted a long and frosty ostracism for the Family's senior-most member, a future in which he would be made to atone for his actions as surely as any prisoner in solitary confinement. His paralysed body would be his cell.

You could almost, Moore thought, pity the old brute.

Almost.

74

The pearl-white Dagenham Seraph stood in the driveway, V8 engine susurrating. With its high wheelbase and pinpoint suspension the car seemed perpetually to be floating; whether in motion or stationary, its tyres seemed only just in contact with the earth. Gravity-defying, it was a limousine that appeared to weigh less than a saloon car.

In the driving seat a chauffeur sat with his gloved hands resting on the steering wheel and a look of perfect impassivity on his face, professionally patient. In the back, Romeo Moore was luxuriating, stretching out his legs, swimming on the calfskin upholstery, relishing every cubic inch of limo spaciousness. One of the rear doors was open, inviting Is to join him inside. She was ready to go, but first there was a farewell to be negotiated, the awkward moment she had forgotten she had been dreading, till now.

There was still a faint glow in the sky, star-clusters pinned to a back-drop of indigo rather than pure black. Clouds of moths hovered around lawn lights, like miniature solar systems, planets orbiting suns. The Seraph's fine-tuned purr was so soft that chirruping insects in the vicinity had no trouble competing with it.

Provender waited. Provender had much to say and no idea how to begin saying it.

'So,' said Is. She raised her hands and let them fall haplessly. 'It's been . . . *something*, hasn't it?'

Numbly Provender nodded. 'It has.'

'Who'd have thought . . . I mean . . . I don't know what I mean. Look, it's better if I just go, I think. Get into the car and get whisked away.'

'You don't have to—'

She held up a finger and darted it towards his mouth. 'I have to. For one thing, they're expecting me back at work tomorrow.' A small lie. The day after tomorrow. 'Early shift. I've a whole life I have to pick back up. Things I have to start doing again. Back to the everyday, the routine. I need that. I need to pretend as if . . .'

'As if nothing ever happened?'

'Don't you think that's for the best?'

'Obviously what *I* think doesn't count. But do *you* think that's for the best? *Did* nothing happen?'

She knew in what sense he meant the question but she answered as if she didn't. 'Fights and dangling off balconies and wrangling with a psychopathic ex-boyfriend and mixing with the Gleeds – I wouldn't call that nothing. But it's not my life. Not what I am. And I'm not sure I'd want to go back and think about it too much. It's just too out of the ordinary. I'm a very ordinary person, Provender. I like normal life, normal things. If I can just somehow push past all of it . . .'

'Erase it? Forget it?'

'Move on. You understand?'

His nod said yes. His eyes said no.

'I'm not saying I'm going to be the same from here on,' she added. 'I could hardly expect to be. But I don't want to be that different, if you see what I'm getting at.'

Is's instinct, the bluntness with which she naturally dealt with life, was urging her to come right out and say it, spell it out to Provender, leave him in no doubt. But she was trying to spare his feelings. Or was she trying to spare her own? Either way, dancing around the subject seemed preferable to tackling it head-on. She couldn't bear to hurt him, but more than that, she couldn't bear to have to see him hurt and know that she was the cause.

'I hope your mother will be all right,' she offered, lamely.

'Yes.'

'I think her chances are good.'

'If you say so.'

That was it. She really could not think of anything else. It was time to leave.

She turned, then turned again and went to Provender and embraced him. Contact. Body on body. Warmth to warmth. His chin against her neck, his breath briefly in her ear. She squeezed. He squeezed back with that tiniest bit more pressure. He straightened away from her, and for a moment their faces were close, nose to nose, mirroring.

'Isn't there anything I could—' he began.

Is looked down, away. Let go of him. Headed for the car, trying not to appear to be hurrying. Stepped in. Shut the door. Did not once look round.

The chauffeur engaged gear and the Seraph glided down the drive, away from Dashlands House into the grounds of the estate, away from light into the boundless warm blue summer dark.

75

Provender watched the car go.

The parting with Is had not gone as he might have wished. Its finality crushed him. Was that it? Was it all over? Just like that?

Peering at the Seraph's dwindling tail lights, he had to fight the urge to sprint after the limo – a mad dash to catch up. He knew he would never make it, and even if he did, what would he achieve? Nothing except make himself look desperate and foolish.

He thought he had proved to Is that he was not just a Gleed; that he was so much less and at the same time so much more. He should just have come out and said it, but, tongue-tied at the crucial moment, he had fumbled and failed.

So, what now?

At the back of his mind there lurked the idea of another book, a follow-up to *The Meritocrats*, possibly a sequel. He had been considering this for a while anyway, and perhaps if he wrote another novel, got it out into the world, spread the Family-sabotaging message a little bit further, Is would be impressed. She would see that he meant everything he said, that he sincerely wanted a better, fairer world, a world where the Families no longer held sway. This grand gesture would surely win her over.

Wouldn't it?

The flaws in the plan were many. Principally, Is hated *The Meritocrats*. It galled Provender to remember this but it was true. She couldn't stand the book, and therefore a second book might not be the ideal way to go about gaining her attention. Besides, it would take him at least a year to write, and then it would probably take another year to percolate fully through the public consciousness. Too long, too slow.

Moreover, Provender no longer believed, as he once had, that a book could change everything, or indeed anything, for the better. This view was based in part on his experiences at the hands of Damien Scrase, which was a case of the law of unintended consequences if ever there was one. Were it not for *The Meritocrats*, would Damien have become quite the fanatic he did? Perhaps he would have, but the book had certainly added fuel to that particular fire.

Also, more relevantly, Provender surprised himself by realising that he didn't resent his Family quite as much as he used to. Was it because he was worried about his mother? Was it because he had faced the threat posed by Great (and Carver) and survived? Was it because he was simply glad to be back with them?

Maybe with time, if his mother's condition improved and he had a chance to gain perspective on things, he would lapse back into his sullen revulsion for all things Familial.

Maybe.

But he thought not.

Great was correct about one thing, at any rate. BOY NEEDED TO DO SOMETHING.

Boy had, with *The Meritocrats*. But it wasn't enough; it wasn't the best way forward.

Boy had also achieved a breakthrough with Stanisław Kuczynski. That was a good sign for the future.

Yet, for all that, boy knew he still needed to do something else, something different, something immediate and concrete.

The Seraph turned a corner, its tail lights winking out of sight. Beyond the aura of the house lights there was nothing now but a blank silhouette of trees and hillside braced against the starry sky. Provender shivered, feeling a small, lonely chill, a foretaste of night.

But he felt, too, a sudden glimmering within. A twinkling amid darkness. The precursor of an idea. A seed of thought, just starting to shoot.

Yes . . .

PART SEVEN

76

Routine was good. At St Fiacre's there was no such thing as an average day, each day was different, each came with its own particular freight of chaos and unpredictability. At the start of a shift you had no idea what lay ahead and for the next eight hours you simply went along for the ride, dealing equally with the longueurs of boredom and the sudden frantic spurts of activity. Nevertheless, in total, one day after another, it amounted to a routine. You got up, did your shift, collapsed into bed. Is welcomed it. It was what she needed. Like the tidal beating of the waves it wore away at the memory of her time with Provender until eventually, perhaps eight or nine weeks later, she could look back on the whole episode without rancour or self-recrimination. She could safely say that it no longer meant anything to her. It was old, done with, tidied away, out of sight.

She slipped back into the swirl of life at the hospital with scarcely a ripple. Several colleagues congratulated her on having the foresight to take a week's leave just when the shit hit the fan. The day war nearly broke out had been the busiest in living memory. By noon the wards were full of panic-attacks and attempted suicides, people whose fragile personalities had cracked under the strain. Then, come evening, when it became clear that peace was going to reign, Accident and Emergency had to cope with a huge influx of alcohol-related cases. The whole of London, it seemed, had gone on a bender, and St Fiacre's was where they ended up to have their stomachs pumped and their lamppost-collision wounds sutured and their brawl bruises daubed with iodine.

Everyone – nurses, interns, residents, registrars – had their war-day reminiscences and wanted to share them with Is. Those of them, however, who got round to asking her what she had been doing during those tense hours, were invariably disappointed by her reply. 'Oh, not much' was hardly a fair repayment for the fraught front-line tales they had regaled her with. But she could not be pushed to say any more, and the assumption was that Is was jealous. She felt left out. She wished she could have been there to grapple with the crazies and the inebriates. Everybody else was part of a remarkable shared experience, bonded by adversity, and she was not.

During the post-Provender period, the long slow process of forgetting,

Is did keep an eye on the newspapers and the TV, and every so often a reminder would pop up, some report or article that briefly brought the whole episode back. There was, for instance, a short piece in one of the Familial columns that mentioned Cynthia Gleed's recovery from a mystery illness. Though still weak, Mrs Gleed was apparently faring well and should be back to full strength in no time. The article gave no clue as to what the illness might have been, although one of the more scurrilous gossip columnists speculated that the Gleed matriarch was most likely going through the Change. A week later, photos appeared in a number of national dailies depicting a wan but smiling Cynthia accompanying her husband at some public function or other. Prosper Gleed had a solicitous hand on his wife's elbow, an arm around her waist. Every inch the caring, attentive spouse. If you knew what to look for, as Is did, you would have noticed how his eyes shone as he gazed on her. What had dwindled to embers had now been rekindled into a blaze.

Then there were the headlines that appeared when information about Damien was finally released to the press. He had been arraigned before a judge on two counts of murder and one of threat to endanger life. Is was not aware, till then, that Damien had killed anyone. All she knew about was his attempt on Provender's life. But it turned out that he had knifed to death a doorman at the Shortborn and also that a body had been discovered at his flat – the corpse of someone called Milner, likewise knifed to death. Milner, it turned out, was a private investigator. In fact, he was an associate of Romeo Moore, a fellow Anagrammatic Detective.

Her horror was great and so, too, was her fear that her involvement in the kidnapping meant she would be regarded as an accessory to murder. For several days she went around on tenterhooks, waiting for the police to come. Whenever her name was called out over the hospital's public address system, her heart would start to pound and her palms would become slick with sweat. At the back of her mind was the thought that Provender, for all his claims that he would protect her, might in a fit of pique do the exact opposite. She had rejected him. He might have no qualms about getting his own back by throwing her to the proverbial wolves. Never mind a woman scorned, what about a man?

In the event, he appeared to stay true to his word. The police did not call on Is. If anyone in officialdom connected her with Damien Scrase, for whatever reason the connection was not followed up. Gleed influence kept her in the clear. She was relieved about this, naturally, but she also felt furtively guilty. It wasn't right that she should be so utterly exonerated. It felt a bit like cheating.

A couple of her nurse friends, who knew of her one-time relationship with Damien, remarked to her about his arrest. He had always struck them as a borderline case, they said, violence lurking below the surface. In fact, they opined, they were surprised nothing like this had happened sooner. At any rate, it was a good thing Is had dumped him when she did. She was well shot of him.

Even her part in his downfall was kept out of the public domain. It was Arthur who took the credit, and he was only too happy to. In an exclusive interview on a popular TV chat show Arthur related at length how he had liberated his cousin Provender from the anti-Familial madman's clutches and then disarmed him and decked him with a single punch. It all took place in the backstage murk at the Shortborn, so there weren't any eyewitnesses who were able to disprove Arthur's claims explicitly. There was no one, even, to pass comment on the improbability of Arthur managing to bring down Damien, a man twice his size, with just one blow. So persuasive was Arthur that he made his account of the incident wholly credible. Perhaps he himself believed it was the truth. That, after all, was what good acting was about, inhabiting a role so thoroughly that you came to feel the part was really you. It was, at any rate, great publicity for his play. *Hamlet* was now sold out for its entire run, and there was talk of taking it on a tour of the provinces and even abroad to the US and Japan.

Damien himself adopted a policy of stony silence. At the arraignment hearing he didn't utter a word, not even answering when the judge asked him to confirm his name and abode. He wore, in the words of one journalist, 'a heavy armour of defeat'. Pictures by court sketch artists confirmed it. In so far as such artists could be relied on for an accurate reproduction of reality, the Damien they depicted in pastel and pencil looked shrunken, hollowed, half the man he had been. He was heading for a fall and he knew it. Is believed that, once his anger had abated and he had had time to reflect on the atrocities he had committed, his conscience had caught up with him. There was blood on his hands. Two innocent lives taken. Whatever his beliefs, no matter how great his faith in his cause, he had killed. There was no getting around that.

Reports of his suicide while in custody came as no surprise to Is. Damien hanged himself in his police cell on the night before his trial was due to commence, using a blanket for a rope and a light fixture for a gibbet.

Deep down she was able to find it in herself to feel sorry for him. Mostly, though, she felt that he had got what he deserved. In a sense, he had shown himself to be decent at the last. A less proud man would have tried to weasel his way out of responsibility for his deeds, blaming the Gleed Family, perhaps, rather than himself. But not Damien. Principled to the end.

She learned where and when his funeral was to be held but didn't go.

And one month became two, and two expanded into three, and Is got on with things because that was what she wanted, wasn't it? A normal life. Wasn't it?

And summer decayed into autumn, and London's few trees took on a brown tinge and there was a knowing nudge of cold in the air.

Then two letters arrived for her, both appearing on the same morning in her pigeonhole at the nurses' lodgings.

The first was in an ordinary-sized envelope which bulged with the several sheets of foolscap folded within.

The letter itself was videotyped and the first page was printed on a sheet of headed notepaper alerting her to the fact that it came from Romeo Moore, Anagrammatic Detective, who could now lay claim to official Gleed patronage. The Family's crest appeared alongside his name and address, motto and split-nutmeg motif stamped crisply into the paper.

For all the impressiveness of the stationery, however, the tone of the letter was anything but proud or gleeful.

```
Dear Is,
    I apologise for contacting you like this, out of the
blue. Finding out where you live wasn't difficult. I am,
after all, a detective. For what that's worth.
    Truth be told, these past few weeks have been very hard
for me and I really need to unburden myself to someone
who I know will lend a sympathetic ear, someone moreover
who was there when it all happened. If you would prefer
not to be that person, I will understand. I remember, in
the car on the way back to London, you said you hoped to
forget about it all. I don't blame you for that. If
that's still the case, don't read on. Crumple this
letter up and throw it away.
    I've been thinking about anagrams a lot, Is. Words have
been whirling around in my brain, settling then taking
off again like flocks of starlings. Words that seem to
have meaning and then no meaning.
    I've been thinking about your name, for one. I feel it
was unfair of me to characterise ISIS NECKER as NICE
KISSER. That was a shallow and dull anagrammatic inter-
pretation. With time and reflection I've been able to
see that ISIS NECKER is also CRISIS-KEEN. You are. You
were. How you dealt with things at Dashlands House that
day, and also what you told me later about how you and
Provender escaped from Damien Scrase . . . CRISIS-KEEN
indeed. A remarkable, resourceful woman you are.
    Mainly, though, I've been thinking about the word
RELATIVES as I sit here in my lonely office through the
long hours of the day. No doubt thanks to our encounter
with the Gleeds, the word has begun to obsess me. Even at
```

night it blurs through my thoughts. Such a VERSATILE word, RELATIVES. IT REVEALS many things.

It tells me about the VASTER LIE that was perpetrated on myself and my colleague Merlin Milner when we were hired by Carver to find Provender. He told us one lie when he praised our track record. The VASTER LIE was that he hoped we would not succeed at all. He intended us to fail in our task.

When I didn't fail, I was exposed to the full vengeful fury of the Gleeds' manservant; a VALET'S IRE.

But what befell me was nothing compared with what befell my partner. You probably are aware that Scrase murdered two people. What you may not have realised is that the first of his victims was my colleague, and friend, Merlin Milner, who succeeded far better than I did at locating Provender. VITAL SEER that he was, he actually tracked down Provender's captor - and was stabbed to death for his pains.

I found out a couple of days afterwards. His corpse lay undiscovered in Scrase's flat until a neighbour noticed. I can hardly bear to think about it. Merlin, dead all that time. Somehow that's the worst part, the loneliness of it. Even dead, to be abandoned like that . . . And I had no idea where he was. I looked high and low for him, fretted about him, and then he turned up. I was the one who had to go to the morgue to identify his remains. Truly that period, those few days between his disappearance and his burial, was and still is the VILEST ERA I have ever had to live through.

I attended Scrase's arraignment. I sat there in that courtroom facing my partner's murderer and I watched his deadened, faraway gaze, his VISTA LEER. (It reminded me, in its way, of the horrible resentful look in Great's eyes when Provender took his signet ring off him, that EVIL STARE of his.) I nearly cheered when a trial date was set and I _did_ cheer when I learned that, on his TRIAL'S EVE, Scrase had killed himself. Even though, if he had gone to prison, it would have been for life - he would never LEAVE STIR - this was altogether better. I'm not by nature a sadistic or uncharitable man, but I truly hope he suffered during his final moments.

What remains for me is to wonder about the Gleeds, whose inner strife reached out and affected ordinary existences like yours and mine, whose squabbling can have a ripple effect, shake the world, TEAR LIVES. What are we to make of people like them who can casually, inadvertently, with a selfish decision, destroy some and leave the REST ALIVE? People who have such power and wield it with such thoughtlessness?

I don't know. It may well be that I'm going mad. The anagrams – my trade, my craft – are closing in around me, ensnaring me. I've been too long inside my own brain and I can't seem to find a way out. Everything makes sense and nothing does.

Maybe, with time, this will pass. Funnily enough, I feel better simply for having typed this out to you, using my brand new videotyper.

I've been getting a lot of offers of work lately, on the strength of my new Gleed patronage. I've been turning them down, but maybe I should take them up. Maybe work is the best cure. Make myself master of the anagrams again, rather than have them be the master of me.

I have money, Family patronage, everything I could possibly wish for. Yet I'd give it all away in a flash, if it meant I could have my friend Merlin back, sitting opposite me, annoying me, one-upping me. Really, I would.

Yours sincerely,
Romeo

P.S. You remember, when we arrived at Dashlands by tram, I mentioned an anagram of Provender's full name which I wasn't able to account for then? I think I can now. PROVENDER OREGANO GLEED – GREEN ROAD DEVELOPER O.N.G. The O.N.G. bothered me. I don't like left-over letters. It's untidy. Then I realised, in the light of subsequent discoveries, that it might well stand for 'On Needle Grove'. You've seen the recent news stories about the estate, I take it. The anagrams twist and turn. They're snaky and deceptive. But in the end, they never lie.

Saddened, Is folded Moore's letter shut and tucked it back into its envelope. Poor man. Half crazy with grief. His world, even more than hers, had been churned up by Damien, and by Carver and Great, and no amount of Gleed kindness after the fact could smooth out the gouges. She resolved to phone him sometime, offer to meet up with him for a drink and a chat. It was the least she could do.

An odd thought struck her. She reopened the letter and reread the P.S. 'Subsequent discoveries'? 'Recent news stories'? She didn't get the reference. She would ask someone at work today what was going on at Needle Grove. If she couldn't find anyone who knew, she'd go to the local library and check back through the newspaper archives. Obviously she had missed something, but then lately she had become a lot less thorough about keeping up with current events. The outside world had ceased to impinge so directly on her, much to her delight.

Then there was the second letter. This one was in a large, card-backed manila envelope, and had apparently been hand-delivered. There was no stamp or frank. She opened it carefully, with fingertip delicacy.

Inside were maps. No covering note, just a sheaf of maps.

Architectural plans, to be precise. Copies of architectural plans . . .

. . . of Needle Grove.

Each plan detailed a section of the estate, and on most of them, though not all, there was a portion shaded in green.

Who had sent her this? She thought she knew, but she discarded the notion, not willing to acknowledge it until she had to.

Some of the shaded portions were large, some small. Each touched the edge of the page it was on. Each formed an irregular geometrical shape.

It didn't take Is long to divine that there was an overall pattern. Cumulatively the shaded portions amounted to something greater. They were parts of a whole.

She cleared a patch of floor in her bedsit and began laying the plan copies out. Her shift was due to start soon and already she could hear other nurses in the lodgings leaving their rooms and clacking along the corridor to the sky-bridge which led across to the main part of the hospital. She was in her uniform and ready to go, but first there was this puzzle, the plan copies like jigsaw pieces demanding to assembled and solved.

On her knees, she shuffled the sheets of paper around, aligning edges, matching up shaded portion with shaded portion. The pattern grew. The geometrical shapes fell together, creating several larger, discrete geometrical shapes.

Then, all at once, she had it, and she sat back breathlessly on her haunches, staring down. The plan copies were spread out in front of her in a rough rectangle, across the middle of which were four capital letters and a punctuation mark picked out in green:

ISIS?

Each character was comprised of streets, roads, walkways, bridges; of plazas, squares, sections of wasteland; of numerous interlocking outdoor segments of the estate, all at different levels. Someone had taken a lot of time, expended a lot of effort, in putting this together. But for what purpose? Why contrive such an elaborate, convoluted way of writing out her name?

'And why do it anonymously?' she said aloud, adding, 'Provender,' as though he were in the room with her.

She peered at the plans again, and it was the question mark that snagged at her and made her think there was more to all this than met the eye. That, combined with the remarks in Moore's letter. Something was afoot. This wasn't merely some sort of declaration she was looking at, a statement of her name . . .

It was an invitation.

She got one of the other nurses to call in sick for her – stomach bug, sudden thing, sorry. She changed into civvies and sneaked out of the hospital. A bus transported her across town, the bus she always used to take when visiting Damien. She knew the route intimately, every stop and turn. Part of her felt she was wasting her time, she was blowing a sick-day for nothing, she had misread the meaning of the plans. Another part of her knew otherwise.

As she passed beneath an entrance arch and stepped onto Needle Grove soil, she flashed back to her and Provender's run-in with the Changelings and a frisson of remembered fear shivered through her. Her throat tightened and her breathing felt constricted. She nearly turned back. Then she spied a group of workmen nearby, gathered in a hard-hatted huddle, studying blueprints. Behind them stood a mechanical digger and a dump-truck whose hopper was heaped high with fresh earth. The sight restored her confidence and refreshed her curiosity. She walked past the men, close enough to overhear one of them, who looked very much like a site foreman, say something about avoiding a gas main when they began excavation. Which was reassuring to hear but not exactly a huge clue as to what was going on.

She continued walking, and was soon drawn towards an area of greenery that shimmered, mirage-like, at the base of the nearest block but one. It looked as incongruous and unreal as any desert oasis: an acre (she estimated) of newly-laid turf which stretched around the corner of the block, with mature pines and cypresses planted in it, clumps of shrubbery, some outcrops of boulder, and even a meandering man-made stream. Several of the estate's residents were out and about among the greenery, some wandering, others lolling on benches or basking on the grass. A pair of Young Moderns were perched on one of the boulder outcrops with that unmistakable air of *our patch* about them, but somehow their cocksure-ness seemed tempered, as though the novelty of their location – sitting on rock, surrounded by grass – was something they were still acclimatising to.

Is ventured further into the estate, and higher, climbing an external staircase until she arrived at a tenth-storey plaza. Here, too, greening had occurred. Huge potted palms and fig trees overshadowed a square of rock garden, at the epicentre of which stood a brand new recreation area for children – swings, seesaw, a climbing frame like a scale-model skeletal city. Kids swarmed everywhere, putting the gleaming equipment to the test. They swung the swings higher than they were intended to go and they clambered like monkeys over the climbing frame and dangled precariously from the uppermost bars. One boy, Is noted, seemed to prefer the rock garden and was busy trying to kick loose a cemented-in stone with his foot. With persistence, he would no doubt prevail. Another boy, no less destructive, was picking at the bark of one of the palms, tearing off small strips.

Probably this would happen more and more, it occurred to Is. None of this new stuff would stay pristine and undamaged. That was just how people were.

But at least someone was making the effort. At least someone (Provender) was trying to brighten up the estate.

If only she could be sure it was purely for the Needle Grovers' benefit and not for his own.

Elsewhere, she came across a small jungle.

A hothouse clustered with cacti and ferns.

A building site which would, when finished, if she didn't miss her guess, be a crazy-golf course.

Another building site which was evidently on its way to becoming a yew hedge maze.

She went higher still, and higher, traversing from block to block, and each time she halted and looked out she saw another patch of the estate that was being or had been transformed, verdured, swarded. Residents she passed were already sounding blasé about the improvements being visited on their home, and several of them assumed that the Risen London Authority was responsible and that, mark their words, this meant rents would be going up, just you wait and see. Their cynicism was ingrained. They couldn't help being jaded about the widespread emeralding of the estate. But still, in their eyes, they did look just that little bit pleased.

Finally Is reached the apex of one block; she could go no higher. From this lofty vantage point she observed that the tops of a number of other blocks now sported roof gardens. She observed, too, how the introduction of lush green areas altered the look of Needle Grove. The blocks no longer crowded side by side in rigid ranks. They were softly connected, cushioned. The greenery brought untidiness, and with that untidiness, relief.

What she could not distinguish, even from so high, was the pattern of her name writ large across the estate. Only a bird flying overhead might perceive it, or the pilot of an aircraft, or God. She had the feeling, however, that because the component parts of the pattern were so disparate, so unalike, the naked eye – even God's – would not be able to make it out. Only someone who had seen the word highlighted on the plans would know it was there.

Provender.

Such a grand gesture. Such a flashy gesture.

What did he hope to achieve by it?

Is knew. She didn't like to admit it, but she knew. What she also knew but didn't like to admit was that – damn him – it was working.

Back at the hospital, there was a car waiting for her. Outside the ground-floor entrance to the nurses' lodgings. The pearl-white Dagenham Seraph. Hovering on the tarmac, its idling motor like the flutter of wings.

The chauffeur stood by the rear door, which was open. He recognised Is and saluted her, nudging the peak of his cap.

Is peered into the rear of the car. It was vacant – nobody on the back seat.

Vacant, expecting to be occupied.

She paused.

The chauffeur now fixed his gaze into the middle distance, under orders not to interfere, not to influence her in any way. Her decision and hers alone.

She continued to pause, knowing that whatever choice she made now, it was irrevocable. The offer being extended to her was, she understood, one-time only. No going back. No room for second thoughts.

The Seraph hummed.

Who was she? What had she done to deserve this?

She was Is. She was nobody.

At long last, she made up her mind.

With solid determination, and just a hint of a smile, she moved as if towards the car.

The chauffeur gently laid a hand on the rim of the door, smiling too.

And then—

Acknowledgements

The author wishes to extend his gratitude – in an ideal world it would be his extravagance as well – to the following:

Simon Spanton (M.S. POINTS ANON) and Gillian Redfearn (AN ELFIN DEAR GIRL) for their insightful, in-depth editing;

Ilona Jasiewicz (IN-CASE-O'-JAIL WIZ) and Krystyna Kujawinska (JINK AWAY, STRAY SKUNK) for their help with the Polish dialogue, especially the sweary bits;

Antony Harwood (A NON-WORDY OATH) and James Macdonald Lockhart (CLAN ADDS TOOL – JACKHAMMER) for being A GENT'S agents;

everyone at Arts Council South East (SALUTE COUTH COIN STARS) for their generous financial support;

and Peter Crowther (WHERE P.C. ROTTER?), Eric Brown (BROWN RICE), Adam Roberts (DR AT SOME BAR), Roger Levy (GREY LOVER), and Chris Wooding (I OWN RICH GODS), for their generous non-financial support.

This book is fondly dedicated to my family, Lou Lovegrove (OO, LUV, LEG-OVER!) and Monty Lovegrove (ROT MY OVEN-GLOVE) . . . and also to my Family.

– James Lovegrove
(ELSE: V. V. MAJOR EGO)

www.jameslovegrove.com